Terror Toll

by

William C. Gamble

Bloomington, IN Milton Keynes, UK
authorHOUSE

AuthorHouse™
1663 Liberty Drive, Suite 200
Bloomington, IN 47403
www.authorhouse.com
Phone: 1-800-839-8640

AuthorHouse™ UK Ltd.
500 Avebury Boulevard
Central Milton Keynes, MK9 2BE
www.authorhouse.co.uk
Phone: 08001974150

This book is a work of fiction. People, places, events, and situations are the product of the author's imagination. Any resemblance to actual persons, living or dead, or historical events, is purely coincidental.

First published by AuthorHouse 01/12/07

ISBN: 978-1-4259-8408-3 (sc)
ISBN: 978-1-4259-8407-6 (dj)

Printed in the United States of America
Bloomington, Indiana

This book is printed on acid-free paper..

Acknowledgements

Since 1993, after the first attack on the World Trade Center, I had wondered when and where the next attacks would take place. I began writing this book in 2001 after terrorists destroyed the Twin Towers and heavily damaged the Pentagon. It remains clear that we have not learned much about the consequences of illegal immigration. It is equally clear that our Congress is unwilling or unable to address the illegal immigration problem in a meaningful way. I am not alone in the belief that another attack is inevitable, but I hope and pray that I am wrong.

This book is dedicated to the thousands of Americans and foreign citizens who have lost their lives as a result of terrorist attacks and to the courageous men and women who serve in our armed forces to keep us safe.

Finally, I would not have been able to complete this work had it not been for the love, encouragement and support of my late wife, Pamela, my two children, Christopher and Morgan and my dear friend Nancy.

-Chapter One-

On the 10th anniversary of the World Trade Center attacks, Martha Burdette Simpson took her two children Jenna and Peter to the Mall of America about eight miles from her home. It was chilly and raining, a good day for shopping and for the kids to visit Camp Snoopy and Underwater Adventure in the world's largest indoor shopping mall.

Martha's neighbor and best friend, Alexandra Petty and her daughter joined them. Maryann, a high school senior, volunteered to accompany Jenna and Peter while Martha and Alexandra enjoyed a nice lunch at Napa Valley Grill, one of the Mall's seven upscale restaurants. Their husbands, Chuck Simpson and Ward Petty decided to watch the Vikings play the Lions.

Some 30 miles from the Simpson residence Ahmad Saleh, Hatem Yousef, Abdulaziz Hassan and Muhammed Khalil had different ideas about how to spend a Sunday. They were members of a sleeper cell who entered the United States two years before September 11, 2001 traveling to the twin cities and settling in with other members of the Muslim community. Saleh and Yousef worked at fast food restaurants; Hassan and Khalil were employed by Krone's Sound Systems. The al Qaeda operatives were ordered by their contact to prepare for the anniversary strike.

Saleh and Yousef disguised themselves as overweight women. They each carried two reinforced Nordstrom's shopping bags containing 50 pounds of HMX, a very powerful plastic explosive hidden beneath a small Nordstrom's gift box. Another 50 pounds of

1

HMX was layered around their bodies and covered by a large raincoat.

Hassan and Khalil drove a truck with the logo *You won't need phones with sound by Krones* on the doors. They wore the blue uniforms of the well-known company that had done business with the Mall since it opened in 1992. Hassan and Khalil had worked for Krones for five years and were familiar to Mall Security.

They pulled their truck into the loading dock and began unloading six large black crates. Four contained the speaker systems for an early evening rock concert. Inside each of the two additional crates were 500 pounds of HMX. The crates were placed on dollies and transported to the four-story Amusement Park Rotunda for set up.

Burt Cassella, a Mall security guard greeted the two workers who smiled and returned the greeting. Hassan and Khalil unloaded the crates and began assembling the sound system. The two worked carefully with the amplifiers and speakers making sure all the wires were connected correctly. By 12:55 only two crates remained to be unloaded.

Saleh and Yousef drove to the mall in separate cars. Saleh parked in the West Parking garage; Yousef on the other side of the Mall in the East garage. In the trunks of each car were two containers, one with 25 gallons of gasoline; the other held 400 pounds of HMX.

A timer was attached to the explosives.

Using stolen handicap designations that they hung from their mirrors, both parked within a few feet of a mall entrance. Saleh checked his watch and ambled to the trunk of his car. After setting the timer in the trunk, he picked up a shopping bag and slowly headed into the Mall to the third floor where he window-shopped near the North Food Court. On the south side Yousef called attention to his apparent bulk by waddling to the escalators. He too got off at the third floor where he walked slowly past the stores on his way to the South Food Court.

Martha Simpson drove her mini-van onto one of the feeder roads adjacent to the Mall. At a stop sign, the kids noticed the Krones Sound truck at the loading dock. Peter asked his mother if they could stay for the rock concert. Simpson asked Alexandra Petty what time the concert started.

"I think it starts at 4:00," Petty replied. "The Sunday afternoon concerts are usually over by 5:15 so people can get home in time for dinner."

"What do you think? Do you want to go?" Simpson asked.

"Maryann, do you have anything planned this evening besides studying?" Alexandra Petty asked her daughter.

"No mom, I did my homework yesterday. I think the Gooneybirds are playing. They're pretty good." Petty's daughter replied.

"OK, you can go to the concert," Alexandra Petty said. "Mrs. Simpson and I will have lunch and meet you at the entrance to Underwater Adventure at 3:45. Is that OK, Maryann?"

"Sure."

Simpson parked the car in the west garage since it was nearer to the Napa Valley Grill. Before the kids wandered off, the mothers repeated the instructions. The kids hurried to Camp Snoopy anticipating the thrilling rides. Simpson and Petty decided to do some shopping before having lunch.

Simpson called her husband and told him of the change in plans. Chuck Simpson was inwardly delighted because he and Ward Petty wanted to watch the second NFL game pitting the Chicago Bears against the Green Bay Packers. Martha Simpson then called the restaurant and made an 11:45 reservation. She placed her cell phone in her purse and the two women headed for Bloomingdale's.

The largest mall in North America was jammed with more than 80,000 people. Saleh and Yousef sat at the entrances to the two food courts and began fanning themselves pretending they were hot and tired. Hassan and Khalil calmly sipped their coffees. Martyrdom was minutes away.

Chuck Simpson and Ward Petty had settled in front of the TV with chips and dip and cold beers. Their spouses had just ordered a second glass of wine and poached salmon for lunch. Their children were sitting at the far end of the food court enjoying burgers and fries along with hundreds of hungry adults and kids.

At 1 p.m. the Mall of America was rocked by a series of thunderous explosions in the Amusement Park Rotunda and the entrances to the cafeterias. The shock waves slammed into dozens of storefronts turning the glass into lethal supersonic missiles. The glass roof four stories above disappeared in tens of thousands of pieces that whined through the air to the far corners of the massive parking lots. Hundreds of shoppers in the Rotunda simply disappeared.

The reinforced glass of the 1.2 million gallon aquarium in Underwater Adventure wavered, then shattered under the massive blast. A wall of water 14 feet high carrying thousands of fish poured through the opening. Camp Snoopy was swamped.

Rides mangled by the explosion were submerged. The badly injured drowned. Some people 100 feet away from Yousef and Saleh were hurled into the food courts; others were catapulted over the railings. The blasts sent live trees and their pots into storefronts the window glass instantly shredding shoppers inside. Park benches and nearby kiosks were fragmented into tiny cast iron and oak shards that killed or maimed anyone in their path. Some of the fury of the blasts splintered the lighting and the glass ceilings, tearing loose their steel supports that crashed onto the floor four stories below.

Twelve of the restaurants closest to the detonations collapsed. Chairs and tables were wrenched from their moorings in the floor and were hurled into the diners. The steel beams and ventilation ducts over the food courts fell onto the dead and wounded. The Mall went dark. Emergency generators kicked in but there were few lights intact.

Maryann Petty, Jenna and Peter Simpson were chatting in happy animation, their table shielded by a major load bearing support beam. The giant shock wave sent pieces of the mall accoutrements into orbit and decorations and restaurant trays whistled overhead. Bodies and body parts flew everywhere, some landing nearby. Maryann shoved the two younger kids under their table as chunks of ceiling crashed around them and onto the table just above them Thick choking dust and smoke rose through the carnage. The smell of blood was overpowering. Peter and Jenna were shaking and crying hysterically. Maryann could see Peter and Jenna crying, but couldn't hear them or the crackling flames fed by the broken gas lines in the shattered restaurants. Blood dripped from her ears.

The Rotunda blast blew the door of the Napa Valley Grille into a dozen diners waiting patiently for a table. The glass wall of the bar and bottles and glasses ripped into the bar patrons and the bartenders.

Three diners who had finished their meal were walking by the corner booth occupied by Martha Simpson and Alexandra Petty. None of them had time to react as the standing diners were driven with stunning force into the table and the wall beyond. Simpson and Petty, protected somewhat from the force of the blast were injured; the other three diners who partially shielded them were not as lucky. Blood saturated the tablecloth.

Hundreds of stunned and bleeding shoppers stumbled through the dust and smoke toward the parking garages skirting the rubble and bodies, ignoring the moans and screams of the badly injured. As they neared the garage entrances on the four floors, two more explosions shook the Mall. Huge pieces of burning cars were flung like Matchbook toys into the Mall entrances on the first floor. Flaming gasoline ignited dozens of them. Within minutes the lower level of the garages became an inferno.

Burt Cassella was in the Mall Safety Center having lunch and chatting with fellow guards. A veteran of the gulf War, he had heard artillery explosions, but nothing prepared him for the concussion that knocked him off his feet and under one of the video surveillance consoles. Dazed and bleeding he and several other guards stumbled to their feet.

"Jesus Christ," Frank Langone said. "What the fuck was that?"

The video consoles went dark and the lights went out.

"My God," Langone's boss, Capt. Pat Fant said, "I think we've been bombed." Fant pulled his radio from its holster and called the security substations, "Station four, come in. This is Fant." He repeated the message three times and then called Station three, then station two. No one replied.

"This is Fant calling anyone on patrol."

"This is Rose Pardow, Pat. I was in the ladies room on the third floor at the west end. I think we've been bombed."

"Rose, tell me what you see."

"It's too dark to see much, but I can hear people screaming. Only the emergency lights are working. There's a big fire down by the South Food Court. And there's lots of dust and shit. And there's water everywhere. God, I think the aquarium's gone." She started to cry.

"Rose get hold of yourself. I want you to try to get to the North Food Court," Fant ordered. "Stay close to the walls. The ceiling may have been weakened."

Pardow took in the carnage. She acknowledged the message and started toward the food court. The windows of every store she passed had been obliterated. After the first store she couldn't look inside.

Jagged steel and concrete made the going difficult. "I don't think I can go any further, Pat," she said. "There's a hole in the floor. There's shit everywhere. And the North Food Court's on fire too. What do you want me to do?"

Fant was on the phone with the Bloomington Police when the bombs in the garages went off two seconds apart.

"My God, another bomb just went off. And there's another," he said to the dispatcher. "You better send everything, every fucking thing you got."

The fire alarms in the Safety Center sounded, indicating a fire in the garages.

"Roger," said the Bloomington Police Dispatcher. "Several units have already reported. We've issued an all hands. Everything we have. The fire department's on the way too."

"Sergeant, the fire alarms are going off everywhere. Tell your people to move their ass. No telling how bad it is or how many casualties. Tell the chief to call the Mayor. You can reach my cell if you have to." Fant gave the dispatcher his cell number then picked up his radio.

"Rose, this is Pat. Sorry for the delay. Try the stairs and get back here. Wait here with Fredericks. You two stay by the phones. I'm taking Martin and Cassella with me. The power is out and emergency power isn't working too well. Be careful."

Pardow made her way to the fire exit. Black, acrid smoke was rolling into the Mall from the garage two stories below her. Downstairs she cautiously opened the door before stepping into the shattered hallway. Ninety yards away dozens of cars were ablaze. Dazed and bloodied shoppers had retreated from the searing heat. Burning bodies lay near the garage entrance. Pardow stood transfixed.

"Help us," an injured woman begged.

Pardow smiled weakly and keyed her mike.

"Pat, Rose. I'm on the first floor. There's nothing left of the garage. The door is blocked. Everything's on fire. There's a couple of hundred people here. Lots of them are hurt bad. Do you still want me back at the control room?"

"No. Stay with the injured. See if you can get them out of there. Get everyone as far away from the fire as possible. If you can't get out, move them into a store. Help's on the way. Lots of it. So, hang on."

Pardow looked at the wreckage that had fallen from the third floor over the entrances. *These people will never be able to get through that.* She got everyone's attention with her whistle. On her instructions they made their way inside a windowless book store. Pardow radioed Fant where they were.

"Rose. Do you have your notebook?"

"Yeah."

"Ask each person to spell their name. Write it down. Ask them if they were with other people and then group people and families together."

"Right."

"Hey Chuck, come here, quick. The fucking mall's been bombed," Ward Petty shouted after hearing the bulletin that interrupted the game.

Chuck Simpson dropped the plate of chips and dip on the kitchen floor and ran to the family room.

A video from a hovering helicopter showed the heavily damaged roof that now resembled a smoking crater and the thick smoke from the raging fires in each of the garages. Fire trucks were beginning to arrive at the scene.

"Jesus," Simpson said. He raced to the kitchen grabbed his keys and a jacket. Petty grabbed his coat and was on Simpson's heels.

"We have no word on casualties," the TV announcer said. "But it must be in the thousands."

Simpson almost forgot to open the garage door. The car roared down the quiet street toward Route 77. Neither spoke.

Martha Simpson slowly came to her senses. A male body was wedged between her and the table. His blood soaked Simpson's jeans and made a puddle on the floor. Simpson's left shoulder, collar bone and four ribs were broken by the impact with the wall. Blood dripped from her head. Her right ankle ached. Alexandra Petty moaned. The left side of her face was mangled by glass from the bar. The upper half of the body of the woman who took the force of the explosion lay on the table; the lower half on the floor, Another body lay crushed against the wall.

"It must have been a bomb," Petty whispered. "We've got to find the kids. Help me move this…oh my God." Petty threw up. After the initial wave of nausea, she turned away. Summoning all her strength, she pushed the torso onto the floor. She stood slowly and tried to pull the body off her friend. "Push, Martha. Help me."

Simpson screamed in agony when she tried to move her left arm. "It's my shoulder. Probably broken," she hissed.

Petty abandoned the effort. Holding her jacket to her head to stop the bleeding, she told Simpson to hang on and gingerly stepped over the body on the floor. "I'm gonna get some help. Stay calm."

A shocked Bloomington Fire Chief Carney Rutherford surveyed the scene from his command helicopter. He phoned his counterpart in Minneapolis, praying he could keep his composure.

"Ken, it's Carney. The Mall's been bombed."

"I know. Are you there?"

"Yeah, I'm overhead. I see major fires in the garages, more inside. The rotunda roof's almost gone. God knows how many people are inside. We need help, every damn thing you can send. You copy?"

Minneapolis Fire Chief Ken Patterson had already begun assessing what he could send. He had tried to prepare his department for a terrorist attack, but nothing of this magnitude. "I'll send everything I can. Any word on casualties?"

"Not yet. My rescue people are trying to get in, but the fires are making it difficult. It's a Sunday. Lots of shoppers. That's all I know. We're gonna need lots of medical help…." Rutherford's voice trailed off.

"Air One from Rescue One," the radio crackled.

"This is Air One," Rutherford said.

"Chief, it's Binford. I'm inside," Lt. Corey Binford said as he sloshed toward Camp Snoopy. "It looks like a slaughterhouse." He looked in every direction describing what he saw. "The south side food court is fully involved. We're ankle deep in water. I figure the aquarium must have let go. Can't get near the garage. Too hot. There's bodies got everywhere and lots of injured too. Never seen anything like this."

Binford spotted movement in a store and ordered one of his men to check it out.

"It's one of the security guards and a lot of people, lieutenant. Most of them are hurt," the firefighter said.

"OK, get them out of there as fast as you can. Tell the ones who can't move, help is on the way."

Using the emergency shoulder, Simpson weaved in and out of traffic. When he pulled into the parking lot, fire apparatus was being deployed everywhere. He parked the car several hundred yards away near the perimeter and he and Petty sprinted to the South entrance. Two police officers stopped them as they attempted to enter.

"Our wives and kids are in there," Petty screamed at one of the officers.

Keeping his cool, the officer replied, "I understand, sir. We have firefighters and rescue crews in there right now. And more on the way. We can't let you in sir. Let the professionals handle this. Let them find your families. It's not safe for you to go inside."

Simpson nodded in apparent resignation and winked at Petty. When the officers started talking to other people who wanted to enter, Simpson muttered to Petty, "Let's go." They turned and bolted past the officers.

"Hey, Stop. You hear me. Stop," one officer shouted.

Simpson and Petty sloshed through the dirty water shouting the names of their spouses. "They were going to the Napa Valley Grille," Petty said. "Come on, it's this way."

"Power's out. We'll have to use the stairs," Simpson said. "Martha. Martha," he yelled.

The silent escalators were littered with debris, but the two anxious husbands worked their way to the second floor and sprinted down the hall to the restaurant. Inside, they were totally unprepared for what they saw. Simpson put his hand to his mouth, gurgled something and vomited. Petty leaned over a broken table and did the same.

"Martha, Martha, are you in here. Alexandra," Simpson said, sick again.

"Here. Here, I'm here," Alexandra Petty shouted. "Over here. Martha's badly hurt."

In the darkness, the two followed the sound of the female voice, tripping over broken furniture and mutilated bodies. Alexandra appeared and embraced her husband. Tears mixed with blood rolled down her cheeks.

"My God, honey, your face. Your face. We've got to get you to a hospital."

"Never mind me. Martha's badly hurt. She's got a broken shoulder and other injuries and she can't move," Alexandra said.

Petty handed his wife his clean handkerchief. He took off his jacket, then removed his shirt and held it to her face. Alexandra dropped her bloody coat and pressed the shirt over the handkerchief.

"Where's Martha, Alexandra? Where's Martha?"

"This way." She led the men to the table. Martha Simpson was slumped and moaning.

Blood oozed from her mouth.

With brute strength, Simpson moved the body that was wedged against his wife. She screamed in agony when he pulled her.

"I'm sorry, honey. I'm sorry."

"My shoulder. I think it's broken. Ribs too. And my right ankle. Get us out of here, please. Got to find the kids. They're in Underwater Adventure or Camp Snoopy."

Ward Petty helped his wife limp out of the bar. "Wait here, Ali," Petty said. He went to the edge of the broken railing and yelled "if there are any firefighters down there, we have injured women on the in the Napa Valley Grille."

"We hear you. We hear you. We're coming," Lt. Binford said. In less than five minutes six blackcoated firefighters were inside. Martha Simpson was placed on a body board and rushed out of the shattered eatery.

"Find the kids," she whispered.

"Honey, you have to go with them. You're bleeding badly," Ward Petty said to his wife.

Reluctantly, Alexandra Petty submitted to first aid treatment. A firefighter gingerly pulled glass from her hair and face and began applying gauze to the lacerations. She moaned. "Ward, go with Chuck. Find Maryann and the kids."

"Sir," said Lt. Binford. "We'll transport your wives to the city medical center," He looked over the remains of the restaurant. "There's nothing more we can do here. You gentlemen better come with us. It's not safe."

"We're not leaving. We have three kids in here and we're not leaving until we find them," Petty challenged

"Ah, fuck it. If I were in your shoes I wouldn't leave either. It's against regulations, but the hell with it. Go with Jack and Tracy. Guys, these men are looking for their children. Stay with them. We'll finish here."

Simpson and Petty and the two firefighters groped their way to the escalator. One of the firefighters turned his flashlight on the silent stairways to check its condition.

"It looks ok, but we better check it first."

When he reached the first floor he yelled to the others to follow. They splashed through the ankle deep water.

"Forget Underwater Adventure. There can't be anyone alive in there," one of the firefighters said. "Let's check Camp Snoopy."

Their search turned up dozens of badly injured mothers and kids. A firefighter reported the location and asked for help.

"We've got lots of badly injured people in Camp Snoopy," he said. " Get some doctors here."

After 20 minutes of wading through dirty water, pulling at loose wreckage and calling the names of their kids, the anxious fathers were soaked and exhausted.

"Maybe they went to get something to eat. They might be in the Food Court," Petty said hoping against hope.

"Yeah, but which one?" Simpson asked. "You check the north, I'll check the south."

"We better stick together," one of the firefighters said. "We'll check the north one first."

Emergency crews were setting up lighting to facilitate rescue efforts. At opposite ends of the Mall firefighters were laying hose to

11

fight the massive fires in the garages. Simpson and Petty hurried to the North Food Court where firefighters had extinguished the restaurant fires. Some rescue teams were sifting through the rubble to find the dead and injured.

"Jenna, Peter, Maryann," the men called out taking turns. The firefighters joined in. Even though they were emotionally overwhelmed by what they saw, Simpson and Petty refused to give up hope and slowly worked their way toward the blown out windows calling out the names of the three children.

"Over here, dad. Over here. Help," Jenna Simpson wailed.

Maryann Petty stood slowly and helped the terrified children to their feet. The smoke and dust prevented them from seeing their fathers."

"We're over here."

"This way, Ward. Thank God, they're alive."

Peter waived at his father.

"I see them. By that beam."

The men rushed to their kids and they embraced. Simpson and Petty examined them for wounds, "Are you alright?" Petty asked his daughter. "Are you OK?"

"I think Maryann hurt her ears, dad," Jenna said. "Peter and I tried to talk to her but she didn't hear us. What about mom? And Mrs. Petty" Are they OK?"

Simpson embraced his daughter and patted her back. "They're hurt, but the rescue squad has them. They'll be fine. We better get out of here."

Simpson held the hands of his kids and Petty put his arm around Maryann. They carefully made their way out of the food court. "Don't look around kids. Just look straight ahead," Simpson said as he spotted a bloody baby stroller still occupied. He fought the nausea that welled in his throat.

"Dad," Jenna said, "Maryann saved us. She got us under a table just before some of the ceiling fell down. I was really scared."

Simpson gently put his hand on the head of Maryann Petty. "I don't know how to thank you Maryann."

Maryann could see Simpson's lips moving but couldn't hear what he was saying.

"What?" she said. "I can't hear you."

Petty noticed the blood dripping from his daughter's ears. "I think her eardrums have been ruptured. We better move. This place could collapse any minute."

As they neared the exit, firefighters and rescuers streamed past them. Outside they took deep breaths. Police, fire and rescue vehicles were everywhere. Overhead, med evac helicopters were being directed to landings in the parking lot. Reporters and camera crews rushed over to the two men and their kids.

"Sir, can you tell us where you were when the explosions occurred?" a TV reporter asked.

"You'll have to talk to other people," Simpson said. "We've got to get to the hospital right now."

"But sir. Just a few questions, please."

"Look, these kids are scared. My daughter is hurt and their mothers are in the hospital. That's where we are headed. Please let us through," Petty said keeping his rising temper under control.

At the hospital, Simpson went to the emergency room desk.

"We're looking for our wives. Martha Simpson and Alexandra Petty. They were injured in the mall explosion," Simpson said.

"One moment sir." The nurse said. She looked at the admitting information on her computer screen. Petty's name appeared.

"Mrs. Petty is in surgery."

"What about Mrs. Simpson?"

"She's in surgery too sir. Please have a seat in the lounge over there." The nurse said.

The families sat down.

A doctor appeared at the reception area, spoke to the nurse and approached.

"Mr. Petty?"

"I'm Petty. How's my wife?"

"She's out of surgery sir. She's lost a lot of blood. We have her in intensive care. She's stable and out of danger."

"What about Mrs. Simpson, doctor."

"Are you Mr. Simpson?"

"Yes."

"Would you come with me please, sir?"

Chuck Simpson rose in a trance. He motioned for his kids to stay with the Pettys and accompanied the doctor to the desk.

13

"Doctor, what about my wife?"

The doctor turned, looked Chuck Simpson in the eye, put his hand on Simpson's shoulder and said, "I'm very sorry Mr. Simpson. We did everything we could. She had severe internal injuries, a ruptured spleen and ruptured kidney. I'm very sorry."

"Noooooo," Simpson wailed. "Nooooo. Please God, no, not Martha." His hands covered his face.

Peter and Jenna watched their father and began to cry. Mary Ann put her arms around the two children. Ward rose and went to his friend.

Outside, ambulance sirens were getting louder.

"We're going to need a lot more help here," the doctor said to the nurse.

-Chapter Two-

Faisal Hamed and Jameel Subaey left their White Plains, New York apartment precisely at 11:30 on the 10th anniversary of September 11. They drove north on the Hutchinson River Parkway to Route 127 then to Old Lake Street where Hamed stopped the car. Subaey moved some shrubbery revealing the small dirt road leading to the rear of Westchester County Airport. After Hamed drove onto the road, Subaey replaced the shrubbery concealing the car from any motorist on Old Lake.

At a small clearing Hamed turned the car around driving through a large puddle spattering water over the dry ground. The men retrieved five crates from the trunk and walked through the new mud to the edge of the clearing about 200 yards from the main runway. When they returned to the car, Hamed picked up two AK-47 rifles and six magazines. Subaey carried the last crate from the trunk. Dividing the crates, rifles and magazines into two stacks, they lay on the ground observing the airport with field glasses.

Satisfied that no one had spotted them, they removed the modified FIM-92A Stinger missile launchers from the crates that were innocently marked "beach umbrellas." At 2:00 p.m., Hamed aimed a stinger at the control tower some 2,000 yards away. Subaey's first target was the passenger terminal.

"Allah Akbar," Hamed whispered.

"Allah Akbar," Subaey repeated as both men pulled the triggers. The missiles, modified to carry 15 pounds of high explosive, more than double their usual punch, roared from their tubes. Subaey's missile slammed into the passenger terminal. The explosion blew out its windows and killed more than a dozen passengers and employees.

The missile fired by Hamed splintered the center window of the control tower before detonating inside. Hamed's second missile leveled what remained of the tower. Subaey's aim was also perfect. A Delta MD-80 aircraft and a fuel truck exploded in a giant ball of flame.

The two terrorists methodically took aim again. Hamed hit a second fuel truck parked near the maintenance building; Subaey's missile zipped into a corporate hangar making a direct hit on a Grumman G-4. Pieces of the flaming wreckage hit three other corporate jets, turning the hangar into an inferno.

Leaving behind the empty crates and missile launchers, the men clutched their rifles and crawled back into the underbrush. One 30-round magazine lay forgotten on the ground. The terrorists returned to their car and made their way back to the Hutchinson River Parkway. As they headed south, emergency vehicles sped by in the opposite direction.

At the sound of the first explosions, Westchester County Police Lieutenant Ted Bates and his men raced outside to the front of the terminal some 75 yards from where the second missile had detonated. The heat was intense. In the distance he heard a third explosion. As he keyed his mike to call headquarters a giant ball of flame rose above the building followed by another blast.

He radioed County Police headquarters and was patched through to Chief. Thomas Farrell.

"Chief, Ted Bates, at the airport. We have had multiple explosions here including at least one in the terminal. Another made a huge fireball at the other end outside the terminal. It may have come from a plane on the tarmac."

"My God! Lt. I'm on the way. Locate the source of the explosions. This may be a terrorist attack and if it is they may hit you again. Issue tactical gear and weapons. Block the entrance to the airport. No one allowed in OR out except emergency vehicles. Understand. The terrorists may still be there."

"Understood, sir."

Farrell and his pilot climbed into the police helicopter in the parking lot of headquarters. An officer came running over. "Chief," he said breathing hard. "Terrorists have attacked a shopping mall in Minnesota. The FAA has grounded all aircraft."

"All? What about police and emergency?"

"Don't know sir."

"Well, we're going." He motioned to the pilot to start the engine. "Sergeant, tell Captain Honeywell to bring in everyone from days off and vacation. Send as many as he can men to the airport."

Without waiting for a reply he ordered his pilot, Sergeant Rick Pagonis to call New York Air Traffic Control. "Tell them we're in the air responding to Westchester Airport emergency."

"New York Air Traffic control, this is Whiskey Charlie Papa Chopper One, Westchester County Police Chief. We are airborne responding to Airport Emergency at Whiskey Papa November. Over."

"Roger Whiskey Charlie Papa One. This is New York Air Traffic Control. Maintain altitude five zero zero. Visibility unlimited. National emergency declared. All non-emergency aircraft ordered to land. Repeat. National emergency. Code red. All non-emergency aircraft are ordered to land. Whiskey Papa November, tower is not responding. Aircraft bound for Whiskey Papa November will be rerouted."

"Whiskey Charlie Papa One. Roger, altitude five zero zero."

After Pagonis touched down, Farrell leaped from the police helicopter. A County Police officer approached and saluted. "Report," Farrell ordered.

The officer began reading his notes. "Part of the passenger terminal roof collapsed. Two of our guys and an unknown number of people are inside. We're trying to reach them, but when the fuel truck and the jet exploded a lot of debris apparently hit the terminal blocking two of the exits. The control tower is gone and there's a big fire in a maintenance building and another in a corporate terminal. Lots of fuel around. Could go at any second," the officer said. "The airport fire department is working at the terminal, but they don't have enough equipment to handle the other fires."

"I know about the control tower. What about outside assistance?" the Chief asked. "Have they been requested?"

"Yes sir. White Plains and Greenwich are responding with major units. Port Chester, Rye, Hawthorne and Harrison are sending help too."

"What about the State Police?"

"On the way."

"Anyone notify the feds?"

"You mean the FBI, chief?"

"Yes, the FBI?"

"Not to my knowledge."

"Have you been able to determine where the attack came from?"

"It had to come from across the runway on the other side of the airport," said the officer pointing across the tarmac. "A maintenance worker claims he saw a missile come from over there."

"A missile? What kind of a missile?"

"Don't know, chief."

"Anyone investigating?" the chief asked.

"Not yet sir. We've got three people at the airport entrance. There are only six of us left plus the lieutenant and everyone here is concentrating on getting people out of those buildings. We've got two officers still inside the terminal."

"Where's Bates?" Farrell asked mentally assessing the chances of anyone getting out alive.

"He was on the radio talking to White Plains dispatch."

"I want to see him right away." Chief Farrell ordered.

The officer raced to the front of the passenger terminal where Lt. Bates was talking on his radio. Bates looked where the officer was pointing, nodded and trotted over to his boss.

"You wanted to see me, chief?" Bates asked.

"Lieutenant, it's my understanding that this might have been a missile attack and that it probably came from the other side of the airport. Is that correct?"

"That's what we believe, sir."

"Any men over there investigating?"

"No sir. I have only six men available. They're assisting the firefighters trying to get people out of the terminal," Bates replied.

"Lieutenant, your assistance won't do anyone any good if there is another attack. Your first responsibility is to secure the area and eliminate any additional threat."

"Sir, I...."

"Lieutenant, I asked you to issue special weapons and other gear. Have you done that?" the chief asked cutting him off.

"Not yet, sir."

"Do it now. Weapons, kevlar helmets and vests. Leave one man here. Take the rest to that tree line and try to find out where the missile came from. Be careful."

The lieutenant trotted back to his detail shouting instructions along the way. Farrell watched as the officers went to their van grabbing their emergency gear. They climbed into a patrol car and raced through the gate onto the tarmac.

"Jesus Christ," Chief Farrell said to Sgt. Pagonis. "What the fuck does Bates think he's doing? If there is anyone over there, one missile will take out his entire detail."

Not waiting for instructions, Sgt Pagonis transmitted the warning. "Lieutenant, do not approach the tree line in the patrol car. Dismount and spread out."

Realizing his mistake, Bates ordered the car stopped and his squad dispersed before beginning their approach.

"Sergeant," Chief Farrell said. "Get me the FBI, please."

Pagonis punched in the code and handed Farrell the phone.

"FBI," came the sweet tones of the operator.

"This is Tom Farrell, Westchester County Police Chief. I want to talk to Terry Daly or one of his deputies in the counter terrorism group right now."

"Assistant Deputy Director Brown's office. This is Sally."

"Is he there? This is an emergency. I'm Tom Farrell, Westchester County Police Chief."

"Sir, he's in a meeting."

"I repeat. This is an emergency. If he's unavailable get me Terry Daly or Roosevelt Ewing," the Chief said, his voice rising.

"They're all in the same meeting, sir."

"I don't want to have to say this again, God dammit. The County Airport has been attacked by terrorists. I need to talk to one of them right now. Do you understand. Right now!

Sally Weathers dropped the phone and walked around the corner to the conference room. She didn't wait for an answer to her knock. "Excuse me gentlemen, Westchester County Airport has been attacked. The County Police Chief is on the phone. He sounds like he's right on the edge."

"I'll take it," Brown said. "Farrell's a damn fine police officer, but he is excitable. And I guess given the circumstances, that's

19

understandable." He punched the button with the blinking light. "This is Carter Brown."

"Carter, the County Airport's been attacked."

"Let me put you on the speakerphone," Brown said. "Terry Daly and RE are here along with other agents. Go ahead chief."

"Gentlemen, this is Westchester County Police Chief Tom Farrell. Terrorists have attacked Westchester County Airport.

"Farrell, Terry Daly. My mother and father were scheduled to fly out of there on Delta today. What's going on?"

"I don't have a lot of information yet, sir. Here's what I know. Several buildings including the passenger terminal and the control tower were hit. Also a passenger jet. It appears to be a missile attack. State and more local police are on the way. Fire and med evac people too. No estimate on casualties, but it may be in the hundreds."

"Jesus," Daly said. "Listen carefully. Put your entire department on alert. Understand. This is the second attack. A large Mall in Minnesota was bombed just a few minutes ago. Where did the attack come from?"

"We think the missiles were launched from the tree line on the east side of the airport. I sent a squad over there."

"OK. We're on the way. Keep us informed," Daly said ending the call. "Carter, order a full alert. Then come with me." Daly opened the door and yelled, "Pat, call the heliport and tell them we need a team chopper in 15 minutes. Then tell Resnik to send a full team to the heliport. Have someone tell Roy Owens where we're headed. I'll fill him in from there. Got that?"

"Sir, Gail Resnik is involved with the mall attack," his secretary reported. "I don't think she has anyone she can spare. She's even getting help from Washington."

"Shit. OK I'm gonna try to reach Owens." Daly dialed the cell phone of FBI Director Roy Owens."

Owens felt the phone vibrate. He looked at the display and saw the word **emergency.**

"Owens."

"Terry. The County Airport in White Plains, New York has been attacked. Missiles they think. Resnik's got all her people on the mall attack. We need help. Can you spare anyone to cover here? I'm headed up there with a team.

"I'll get them from Newark and Philadelphia," Owens said. "Good luck."

Jameel Subaey tuned the car radio to an all news station. He and Faisel Hamed didn't have long to wait.

"This just in. Several explosions have rocked Westchester County Airport. According to authorities, several buildings are involved and emergency medical and fire apparatus have been called in from surrounding municipalities.

"We're on the phone with Lieutenant Dan Sykes at County Police headquarters now. Lt. Sykes what can you tell us?" the radio newsperson asked.

"As far as we can determine, the control tower and a plane have been destroyed. There were explosions in or near the passenger terminal, the maintenance building and in one of the corporate terminals."

Do you have any estimate on casualties?"

"We don't. But we're sure the numbers in the passenger terminal will be significant as two planes were on the tarmac. One was loading passengers. The plane that exploded was being refueled. I can't talk. Have to go." Sykes instantly regretted being so forthcoming.

"Thank you lieutenant. That was Lieutenant Dan Sykes of the Westchester County Police. Repeating this breaking story: in what could be a second terrorist attack today, several buildings at Westchester County Airport including the control tower and the passenger terminal have been wracked by explosions. No word on casualties. Stay tuned."

Hamed and Subaey congratulated one another.

"We should be hearing about the others shortly," Subaey said.

"Maybe we can catch it on TV," Hamed replied. "As he turned off the parkway, a huge black cloud rose rapidly into the sky behind. He smiled.

21

When Port Authority Police Chief William Reilly learned of the national emergency, on his own authority he ordered all city bridges and tunnels closed. No one challenged the decision. Subway, commuter trains and ferry service were also halted.

At the Westchester Airport, Chief Farrell stood next to the chopper watching fire apparatus arrive from nearby communities when Sgt. Pagonis handed him the phone. "It's Governor Pointer. You asked me to call him," the sergeant said. Farrell quickly reported the situation and obtained permission to close the Hutchinson River Parkway and the southern end of Route 684 except to emergency vehicles. The governor said he was calling up units of the National Guard. Farrell thanked the governor and handed the phone to Pagonis.

"Rick, call all PDs whose borders touch the Hutch. Have them block the northbound entrances. Nothing but emergency vehicles are allowed. Then request the same assistance from Greenwich for southbound traffic. If they need to pull in off-duty people tell them it's a federal emergency."

Pagonis dialed the emergency broadband number and broadcast the message to the local police departments. Farrell radioed Lieutenant Bates.

"Bates," the lieutenant said.

"Farrell. What's the status?" the chief asked.

"We just got here. We're starting the search now"

"Hold up until that chopper lands," Farrell said, referring to the helicopter in the distance. "Be careful. These guys may have had military training. We don't know what we're up against."

"This must be the FBI," Pagonis said as a large black helicopter made its approach from the south. It flew over the chief's chopper, circled and landed on the parking ramp about 100 feet away. Six men and three women dressed in blue battle dress and helmets emerged. Each carried MP-5 automatic weapons. Daly walked over to Farrell.

"Chief, Terry Daly, FBI. Anything new?" Daly asked, shaking hands.

"I don't have all the details. We have police at the tree line over there where we believe the attack came from. We may have lost two men in the terminal. Two planes were being loaded for departure.

One was hit. Fires are still out of control. More fire equipment's on the way. I've never seen anything like this, sir."

"Neither have I. Tell your men over there to secure anything they find and to wait for us," Daly ordered. "Carter, take four agents and get over there. Use the chopper."

"Right. Okay, you three and you, let's go," Brown barked. As the agents climbed into the chopper, Daly moved closer to the blazing terminal building. Farrell and two agents kept pace. Sgt. Pagonis and one agent stayed with the police chopper. The FBI chopper roared overhead and banked away from the flames and smoke.

Daly removed his sun glasses and wiped his eyes.

"Anything wrong?" the chief asked.

"I think my parents are in there."

"My God. I'm very sorry." Another section of the terminal roof collapsed sending cinders and a ball of flame skyward.

Tears rolled down Daly's cheeks. He wiped them with his sleeve and put on his sunglasses..

Farrell's radio crackled. "We've got something, chief," Lt. Bates said.

"What?" the chief responded, forgetting he had ordered Bates to wait for the FBI.

"Six launchers. Empty. Looks like Stingers. And their crates are here too."

"The FBI chopper is on the way. They'll take over. Follow their orders. Understood?"

Before Bates could reply, an officer tapped him on the shoulder, "Lieutenant, look at this." He pointed to the magazine,

The lieutenant glanced at it. "Chief, we also found a fully loaded magazine."

The FBI chopper landed noisily and the agents dismounted and ran into the woods. Carter Brown approached Bates and Romano.

"FBI, lieutenant. I'm Brown, Counter Terrorism," he said shaking the officer's hand. One of his agents started taking photos. Two others, wearing surgical gloves, began dusting the launchers for prints. "We'll handle things here. See what's down that road. If you find anything, give me a shout."

Led by Bates, the uniformed officers with weapons at the ready walked double file along the path as the FBI team continued with photographs and fingerprints. Brown began writing in his pad.

"Agent Brown?" one of the officers shouted as he trotted back to the scene.

"I'm Brown."

Not knowing if there was any protocol, the officer saluted before reporting. "Sir, we found tire tracks and some foot prints."

"Where?"

"About 75-100 yards from here," the officer replied pointing.

"Good work. Did you see anyone?"

"No sir. No one."

"Go ask the lieutenant to check both sides of the road for anything suspicious. Try to find out how they came in." Turning to the toiling agents, he said, "Bob, you finish with the prints. Cynthia, you and Larry get the plaster kit from the chopper and follow this officer."

The two agents picked up the suitcase containing the materials Brown requested. They followed the officer to the clearing and began making impressions.

"Rover, this is High Point," Brown's radio crackled.

"This is Rover, go ahead High Point," Brown said to Daly.

"What have you got, Carter?"

"Looks like six missiles. We have six empty FIM-92A Stinger missile launchers, six crates marked "beach umbrellas," and what appears to be an AK-47 magazine. Fully loaded. We're lifting prints now. The PD also found tire tracks and footprints. Cynthia and Larry are taking impressions."

"Stingers, eh. Sure would love to know where they came from. When you're done, put everything in plastic. I want to get that stuff to Washington. Any witnesses?"

"The uniforms are looking for witnesses. How's it going back there?"

"They're using foam on the terminal fire and it appears to be working. The entire roof collapsed. We're still getting small explosions from the hangar. It's going to be too hot to do anything for awhile. Listen, Carter, ask Arnie to radio New York. I want more agents here first thing tomorrow morning. You'll have to wait until things cool off. "

"Will do. We should be through here in about an hour or so. I'll ask the PD to put up yellow tape. I'll have Arnie radio New York right now. Rover, out."

Daly put his radio into its holster.

"The cowardly bastards," Farrell said. "All those people. They didn't do a thing to deserve this."

"God knows how many at the mall in Minnesota. Maybe now this country will wake up and remember that we're still at war," Daly said.

"War with what? We don't even know what country these cowards came from."

"We'll find them. Take that to the fucking bank," Daly said.

The two watched the assault on the flames unable to do anything. Across the airstrip the FBI chopper became airborne. Daly and Farrell shut their eyes to avoid the swirling dirt as the chopper approached. When it touched down, Brown jumped out ahead of the other special agents and trotted to Daly.

"Looks like usable prints from the missile launchers, boss, and the foot prints may yield something too," Brown said. "But we hit the jackpot on one of the crates the missile launchers came in."

"What do you mean?" Daly asked. Farrell edged closer.

"One of the crates is addressed to the Saudi UN Mission on Lexington Avenue. It has a diplomatic stamp and a customs receipt stapled to it."

"Are you certain?"

"Absolutely. It's in the chopper." Brown led the way as the three walked swiftly to the aircraft. Brown unzipped the plastic bag .

"Fanfuckingtastic," Daly said. "Owens will enjoy seeing this and Secretary Mooreland will positively salivate. Get some photos in case the crate is lost or damaged."

"Already done, boss, from four different angles in the position where they were found. And I even have establishing shots showing the location of the crates with the fires in the background."

"Good work, Carter. Daly turned to Farrell. "Please impress upon your men the necessity for keeping the information about the missiles completely confidential. It's vitally important, chief. We don't want the media to know anything about this."

"I agree fully," the chief said. "And I'd like you to tell them so they know that this is serious."

When the patrol car pulled up, the chief introduced Daly to the officers.

"Lieutenant, I want to thank you and your men," Daly said.

"It took real courage to approach those trees. I'm proud of all of you. But please understand you are to tell no one about what you saw in the woods. No one. Not even family. The explosions and fire are public knowledge. What you found is top secret. Do you all understand how vitally important secrecy is?"

"Yes sir," they responded in unison.

"Thank you gentlemen." He congratulated each officer individually. When the formality concluded, Daly told Brown he was returning to the office and would order the chopper to return with supplies to get them through the night.

"I'll bring Roy up to date when we're airborne. If you come up with any new evidence or witnesses let me know right away," Daly said. "Another crew will relieve you guys in the morning." Turning to the pilot, he said, "Call New York. Tell them to meet me at the heliport with a van. I want this stuff on a flight to Washington soonest. And tell New York, to have a van meet that flight. I want a super double rush effort from the lab on fingerprints, footprints, tire prints and an analysis of everything else. I'll be with chief Farrell."

-Chapter Three-

Tens of millions of Americans were riveted to the TV screens as local reporters described the horrific scenes at the Mall of America and the airport.

The governors of Minnesota and New York responded quickly dispatching National Guard troops and State Police. Local highways near both disaster scenes were closed to all civilian traffic. Ambulances, rescue workers and firefighters arrived at the Mall from as far away as Chicago and Milwaukee. One of Bloomington's schools was turned into a morgue; another became an emergency shelter for the injured awaiting transport to hospitals. At Westchester Airport, eleven surrounding communities sent emergency equipment, firefighters and medical personnel. One of the corporate hangars was turned into a morgue; another became a trauma center. Ambulances and EMS Units lined the curb.

Around the country, malls closed, airline and rail service was suspended and traffic at toll bridges and tunnels was halted.

President Harold Barnes was meeting with members of his cabinet and senior staff reviewing the staff assessment of the recent Congressional refusal to make requested changes in immigration policy when his Chief of Staff Fred Randolph returned and approached.

When Randolph whispered the news, the President was visibly shaken. "Oh my God," he managed.

"Sir," Randolph continued, "The FBI found empty missile launchers and their packing crates. One had a tag with the address, UN Mission to Saudi Arabia, Lexington Avenue, New York."

"Are you sure?" the president asked. "No mistake."

"That's what the report said. The address was written in Arabic and English. And the crates were labeled Beach Umbrellas."

"Repeat what you said," the president ordered.

After completing his report, Randolph added. "Mr. President, I've asked the Air Force to put up fighter cover over the New York metro area until we have a better handle on this." Barnes nodded his approval.

"Mr. President," Nancy Hanks, the National Security Advisor interrupted. "Sir, you should move to the Crisis Command Center. Now. This could be just the first of many attacks." She buzzed the Secret Service outside the door and called the duty officer.

Three Secret Service officers appeared in the conference room. The President rose and said, "Very well, we'll all go down. Fred, we need information, as much as you can get, and as soon as possible. Nancy, get the vice president airborne."

Homeland Security Secretary Philip Mooreland excused himself and called FBI Director Roy Owens.

Additional Secret Service agents appeared and surrounded the President. Two agents led the way to the Crisis Command Center deep beneath the White House. Hanks stayed behind and called the vice president. Within minutes he was whisked from his residence to a waiting chopper.

The group assembled in the Center and settled in. While Randolph gathered information on the two attacks, the president asked that the overhead TV screen be lowered. For 35 minutes the group watched news reports in silence. When Randolph entered the room the president began, "It would appear that we now have what the media call a smoking gun," the president said. "The question is what the hell do we do with it? Do we let the world know? What do we do about Saudi Arabia?"

"Mr. President, the Saudi Mission address doesn't by itself implicate Saudi Arabia, sir." Senior Military Advisor General

Beverly Watson said. "Before we make anything public we ought to at least ask the ambassador to explain."

"General, the Saudi Ambassador will deny everything and claim that someone put the address tag on the box to try to discredit the Saudis." Secretary of State Alan Collins said.

"There is one sure way to find out," said Randolph. All we have to do is find out how those missile crates were delivered. If they were picked up at the airport, the customs receipt would indicate who picked them up."

"Good thinking, Fred," the president said. "No one has claimed responsibility yet. But the FBI is certain it was the work of terrorists in both instances. There were several explosions in different parts of the Mall. And missiles were used at the airport."

"Jorge, shut that off, please," President Barnes said to Senior Advisor Jorge Rivera. The group turned their attention to Barnes. "It would appear these attacks are worse than the one on the Towers certainly in terms of casualties and the effect on the national psyche. Tell Governor Holmes and Governor Pointer I'll be speaking with them shortly. And alert FEMA."

"Sir I think you should consider addressing the nation tonight. You have to say something reassuring," Randolph said. "Americans don't just want to hear how sorry you are. They want you to show some leadership."

"I agree," senior political advisor Donald Paterson said. "This may have wide ranging repercussions. Some members of Congress will be looking for a scapegoat, someone to blame. And there may be some panic."

"What can I tell the American people? How many casualties have we suffered? What should we tell them about their future? Will there be more attacks? How come we didn't see this coming? What is Congress going to do? I need some answers."

"Sir," Randolph began as he was handed a report from one of his assistants. "I've got more information. The preliminary report from the airport at White Plains indicates missiles were used by at least two terrorists. They were fired about two miles away from the buildings. Damage extensive, the control tower, the passenger terminal, a plane being refueled and a corporate terminal, destroying several planes inside. Two police officers killed. Civilian casualties between 200 and 500. Nearby municipalities have responded with fire, police and medical help. Gary, anything else from White Plains?

"No sir," said Gary Flowers, assistant to the Chief of Staff. "The report from the mall is coming in now."

"Can anyone speculate as to why terrorists would hit a small regional airport in a state with one of the busiest, most important airports in the world?" the president asked. "I just don't get it."

"There may be several reasons," Mooreland said. "First, our security at the more well-known facilities like JFK and LaGuardia may have forced them to seek targets where the security isn't as tight. Or, this may have been just one of a number of planned attacks that either haven't happened yet or were called off for some reason," Mooreland said.

"Are you telling me there may be other attacks on the other airports?"

"It makes sense. Coordinated attacks would isolate the New York-New Jersey metro area for weeks," Mooreland replied.

"Not to mention confidence in flying," said Hanks. "Such a scenario would have disastrous consequences. Hell, after what happened in Minnesota it may be months before people return to shopping malls in any significant numbers. If they are looking for a way to damage our economy, they sure as hell found it."

"Additional attacks aren't likely now," Mooreland said. "Special counter terrorism procedures are automatically activated in the event of a warning or an attack. Security is at code red at all airports now. They're all closed."

The president removed his glasses, putting them on the long polished conference table. "You know, what's puzzling me is why did they attack a mall and an airport separated by a thousand miles? Is it possible several cells acted independently of each other?"

"Mr. President. I'm guessing, but I'd bet that these two attacks were independently planned and executed," said Mooreland. "Roy told me the FBI has picked up no increased elint."

Randolph was scanning the report from Minnesota when the president asked, "is that the latest from the Mall?"

"Yes sir. The preliminary FBI report indicates at least five separate explosions of significant power. No one has claimed responsibility. Casualty estimates are ghastly, 50,000. Maybe more."

"Fifty thousand! Jesus Christ, that's incredible. That many are dead?" the president asked.

"Not sure, sir, but I believe that would be both dead and injured. Security at the mall says attendance was between 70 and 80 thousand. There are large fires and one of the bombs destroyed the large aquarium. The water is four feet deep in some places. Many of the injured probably drowned. The FBI Agent in Charge said dozens of cars exploded. The fires prevented shoppers from using those exits and that may have contributed to even more casualties. And it appears bombs were deliberately exploded near the North and South Food Courts. It was lunch time."

"Those fucking cowardly bastards," the president said in a low tone. "I'll tell you right now if we can pin this on any country, they will pay a very dear price."

"Mr. President, the FBI AIC says access security to the mall was almost non-existent," Randolph said completing the report. "No one checks shopping bags for anything let alone weapons."

"I'm not surprised," said the president. "Don, how does that translate politically?"

"It will be hard for Congress to attack you on that point, sir. You cannot order Malls to install better security systems. Our political weakness may be the airport depending upon what the FBI finds," said Paterson.

"Hell. Didn't that fathead Senator Featherstone tell me he would not consider the personal X-Ray to improve security? I think he called it an invasion of privacy. Well, so is a bomb that takes off a leg or an arm."

"Sir, but this attack happened because of a breakdown in perimeter security. That's the airport's responsibility in conjunction with local police. And Sen. Featherstone might find a way to make you take the rap for that," Paterson said.

"Phil, you know what we need? We need more evidence that will directly connect Saudi Arabia to this. Now the question is, how do we get that?"

"My guys are doing everything they can, following every lead," said Mooreland.

"Suppose we resorted to things that are not Kosher to help us get that evidence?" the president asked. No one in the room responded. "Look, we sure as hell aren't winning the war on the home front. We can't find these bastards despite my pleadings and Congress isn't doing much to stop the influx of people who might do these kinds of things. So we have to think out of the box."

"Are you suggesting, Mr. President, that we, ah, stretch the limits on…….."

"Well, I'm not sure what I'm suggesting. But I am sure of two things. The first is we are still at war. And the second is we have been attacked again. In a war I don't think being politically correct is very helpful. You know what's been troubling me? A former president declared three countries as the axis of evil and put some cosmetics on the immigration problem. And he named a number of other countries that support terrorism in one way or another. But what the hell have we done since?" the president asked.

"Nothing. We still accept visitors and residents from Iran, Iraq, Egypt, Somalia, Libya, Syria and the Sudan. And North Korea too. And thousands still cross our borders illegally every day. Hell, we have a visa lottery that is nothing more than an engraved invitation to our enemies. I've never heard of anything so stupid in my life."

"Sen. Poindexter, Sen. Gomez and their group won't go for any changes in immigration, Mr. President," Paterson said. "We've been down that road."

"I know. Their only concern is getting re-elected and illegal immigrants represent future voters," the president replied.

"But, the Visa Lottery system might give you something to talk about. Not many people in this country know very much about that. Discussed in the right context, it might embarrass certain members of Congress," said Paterson.

"Don, are you suggesting I make a political pre-emptive strike in my speech tonight?"

"It's worth considering, Mr. President. You have asked for changes in the immigration laws on two occasions and been turned down on both."

"Featherstone and Poindexter aren't going to like that," said Randolph.

"They'll try to make political hay," Paterson said. "But if you point out a glaring weakness in our system and can lay that at the feet of Congress, it mutes their argument."

"OK. Now what do you think about closing some embassies and UN missions, kicking some of these trouble makers the hell out of here? Alan?"

"Mr. President, we can't do that without good reason." Secretary of State Alan Collins asked.

"We've got good reason. Two of them. Let's start with Hammas, the Palestinians. We should have gotten rid of them years ago. And what about Iran, Syria, Somalia, the Sudan and Libya?"

"Mr. President, those countries have missions under the auspices of the United Nations. We can't close them," Collins said.

"Why the hell not? This is a God damned national emergency. No other country has suffered this level of terrorism. As president, I see these people as a threat to National Security. If the UN wants one of their representatives here for a vote or for some cocktail party, they can ask State for permission to fly someone here. But other than that, let's make them persona non grata."

"Mr. President, don't you think that is a little precipitous?" Collins asked.

"Alan, America took it on the chin ten years ago. The President then said to the world, you are either with us or against us. If you befriend the terrorists, you are our enemy. Well now, by God, we're going to back that up. We've taken two more body blows. And if the reports of the Mall attack are accurate...." He stopped, shaking his head.

"We know who's behind it. We know who trains these murderers, who finances them and where they are hiding. Trouble is we can't prove it. Yet. Well, in the meantime, we don't have to sit with our thumbs hiding in our body cavities. We can do something and by God we will."

"Sir, I must advise you in the strongest possible terms not to do this," Collins said. "The United Nations will take a very dim view of any unilateral action to close any missions."

"Good. It's about time somebody stood up to the high and mighty UN. They don't see fit to condemn PLO sponsored attacks in Israel, yet they condemn Israel for hitting back. They didn't think it necessary to declare Iran an outlaw nation when it stormed our embassy and held our people hostage. They didn't insist that Iraq obey the Gulf War Treaty. They make a mockery of the Oil for Food program, allow Iran to develop nuclear weapons and then make Libya, Syria, and China members of the UN Human Rights Council. Do you want me to continue? In short, I have no particular use for the UN," the president said. "It's a U.S. bashing cocktail club. And I'll bet that if we were to take a poll of Americans right now, they'd vote to kick the UN out of New York.

"Supposing I told the American people I would be sending legislation to Congress requesting, no make that demanding tough immigration laws to enable us to monitor the movements and the phone conversations of all immigrants? It would be difficult for Congress to say no after today."

"Mr. President, in my opinion even after the attacks, the senate won't go along with any change to 241i," Randolph said.

"God damn it, Fred, these killers use our own laws against us. They sneak into our country and we let them stay because they find loopholes. Then they show their gratitude by murdering us by the thousands. If that doesn't piss you off, I'd like to know what does," the president said. "We probably can't eliminate terrorism, but we damn sure don't have to help them."

"I agree, Mr. President," Mooreland said. "There are a number of things we can look at. One is a national ID card, a card for everyone including all foreigners. People who don't have a card should be detained and deported if they are here illegally."

"A national ID card? Mr. Secretary, most Americans won't stand for that," Paterson said. "A lot of people already see government as big brother and a national ID card will positively inflame them."

"I disagree," the National Security Advisor said. "Couched in the right terms I think we can sell it. Right now I think we can sell anything. A national ID card is no different in many respects than a driver's license. It will be helpful in tracking foreigners and I think the FBI could use the help."

34

President Barnes buzzed his secretary. "Lucy, ask Lisa Cunningham to come to my office. I want her to get to work on a short address to the nation tonight."

"Yes sir."

"And get me the Minnesota governor, please." Barnes resumed talking to the group, "I'm zeroing in on three things: diplomatic action, tougher immigration laws and a national ID card," Barnes said. "Any other suggestions?"

"Mr. President," Rivera said. "I agree with Don, sir, the ID card is a bad idea. It won't sit well with a lot of minorities, especially those who here illegally."

Lucy Vernon knocked and entered, "Mr. President, excuse me, Governor Holmes is on the line and Lisa Cunningham is here."

"Very well, Lucy. Tell Lisa I'll be right with her. Ladies and gentlemen, thank you for your input and your good wishes. Phil, Fred will you stay, please."

Mooreland and Randolph remained seated. The others put their papers in brief cases and filed out. The President picked up the phone.

"Governor Holmes, President Barnes. I want to express my sincere condolences on behalf of the nation. Our prayers are with you, all of you out there. Is there anything you need? Anything at all?"

"Thank you Mr. President. In all my years of public service and in the military I've never seen anything close to this. Mall officials estimate upwards of 80,000 people were in the mall. The carnage is horrible. The dead and injured number in the tens of thousands. I've activated the entire National Guard but what we desperately need are doctors, nurses and med evac choppers. Our medical facilities are overloaded. Can you send us medical supplies and doctors and nurses?"

"Governor, I've asked Fred Randolph my chief of staff to coordinate federal efforts with your office. He'll get you whatever you need. The folks from FEMA will be arriving tomorrow."

"Mr. President, Governor Pointer is on line 3."

"Thank you Lucy. Goodbye governor. Lucy, ask Lisa to come in, please."

"Governor Pointer, President Barnes. On behalf of this country I want to offer my condolences to your great state. Our prayers are with you. I also want you to know that we'll send you anything you need." Barnes said.

"Thank you Mr. President" Gov. Pointer said. "We still don't know the number of dead and injured. I've heard some estimates as high as five or six hundred. Westchester isn't a big airport, but it means a lot to the economy of Westchester County. I've activated units of the National Guard to supplement State, County and local police. "

"I understand, Governor. I've asked Fred Randolph my chief of staff to coordinate federal relief efforts with your office and FEMA."

"Thank you Mr. President."

"I'll also schedule a trip up your way later this week or next week."

"Your visit will mean a lot, sir."

"My office will be in touch. Good luck governor."

"Thank you, sir."

After the president hung up, Lisa Cunningham spoke up, "Mr. President. Mr. Secretary. I want to express my sorrow and my condolences about what happened today. It's sickening."

"Thank you. Lisa, I want to talk to the nation tonight. I've got some ideas. I want a draft of a speech that shows what action we are taking. I want it forceful, but not too hard edged. I want it to show the American people and the rest of the world that we are angry and we will fight back. I've asked Secretary Mooreland and Fred Randolph to help."

President Barnes began his speech at 8 p.m. central time.

"Good evening. As many of you know, earlier today, at about two p.m. Eastern Time on the 10th anniversary of the world Trade Center attacks, a series of bombs were detonated by suicidal terrorists at the Mall of America in Bloomington, Minnesota," the president said. "At just about the same time, a regional airport in Westchester County, New York was attacked by terrorists using shoulder fired missiles.

"Hundreds of rescue workers, medical personnel, police and firefighters are doing everything they can for the injured and to rescue those who may be trapped. At this point we do not know how many casualties there are but the estimates of the dead and injured may run as high as 50,000. Perhaps even more. Both the mall and the airport were heavily damaged.

"To the people of Minnesota and New York, the thoughts and prayers of all Americans and millions of other decent peace-loving people around the world are with you tonight.

I have received messages of condolences from the heads of more than 60 nations including the United Kingdom, France, Germany, Italy, Japan, Russia, China and many more. This afternoon I spoke with Minnesota Governor Holmes and New York Governor Pointer. I assured them that they will get whatever help they need from Washington.

"Today's attacks on American soil are the worst in the history of our great nation and may be the worst terrorist attacks ever. They were carried out by cowards, people who have no regard for life, who will slaughter innocent men, women and children. These people claim their acts in the name of their religion," President Barnes said.

"This has nothing to do with religion. These were despicable acts of hate and evil. They hate our culture and they hate us because we are tolerant of all religions. They hate the fact that we are free, that we are diverse and that we cherish our differences and are strong because of them. They hate us because we are wealthy. And they hate us because we treat men and women equally. By committing these unspeakable acts, these terrorists believed they would become martyrs. They will not. They are nothing but cold-blooded murderers.

"They have hurt us. But they cannot defeat us. Today's attacks will not go unavenged. The despicable people who mastermind these senseless attacks, the people who fund the terrorists, and the countries who harbor them will pay a fearsome price. As of this moment, the policy of this administration will be to treat a terrorist as a representative of his country. And that country will be dealt with severely. To you who would befriend terrorism I say listen to my words very carefully.

"Seventy years ago, with God's help, America and her allies wiped the scourge of Nazism from the face the earth. It took courage and enormous sacrifice and an indomitable spirit. As Nazism was the scourge of the 20th century, terrorism is the scourge of the 21st.

And it too will be wiped from the face of the earth. No matter what cave you hide in or what rock you have crawled under we will find you. Do not expect mercy. For your actions transcend mercy. Expect death and destruction," Barnes said.

"This great nation has always been a beacon for the religiously persecuted and politically oppressed, the poor, the unfortunate and all those who seek a better life. Since the attacks on the World Trade Center ten years ago, your government has been hard at work developing new measures to deal with immigration that would help ensure that honest, decent, hardworking people would continue to be welcomed while those who would cause us harm would be denied admittance.

"Tonight, I am announcing the following steps:

"First, on my orders, the United States has broken diplomatic relations with the Palestine Liberation Organization, the Sudan, Iran, Syria, Somalia and Libya. These people harbor terrorists and permit training camps on their soil. Their missions and embassies in New York, Washington and elsewhere in this country will be closed and their personnel ordered to leave our shores," President Barnes said. "I have ordered our personnel in those countries where we have embassies to come home. All Americans who are traveling in those countries are strongly advised to leave and to return home.

"Second, for the foreseeable future, our borders will be closed to citizens of Iran, Syria, Libya, Somalia and the Sudan. Citizens from those countries who are currently in our country will be ordered to report to the nearest office of the Federal Bureau of Investigation. No American will be permitted to visit any of those countries.

"Third, within the next few days this administration will send to the Congress a proposal for new laws dealing with immigration. I will ask Congress to make it a serious federal crime to enter this country illegally or to stay in this country once an individual's visa has expired," Barnes said.

"Those individuals who have entered this country illegally or those whose visas have expired will be deported instead of being given an opportunity to apply for permanent residency. People who are here illegally clearly are not playing by the rules. And that applies to business owners who employ illegal aliens. They will be required to notify law enforcement officials. Foreign students will be required to report their student status and residency every quarter," Barnes continued. "If they fail to do that, they will be deported."

"Currently, there is an immigration law on the books that is counter-productive to our national security. It provides for a visa lottery that permits 55,000 people each year to enter this country if they are selected. And this includes people from the countries that I mentioned earlier. This law was enacted years ago to give people greater access to our shores, but the law gives lottery winners an unfair advantage over those who undergo normal background checks and processing," the president said. "We will seek to have that law repealed."

"Since that tragic day ten years ago, it has become increasingly clear that there is indeed a profile of the individuals who would try to destroy our nation. In an effort to be politically correct airport security personnel and law enforcement officials around the country have been focusing many who do not fit the terrorist profile rather than on those who do. This is not only unfair to those involved, it is also inefficient and ineffective.

"To address this problem and to tighten homeland security, I will ask Congress for a new law requiring all American citizens over the age of 12 to carry a national identity card. Foreign-born visitors who are in this country legally also will be required to register and obtain this form of identification. The card will include a photo, name, address, date of birth and the individual's nationality if he or she is not an American. A digitized code will ensure the card cannot be copied and that it can be read easily by special machines in much the same way as machines at supermarkets now read the digitized information on the products we buy. This will take some time to implement, but we will put a high priority on it.

"In the case of foreign visitors, the individual's fingerprints will be on the back of the card," the president continued. "This card must be carried by everyone over 12 at all times and must be produced when requested by law enforcement officials at the federal, state and local levels. It must be shown to officials before entering a terminal to board a bus, train or plane or when registering at a hotel or motel. Similarly, the card must be produced to gain entry to sports facilities, shopping malls, and theaters.

"This card in most respects is no different than a driver's license. Machines will be able to read the information on it electronically. In the coming months card readers will be available at airports, sports arenas, theaters and shopping malls," the president said

"The United States is admired around the world. It is one of the few nations whose citizens are not packing to leave. Instead it is a beacon, a magnet for those seeking freedom and opportunity.

"The proposals I will be sending to Congress will not prevent those seeking a better life from coming to our shores. Instead, it will make the opportunity even more attractive by helping to ensure the safety of all people who live here now and in the future.

"Now I ask that you join me in a moment of silent prayer for the victims and their families in New York and Minnesota and for the men and women who are working valiantly to assist them. Thank you, and may God Bless America!"

"That son of a bitch," Sen. Featherstone said.

-Chapter Four-

The day after the attacks Terry Daly, Director of the FBI's Counter Terrorism Division was in his office at 26 Federal Plaza by 6:30.

At 6 feet four inches tall, Daly was just under the maximum height. A former Green Beret, Daly used the Army bonuses to pay for his education, majoring in accounting at University of North Carolina in Chapel Hill where he met his wife, Ellen. The two fell in love and married. After graduating, Daly passed the FBI exams and entered the FBI Academy where he excelled, finishing number two in his class. He was offered a choice of two positions, an instructor at the academy, or field work in Chicago near Glenview where Ellen's parents lived.

Over the next five years, the Daly's had two children, Beth, now 8, and Terry, Jr., now 5. Daly quickly demonstrated his investigative and leadership skills as a Special Agent in the Chicago office. After the 9/11/01 attacks he received an offer to head the Counter Terrorism Department. His supportive wife, Ellen was thrilled at the prospect of moving to the New York area. The promotion carried an increase in salary enabling them to find a modest house in the northern suburb of Larchmont in Westchester County just a few miles from the badly damaged airport.

After making a pot of coffee, Daly called the county police for the latest information. Lt. Bates told him it was unlikely they would find the bodies of Daly's parents because of the intensity of the fire.

"I'll call you if anything changes, Mr. Daly. I'm very sorry."

"Thanks. I appreciate anything you can do." Daly began reading the report on the attack on the Mall in Minnesota. He was looking for similarities or patterns to measure against what he knew about the attack on the Westchester Airport. When his two deputies arrived at 7:30, he was listening to a voice mail from Roy Owens calling a meeting in Washington of the top FBI people.

"Good morning, Terry," Carter Brown said as he poked his head in the door. "I'm sorry to hear about your parents. Is there anything I can do?"

"Morning, boss," said Roosevelt Ewing. "Carter told me about your folks, Terry. I'm very sorry. Is there anything we can do?

"Thanks. Ellen is going to handle things for the next few days until we sort out what happened. Then I'll take some time to get their affairs in order."

Both Brown and Ewing were older than Daly and each had five more years' experience with the Bureau. Brown had been a Special Agent in Philadelphia prior to joining the Counter Terrorism Division that Daly headed reporting directly to Owens.

Ewing was a Special Agent in New York and had participated in several successful investigations of organized crime leading to some important convictions. Daly liked them both and had hand picked them for the Counter Terrorism Division.

Brown was 6 feet 1 inches tall. At 200, he was trim, if not lean, some 20 pounds lighter than his boss, and his weight never varied. A graduate of Michigan, Brown played college football and Lacrosse for three years. After Michigan, he married his high school sweetheart and went to law school at Fordham, graduating in the middle of his class. He had difficulty with the bar exams the first time, but passed on the second.

His hero was his father, a retired New York City Police Captain. Brown developed the love for law enforcement from his father and chose the FBI so he could use his legal training. His wife was disappointed, but he told her if it didn't work out he could always become a shyster lawyer. Lisa Brown soon got used to being the wife of a Special Agent.

Since they couldn't have children, she went to law school and passed the bar on the first try. Lisa decided NOT to tease her husband about the bar exams. And she also decided NOT to become a Special Agent.

"I'll be the shyster lawyer in the family," she joked.

The Browns lived across the Hudson River in Leonia, New Jersey in a well kept, modest home near Overpeck Park, a recreation area reclaimed from the meadows. Lisa and Carter jogged on the track there several times a week.

Lisa worked about five miles away in a law office in Hackensack, the county seat, where she specialized in divorce proceedings.

Roosevelt Ewing, known as RE to his colleagues, was different in almost every respect. He was 5 feet, eight inches tall and weighed 170. Although he worked out regularly as required by the Bureau, and was in terrific shape, Ewing preferred working with figures, studying tax returns, corporate finances and the like. A CPA, Ewing majored in accounting and had graduated second in his class at Miami of Ohio. After college, he earned a master's degree in computer programming and quickly became a systems expert with the title Cisco Certified Internet Expert (CCIE).

With a nose and a computer to sniff out money laundering, covert bank accounts and illegal offshore investments, activities practiced not only by white collar criminals, but also terrorists, he was an invaluable member of the team. He was also an integral part of the government team that went after hackers who penetrated federal computer systems. Ewing loved outsmarting them.

He was single and often worked well into the night. He rarely carried his service weapon, keeping it locked in the drawer in his desk. Not carrying it outside the office was a Bureau violation, but no one objected.

Both Brown and Ewing respected Daly's Special Forces background and leadership. They were intensely loyal to their boss. All three were fanatically dedicated to fighting terrorism.

Brown and Ewing settled into the chairs at Daly's conference table on the 15th floor of the New York FBI office. Daly poured himself another cup of coffee and set it on the table. He retrieved some papers from his desk and sat down.

"OK I've got a report from Fran Denton at the mall that I'll share with you, but first I want to hear what you found at Westchester. Carter."

"You know most of this. Not much has changed since you left yesterday. The control tower was destroyed. Judging by the wreckage, it might have been hit twice. Most of the main terminal building was also destroyed. We were able to get the passenger manifests for both planes, but that doesn't mean all those people were victims. One of the planes had not arrived when the attack occurred and some of the passengers may not have checked in," Brown said referring to his report.

"There were five survivors from the main terminal building. All are critical. Westchester doesn't have any jetways, so the planes and service equipment are fairly close to the terminal. The MD-80 was probably 75 feet away from the terminal gate and the fuel truck was alongside. Apparently the missile hit the fuel truck and the explosion hurled a huge piece of wreckage onto the roof near the front door of the terminal and the roof collapsed trapping everyone inside. There was a secondary explosion a minute or so later when one of the wing tanks let go. The fire caused by the fuel was so hot it melted the beams in the ceiling.

"These guys were experts," Brown said. "They took their time and they didn't miss. One of their targets was a hangar housing a Grumman G-5, three other corporate jets and a helicopter. The explosion sent shrapnel and flaming wreckage all over the hangar. The sprinkler system in the ceiling apparently was destroyed by one of the explosions because it never worked. There's not much left of the hangar or the aircraft. Another missile hit a fuel truck near a maintenance building.

"Casualties?" Daly asked.

"Not sure yet, boss, but between 400 and 600 is a good guess. That includes two county uniforms," Brown said. "We have 10 people there today. As you know, yesterday, agents took some impressions of some pretty clear footprints and tire tracks on a muddy portion of a dirt road on the far side of the airport. They also found a fully loaded banana clip from an AK-47. The piece de resistance was the address of the Saudi UN Mission on one of the six Stinger missile crates left at the scene. It was written in Arabic and English and had a customs number on it."

"My God," Ewing said. "That's a smoking gun if there ever was one."

"Right," said Daly. "On my orders, Carter sent a secure email to Owens and Mooreland and the White House Chief of Staff. Keep this to yourselves. I'm not sure what the president will want to do with this.

"Thanks Carter. The report I got from Francis Denton in Minnesota looks like a casualty report from a major Civil War battle. Fran said they believe there were five detonations, one in the main section of the mall, one in each of the food courts and one at the mall entrances to each of the garages. She said the explosion in the main section was so powerful steel beams in the ceiling were buckled upward and nearly all of the glass was blown out. The security chief who is a Vietnam vet said he has never heard an explosion that loud. The floor in his office rippled and almost all of the video monitors broke free from their mountings. Preliminary findings suggest the fires in the garages were accelerated by additional fuel," Daly said. "Some of the cars were partially melted.

"They found the remains of a truck owned by a company called Krone's Sounds or something like that. The panel was badly singed. One of the security guards said he talked briefly with two guys from Krone's who were setting up the sound system for an afternoon concert. These guys could not be located and no one answered the phone at the company offices. Probably closed because it was Sunday. Anyway, the two guys are missing. Our team will question the Krone's people today.

"Fran said hospitals are reporting upwards of 20,000 injured. They won't have an accurate figure on the number of dead for weeks until we get missing persons complaints from the families of the victims. In the cases of whole families being wiped out, the wait may be longer.

"They'll begin building a picture based on the number of undamaged cars that haven't been driven from the parking lots. By the way, one of the casualties was a woman named Martha Simpson. She died at the hospital. Her father is Bill Burdette, CIA Director," Daly said. "You guys know Bill."

"Ah jeez," said Brown. "I met Martha several years ago. Bumped into her and her father with the kids at the Museum of Natural History. She was a doll. What a damn shame."

"I'll call Bill next week," Daly said before resuming the report. When he finished no one spoke for several minutes. Daly broke the ice changing the subject.

"As you might expect, the president will be on the Congressional hot seat very quickly. Mooreland is going to try to meet with the President late this week and he wants the Counter-Terrorism team to give him our assessment of security at the other three New York area airports. Apparently there is some thought the terrorists are still going to attack them. He wants to know everything about security and that includes entrances and exits, parking, ticket counter, baggage, passenger screening, catering, ramps, and aircraft maintenance. Oh, and he wants to know what we've done about perimeter security."

"Shit," said Brown. "He's not going to like what he hears about JFK. I've got 11 agents working that place. So far they have smuggled knives aboard aircraft, suspicious materials in luggage and have wandered just about everywhere through baggage and maintenance, including the hangars without being challenged. And, LaGuardia isn't much better. One of my guys just walked into the Delta hangar unchallenged."

"Your fucking kidding," Daly said. "You mean no one asked him what he was doing?

"Hell no," Brown said. " He could have sabotaged a plane, planted a bomb, anything. And no one challenged him. By the way, the LaGuardia report hasn't been completed. We still have information coming in. But if it is as bad as what we found at JFK, the shit is going to hit the fan."

"Boss, I know you are aware we have a bit of a political situation here. The security people are essentially the same group of somnambulists we had before they became federal employees. If we come down too hard, we're going to create a field day with the media and embarrass some senators and congressman who thought federalizing them was a good idea."

"I know," Daly agreed. "We know these airports are a fucking time bomb. And I sure as hell don't want my family in one of them when some asshole lights the fuse under his shirt. What about Newark? Is that any better?"

"Perhaps," said Brown as he opened the red folder labeled EWR Security/CLASSIFIED. "Thanks to the security breaches uncovered at Newark about four years ago security is tighter. But that may be in part due to the location of the airport with fewer roads in and out. Newark is newer and has more modern detection equipment. And it doesn't have a parking garage." He turned a couple of pages. "But we did uncover one serious flaw. Two of my guys were successful in driving right into the Celestial maintenance area."

"How the hell did they do that?" Daly asked

"They were wearing Celestial aircraft maintenance uniforms."

"Didn't anyone ask who they were? New faces and they go unchallenged?" Daly wondered. "How did they get down to the tarmac?"

"They followed a Celestial employee into the break room, hung around by the bulletin board for a couple of minutes and then walked out to the tarmac," Brown reported. "It gets worse. A guy in the refueling truck must have thought they were ok because he saw them come out of the break room. He laughed when they asked if they could borrow his truck to pull a prank on someone. The man said 'sure, go ahead. It's my break anyway.' He hopped out of the cab and walked into the break room. And the agents drove the truck to the hangar. The truck had 6,000 gallons of jet fuel in it."

Daly slammed his fist onto the table.

"They have tighter security at Starbucks. That fucking refueling driver should be canned. And his fucking supervisor too." He walked to his desk and pressed the intercom.

"Pat, get me the director of operations at Celestial Airlines. If he's not there get me his deputy. If he's not there, get me...... wait a minute. Carter, who is the CEO of Celestial?"

"Ah, it's Walter Amberly," Brown replied.

"Thanks." Pressing the intercom, he said, "Pat, get me Walter Amberly at Celestial Airlines right away. Interrupt me when you have him on the line. And don't let some lackey prevent you from reaching him."

"Right away," Pat Clinton, Daly's secretary, said.

"You know, Mooreland's going to shit when he see this report. It won't be pretty when he tells the President. I love seeing Mooreland sitting on the hot seat. He's in over his head. Way over," said Brown.

"Remember something, Carter. You too, RE. Shit always rolls downhill," Daly declared. A knock interrupted Daly.

"Come in," he said. Daly's secretary Pat Clinton appeared.

"I couldn't get Mr. Amberly," Clinton reported. "His executive assistant said he was in a meeting and could not be disturbed."

"Did you tell him the FBI was calling?"

"Yes sir."

"Call back and let me talk to the assistant."

"Right away." She went to Daly's phone and punched in the area code and private number of the CEO of Celestial. Then she handed the phone to Daly.

"Celestial Airlines, Mr. Amberly's office," came the saccharin voice.

"Who's this," Daly demanded.

"Mr. Amberly's executive assistant," came the reply.

"Do you by chance have a name? This is Terry Daly, FBI."

"How do I know you're not a crank caller?" the assistant asked.

"You don't. But I am calling on Mr. Amberly's private line. I assume he doesn't give his private number to crank callers. I have to talk to him right away. So either interrupt him now or tell him to call me back right away at the FBI office in New York City."

Daly gave the assistant the switchboard number and hung up. He folded his arms and rested his butt against the edge of the desk.

Midway through the first ring Daly picked up the phone,

"Daly."

"Mr. Daly, it's Walter Amberly, Celestial Airlines. What the fuck is so important that it couldn't wait 10 more minutes? I don't like Gestapo tactics."

Daly waited five long seconds before responding. "I'll tell you what is so important. You have a real serious security problem over there, Mr. Amberly. And I mean real serious. If you like, I'll send Assistant Deputy Director Brown over to explain it, or you can come here. Either way, I want you to fix the problem. Because if you don't, the Secretary of Homeland Security is going to ground your airline."

"I see," said Amberly, taking a conciliatory tone. "OK, sorry for my abruptness. What's the problem?"

"I'm going to put Carter Brown on. He heads the airport security section for the Bureau. Carter."

Brown began. On the other end, Amberly listened.

When Brown finished, Amberly asked him what he wanted done. Brown handed the phone to Daly. "He wants to know what he should do. I figured it would be best coming from you." Brown chuckled as he rejoined Ewing and Clinton at the conference table.

"Mr. Amberly, I don't have the authority to discipline any of your employees, but we can make your fuel truck driver, your operations director and director of security mighty uncomfortable. And when Secretary Mooreland reads the report and I have to tell him that you did not take DRASTIC action, I'll bet next month's pay he grounds your ass."

"I'll look into it," Amberly said. The tone of his voice indicating severe disapproval of the way Daly addressed him.

"Please do. And let me know by the end of the week what action you have taken."

"I don't think we can act that fast," Amberly said.

"Perhaps not. But you'll be very surprised at how fast we act, and even more surprised at how fast Mooreland acts."

"Shut down Celestial for a minor security lapse? You've got to be kidding. The president will take a public roasting for that from a lot of angry passengers. And there are two senators over here in New Jersey who will light the fire."

"Amberly," Daly said. "First, this was not a minor security breach. Second, consider this. Do you think the passengers will be angry with the president, or at Celestial for risking passengers' lives. You may see a lot of your passengers suddenly flying Delta or American and it may be some time before you can get them back, if ever. Your stockholders won't like that one bit."

Daly hung up.

"I'll bet he's one pissed off dude," Brown said. "CEO's don't like people talking to them like that."

"I hope he gets pissed off at his security people and at that driver. Carter, when will you have the LaGuardia report?"

"Sometime this afternoon, boss."

"Good. OK, that's it for now.

"Pat, I want to talk to Bill Reilly. Would you get him on the phone for me, please.

"Sure. Right away."

New York Port Authority Police Chief Bill Reilly was chatting with New York City Mayor Michelle Bloom when his first deputy motioned that he had a phone call.

"Excuse me, Michelle, who is it Pete?" he called out to Peter McIntosh.

"It's Terry Daly, FBI Counter-Terrorism director, on your private line. He says it's urgent. Will you take it now or should I tell him you'll call back?"

"I'll take it now. Michelle, sorry, it's the FBI."

"Go ahead, Bill. We're finished anyway."

"Right." As the mayor walked out of the office, Reilly picked up the extension on the sideboard of the conference room. "Terry, I hope you are not calling to tell me there's been another attack."

"No. But I do have some stuff we need to discuss."

Reilly motioned for Peter McIntosh to come into the conference room, "Shut the door, Pete. OK, my deputy Pete McIntosh is here with me. You're on the speaker. We're all ears."

"Good morning Pete. Terry Daly here. Bill, before I begin can you bring me up to speed on what your guys have done?"

"Sure. As you probably know the FAA closed all the airports. They'll probably stay closed at least through today. I closed all the bridges and tunnels into the city. Created a monumental traffic jam, but I'd rather have that then....... This morning we reopened all the bridges and tunnels but our officers are searching almost every vehicle," Reilly said. "I was just with the mayor when you called and she has warned people to use mass transit to avoid sitting in traffic for hours. The MTA closed Grand Central Terminal and stopped all subways, but they should be running today. The NYPD has stepped up its security to level one. We have had no incidents and no arrests have been reported."

"That's good news. I know you have lots to do so let me get to it. You know my airport security detail has been nosing around LaGuardia, JFK and Newark even before the attack at Westchester.

"Yeah. When you told me I thought that was a good idea. Too bad Westchester wasn't part of that investigation," Reilly said.

"Anyway, we found major problems with security. I have the reports for JFK and Newark in front of me and I'm having copies delivered to you within the hour. One of the problems at Newark is being, ah, shall we say, looked into by Celestial Airlines, at least I hope it is. I had a heart to heart with Celestial's chairman Walter Amberly after a refueling driver actually let two of my men borrow his fuel truck. They drove it to the hangar," Daly said.

"My God! In the hangar?"

"Yeah, with 6,000 gallons of jet fuel and two 767s in the hangar being serviced. Anyway, he went political when I strongly suggested he act on it and fire that clown right away or risk having his airline shut down by Secretary Mooreland."

"What do you mean political?"

"He told me the two New Jersey Senators and American public would not like having a major airline shut down."

"Jesus. He's got balls, I'll give him that. Did you give him the security lecture?

"Yeah. But I think he got the message. I gave him until the end of the week to fix the problem or his airline gets shut down."

"Do you have the authority to do that?"

"I don't but Mooreland does. Anyway I wanted you to hear it from us, not Amberly."

"Thanks, for the heads up, Terry. Amberly is an arrogant son of a bitch. It'll do my heart good to watch him squirm. But you know, I think the only way to make airports secure from ground threats is to put a fucking 100 foot wall around them. What about JFK and LaGuardia?"

"The LaGuardia report should be finished later today. I'll send it separately after I've read it. I think it's fair to say that security is poor everywhere we have untrained or partially trained people. The weakest links are the people who screen passengers. In an effort to be politically correct and show they aren't profiling anyone, they deliberately go to great lengths to screen a 95-year-old woman with a walker and give a cursory look at a 35-year-old Middle Eastern male. My agents have gotten by them carrying knives, razors, mace and, in one case, at JFK a 9 mm pistol. It was plastic, but what the hell, a pistol is a pistol."

"How the hell could that happen? The cartridges are metal and the machines sensitive enough to read even one bullet. Hell, they can identify a passenger with braces for Christ's sake."

"I know, but one of the agents, who was shielded by his partner, used a newspaper to hide what he was doing. He dropped his gun in the personal effects basket and covered it with a lot of shit like a cell phone, a pager a CD player, keys, a watch, a glass case, three extra CDs and his handkerchief. Another guy created a diversion by dropping change all over the carpet, creating a mad scramble.

The gateway passenger screener was so rattled, he didn't even check the stuff in the basket. So a gun gets through and any one of those other things could easily have been a bomb. That's scary."

"Doesn't the passenger screener work for Homeland Security, Terry?"

"Technically, yes and that makes the federal government part of the problem. They are the same people working the same jobs they did before the world Trade Center Attacks. Then Congress made them federal employees and gave them more money. No extra training, just more money. And because they work for the government, they're practically fire proof no matter how ineffective they are. Shit, someday, maybe tomorrow, we're gonna have another hijacked airliner come down in this town because some, some nutcracker didn't take the time to look through the personal effects basket."

"Getting that gun through security may be the catalyst, Terry. At least to get them better trained. One thing for sure, it's tough to fire them"

"Any son of a bitch who is that derelict sure as shit should be. Anyway I hope we can send up some serious alarms at the meeting in Washington. When Secretary Mooreland briefs the President I'm sure there will be changes. After all they are Mooreland's employees. That means federal legislation.

Oh, by the way, we also have reports on security at the river crossings, Penn Station and Grand Central."

"That's the jurisdiction of the MTA, Terry."

"I know, I know. But technically, the Hudson River crossings, Grand Central and Penn Station carry interstate traffic and that is the purview of the federal government. I'm not trying to overrule your people, Bill. I want to work with them. God knows I don't have enough men to handle our current load. But I thought you'd like to know. I'll talk to the MTA. Keep what I said under your hat, OK?

"Those reports won't go any further than us," Reilly said.

"Thanks. Oh one more thing. I think Mooreland will be recommending new laws to enhance security at airports, bridges, trains stations, tunnels and large public gathering places. Roy Owens told me Mooreland has already hinted at this and he believes the president will buy into it.

"No one is blaming you, Bill. We are pointing out problems that will require new laws and lots of money to solve. If you have any anecdotal evidence you wish to share, please do," Daly said. "We have a lot of evidence, including photos, and videotape to support our conclusions that we need to change the way passenger check in is handled, but whatever you can add will be appreciated. We have to impress upon Congress how critically important this is."

"Terry, I've known you for 11 years. And even though this doesn't reflect too well on the Port Authority, I trust your judgment. You can count on me."

"Great, Bill. Thanks. I'll have the reports on the river crossings and the rail stations sent over right away. Labeled your eyes only. Daly put the phone down. "Carter, what's on your plate for the rest of the day?"

"I'm finishing the LaGuardia report." Brown said. "Should be finished in an hour or so, give or take."

"I'm still on the Adnan Fahad case. But I can spare some time. What do you need?" Ewing asked.

"Ask Pat to arrange a video conference call on the secure line with Fritz Thompson, Eliot Schweikert,, and Phil Maranda. Oh, and see if you can also get Chris Boggs in Detroit. Tell them it's about a meeting in Washington and that it is Level 5."

"What about Roy? Don't you want him in on this?" Brown asked.

"No need to include Roy. This is just an exchange of regional information. We're meeting with him and Secretary Mooreland tomorrow. But I do want you two in on the conference call."

Brown left the office and told Pat Carter to set up the calls. She accompanied Brown to the video conferencing room where she made the calls to the District Directors and Brown directed the Audio Visual technician to set up the equipment. Within 22 minutes all five were on the line.

"Gentlemen, before Terry comes in I want to tell you that he lost his parents in yesterday's attack on the airport in Westchester," Brown said.

"My God," said Maranda, the Special Agent in Charge in Miami. Before anyone else could weigh in with expressions of sympathy, Daly entered the room.

"Good morning, everyone," Daly began. He was now wearing his suit jacket and his tie was straightened for the broadcast. "Thanks for answering my call so quickly. I'll be brief. So we are all talking from the same page at the meeting in Washington, I want to share some information with you about the attacks and then discuss New York City area airport security and then see what you have."

"Terry, before you begin, I want to tell you how sorry we are for the loss of your parents," Miranda said. Each of the others offered similar expressions.

"Thanks. I appreciate that. I'll probably take some time later in the week, but for now Ellen is handling things. OK, let's get started."

Daly gave his colleagues all the information he had on the two attacks including the information about the missile crates. There were few questions. "OK, let's move onto airport security." When he finished he asked if anyone had information to share. .

"Yeah, I'll start, if I may," said Eliot Schweikert, Special Agent in charge in Dallas. "I'll start with the U.S. Mexican border. Because of the partial wall and more border patrol agents, it's a lot tougher for illegal aliens to get across the border here, but all that means is the numbers have slowed to 800-1,000 a day.

"The fixed border crossings are tight and traffic is often backed up for hours waiting for customs clearance. But we still have hundreds of miles of unpatrolled or partially patrolled areas and they sneak across to waiting trucks for movement to, well hell, anywhere.

"And as bad as that sounds," Schweikert continued, "the situation at Dallas-Ft.Worth, Houston International and the other major airports isn't any better than what you described in New York. One of the airlines here is almost as bad as what you have in Newark. You know the planes all have reinforced cockpit doors. Well one of our sky marshals observed a flight attendant taking coffee to the cockpit crew while two passengers were waiting to use the first class restroom. Reinforced doors don't help if they're open.

"We've had all kinds of problems with baggage check-in and a couple of potentially dangerous incidents while aircraft were being serviced. Passenger screening is working slightly better, but it has a long way to go," Schweikert said. "We test it several times a month and you would be surprised at what we can get through."

"Eliot, are your guys using a lot of overtime?" Daly asked.

"Shit yes. Most of our guys are working 65-75 hours a week. They aren't complaining, but they wonder how much good they can do when they see all the weaknesses."

"What about the rest of you guys. Overtime?"

One by one they reported using hundreds of hours of overtime each month. Daly was taking notes and trying to do the math in a rough manner. He crossed out the figures and asked each one to be prepared to quote overtime figures for the meeting.

Thompson and Boggs, the assistant deputy directors in Los Angeles and Detroit respectively and Miranda in Miami then made their reports essentially echoing what Schweikert had said.

"It would appear we have a lot of work to do," Day said. "And we're going to need a lot of help. That's all I have, gentlemen. If none of you have anything to add, I'll see you in Washington," Daly said.

-Chapter Five-

Larry Kirkman and some of his neighbors and other residents of the New York village of Chappaqua regularly rode the 7:08 Metro North commuter train to New York City. The MTA, Metro North's parent organization had improved service, upgraded the stations, laid new tracks, modernized the rolling stock and kept fare increases to a minimum. Commuting was now almost pleasurable, because the worry and stress had all but disappeared. Then came the attacks on the mall and the regional airport just a few miles away from the commuter line Kirkman and his neighbors were now riding.

The attacks and the inevitable speculation about the future often came up in their conversations when train service resumed. When the subject turned to business travel, everyone had an opinion and a concern. "I know one thing," Kirkman said to a friend and business colleague Robert Costa. "I've flown out of Westchester Airport half a dozen times. I'm not flying from there again unless I have no choice."

A former lobbyist in Washington, Kirkman, and Costa were partners in the law firm of Silverstein, Watkins, Hirschfeld and Fowler that they had joined in 1995. Costa had been a trademarks lawyer at another firm in New York. By coincidence, both lived on the same street and both were active locally. Kirkman was president of the Board of Education; Costa was a councilman.

Seated in the same five seat configuration was Lois Ryan, a brilliant stock analyst at Marshall, Feldstein and Winston who, at 38, was some 10 years younger than the two men. She and her husband Spencer were childless, still working on their careers.

They sometimes talked about starting a family, but neither wanted to give up their lifestyle and the freedom to spend weekends at one of their vacation residences.

"Lois, I'm curious, did the Mall bombing affect the way you shop?" Kirkman asked.

"Sure. I haven't been to The Westchester, Stamford Mall or any other shopping center since. Spence says we shouldn't let it affect us, but it's hard not to," Ryan replied. "What about you?"

"Fran and I haven't been to any of the malls either. We shop locally, now."

"What about you, Bob?" Ryan asked.

"Do you remember when the movie Jaws first came out? I remember being at the Jersey shore and no one was in the water beyond their knees. And the water was perfect. Well, that's the way I feel about shopping in malls now. I know I'm paranoid, but I can't help it after seeing the TV shots. At least 50,000 dead and injured. That's double the size of Chappaqua, and as many as were killed and wounded at Gettysburg." Costa said. "No malls and no flying for us."

"I feel the same way," Kirkman said. "That's why I'm very glad we have that place in Chatham on Cape Cod. It's less than a five hour drive."

"Only been to the Cape once and that was in Falmouth. What's Chatham like?" Ryan asked.

"It's a quaint little village, in many ways a typical New England community. Most of the shops and stores are gray with white trim. Fran calls it charming," Kirkman said.

"May be, but in the summer it's inundated with tourists from New York and New Jersey and folks who come down from Boston to their summer homes. We like it though, because we have Nantucket Sound in our back yard, and on Ridgevale Road where our house is, there is a shallow lagoon that the kids swim in and ride the tide out to the sound.

When we bought it, we added a large extra bedroom and bath that's now the master bedroom. The next year, we extended the other end with a matching bedroom and bath for guests. And last year, we replaced the deck with a large two tier affair.

Ryan waited until Kirkman had finished. "Bob, I recall hearing you say something about not wanting a vacation place. How come?"

"Leslie and I thought about it, but we agreed it anchored us in one spot. We like to travel, though not as much since 9/11," Costa replied. "We used to love cruises, been all over the Caribbean and through the Panama Canal. And we love to ski. So we rented for a week or two at a time, but never in the same place. We liked the variety and the internet made it easy. But all that has changed. If we can't drive, we won't go."

"What do you guys think of how Barnes is handling the situation?" Kirkman asked.

"I think he hit the nail on the head, but I don't think Congress will act on most of his proposals. Our senators won't do a damned thing even though we have millions of illegal aliens in this country," said Costa. "They see the illegals as future votes. And you don't have to be a nuclear physicist to guess what party the illegals will support.

"Very few pay taxes, but they send their kids to our schools and get free medical care. We know a guy married to a Costa Rican woman. He couldn't get his wife in here legally for more than a year despite the fact the two kids were married," Costa said.

"That doesn't make sense. His immigration ideas are as bad as Bush's. But he did kick the PLO out of here and those other countries too," said Kaufman. "That was long overdue. Too bad we can't get rid of the UN. Move it to Switzerland. They're nothing but a bunch of spineless US bashing martini drinkers."

"I don't think Barnes went far enough," said Ryan. "I think he should have broken off relations with Saudi Arabia too. I agree with my husband. Anyone who deals with terrorists is a terrorist and should be treated as such."

"I agree," Kirkman said. "I think Saudi Arabia is very involved in this. Fifteen of the 19 hijackers who destroyed the world Trade Center were Saudis, Bin Laden is a Saudi. So is Omar. And more than half of the Taliban and al Qaeda fighters that our guys captured in Iraq are Saudis."

"I wouldn't kick them out," said Costa. "I'd use them the same way they use us."

"What do you mean 'use them'?" Ryan asked.

"Remember what Abe Lincoln said," Costa replied. "Keep your friends close. And keep your enemies closer. We should keep the Saudis close, bug their embassy, go through their diplomatic bags, monitor their messages and do anything else to gather evidence to prove to the world what they really are."

"That's against international law," Kirkman said.

"Sure it is. So is terrorism," said Costa. "I don't see the UN denouncing terrorists or their supporting nations. Why is it that we have to obey international law and countries like Libya, Iran, Syria, North Korea, the Sudan, Somalia and Saudi Arabia don't?"

"You know what I'd do?" said Kaufman. "I'd send a group of our guys down to that prison in Cuba, kick the press out of there and then let them have their way with the al Qaeda. They'll be singing like opera stars."

"You mean torture?" Ryan asked.

"Why the hell not? These guys raped innocent women and girls, they brutalized women and murdered men, and they took away all their freedoms. What goes around, comes around."

"I never thought I would ever agree with that kind of thinking," said Costa. "But after seeing the pictures of what happened at the Mall and the airport I have no pity for those murdering bastards. We're at war and they aren't wearing uniforms. They don't obey the rules of war, so why should we?"

"So what should we do with them after we catch them, Bob? Should we use military tribunals, or the civilian criminal courts?" Gray Bostwick asked. Bostwick was creative director at a leading advertising agency

"Neither," said Kirkman. "After we get the information we need and we should verify it to make sure they aren't playing games. If the information is accurate and we no longer need them, get rid of them."

"That's stooping to their level," said Brianna Russell, a public affairs director at Altria.. "We're better than that."

"Well how do you feel about illegal aliens, Bree?" Kaufman asked. "We've got at least 25 million of them and several hundred thousand are from Saudi Arabia, Syria, Libya, and Iran?"

"I think they're necessary," Russell said. "They do a lot of the work that most Americans don't or won't do."

"That's true," Kirkman said. "I'm sure my neighbor's landscaper's workers are all illegal aliens."

"Do you know that or are you guessing?" Bostwick asked.

"I was thinking about using the same landscaper. So I told the landscape guy that if his men had green cards I'd talk about hiring them. I didn't want using illegal aliens to come back to haunt me later. The guy said he was sorry he couldn't help. He also said all the other landscapers were just like him. Couldn't afford to hire people at better wages without raising prices," Kirkman said.

"It seems to me that if we get rid of all of them we'd be better off," said Costa. "First, we'd probably be deporting a lot of terrorists. Our schools wouldn't be so overburdened with their kids and a lot of the elite and celebrities would have to mow their own grass. I'd love to see loud mouthed liberals like Barbra Streisand and Rosie O"Donnell mowing their own lawn."

The discussion died away as the train entered the tunnel. The lights went out momentarily and then flickered to life along with the conversation.

"It's hard to remember what life was like before the first 9/11. So much has changed," Costa said turning away from the window as the train sped toward Grand Central."

"I know. I don't think I'll ever get used to not seeing those towers," said Russell. "I was looking out the window of my office after the first tower was hit. I was mesmerized, so fascinated I stayed at the window and I actually saw the plane hit the second tower. Do any of you remember what you were doing that day?"

"I'll never forget that day," Costa said. "I was in my office."

"Me too," said Ryan. "One of my colleagues told me what happened and we ran to my boss's office because it overlooked the Trade Center. We were lucky. Our company moved out of the South Tower to mid-town about a year before 9/11."

"I was in Albany," Kirkman said. "I didn't hear about it until after the first tower collapsed because I was in a meeting with the assembly speaker. We didn't get a lot accomplished after that."

"We didn't either," said Ryan. "In fact, we were told to go home at noon and we stayed home the rest of the week."

"I was on vacation in New Hampshire," said Harry Kaufman. "My wife and I didn't hear about it until late afternoon when we stopped at a bar for a glass of wine."

Kaufman managed the dining facilities at Altria. He and Russell worked in the same building at 41st and Park.

The other Chappaqua passengers who sat nearby included Dr. Keith Slack, an eye surgeon, and Walter and Vera Perry, an African American couple. Walter was an accountant at a mid-town firm and Vera was a senior editor at Time Warner.

Walter Perry read The Times; Bostwick read *Ad Age*, Vera read manuscripts and Dr. Slack immersed himself in medical journals on the latest advancements in lasik surgery, his very lucrative specialty. He listened attentively to the banter about summer homes, a luxury he could now easily afford.

Bostwick was a stunning woman of 27 who was not only beautiful and bright, but also sweet and charming. She was always immaculately dressed in form fitting slacks or skirts that exposed her well-shaped athletic legs drawing smiles of appreciation from every man. Vera Perry pretended to ignore her husband's stares. Bostwick was responsible for ad campaigns for a leading German auto manufacturer and the world's largest soft drink manufacturer. She completed her undergraduate studies at Duke University before she was 20. A year later she was awarded an MBA from the Wharton School at University of Pennsylvania.

A hard worker who often put in 12-hour days, she still found time to work out four times a week to maintain her luscious figure. She played as hard as she worked. On weekends she was often the guest of the rich and famous at their estates in the Hamptons or on the slopes in Aspen. She made no attempt to rid herself of the soft southern accent she picked up at Duke and that helped her charm CEOs, governors and senators and the Hollywood glitterati. She didn't need to sleep her way to the top, but the fact she loved sex, particularly with marquis stars, didn't hurt her career.

Russell was envious. She was 43 and had not had a date in four years, a fact she attributed to her being about 40 pounds overweight. A graduate of Georgetown, Russell had worked in Washington for five years on the staff of a Democratic Congressman, following a two-year stint with the *Washington Post*. Her father was a wealthy party contributor and managed to get her both jobs. She enjoyed the power associated with her role, but she drew the line at sleeping with her boss. When her father died, the Congressman replaced Russell with a southern woman 12 years younger and a lot more willing. Russell used her networking abilities and soon landed a job as a public affairs director with the largest tobacco company in the world.

She used some of her inheritance to buy a three-bedroom condo in the same complex as Bostwick. Until recently, neither knew they were neighbors. She knew Kaufman because she ate in the management dining room, one of the eating facilities he managed.

Ryan was grateful for the competition. She also was very attractive, but was uncomfortable with the attention it brought.

The Perrys, he almost 41, she a year younger, had been Chappaqua residents for nearly three years. Former Manhattan residents, both had been divorced. They met through an internet dating service, had lunch at an Italian restaurant in the city and began dating. Five months later they were married. Walter had two children who were living in Los Angeles with their mother.

They were an interesting couple. Walter, who held an MBA from New York University, was a CPA, a partner in his firm. A former athlete who stayed in shape, he was a basketball official in a youth league and a Little League coach in the summer. Vera, held a master's degree from Columbia's Journalism School and taught English for several years before entering the magazine field. She was a member of the Friends of the Library. The Perrys were active in the Episcopal Church.

Dr. Slack, a 36-year-old ophthalmologist, Board certified in both New York and New Jersey was driven by money. When he read about the benefits of lasik surgery, he called a colleague, a lasik pioneer with a practice in nearby River Edge, New Jersey, who agreed to train him for six months in exchange for pro bono professional assistance one day a week.

He took a second mortgage on his house to pay for the expensive laser surgery equipment and repaid it in just eight months. Dr. Slack was on the gravy train that was fueled by vanity.

When not engaged in his practice, he poured over investment articles and chatted daily with his broker. He had no time for community. He and his trophy wife, Midge, rarely saw each other during the week. In fair weather, she played tennis or golf. When it rained, she enjoyed three-hour lunches with her equally snobbish friends at their club discussing, among other things, Broadway, vacations, and vacation homes.

"This is Grand Central Terminal, last stop on this train," the PA system blared. "Please remember to gather your personal belongings from beneath the seat in front of you and from the overhead rack. Watch your step leaving the train and have a pleasant day. Thank you for riding Metro North."

Rail commuting becomes mindless in a few months. The Chappaqua commuters were already on their feet with their briefcases in hand well before the train stopped.

One by one, the passenger stepped from the train. Russell fell in beside Kaufman as they made their way up the platform and across the concourse toward the corporate headquarters of Altria about a block away.

"What's the lunch special in the management dining room?" Russell asked.

"Grilled salmon with dill sauce and field greens. Do you like salmon?"

"It's OK. How come we never get lobster?"

"Lobster? Are you shitting me? Jees your lunch is paid for by the company and now you want lobster?"

"Just a thought. I'm not greedy. Hey, do you get your lunch free?"

"Sure. How do you think I got this gut?" Kaufman laughed.

"I need to lose some weight too. I guess I'll have the salmon and the salad and maybe some yogurt tonight."

"No date?"

It really wasn't a question from Kaufman, but Russell felt compelled to talk about her personal life. "No. I don't date much. I don't have time with my job and the traveling," she lied.

Kaufman fell silent as the two walked south along 41st street past the windows of the Whitney Museum. Moments later they passed through the revolving doors into the Altria lobby. Russell fumbled through her purse for her magnetic ID card as Kaufman slapped his on the reader enabling him to pass through the turnstile. Russell was right behind him.

"Will you be on the 5:27?" he said over his shoulder.

"Should be."

"I'll be in the fourth car. Maybe I'll see you at lunch."

Kaufman went down the hall towards the elevator to the cafeteria. Russell turned to the ground floor elevator lobby.

-Chapter Six-

Antonio Rodrigo sat at his kitchen table sipping a Pepsi. A bachelor, he and the other members of his cell had been inactive since September 11, 2001. On the 10th anniversary of that attack, his cell was ordered to attack several New York City targets in a coordinated cataclysmic nationwide strike.

He received his orders from Talal Farhan, a Saudi UN Mission official codenamed Atta in honor of the man who led the World Trade Center attacks. But early on the morning of September 11 Rodrigo called off the new attacks. His explanation to his superior was that the quantity of explosives in storage was insufficient to destroy all four targets. Either more explosives were needed or the number of targets reduced. Accepting the explanation, Farhan ordered more explosives.

While Rodrigo's cell was inactive, another, acting on orders from inside the mission, had attacked Westchester County Airport. A third had destroyed a huge mall, another symbol of America. Three others had been captured. Farhan's boss, who controlled al Qaeda activities in the U.S. was disappointed and skeptical, but took no action against Rodrigo because of the two spectacular successes and the fact that Rodrigo's cell had not been discovered. Instead, he ordered Farhan to assume tighter control. The media was saturated with stories about the attack and alleged terrorist activities, but no arrests were made and there was little speculation about other potential targets. His new orders: *Resume normal routine.*

Rodrigo, who possessed an IQ of 155, studied graphic arts at Rhode Island School of Design, graduating first in his class with a 4.0 average. The speaker was William Burdette, Under Secretary of State for the Middle East. After the ceremony, Rodrigo, as Valedictorian was invited by the president of the college to a luncheon with Burdette who was struck by Rodrigo's demeanor, maturity, intelligence and the fact that he spoke fluent Arabic which Rodrigo said he learned during summer vacations.

Unknown to Burdette, Rodrigo, was a Saudi whose Saudi name was Abdelaziz Hakim. He was born in al Khobar on the East coast to Jason Rodrigo, an American and his Saudi wife, Assan. He spent the first 17 years of his life in Dhahran where his father taught Arabic to American and European employees of the Arabian American Oil Company. Rodrigo was able to attend the American run schools in Dhahran where he learned many American customs. His father persuaded his mother that it was best he keep his American name so he could keep his American passport.

After graduation, Rodrigo returned home to Dhahran where he reverted to using his Saudi name to help him find a job designing packaging for fledgling businesses. In a job interview with Khalid al Mahid, the local businessman was impressed by the young man and asked him what he thought of America. Rodrigo's sixth sense told him al Mahid was not looking for glowing descriptions.

"They are a decadent people who have little regard for anything but money and the pleasures of the flesh," he replied. "I only went there to study and returned home as soon as I graduated."

"Do you like Americans?" al Mahid asked. "Did you make any friends in school?"

"I sometimes went out for pizza with some of the guys, but I never got close to any of them. I think most of them were gay."

"What about the women? Did you have any close female friends?" al Mahid asked.

Rodrigo knew he had to be careful. "I went to the library with a couple to study and occasionally I'd get together with a couple of them to discuss our work," Rodrigo replied.

"I never developed a close relationship, if that's what you mean. After all, they were infidels."

Al Mihadi's smiled. "I know a number of bright young men like you who don't like Americans. Some of them studied there and feel the same way you do. And while in America they could only read the anti Muslim stories, not the truth. Do you know what I mean?"

"Yes."

"Abdelaziz, have you heard of al Qaeda?"

"Of course."

"Do you believe what the American media says about al Qaeda?"

"No."

"What do you believe?" al Mihad asked.

"The American media is prejudiced. I think al Qaeda wants to keep Islam pure," Rodrigo replied.

"Yes. And to do that often requires sacrifice and even violence."

Even while talking with al Mihad, Rodrigo was remembering some of the cruelty he had experienced in Dhahran at the hands of the American kids and at the outright rejection he had often experienced in college. His male classmates often bragged about their sexual conquests but Rodrigo felt insecure with women. He wondered why and now he was beginning to suspect it was because he felt they were immoral and unworthy.

Over the next hour, al Mihad talked about Islam sprinkling the conversation with short details of the martyrs of al Qaeda. Rodrigo had long been fascinated by the idea of someone sacrificing himself. He wondered if he would ever have the strong conviction needed to do that. Yet he loved his religion and almost every day in America he prayed five times a day. Some of his classmates viciously teased him about that and he had even come to blows on two occasions. After the fights in which Rodrigo was clearly the winner, the two classmates never spoke to him again and worked to poison his relationship with others.

The final insult took place in a class when a professor, who apparently did not know Rodrigo was a Muslim, preached venomously about al Qaeda's destruction of Buddhist icons reviling the Muslim religion that he said not only condoned such sacrilege but supported it in his view.

Rodrigo wondered how to handle that, whether to report the professor or to confront him. In the end he did neither, deeply regretting his inaction, but also understanding that in the U.S. people were free to say what they liked whether right or wrong.

Al Mihad asked Rodrigo if he knew anyone associated with al Qaeda and when Rodrigo said no, al Mihad simply countered with "yes you do. I am al Qaeda."

Rodrigo smiled and al Mihad related some of his experiences exciting the adventuresome side of Rodrigo. He was completely surprised when al Mihad asked him if he would like to talk with others in al Qaeda. Rodrigo said yes.

In three months Rodrigo was in Afghanistan for indoctrination and training with the Taliban. The two years in the mountains and caves had been very difficult. He often ate only one meal a day and slept 3-4 hours, enduring severe temperatures and hostile weather. His clothing was barely adequate against the sub zero winter. But he never complained.

On several occasions he was observed by al Qaeda leaders Osama bin Laden and Abu Musab al Zarqawi who took note of his intelligence, nearly infallible memory, language ability and the fact he was educated in America. Once he was captured by a Special Forces unit, but while he was being interrogated attacking helicopters mistook his captors for Taliban killing or wounding most of the Green Berets. Rodrigo escaped while the uninjured helped their wounded comrades.

Rodrigo was rewarded with special ops training in Syria where he studied Spanish and team management. He then was sent to Mexico where he reassumed his American name Antonio Rodrigo and given a passport, letters of credit identifying him as a businessman, formerly from Madrid, a New York driver's license, two credit cards including an AMEX card with unlimited credit, a forged Social Security card and the names of contacts who provided him with a legitimate address.

Because of his fluency in Spanish and the porous border between Mexico and the United States, he was told to avoid the official entry points where he might be subjected to questions.   Wearing a backpack, Rodrigo became one of the millions of faceless illegal immigrants, and one of several thousand al Qaeda in the United States. After crossing the border, he changed his clothes and hitched a ride to Laredo, Texas.

His New York driver's license and a credit card enabled him to rent a car that he drove to San Antonio. After dropping off the Enterprise car, he booked a flight to New York and took a taxi to the Super 8 Motel near the airport. Next morning, he called his New York contact to arrange for pickup and caught a United Airlines flight to LaGuardia Airport. Rodrigo was relieved and amazed at the ease in which he had accomplished the entry phase. A man, who had purchased an apartment for him, met him at the airport.

Rodrigo's two-bedroom apartment was on the third floor of a five-story building in the Bronxville section of Yonkers, about 25 miles north of Manhattan. Bronxville, the neighboring town his neighbors identified with, was an affluent bedroom community a short 30-minute train ride to his job in the city. One bedroom he used as an office. Since he never learned to cook, he rarely used the kitchen, eating out every night in local restaurants and in the city at The Palm and Palm II, and Peter Luger's.

Rodrigo chose not to draw attention to himself. He was very careful about what he wore. In warm weather, his $60 polo shirts were similar to what other men wore. In cooler or wet weather, Rodrigo wore an expensive English Burberry raincoat into which he could insert a lining. The coat helped him blend in with other commuters.

There was little discernable difference between Rodrigo and his fellow commuters. Each morning, Rodrigo bought a Danish or a roll, coffee and the Wall St. Journal before he boarded the train. Outwardly, he was a New Yorker in every respect.

As the chief of his cell, Rodrigo was responsible for communicating with the other members as well as monitoring and coordinating their efforts. He was also entrusted with finances, cash for expenses that averaged nearly $30,000 per month. After the New York Times had revealed how the government monitored their finances, his organization, and others like his, changed their methods. Money again flowed freely enabling each to live quite comfortably in nicely furnished apartments in middle class neighborhoods. Each drove mid-sized cars. Nothing flashy.

Rodrigo was given few rules, but one was paramount: the group should *never* meet until given their orders lest they attract unwanted attention. Instead, whenever Rodrigo had instructions for them, he would use impossible-to-trace instant messaging on the internet, that was preceded by a cryptic email warning of the date and time of the IM.

Each had his own personal computer connected to America on Line where they could hide their communications in their own chat rooms. Mindful of the need for speed and security, each used an expensive T-1 line. On rare occasions, Rodrigo would arrange a meeting, but never with more than one at a time.

A second rule governed appearances. No beards. Mustaches were discouraged but a mustache was permitted if it was neat and trimmed. Hair must be groomed and never long. A sports jacket or a suit was mandatory unless their employer permitted something less formal. "Look like a successful businessman. Always wear shined shoes, conservative white or blue shirt and a Brooks Brothers tie. Observe what impressive Americans wear and imitate them," Rodrigo stressed. Cologne too was mandatory. But not the strong scents favored by Arab males. Rodrigo's group shopped only at Brooks Brothers, Lord & Taylor and other fine stores.
Some subjects were never discussed.

"NEVER engage in a discussion about religion or politics, particularly Middle Eastern politics," Rodrigo reminded them. " 'I don't know very much about that' or 'I dislike politics at any level' are ready made answers. Resist the temptation to give anyone your opinion because it might reveal your feelings and escalate into a heated argument that might draw attention to you and jeopardize the mission."

Macho behavior with women, he reminded them, is rude. Be charming, polite, complimentary and a gentleman. Discourage friendships, but be friendly. "If you make friends with other men, they may want you to join them for a movie, dinner or to go to an athletic event. Be vary wary of who you invite to your apartment.

This applies to women," Rodrigo repeated, though he wondered if that rule should apply to him.

Rodrigo and co-worker Angela Hart had exchanged phone numbers. Rodrigo put hers in his wallet. On an impulse, he retrieved the slip of paper, grabbed the phone from the kitchen wall and dialed Hart's number.

"Hello, you have reached Angela," came the recorded message. "I can't come to the phone right now, but if you leave your name and number, I will return your call as soon as possible."

Rodrigo started to hang up, but changed his mind.

"Hi Angela, this is Tony. I wanted to ask you at work today, but....it's supposed to be a beautiful day tomorrow and I thought you might like to go to the zoo with me. I've never been there, and...."

"Tony, it's me, don't hang up. I was screening calls. I'd love to go to the zoo, but I have a 8:30 appointment to get my hair done. Can we make it after that?"

"Sure. When will you be finished? I'll pick you up. Where do you live?"

"I should be home by 10:30. I live at 146A California Road in Eastchester." She gave him directions.

Rodrigo was now having second thoughts. *What if new orders were sent?* He did not know when the next attack would be ordered. *What if there was a problem?* Unlikely, he reasoned.

He turned the can upside down in the sink, removed his shirt and strode to the bathroom.

Each of Rodrigo's hand picked cell members was dedicated, well educated, highly trained, and spoke flawless English. Each had been assigned specific tasks and each was forbidden to discuss it with the other members.

Yousef al Hafra, a former Saudi hotel manager now working at the Saudi UN Mission on Lexington Avenue, was the "product" manager. At 29, he became a diplomatic courier, and used his immunity to import to New York what was referred to as "product" in diplomatic bags and innocent looking packages. Anything but innocent, product was HMX, a plastic high explosive that could be molded to almost any shape.

The amount of "product" in each package never exceeded the 30-pound limit dictated by Riyadh. Al Hafra was a regular passenger on Saudia Airlines between New York and Riyadh. Each time he landed at JFK Airport, 210 pounds of "product" in seven packages were successfully added to the terrorist arsenal. Al Hafra had just completed his 44th trip.

Married to two women, al Hafra had six children. On each trip to Riyadh to pick up "product," he would visit each wife and their children bringing them gifts. His visits included one night at each residence and one night with his Director. At about the halfway point between New York and the Saudi capital, al Hafra would change into the traditional thobe and ghutra becoming just another Arab passenger.

On the return trip to New York he would reverse the procedure, donning a suit. An attaché case completed his appearance. It always contained faked letters addressed to the Ambassador or the Foreign Minister and stamped Diplomatic Correspondence to prevent the authorities in New York from opening an envelope that sometimes carried instructions meant only for the eyes of Atta.

For security Al Hafra was completely unaware of the content of the bags and containers that accompanied him. Because of the number of parcels and their special content, he was always met at the airport and driven to the Saudi mission in Manhattan. Rodrigo kept a written record of the number of deliveries to be certain there was enough product to destroy each target. He calculated four more trips were needed.

Al Hafra was chosen for his role because he was fanatically loyal and kept his mouth shut. When necessary, he was charming and had a broad sparkling smile that disarmed most of the people with whom he came in contact. He was tactful, polite, well dressed when in western garb, and he was patient, a characteristic that served him well at airports.

Ahmad Humaidi was an engineer educated at King Abdelaziz University. A thoughtful man of 30, Humaidi had never seen the inside of a terrorist training camp or raised his hand in anger against anyone. His assignment was to find the best way to approach each target and the most efficient way to destroy it. For nearly three years he had read everything he could get his hands on relating to their construction. He also studied security arrangements and traffic patterns during the morning and evening rush hours. The book he carried, The War for American Independence, was an ironic cover prop.

Only a close observer would notice that he talked to himself. His conversation, however, wasn't the verbal meanderings of a schizophrenic, but that of a highly educated engineer and a careful tactician. Inconspicuously pinned to his shirt was a microphone that was attached to a voice-activated dual media recorder strapped to his waist. Earphones conveyed the impression Humaidi was listening to music. When he said "PLAY" the device would record his words. "STOP" and music would flow through his earphones. The dual capability was his own invention.

The fourth member of the cell was Tariq Dossari. A former Iraqi lawyer, Dossari, at 48, was the oldest. He had been recruited by Sheik Omar, Osama bin Laden's lieutenant, who thought his nearly perfect English and negotiating skills would be useful. Dossari had received his undergraduate degree from the University of Colorado and a law degree from the University of Houston where he was captain of the debate team.

But there had been little use for his legal background in Iraq after Saddam Hussein assumed power. Over lunch, Dossari and Omar frequently talked about the Gulf War and how the oil embargo had created so many problems in Iraq. It was an easy step to blame America, and not Saddam for his inability to care for his three wives and 11 children. Naturally, Omar did nothing to dissuade him from that belief. Instead, he methodically fed Dossari's disenchantment until it became anger. When the time was right, Omar made his offer. Dossari accepted gratefully.

His assignment was to furnish transportation to carry out the mission, perhaps the most complex assignment of all. His first step was to rent a small building at 705 Cedar Lane in Teaneck, New Jersey to give him a business address.

On the front window was an elaborately painted sign **Frank's Used Furniture and Furniture Repair** owned by Frank Petrocelli, Dossari's alias. The office was furnished simply but efficiently.

Cards and stationery were printed and a business checking account opened with deposits of $8,000 in three different banks in Teaneck. Four mini-vans were leased, each one displaying the name of the fictitious company on the side panels.

Petrocelli's office had a rear entrance with double doors that opened to a parking lot for the mini-vans. Each day, he would back a different van up to the doors and load six two-drawer filing cabinets securing them with webbing. Then, he would drive off, returning to the office in late afternoon with the same cabinets that he dutifully unloaded. While he was away from the office, he made short stops at random mailboxes all over Bergen County, depositing one envelope in each. The envelopes containing phony invoices were addressed to his company on Cedar Lane. This created the ruse of business traffic.

He also drove into New York City at least three times per week using one of the tunnels or the lower level of the George Washington Bridge. His truck was now registered in the data banks of the Port Authority Police. Inspection of his vehicles was a cursory formality when they even bothered.

-Chapter Seven-

Tony Rodrigo drove slowly along California Road looking for the number 146A. It was 10:25. A sign said "Apts 142-148." He stopped and backed into a parking space. Angela Hart, who had been looking out her living room window on the second floor, bounced down the front porch stairs to the sidewalk and waived at Rodrigo as he got out of his car.

"Hi," she said smiling. "You're right on time." She wore a Yankee t-shirt, emphasizing her breasts, short shorts and Nike walking shoes.

Rodrigo, mindful of his orders about how to treat women, opened the car door and got a good look at Hart's bottom and legs as she sat in the car. Inexperienced with women, he felt a stirring in his groin. "I try to be on time, especially when I'm with an attractive woman," he said as he shut the right front door of the Camry.

"New?" Hart asked, as she smelled the unmistakable aroma of new leather.

"It's a few months old. I traded in my old Buick," he lied. "Got a good deal and the payments are reasonable." Rodrigo started the car and pulled out onto California Road, his mind racing to find a cover if it became necessary.

"How do I get to the Bronx River Parkway?" he asked, changing the subject quickly. He turned left onto Mill Road as she directed. "So when was the last time you went to the Bronx Zoo?" he asked.

"It's been a few years, probably five or six. They've made some great changes. How come you've never been?

"Just never had anyone to go with," Rodrigo said. "I'm glad you said yes. What's your favorite animal?"

"The otter's my favorite. They're cute and they seem to have so much fun all day long. I don't know if the zoo has otters. I also love the seals and sea lions. What about you? What's your favorite?"

"The leopards and the tigers," Rodrigo said. "They are really beautiful. And dangerous. I like that."

Hart let the remark go and turned to look at Rodrigo. When he returned the glance, she smiled, "You smell good."

"Thanks," he said. "It's Aramis." He turned left onto the south-bound Bronx River Parkway and settled into the traffic pattern. He stole a quick look at her chest and legs and felt the stir in his groin again.

"My old boyfriend used Aramis. I thought it smelled familiar"

"Did you say *old* boyfriend? How old was he?"

"I meant old as in former boyfriend. We're about the same age."

"Oh, right," Rodrigo recovered, silently admonishing himself for not remembering the expression. "I was just kidding. When did you guys split up?"

"About three-four months ago," Hart said. "I caught him in bed with my girlfriend. Can you imagine? What an asshole. Both of them are assholes. I hope they are happy together."

"And you haven't dated since?" Rodrigo said, his hopes rising.

"Nope. You're the first. I've been wondering if you were ever going to ask me out. I'm glad you did. By the way, I never asked. Do you have a girlfriend?"

"Uh huh. Haven't had much time, really. I'm not into the bar scene so I don't get much of an opportunity to even talk to women. I had a girlfriend, but we had a fight and broke up." Rodrigo lied.

"Hey, there's the exit for the zoo," Hart pointed.

Rodrigo exited the parkway, and rolled up to the parking lot entrance.

"Fifteen dollars, please," the attendant said.

Rodrigo fumbled for his wallet and Hart quickly pulled a $20 bill from her purse. "Here, you can pay me later."

"OK, thanks," he said, taking the money, handing it to the outstretched hand of the attendant. After passing the change and map to Hart, he parked the car, got out and opened the passenger door.

"Thanks Tony," Hart said as she stepped out. "I see chivalry isn't dead." She took his hand and they began walking.

The sign at the gate said "Admission $15.00." Rodrigo removed a $50 bill, passing it to the cashier requesting a ten and two fives in change. He handed Hart $15

"Thanks," she said, opening the map. They began walking.

"I think the sea lions are closer. Wanna do them first? She asked.

"Sure. Then let's find those otters. I've never seen an otter. How big are they?"

"They actually quite small, about the size of a house cat or maybe a small dog," Hart said. "But they have long bodies and a long tail. They swim all day."

"I hope they have some."

"The sea lions and seals are up this way," Hart said pointing to her left at the trail that disappeared over a small rise. "Can't be far away."

Rodrigo made several quick looks at the way Hart's breasts bounced. She caught him staring but decided not to say anything. Besides, she liked him and she liked the attention her breasts brought her. At the top of the rise there were three trails.

"This way," Hart said. Rodrigo turned to the left in the direction of the jungle cats. "Hey, Tony, where are you going?

The sea lions are this way."

"Shit, You're right. I don't know what I was thinking," he uttered as he walked swiftly to her side. They fell silent and resumed walking.

"There it is," Hart said pointing to the large outdoor pool where the sea lions romped. They could here the animals barking. "Not much of a crowd. That's good. We can get a good look." She hurried her pace and as Rodrigo fell behind, he dropped to one knee to adjust a lace that didn't need adjusting and got an eyeful of Hart's tight buttocks enclosed in the shorts.

When she turned and put her hands on her hips, Rodrigo got to his feet and trotted to her side. "Sorry, my lace was undone."

She took his hand again and they approached the aquarium. Several dozen sea lions swam in and out of the rocks in the cool water. Others lay taking in the warmth of the September sun. Rodrigo freed his hand from hers, putting it around her waist. She moved closer.

"Aren't they cool," she said referring to the sea lions. "Look at that big guy. I'll bet he's the boss." As if on cue, the 1,000 pound male roared.

"He's the man." Rodrigo said. "Nobody's going to mess with him."

The pair watched in silence and admiration for nearly half an hour. Rodrigo glanced at his watch and suggested they move to another exhibit.

"Anywhere you want to go is cool," Hart said. "Except for the snakes. I hate snakes."

"I don't like them much either," Rodrigo said. He took the map from Angela and pointed to a walkway. "The cat house – whoops pardon me, I mean the jungle cat house - is over there," he said turning slightly red.

Hart ignored the ribald reference. "Let's hit it," she said.

On the way they passed the monkey house and decided to stop.

"These are my third favorites," Fronteiri said as they stood in front of the chimps. Several screeched and jumped from limb to limb as if in some game. Hart and Rodrigo laughed.

"They certainly look like they haven't a worry in the world," Rodrigo said.

At the jungle cat house, they lingered for more than 20 minutes at the cage of the magnificent Bengal Tigers fascinated by their size and coloring. One male paced back and forth snarling. In another cage, two females lay sleeping on the cement floor.

Rodrigo wondered about the brute strength of the huge male, but his thoughts softened as his gaze swept over Hart's back as she read the information panel. He suddenly wanted to put his arms around her and hold her lush body next to his.

"It says these tigers are an endangered species and they are still hunted." Rodrig's mind was on other things.

"Tony, did you hear what I said?"

78

"Yeah. Sorry. It's a shame. He's such a beautiful animal. He must be 700-800 pounds."

Hart finished reading, noting that the male was indeed 800 pounds and asked, "Are you hungry? I'm starved. I only had coffee this morning before my appointment."

"I could use a bite. Where do we go? He asked as he produced the map from his pocket. "There's a cafeteria in that direction, about 3-400 meters."

"Meters? You mean yards?"

"Yeah. I mean yards. I sometimes say meters because a college professor of mine wouldn't let us say yards. Told us that meters, grams and liters were a pure form of measurement preferred by most other countries. And he drummed it into us. Wouldn't let us forget," Rodrigo said hoping that Angela would accept his explanation.

"I seem to remember there was an effort here in the U.S. some years back to get us to change to the metric system," Hart said. "I don't know why we never did, but that effort died. We do have some metric system references – you know two liter cokes and 1.5 liter bottles of liquor. But gas is still measured in gallons."

Inwardly, Rodrigo breathed a sigh of relief.

When they arrived at the cafeteria, Rodrigo and Hart looked at the menu on the wall.

"You get the food and I'll find a table. I want a salad with Russian dressing and iced tea."

In a few moments, he joined her, carrying a tray with a salad, iced tea, a hamburger, French fries and a large coke. He sat down and they hungrily ate watching the sparrows grabbing the scraps left by other diners. Rodrigo tossed a French fry at the birds that quickly scattered, gathering again seconds later near the new treat.

"What do you want to see next?" Hart asked as she picked at one of his fries.

"The snake house!" he hissed. "I want to see the big slithery snakes."

Hart almost jumped at the bait. "Well, you can if you want to. I'll wait outside. Snakes make my skin crawl. I hate 'em." She shivered.

"I was kidding," he said apologetically. "Don't you want to see the otters?"

"Absolutely. And we can use the monorail to get to that part of the park," Hart said as she gathered the paper containers, plastic cups and used napkins. She rose and carried the trays to the receptacle.

"Angela? What are you doing here?" a male voice asked.

Hart turned and recognized the speaker. "Oh my God! Terry. Hi, this is a pleasant surprise. I'm here with a friend from work," she said gesturing toward Rodrigo who rose and joined them.

"Tony, this is a friend, Terry Daly. Terry, this is a colleague, Tony Rodrigo."

The two men shook hands. "Terry, I'm very sorry to hear about your parents. I know you and your dad were close. He was a nice guy. And your mother was very sweet and very nice to me. I'll miss them," Hart said.

"Thanks, Angela. I'll miss them too. It's especially hard on the kids. They really liked their grandparents. That's one of the reasons why we brought them here today. We're going to have a memorial service for them soon. I'd like you to come."

"Thanks, Terry, I'd like that."

Daly looked at Rodrigo. "You look familiar Tony. Do you live in Eastchester?"

"No. Bronxville."

"Oh. Well maybe I've seen you at Little League games or something like that?"

"Never been to a Little League game," Rodrigo said. "I don't have any children."

"Right. Of course. Maybe it was church. Do you go to St. Joe's in Bronxville?"

"No."

"Don't pay any attention to Terry," Hart said. "He's an FBI agent and asking questions is second nature to him. Whoops, sorry, Terry, I think I spoke out of turn."

Daly gave Hart a hard stare.

Rodrigo froze at the sound of the letters FBI. He recovered and said lightly, "Never met an FBI agent before. I somehow had the impression you were all seven feet tall and built like an NFL linebacker. Do you carry a gun?"

"Angela, I'm sorry, I have to run. My wife's probably wondering where I am," Daly said. "Very nice to meet you, Tony. Good to see you again, Angela. You look fabulous. Excuse me, please." He strode off in the direction of his family who were getting ice cream.

"Bye, Terry. Say hello to Ellen for me," Hart yelled. He waived without turning around. "You should have seen the look on your face when I mentioned Terry was an FBI Agent, Tony."

"I was surprised. I have never met an FBI Agent. I guess I was a little in awe."

"I don't blame you. I'm in awe too," Hart said. "He's so good looking, and so is his wife, Ellen. I used to baby sit the kids every now and then. They are a nice couple."

"I'm sure. He is a handsome guy. Sorry about the dumb remark about FBI people being seven feet tall and all. What happened to his parents?"

"They were both killed in the terrorist attack on the airport. They were headed home after a visit."

"Wow. That's tough. What does he do for the FBI?"

"I asked him that one day and he told me he couldn't tell me what he did," said Hart. "So one day I asked Ellen and she told me but asked me to keep it a secret."

"Oh. Must be some sort of spy."

"No. I shouldn't tell you this. But he's the head of the Counter-Terrorist Department. They're based in New York City."

"Oh," Rodrigo said trying to be as matter of fact as he could. He put his hands in his pockets. "I guess he's involved with the airport investigation."

"I honestly don't know what he does on his job, but Ellen says he takes it very seriously. He lost a brother in the World Trade Center 10 years ago and Ellen lost her father. Now he's lost his parents."

"That's tough," Rodrigo said. "Did you lose anyone close?"

"No. Some people in my town were killed ten years ago, but I didn't know any of them. "You?"

"No friends, but a couple of neighbors," Rodrigo responded.

"If we're going to the see the otters, we'd better get started," Hart said.

The Daly family was 200 yards ahead walking in the same direction. Normally, Daly would have told his wife he had met Angela, but his mind was sifting through information. *I have seen this guy's face before. Where? Where?*

Seeing the direction Daly was headed, Rodrigo not wanting to risk being seen with an FBI agent stopped and said, "I'm getting a headache, Angela. Must be the sun. Would you mind if we went back to the car? We can see the otters another time."

"Not at all. You can take a nap at my place if you're not feeling ok. In fact, I'll make dinner. How's that sound?"

"Thanks for being so understanding. I'd like that," he said as he took her hand. They started walking. "Let's stop and get some wine too."

All the way home, Terry Daly tried to place the face of Tony Rodrigo. His wife sensed something was troubling him when he nearly missed the exit. "Honey, is something wrong?"

Ellen knew better than to ask about work, but her husband volunteered.

"I bumped into Angela Hart while you were getting ice cream. She was with a guy named Tony Rodrigo who works with her. I have seen that guy's face and I can't place where. He's not some non-descript looking guy. He's very good looking. He's got a dark complexion and nearly jet black hair. And he spoke perfect English."

"Well why wouldn't he?" Ellen asked.

"No reason, I guess, Terry Daly said. "Hey, maybe you could call Angela and schmoos with her. You know, I hear you were at the zoo with a fellow. What's he like? Where's he from. Try to get some information about him."

"You mean spy on her, don't you?"

"No, I don't mean spy," Daly said emphatically. "You two are friends and you are interested in her happiness. That's all."

"I'll have to think about that." Ellen turned her attention to the kids to see if they enjoyed the outing. At their home in Larchmont, they went to their rooms and logged onto the internet to check their email messages. Ellen got out of the car and put her arms around her husband.

"Honey, why don't you fire up the grill. I'll make the drinks and the salad. I'm famished."

"Deal."

The Daly's kissed passionately.

"Hey lover, feed me first," Ellen said, breaking the embrace.

"Aw," He swatted her fanny as she turned away from him.

-Chapter Eight-

Rodrigo and Hart made their way to the Bronx Zoo parking lot. Rodrigo pressed the auto unlock twice and opened the door for Hart who gave him a light kiss on the cheek as she slipped past him into the car.

"Thank you," she said softly. "You are a perfect gentleman."

Rodrigo got in beside her. He backed the car out of the parking space and exited the lot, heading to the northbound Bronx River Parkway.

"What are you planning for dinner?" he asked.

"I don't know, what would you like?"

"Well I like beef, chicken and fish. And lamb too. But I don't like pork."

"You don't like pork chops?" Hart said. "You don't like pork loin? Or ham? They're delicious."

Not wanting to draw too much attention to the matter, Rodrigo said, "I guess it's ok, but it's not on my list of favorite things. I much prefer a good steak, or roast chicken. Do you have a grill?"

"Yes, it's in the back yard. I don't use it much because I'm on the second floor..

But we can grill a steak and sit outside with the wine while it's cooking."

"Ok. I'll cook the steak and you make the salad. What else?" Rodrigo asked.

Hart liked Rodrigo. Soft spoken, very bright, quiet, and very attractive, she thought. She liked dark men and Rodrigo looked as if he had a permanent tan.

"You remind me of a movie actor," she said.

"What? How so?"

"I'm talking about that movie actor, George something or other. He always has a gorgeous tan."

"Oh. I don't go to a lot of movies. But this isn't a tan. It's me. I have a dark complexion."

"I know, silly. It's great. I'm attracted to men with dark complexions. Must be your Spanish heritage."

"You're right." Rodrigo smiled broadly, but again changed the subject. "OK, we can shop in Bronxville, or in Eastchester, what's your choice?"

"Eastchester has a Stop and Shop about a mile from the parkway and there's a liquor store nearby. Get off at exit 17," Hart directed.

Rodrigo mumbled agreement. "Angie, what do you like to do, you know, when you're not working."

"I love the beach and in the winter I like to ski. I like all kinds of music and I love romantic movies. Tony?"

"What?"

"Please don't call me Angie. Call me Angela. OK?"

Rodrigo looked at her and smiled. "Sure. Sorry."

He exited the parkway and on Hart's order, made a left at the traffic light and another left onto Mill Road. "Just go straight for a while," she directed. "I'll tell you where to turn."

He followed her directions and soon they were in the supermarket parking lot. Rodrigo grabbed a basket. "Why don't you get the stuff for the salad and I'll get the steak. What kind do you like?"

"I love filet mignon. It's my favorite. But it's expensive."

"Filet mignon it is. How about baked potato? Can you do that?"

"Sure. I'll wrap them in foil and we can cook them on the grill too."

"I'll meet you in the vegie section," he said and hurried off to the meat counter. Hart went to the produce section. Out of sight of Hart, Rodrigo pulled his cell phone from his belt and dialed his number punching in the code for messages. "You have no new messages," the mechanical female voice responded. Relieved, he punched the code for email and received the same response.

"Can I help you?" the meat clerk asked.

"What? Oh, yes, I'd like three filet mignons, please, about this thick," Rodrigo said as he held his thumb and forefinger about two inches apart.

The meat clerk cut, weighed, and wrapped the steaks putting the sticker on the pack. Rodrigo thanked him and headed for the produce section where Hart was still gathering the materials from the ample salad bar. "Hi. I see you got the meat. Do you like avocado," she asked pointing to the basket that held a plump avocado.

"Never tried it."

"You'll like it. And it's good for you." She closed the lid on the plastic salad container and put it in the basket along with the potatoes. "All set. Let's go."

At the liquor store, Rodrigo picked out a red wine that was suggested by the clerk.

"I didn't realize how hungry I was," Hart said. "I'd also like a drink. What do you drink besides wine?"

"Beer. I also like Jack Daniels, manhattans, martinis and vodka on ice."

WOW! Me too," she said. "I love vodka on the rocks. I've got some Smirnoff. It's not Stoli, but it's still good."

They fell into a discussion about food and restaurants. Hart was impressed with the names of the places that Rodrigo said he enjoyed. "My favorite is the Gourmet Fish Market in Eastchester. Great seafood, wonderful presentation and moderate prices. I bet you'll love it," she declared.

"I love seafood, especially Hamour."

"Hamour? What's that?"

"That's what we.. ah. That's another name for grouper."

"Oh. Hamour, eh. Never heard of that. I don't know if I've had grouper," Hart said.

"It's a mild white fish from the Arabian Sea." *Damn, why did I say that?*

"The Arabian Sea? Where is the Arabian Sea?"

"That's another name for the Persian Gulf."

"Oh. Well when did you have Grouper."

"When I was in Egypt. A friend and I visited the Pyramids."

"Oh. I've never been to Egypt. I'd like to go sometime," Hart said.

When they arrived at her apartment, she took the groceries and wine and entered the apartment leaving the door open. Rodrigo parked a few hundred yards down the block and quickly walked to the front door of the building. He took the stairs to her apartment two at a time.

"I'm in the bedroom, Tony. I'm changing. Be there in a sec. Why don't you make us a drink. The vodka is in the cabinet next to the fridge. Glasses in the cabinet just to the right of the sink."

Rodrigo found the vodka and the glasses, put three ice cubes for each glass and poured two generous drinks. Hart joined him and accepted the glass he offered. "WOW! Are you trying to get me drunk?"

"Mostly ice." He took a healthy swallow that she imitated.

"Hmmmm. That feels good."

Rodrigo put his glass down and took the glass from Hart and set it alongside his.

He put his right arm around her waist and pulled her gently to him. They kissed for a second or two, withdrew and looked at each other. Then they embraced and locked their lips together hungrily.

The phone jolted them from their passion.

"Shit," Hart uttered. She grabbed the receiver from the wall. "Hello."

"Angela. Hi, it's Ellen Daly."

"Hi Ellen. How are you?"

"Fine, thanks. Listen did I get you at a bad time? I only need a second or two."

"I can talk for a few minutes. Tony and I are having a drink before we make dinner. What's up?"

"Tony? Is that the guy with you at the zoo this afternoon?"

"Yeah, why?"

"Never mind. Listen we can chat later. I'm sorry to interrupt."

Hart liked the Dalys and enjoyed the occasional lunches and shopping with Ellen.

"It's ok, I can talk for a minute or two." Turning to Rodrigo she said, "Please excuse me. It's a good friend. I'll only be a minute." Hart walked into her bedroom and shut the door.

"OK, I can talk. What's up?

"Angela, this is between you and me. Don't breathe a word to anyone. OK?"

Hart was a little apprehensive, but knew that Ellen Daly could be trusted. "OK."

"Good. Look, I don't want to pry, and I know it's none of my business. But Terry asked me to call."

"Terry did? What for?"

"When you introduced this fellow Tony to Terry this afternoon, Terry thought he recognized him from somewhere. And it has bothered him all day. His last name is Rodrigo? Is he Spanish? How much do you know about him?

Hart was slightly annoyed. "Does Terry think he's a criminal or something?"

"No. Nothing like that. But he gets crazy when he can't place a face with a name."

"I've worked with Tony for about five years. He's a graphic artist, and a pretty good one too. This is the first time we've been out together so I don't know very much about his personal life. He lives in Bronxville, about 2-3 miles away, and he's older than me. I'd say he's about 35-36, something like that. What else do you want to know?"

"Do you know where he worked before he joined your company?" Ellen asked.

"No. But I can ask."

"No, don't do that," Ellen said sharply, then in a calmer voice said, "No need to, really. Look, I'm sorry I bothered you. I'm sure it will come to Terry eventually, Listen I'll call later this week. Maybe we can get together. OK?"

"Sure Ellen. Sorry I couldn't help. I should be home after work every night this week. Nothing planned yet."

"OK talk to you later. Have a lovely dinner."

"Thanks. Toodles." Hart pushed the off button, put the phone down and returned to the kitchen and her drink. Rodrigo was in the living room watching the Yankee–Baltimore game, now in extra innings.

"Everything OK?" he asked, not wanting to raise her suspicions that he had heard her talking about where he lived and guessing his age." He made a mental note to be more circumspect talking about himself.

"No everything is fine. It was a friend wanting some information, that's all," Hart said.

"OK. I need another drink. You're one behind."

"Help yourself. I'm going to make the salad."

Rodrigo switched off the game, but Hart asked him to turn it back on. "I like the Yankees."

"I don't know much about baseball," Rodrigo said. "Football is my sport." He followed Hart into the kitchen and made another drink. She took two long swallows and handed him her empty glass.

"I'm ready for another," she said as she removed the lettuce, tomatoes, and onion from the plastic container, placing them into a wooden bowl.

He took her glass, put it down next to his and pulled her to him.

"Wait." She put the rest of the salad ingredients on the counter, dropping the green pepper on the floor. The two fell into each other's arms in a passionate kiss.

"You're making it very difficult to think about the salad," she hissed slowly after breaking off the kiss. They kissed again. His hands cupped the cheeks of her bottom and she moaned softly. "Tony, this is our first date. I'm not that kind of girl."

His hands lingered before he slowly removed them and took a half step away from her. "I'm sorry. It's just that I thought..... I mean the kiss earlier...I'm sorry....you're so beautiful, I couldn't help it," he stammered.

"I'm not blaming you. You didn't do anything wrong. And I am very flattered by your compliments. But we should take this a little more slowly."

"Sure."

They bent down simultaneously to retrieve the green pepper bumping their heads as the pepper rolled toward the dining room. Startled, but unhurt, they rubbed their foreheads and laughed.

Rodrigo picked up the pepper, ran some water over it handed it to Hart who was washing the tomato. "That door goes downstairs to the back yard. If you go down and light the grill. I'll finish the salad, wash the potatoes and join you."

"I have a better idea," he laughed. "I'll wash the potatoes while you do the salad. Then we can both go down and light the grill."

"What a team," she said. "You know, sir, I have to tell you something. I have admired you almost as long as we've known each other. You are very good looking. You are bright and interesting… and, well, I like you."

Rodrigo approached, but Hart put her hand against his chest and gently admonished him, "Let's have our drinks and eat first. Then we'll see what happens."

Rodrigo threw up both his hands in mock surrender. Hart stepped back from the sink and Rodrigo stepped in and quickly washed both potatoes. Then they switched and his gaze fell on her bottom. He felt the familiar stirring in his groin.

"OK, all done," Hart said wrapping the lettuce in paper towels. She put the bowl and the lettuce into the fridge. Next, she dried both potatoes, penetrated them with a fork and wrapped them in foil. "Let's go downstairs and relax."

Outside, Rodrigo admired the new Weber. "How do I light it?"

Following Hart's instructions, Rodrigo lifted the cover, turned on the gas and burner and pushed the ignitor. .

"This looks new," he observed.

Hart settled into her chair after making sure both were clean and dry. "It's a couple of months old, a gift from an old friend. I am paranoid that someone's going to steal it. I told my downstairs neighbor he and his wife could use it if they kept an eye on it. He doesn't grill much."

Rodrigo put the potatoes on the grill. "How much time for the potatoes?"

"Put them in the middle and turn the front and back burners on high," she replied. "Let 'em cook for 15 minutes and then put them on the rack in the back while we cook the steak."

Rodrigo sat down, setting the timer on his watch. "You know that guy we met this afternoon, the FBI person? He ever tell you what it's like to work for the FBI?"

"No," Hart responded. "He doesn't talk about his job at all. But sometimes Ellen does. That's his wife."

"So, is his job exciting? What kinds of crooks does he catch?" Rodrigo asked hoping Hart would give him more information.

"Noooooo," she mocked. "Police officers do that. Don't you know anything about the FBI?"

"Not much, and apparently you don't either," he said.

"Well, I do know that he heads up the anti-terrorism group. And he has met the president and vice president. I guess that means he is pretty important."

Rodrigo was sipping his drink when he heard the words "anti-terrorism." Reflexively, he swallowed quickly and began coughing. When Hart got up and began slapping his back, he waived her away saying he was OK. His mind raced as he lifted the grill cover to check on the potatoes. *What did I tell her? How much did she tell that guy's wife?* He wiped his mouth and sat down.

"Terry is a really nice guy, Tony. You'll like him. I'll invite them over for dinner soon and you can chat about the FBI. I'm sure he'll tell you some of the stuff that isn't secret."

That meeting will never happen

"Yeah, that might be interesting. Does he carry a gun?"

"Most of the time, I think so."

"I wonder if he ever caught a terrorist?"

"He hasn't, but one of his colleagues in Miami caught some guys who belonged to Al Kana."

"al Qaeda," Rodrigo corrected, simultaneously wishing he hadn't.

"Al whatever," she said.

"Where are the people he arrested?"

"He didn't say."

"No matter. Hey, how do you like living in Eastchester?"

"It's not as pricey as Bronxville. Not as snooty, either. It's OK. I was thinking about joining Lake Isle, the town country club, and taking up golf."

"Why didn't you?"

"Never got around to it. And I don't have a partner to play with. It's more fun with a partner. The potatoes should be about ready," Hart said.. "I'll get the steaks. You want another drink?"

"Are you having one?"

"I better not, not if I'm having wine with dinner."

"You can bring me one if it isn't too much trouble." *I don't plan on driving tonight anyway.*

Hart reappeared with the steaks on a plate in one hand and Rodrigo's drink in the other. "Pour a little of that into my glass," she told Rodrigo.

Rodrigo grabbed the platter, set it down on the side of the Weber, and dropped the filets on the fire. He poured a little of his drink into her glass.

Hart felt the potatoes and placed them on the warming rack. "Turn off the back burner and turn the front and middle burners to high," she said. "I like my steak medium. How about you?"

"Medium's fine. But we need some utensils, Angela. Tell me where they are and I'll take this plate upstairs and wash it."

"Oh shit. Sorry. You sit. Tony. It's easier for me to find them."

She brought a clean platter, a large barbecue spatula, a knife and fork and handed the utensils to Rodrigo.

Twenty-five minutes later they ate hungrily.

"More wine, Tony?" Hart asked as she poured a half glass for herself.

Rodrigo held out his glass.

"This is really good. Very tender," Rodrigo said.

"Filet mignon is my favorite. Very tender and very tasty. AND very expensive. How much did you pay for this?

She's beginning to slur her words a little. Rodrigo partially refilled Hart's glass and emptied the bottle into his. He settled back and wondered: *How do I get her to ask me to stay?*

"You better go easy on that," Hart said. "I don't think you want to get stopped for DWI. Are you OK?"

"I think so. I'm not much of a drinker," he said.

"Well, I'm feeling a little light headed. And you've had more to drink than me. Maybe you should sleep on the sofa... if you promise to behave."

I don't want to make you uncomfortable even though we've known each other for quite a while. Besides I don't have a tooth brush."

"I trust you. Besides you'll be here on the sofa and I'll be in my room. And by the way, I have an extra toothbrush."

Perfect.

He cleared the table as she sipped her wine. "I'll run down and cover the cooker. Do you want me to wash the grates?" he asked.

"No, thanks. I'll wash them the next time I use the thing. I'll take care of the plates and glasses, if you'll put the salad in a plastic bag – the bags are in that drawer."

Rodrigo put the remainder of the salad in the fridge, went into the living room with his wine and clicked the remote to turn on the TV. Hart rinsed the dishes, put them in the washer and followed. She put her wine on the table and almost sat in his lap. He casually slipped his arm around her as he appeared intent on the screen.

Hart dropped her head onto his shoulder and the two remained quiet for a few moments. Rodrigo wondered what to do next and was interrupted by Hart's snoring.

Disappointed, but with an eye to a more fruitful future meeting, he rose lifting her into his arms and carried her into her bedroom gently putting her head on the pillow. Removing her shoes, he thought about undressing her. Instead he took half of the blanket from the far side of the bed and gently pulled it over her. At the last second, he unbuckled her belt and top button of her jeans.

Then he picked up the spare blanket, turned out the light and retreated to the sofa. In a few moments he had finished his wine, turned off the TV, removed his shoes, laid down and closed his eyes.

"Tony."

Rodrigo opened his eyes and sat up as Hart called his name again. She was standing in the door in her panties.

"I don't want you to sleep on the sofa."

-Chapter Nine-

They embraced at the entrance to her bedroom. Breathing faster, she pulled his shirt over his head and unzipped his shorts.

He scooped her up, dropped her gently on the bed and hungrily began kissing her breasts. As his fingers pulled at her waist band, she lifted her hips allowing him to ease her panties down past her knees. He dropped them on the floor.

Her hands ranged over his body and down inside his underwear. "WOW," she gasped huskily.

"You make me that way. I want you," he said as he helped her remove his undershorts. Their tongues explored each other's mouths.

Later, they lay in each other's arms. Hart broke the silence, "Tony, I hope you don't think I'm a slut. I've never slept with a man on the first date before. You're the first."

"I don't think you're a slut. Besides, we have known each other for a long time."

"Can I tell you something?" she asked.

"Sure."

"I've only slept with four men in my life, now five counting you. And you are the first to take the time to satisfy me. You know, make me climax. The other guys just wanted to get laid. You're different."

"Angela, I like you. You always talk to me at work, not like the other girls. I think you're sweet. And warm. And you have a beautiful body."

She kissed him and put her head on his chest. "We should get some sleep," she purred. "Maybe we can make love again in the morning."

He reached down and caressed her bottom with his right hand. "I just thought of something."

"What?"

"I didn't use any protection"

"I'm on the pill. Don't worry."

Rodrigo was awakened by the sunlight on his face. He reached over to the other side of the bed. Hart wasn't there. Startled momentarily, he relaxed when he heard her in the kitchen making coffee. Slipping behind her, he cupped her bare breasts in both hands and kissed her neck.

"Good morning," she whispered, turning to meet him. "Hmm, I see you are glad to see me, but before we make love I want to shower. Want to join me?"

Hart led the way. They playfully washed each other at first but soon their movements became more purposeful and their excitement grew. They barely had time to dry each other before running to the bed to finish.

The two lovers sitting in their underpants were enjoying their second cup of coffee. Hart was reading the Sunday paper's entertainment section; Rodrigo was scanning the front section looking for stories about terrorism. On page three a headline caught his attention:

Congressional Panel
To Hear Testimony
On Anti-Terrorism

In the seventh paragraph, Rodrigo spotted the name Terry Daly. "Hey, that FBI agent we met at the zoo is in this story?"

"Terry Daly. Really? He's got your interest, doesn't he?" She kept reading.

"A little. Didn't his wife ask you about me?" Rodrigo asked, his voice under control as he devoured the story.

"How did you know that," Hart asked raising her head. "Were you eaves dropping on me?"

"No. But I couldn't help overhear you. What did she want to know?"

"She told me her husband thought he recognized you and wanted to know where you two might have met. She also asked if you were Spanish since you have a Spanish name. I told her I didn't know, but I assumed so. That's all. No big deal."

"OK. I just wondered."

"You know Tony, we've worked together for five years and I still don't know very much about you. Come to think of it, I hardly know anything about you."

And that's the way I want it!

"Nothing to tell, really."

She took his hand. "We work together and we just became intimate. I'd like to know something about you, where you come from, where you went to school, are your parents still alive, where do they live? Heck, I don't even have your phone number or know where you live exactly."

Rodrigo gently pulled his hand from hers, lifted her chin and kissed her lightly. His right hand slid upward along her leg. She stopped it just before he reached the top of her thighs. "I'm serious, Tony. You know a lot about me, where I live and all. It's only fair that you tell me something about the man I've had sex with twice."

Looking for a diversion, Rodrigo glanced at the clock on the kitchen wall and whistled. "Oh shit, I almost forgot. I have to finish up the layouts for *Single Maltings*. But I promise, I'll tell you all you want to know tomorrow. You wanna have lunch?" His hand touched Hart's knee. This time she parted her legs.

As his hand found her, she put her hand behind his head and kissed him hard on the mouth for a moment. "God you are insatiable. OK, You said you gotta go, then go. I'll see you tomorrow and we'll have lunch."

He removed his hand, rose and went to the bedroom where he put on his shirt and pants. After locating his socks and shoes he returned to the kitchen where she was standing, still topless with her arms across her chest.

Rodrigo pulled her arms away and put them at her sides. He stepped back and admired her lush form. *She is beautiful.* He enfolded her in his arms and they kissed. She moaned softly as Rodrigo's hands gently squeezed her buttocks. Then he pulled away.

"I'll see you tomorrow, Angela. Dinner was great." *And you were a great lay.*

When Rodrigo opened the front door, she stood behind it to hide her nakedness. "Bye, Tony. Safe home."

Rodrigo walked to the sidewalk and then jogged to his car, his mind racing. *Stupid fool. You never should have gotten involved.*

He quickly got in and picked up his cell phone. I wonder if she's watching. I better not look back. No, I should wave. When he turned, her door was closed. Of course, she's not going to wave. She's naked!

Rodrigo checked his voice mail and his email. He had one message. *From Atta!*

"Media indicate competition meeting."

Rodrigo knew not to reply on the phone. When he got home he, turned on his computer and opened his email. Atta was waiting for him. *Read story on competition in morning paper. Can see no effect on business plan. Need to confer with you. Call and leave number!.*"

Rodrigo shut down his computer, gulped a glass of water and made his way hurriedly to the pay phone near Lawrence Hospital. He called the number, left the pay phone number and hung up. When the phone rang it startled him.

"Yes," he said.

"Juamah," Atta said.

"Dhahran," Rodrigo replied. He composed himself and began, deliberately leaving out the part about sex with Hart. When he finished, he said, "I'm not sure it's anything to worry about, but I'd rather be safe than sorry."

"What are you planning to do?" Atta asked.

I'll go to work today and clean out my desk. Then I'll call in tomorrow and tell them I quit. I don't want this woman to get too nosey, not with the FBI asking her questions."

Atta thought for a moment. "Quitting is not wise."

"It's the only way I can think of to avoid questions," Rodrigo said.

"If you quit your job, this woman will wonder why. If you don't say goodbye and give her a good reason for suddenly leaving, she'll go looking for sympathy and will tell her friend who will certainly tell her husband, the FBI agent. Then they'll start asking some serious questions. They'll get your address from your employer and pay you a visit."

"I'll find another place."

"NO. If you do that the FBI will know something's wrong and will certainly start searching for you. You'll jeopardize everything. Stay put and go to work," Atta demanded. "Don't change your routine."

"OK. Any idea when...?" Atta didn't reply. He hung up, walked to the communications room and called the U.N. mission..

"Ambassador Sulieman's office. How may I help you?"

"Talal Farhan here," Atta said, using his Saudi name. "Please put him on the phone."

"Right away, sir."

"Yes," Sulieman said in his rich deep voice.

Atta explained the situation in careful detail including his orders to Rodrigo.

Sulieman was silent for a long moment. "You were right. He shouldn't leave his job or his residence," the Saudi ambassador said. "Something may be wrong. This isn't like Hakim. I know him. He doesn't panic."

"I don't think he's going to panic, your excellency. He has little experience with women and this woman apparently got to him somehow. Remember, he lost his wife and family some years ago," Atta replied.

"It may be a problem. Stay in close touch. Give him all the help you can, but do not meet with him. We are too close to make a change now."

"I understand, your excellency. Any date in mind?"

"Not yet. You will know soon enough."

"Yes sir."

"Anything else for me?" Sulieman asked.

"No sir."

"Good. We will be receiving four students very shortly. They will help you with the deliveries. When they arrive in New York they have instructions to come directly here. One of them will have instructions for you. In the meantime, keep me informed if anything changes. Anything at all." Sulieman hung up.

"Yes, sir," said to the dial tone.

After the students arrive we won't have long to wait. I won't alert Rodrigo until they get here. No need to put any more stress on him.

-Chapter Ten-

"Good morning," Terry Daly said to his two deputies as they sat at the conference table for the Monday morning staff meeting. "Before my meeting with Owens and Mooreland, but I want to share something that occurred over the weekend and see what you make of it.

"On Saturday I took the family to the zoo and ran into a woman named Angela Hart, Ellen's friend who used to attend our church. She had a guy with her she introduced as Antonio Rodrigo. I believe that's a Spanish surname, but this guy was no Spaniard or of Spanish background. This guy was an Arab."

"I don't understand," said Brown. "What's the problem?"

"Why would an Arab be using a Christian Spanish name?"

"How do you know he's an Arab? And besides what if he is? Didn't the Moors settle in Spain? Perhaps he comes from a family of Moors. It's not against the law and his having a Christian name isn't against the law either," Brown offered.

"Well it might be, if he's using an alias to cover something," said Ewing. "He could be an illegal alien. Do we have anything on him?"

"What bothers me," Daly continued, "is that I have seen this guy's face before. I know it. I am absolutely sure. I just can't place it."

"Forgive me for suggesting this, boss, but we do have more important things on our plate. And I don't think this Rodriguez fellow was the reason you called this meeting," Brown put in. "But if it really bothers you, ask Pat to run a check."

"Right. And it's Rodrigo, not Rodriguez. Sorry, but this bothered me all weekend. Ellen talked to Angela Hart. She didn't have a lot of information on him. But I can't shake it. I know this guy. Anyway, think about it. I've got to get to the meeting.

"Oh, boss, before you go. We haven't heard from Walter Amberly at Celestial," Brown said.

Daly paused. "Alright. I'll give him the benefit of the doubt. Call him back."

Homeland Security Secretary Philip Mooreland and FBI Director Roy Owens listened as Terry Daly briefed them on security problems and the continued lack of cooperation between the nation's law enforcement and governmental agencies. The briefing went on for nearly four hours with occasional breaks. When Daly finished, Mooreland walked to the window and looked through the curtains at the Washington Monument. It was drizzling.

"Not a very pretty picture, you're painting," Mooreland said. "It's been ten years and we seem to be no better off than we were then. Why couldn't we prevent these latest attacks? Why was there no warning? And what assurances do we have there will be no attacks in the future? That's what the president will want to know."

"Mr. Secretary," Owens said. "Before I address your specific questions, I'd like to address the morale issue of the FBI. We've taken the fall for just about every governmental screw-up. When a presidential candidate's background fails to reveal he smoked pot 25 years before or received a speeding ticket or was caught in a panty raid in college, we get nailed. When an FBI memo is leaked by Congress, we get the blame for that. And, of course, I'd be remiss in not blaming the FBI for the latest terrorist attacks.

"Unfortunately, our most vocal critics are the Congress, the very people who have tied our hands since the 70s when they thought we were abusing our powers. They disemboweled the bureau and made it illegal for us to collaborate with the CIA, made it illegal for the CIA's intelligence experts to work here in the States, disemboweled the Patriot Act and cut both of our budgets," Owens said. "So now we have an almost non-existent intelligence network, damn few agents who speak Arabic or Farsi, computers that are obsolete and a

Bureau where CTA has become more important than fighting crime and terrorism.

"That's just part of the problem," Owens continued, warming to his subject. "The State Department still insists on granting visas to people who may well be terrorists even though the Justice Department has asked State to halt that practice. To make matters worse the U.S. Citizenship and Immigration Services acts like a traffic counter rather than an enforcement agency."

"I'm, ah, we are aware of that," Mooreland said. "Please go on."

"What I'm saying, Mr. Secretary is that for all intents and purposes it would appear we are lacking a national focus. The last I heard we were at war, but no one agrees how to fight that war and Congress can't or won't give us the tools. The FBI is engaged in chasing down more than 20 million illegal aliens who, if our system was working right, wouldn't have been here in the first place. Does it make sense that an illegal alien isn't breaking any laws? Hell, he's here illegally. But the politically correct assholes call them undocumented workers, or out of status. Does it make sense that an illegal alien convicted of beating a baby to death is not deported because a group of unelected judges says the crime wasn't violent?

Does it make sense that we are still allowing students into this country from Iran, Syria, Libya and other terrorist havens? Do you want me to go on?"

"Yes, please do," Mooreland said.

"Mr. Secretary, the CIS is a serious problem," Owens said. "Their mistakes, their disinterest, their failures are overwhelming us. We have to track down all the illegal people they don't keep track of. God only knows how many terrorists we have in this country. Illegal aliens actually outnumber legal foreign visitors and by a substantial number. The sad things is that CIS reports to you.

"When the Bureau or the Border Patrol nails an illegal alien he is turned over to the CIS. The guy has a hearing and if he is ordered deported – and that's a big fucking if – he can appeal. And while he's waiting for the Board of Immigration Appeals to do something, he isn't even detained. So, if he really has something to hide, he disappears. And even if he has committed a criminal act, the Board of Immigration Appeals in nine out of ten cases will overrule the CIS and let him stay," Owens said.

"The situation is so sad it's a comedy or a tragedy depending on your point of view. Our problem, Mr. Secretary, is that the Bureau is spending hundreds of thousands of hours tracking down these bastards for nothing. Let me give you an example, one that ended in tragedy. Do you remember the two snipers who terrorized the Maryland and Virginia countryside, DC too, about eight years ago?"

"Of course. You had more than 800 Agents working on that case. What about it?" Mooreland asked.

"One of those snipers was an illegal alien from Jamaica. He was a stowaway who jumped ship in Miami in June 2001. He was nailed by the Border Patrol in the State of Washington about six or seven months later.

"According to the record, the then INS in the Seattle District let the bastard go and that was a clear violation of federal law. This guy was a stowaway and according to federal law he should have been deported without even a hearing. But instead, he was freed without bond. Ten months later 11 people paid the price with their lives and hundreds of thousands more, hell, maybe millions, were scared to death for weeks. We've got to fix that problem, Mr. Secretary. Until this government gets its act together, we are wasting our fucking time.

"We need new tough laws, the new technologies, more agents and a completely new computer system, not one that is State's leftovers. And that is just the start," Owens continued "We won't ever be truly effective until Congress unties our hands and until the President sits down with the CIA, State, Justice, the Border Patrol, the ATF and the dozens of other federal agencies and demands cooperation.

"Look, I agree with you about the CIS and I am trying to solve the problem. But what's needed are changes in the laws. And I'm sure you know there are other considerations in play here," Mooreland said.

"You mean political considerations?"

"Well, yes."

"Pardon me, Mr. Secretary," Owens said, "what's more important, American lives, or politics? We're talking about National Security. We're talking about more than 40,000 people murdered

103

and another 30,000-40,000 injured. And we're talking about agencies that either don't cooperate with each other or aren't allowed to.

"CIS can't find its ass with both hands. And another knowingly allows terrorists to enter this country. You know the real reason why attacks are so infrequent? I'll tell you. The terrorists are laughing too hard to do anything. National Security is a National joke," Owens said.

"Look, I understand you are upset. No one can blame you. Your own staff has lost relatives to terrorists. But we have to face political realities."

"You want realities. Here they are," Owens interrupted. "We need to fight fire with fire, let us by-pass the CIS and deal directly with the aliens we suspect of being terrorists. No more kid gloves. No more Miranda crap. Since they're not citizens, they shouldn't have any rights or privileges. No driver's licenses, no free school and no medical care. Without the freebies, they might go home without our insistence.

"The only right they should have is a hearing before a military tribunal and a fast execution or a fast exit. Untie our hands. Untie the CIA too. They still have an intelligence network that can help us. And we can help them," Owens said.

"Here's another example. The airport security agents are trying to do their jobs. But the politically correct liberal assholes criticize them for what they call profiling because they were taking long looks at Middle Eastern males between the ages of 20 and 40. Hell, that's not profiling, that's common sense. .

"That is the group that carried out the attacks on the towers and at least two of the bombers at the mall were in that age category. Instead, they're wasting their fucking time frisking 85-year-old ladies in wheel chairs. It's ludicrous. It's, it's, it's wrong, and someone has to have the guts to tell Congress."

Mooreland's jaw tightened and his eyes narrowed. "Terry, do you feel this way?

"Yes, I do, Mr. Secretary. I never thought I would hear myself say that, but there is so much that needs to be done, and no one is listening," Daly said.

"My God, what's come over you people?" Mooreland asked. "This is not a game where if we don't play your way, you'll take you bat and ball and go home. Jesus Christ, Roy, you know where Congress stands on this. This is not the kind of conduct I would expect from you and your team. You're professionals, all of you. This is a country of laws. We have to obey those laws."

"Tell that to the CIS. They broke the law in Washington and it had tragic consequences. But, I'm not talking about breaking the law," Owens said. "I'm talking about tougher laws and insisting that the CIS obey them for Christ's sake. How many more thousands of Americans have to die before we decide to fight fire with fire?"

"To protect our country effectively, we need to close the loopholes in existing laws, and we need to deploy all the technology we have. We're in a war. But those smug bastards bloat the budget with pet projects instead of giving us what we need to win. A 10 million dollar court house in West Virginia and a $278 million bridge to nowhere in Alaska are more important than national security."

"I know how you feel," Mooreland replied. "But Congress pays attention to the voters. And most voters take a dim view about sacrificing personal freedoms."

"You asked me earlier what we had to do to prevent another attack," said Owens. "Without new laws, greater cooperation and greater freedom to act, we simply won't be able to prevent another attack. It's that simple. And you know what is going to happen? If, or rather when, there is another attack, the bastards on capital hill will point fingers at the president, at you and the FBI , the CIA, Justice, the Border Patrol, everyone, but themselves. They're the real culprits. I'm sure it bothers you. It sure as hell irritates the shit out of us."

"Mr. Secretary, I have a couple of things I'd like to say. But first I want to assure you this isn't a palace revolt," Fritz Thompson, L.A. Assistant Deputy director said. "If we aren't given the freedom to act and the tools and laws we need, we can practically guarantee another attack."

"I'll be specific," Daly said. "And the president said it the other night. First, let's deal with the illegal aliens. Round them up. Deport them and deport all legal aliens who break the law. Once they are released from jail, they should be escorted by a U.S. Marshall to the airport or the border. If an alien is ordered deported, deport him. And if he comes back and we catch him again, send his ass to jail for 10 years. And if we need more judges, jails and administrators to get this done, then let's hire them.

"In 11 states, illegal aliens can get a driver's license and in nearly every state they can send their kids to school and get free medical benefits. Some states even give them preferential treatment on college tuition. Talks about incentives for more of them to come here. It's ludicrous.

"Only legal immigrants should be able to get a license. When a visa expires, the license should too. We want a law that requires all 50 states to link their motor vehicle computers with the FBI.

"That will help a traffic cop determine who the motorist really is when he's stopped for a traffic offense. And while we are at it, let's get rid of the Board of Immigration Appeals. Illegal aliens should have the right to life and the pursuit of happiness in their own country," Daly said. "They should not have the right to be here illegally and they certainly shouldn't have the right to appeal.

"To that point, let's get tough on foreign students. I simply cannot understand why we are issuing visas to students, hell, to anyone from Iran, Somalia, Syria, Cuba, Libya or North Korea? And North Korea and Iran both have nukes. Schools and universities that have foreign students here on visas should be forced to keep track of them on a monthly basis. You come here as a student, you attend classes. You don't, you go home.

"Our borders are wide open," Daly continued. "We need a fence in the north and more and better fencing in the south. That 700 mile fence they put up a couple of years ago still leaves more than 1,500 miles of the border without a fence.. We also need more border patrol officers. And we should give them special vehicles that can navigate difficult terrain, better listening devices and aircraft drones with video and infrared. And empower the border patrol to shoot back when fired upon." Daly said.

Owens raised his hand and Daly fell silent. Owens picked up the subject. "The bureau would like all citizens over the age of 10 to carry a digitized national security card, one that cannot be altered or forged. Every theater patron, every mall shopper and sports fan and every driver should produce this card to enter a public facility or to get through a toll plaza. Anyone not carrying a card should be detained and checked out.

"There is absolutely nothing in place that can stop a terrorist from walking into any crowded public facility and blowing himself up. We just got proof of that."

"OK. I've heard enough," Mooreland jumped in. "We've been over this ground before. We know what we need. And we know what needs to be done. But we don't make the rules. Congress does. And I'm already hearing that Congress is angry at the President's tough speech. It's likely they won't go along with suggestions that even hint at affecting personal liberty."

"Phil," Owens dropped the formality of Mr. Secretary. "If we had a National ID card and rules governing employment of illegal aliens, at least two of the murderers who blew up the mall would have been deported. Our agents in Minnesota interviewed the management of the Sound System Company and found out after these murderers were hired, their visas were never rechecked. One of the owners said it wasn't his problem. If a visa expires, the government should do something. Well, he's right. We should.

"Those two technicians worked here illegally for years and no one cared. I just cannot understand opposition to a national ID card. When Americans travel abroad they have to carry a passport. Why shouldn't foreigners be required to carry a government ID? What the hell is the difference?" Owens said.

"I would rather give up some of my personal freedom and be inconvenienced and know that my family is safe from murdering lunatics. Sure, leisure activities, shopping and commuting will be affected. Will people care if they know they'll be safe? What do you think?" Owens asked.

Mooreland sighed, put his hands behind his back and let his men continue to vent their spleens. Owens didn't disappoint. "Besides metal detectors and the like, we should be employing all the new technology including Carnivore Two, low frequency radar, side scan radar, the new personal x-ray, the new baggage x-ray, infrared digital video, and aircraft drones. And we need a lot more bomb sniffing dogs."

"No one, particularly a woman, is going to allow a security guard to see their bodies as if they were naked," Mooreland said. "The President won't touch personal x-ray. And he probably won't touch Carnivore Two either. Too risky, politically."

"Phil, you asked us here to brief you. We're doing that, telling you why things are the way they are. And we haven't even talked about our commercial harbors because that's not our responsibility. But that situation is frightening. Hundreds of cargo ships a day enter this country. Each holds as many as 200 containers the size of trailer trucks.

"We estimate as many as 250 illegals enter our country every month by stowing away in these containers. And if one of those is loaded with explosives it could destroy most of a good-sized port facility. The problem is we don't have the manpower to search every container on every ship," Owens said.

Mooreland responded. "That would mean hiring another 3-4 thousand people and it would mean inordinate delays, perhaps weeks, while the cargo is searched. So in this instance we have to rely on technology."

"What about the oil tankers?" Daly asked. "Dozens arrive every day. While the super tankers are too large to get near our harbors, if one was attacked even off shore, crude delivery to the entire country would be shut down for days or weeks. That would a disaster.

"The supertankers offload to smaller tankers for delivery to our refineries. These smaller tankers carry up to 80,000 barrels. That's about 4.4 million gallons of flammable material. Who checks the crew? What prevents terrorists from infiltrating these crews over the years? Four million gallons of oil can make a hell of an explosion and it also burns on water."

"Phil, these bastards have the advantage of surprise. It's just a matter of when and where. There is no urgency for them to act right away. As time goes on, we lower our guard more and more, little by little. In a year or so public apathy will increase fueled by the belief that the government is again vigilant " Owens said. "Then one day, we lose a harbor, or another airport, or another mall. Congress has to act NOW!"

Daly jumped in again. "These guys who attacked Westchester are probably laughing themselves silly over our security. But there are many targets just as important, maybe just as big in terms of people and national impact where the security can't be improved without creating terrific headaches.

"If I wanted to create a huge problem for this country, perhaps even more cataclysmic than what just took place, I would look at the hundreds of easier targets with little or no protection. And I would find a way to link them." Daly said. "In many ways some of the targets I have in mind are every bit as important as the World Trade Center and just as symbolic."

"Like what, Yankee Stadium" Phil Miranda aske, half kidding.

"That's one," Daly said. "Seriously, the list is endless. If there is a chink in our armor, these people will find it. We were busy making it safe to fly again but they still managed to destroy an airport and the world's largest shopping mall."

"Well we are a target rich environment," said Fritz Thompson.

"Right. Fritz, do you remember the Sheik Abdel-Rahman case in New York back in, ah 1995-96?" Daly said.

"Vaguely. Wasn't he involved with the first World Trade Center bombing?"

"Probably. But he was convicted in '96, I think, of plotting to blow up a number of critically important places in New York City," Daly said. "They may still be plotting to do that."

"I admit I'm as concerned as you. And a lot of this makes sense," Mooreland said. "I'll bring your concerns to the president. If he buys it, he'll have to convince the congress."

"Mr. Secretary," Owens switched back to the formal address. "Please tell the president we strongly believe we must have these new laws and tools to give us a fighting chance in this war. Without them we can positively guarantee there will be another attack."

"I'll relay your warning, Roy. Gentlemen, if you'll excuse me," Mooreland said ending the meeting.

"Mr. Secretary, one more thing, sir." Daly recounted the story about Celestialal and Walter Amberly. "We gave him until Friday to take some action. He hasn't done a thing."

"What do you propose we do?" Mooreland asked.

"I think you should speak to him, get his commitment on some action. If he fails to act ground his airline," Daly said.

"I can't do that Terry. The administration would be severely criticized by the media, passengers and by those two high and mighty senators from New Jersey.

"So we do nothing?"

"Did they break any laws?"

"Technically, no. But their laziness is putting thousands in danger."

"Then there's nothing to do. I'll brief Roy after I talk to the president," Mooreland said. "Roy, walk me out."

After Mooreland and Owens departed, Daly and his assistants sat in disbelief. "I cannot believe what I just heard," Brown said. "This whole country is out on a very thin limb and there's a committee of beavers eating the trunk of the tree."

"If Congress does nothing we may have to get creative," Daly told his assistants.

Everyone looked at Daly. Not a word was spoken.

Later, at the White House, President Harry Barnes sat stonefaced as he listened to Mooreland's report on national security and the FBI requests. Keeping his emotions under control, the president said, "I am as upset as you are, Phil. Many of us realize we are in a national emergency. Nevertheless, I don't think Congress is going to be disposed to act in a meaningful way.

"The fact of the matter is certain members of Congress don't want to crack down on immigrants because they know these immigrants will be voters and they traditionally vote for one party. Hell, they've been reaping the rewards at the ballot box for years. Poindexter and Featherstone and others are so paranoid, the last thing they want is a more powerful FBI and CIA that communicate with each other.

"Restricting personal freedom is also a concern. That's the bottom line."

"Sir, you and I have been friends for almost 20 years. So I'm not going to bullshit you. I got the sense that some of my guys are not only worried, they are scared. When Terry Daly mentioned train stations, movie theaters and baseball parks as potential targets my blood froze. After Mall of America was attacked, anything appears to be fair game."

"I don't even want to contemplate something that horrible," the president said.

"Roy Owens told me he is sick to death – his words – of the FBI being blamed by Congress, the same group that hamstrung the FBI in the first place. The Foreign Intelligence Surveillance Act effectively prevents agents from each agency from talking to one another and sharing information on different cases even though the information may be vital in protecting our country," Mooreland said.

"Under the current law if they want to wiretap foreign spies or terrorists they have to get permission from a secret FISA Court, a court that has prevented the FBI from being an effective anti-terrorist force. The FISA Court's guidelines are known as The Wall. One of the terrorists who hijacked an airliner in the first 9/11 attacks would have been apprehended before 9/11 if the agents had not been prevented from sharing evidence. Mr. President we need that act repealed."

"I'm well aware of The Wall, Phil. The attorney general and I have discussed it at length and you know he is of the same opinion as you. And I share that opinion. But the simple truth is that the liberal media will scream that it will be an abuse of individual's rights. And the fucking ACLU will have a field day. But I'll raise it with Walter Poindexter just before I send the package to Congress."

"Sir, some of what the FBI is asking for is doable by executive order. You have the power to demand close cooperation between federal agencies and you can order State to stop handing out visas to people whose countries are harboring terrorists bent on blowing up our buildings and murdering our people. I'm going to jump on the CIS. But we still need laws and allow us to employ all the new technology that is available," Mooreland said. "And if Congress calls me to testify I'll be as forceful as you want me to be."

"Phil, right now there are any number of groups in this country who think the federal government is trampling all over their rights. Most people consider them to be right wing nuts. But if we insist on things like the personal x-ray, Carnivore and the National ID card, women will join in and so will the National Rifle Association and other groups. That's a lot of votes. Congress isn't going to go up against that."

"Mr. President, you know these tools are not invasive. Carnivore Two enables us to zero in on major suspects, determine their plans, and track their activities. Since SWIFT was exposed by the damn New York Times, we are having a tough time monitoring terrorist activities. Carnivore Two will save many lives. It's a vital tool in our arsenal if we are to go on the offensive.

As far as the personal x-ray, I am aware that the women will take issue with it. Hell, men will too. But if we employ same gender operators, it may be enough to appease them, particularly if we keep repeating the message on what is likely to happen if we don't."

"The National ID Card shouldn't be a difficult problem politically either. Polls show we should be apprehending illegal aliens and deporting them. If we carefully explain how the new tools will increase results I think that would be welcomed politically," Mooreland continued.

"I'll be frank. The FBI doesn't need legislation to do some of the things we talked about. Carnivore Two is a valuable tool and I believe it should be employed against those on the terror watch list. If we get something substantial, we can be a little slow on allowing them to get a lawyer.

"Are you asking me to give you permission to break the law?"

"No sir. I'm merely suggesting that we use the new tool and that more time is needed for interrogation."

"So you want to suspend the legal rights of suspects," the President said.

"Only for illegals and those with expired Visas from certain countries."

"Just how far do you intend to go?" the president asked.

"Only for 72 hours. And if we find anything substantial, we'll make the arrest and notify the CIS. Because of the arrest and formal charges, the CIS will be unable to do anything," Mooreland said.

"As the president, I can't condone this or authorize it. But I don't have to know about it either. Anything else?"

"The FBI is not an intelligence gathering organization per se, but it has assumed an intelligence gathering role. One problem is our computers are woefully out of date. We need high- speed computers linked with State, Justice, Defense and Treasury and other agencies. And we need some Arabic speaking agents."

"Thanks, Phil. I'll request the computers. That's not likely to be rejected. And I'll think about better cooperation between the agencies. You know, according to what I read the in the Times and the Post, it wasn't the terrorists that blew up the mall and the airport, but the administration. Imagine! Well, We are building a case against Saudi Arabia. I'll ask Burdette if has any spare Arabic speaking agents. Once we get the evidence we need, I am certain we'll get whatever we need from Congress."

"And if not?"

"I've said on more than one occasion that I believe my most important responsibility is to protect and defend this nation. And that is exactly what I intend to do. Thanks for coming by, Phil."

-Chapter Eleven-

The electronically secure hearing room in the capitol was jammed. Forty-eight members of the joint Senate and House Homeland Security Committee sat in two rows. The Senate as the host group occupied the top row. Staffers for both senators and representatives hovered behind. Conspicuously absent were members of the media.

"This meeting will come to order," Senator John Featherstone declared, banging the gavel. I am pleased to welcome Mr. Philip Mooreland, Secretary of Homeland Security and Mr. Roy Owens, distinguished director of the Federal Bureau of Investigation. "Mr. Secretary, Mr. Director, on behalf of the special Joint Homeland Security Committee we are delighted to have you both here today. Because of the sensitivity and classified nature of your testimony I have directed that this be a closed-door meeting. I'm John Featherstone, Chairman of the Senate Homeland Security Committee.

To my left is Charles Fumer, the senate's ranking minority member. Immediately to my front is Cecil Bartholomew, Chairman of the House Homeland Security Committee and Representative Joyce Kershaw, ranking minority member.

Mr. Secretary, Mr. Director and distinguished members of your organization, this committee thanks you for agreeing to appear before us. We've asked you here today because we are anxious to learn why the attacks of three weeks ago were not anticipated and prevented and what you have done to address the inadequacies or problems that you have uncovered.

"In the interest of time, Mr. Bartholomew and I asked all committee members to waive their opening statements and they have graciously consented. Ladies and gentlemen we thank you for that. I want to assure you that you are free to ask questions at any time. Having said that, let's get to it. Do you have an opening statement, Mr. Secretary?"

"I do, Mr. Chairman, but before I present my statement, on behalf of the president, FBI director Roy Owens and the gentlemen with me I want to thank this committee and you Mr. Chairman for the opportunity to be with you today," said Mooreland. "I want to share this information with you in the hope that we can work together to ensure our country remains strong and united against those who would attempt to destroy us.

"Because the information we will be giving today contains sensitive information that could lead to finger pointing, and a serious erosion of public confidence if the media were involved we are grateful to you Sen. Featherstone and Rep. Bartholomew for agreeing that this be a closed door meeting. I have also been assured that what we say will not be given to the media."

"Thank you, Mr. Secretary" Sen. Featherstone said. "On behalf of the joint committee, I want to convey our appreciation to the president for his consideration. We are also grateful you brought along members of your distinguished staff. We are anxious to hear what you have to say and will give it every consideration. Will all of you who plan to give testimony before this committee please stand and raise your right hands."

"Thank you gentlemen," Sen. Featherstone said after administering the oath. "Mr. Secretary, please begin with your opening statement?"

"Thank you, Mr. Chairman," Mooreland said. "I think all of you on this prestigious committee would agree that nothing is more important to this country than its security. My Homeland Department colleagues in the Federal Bureau of Investigation, the

Customs Service, Coast Guard, Secret Service, Bureau of Alcohol, Tobacco and Firearms and the other agencies involved in the security of the nation do not scare easily as you might imagine. But they are deeply concerned. We all are.

"Mr. Chairman, national security begins at our borders and incorporates the fundamental ways we deal with immigration and the visitors to our shores and with the procedures in place for the importation of foreign products. For nearly 10 years we had been successful in preventing terrorist attacks, but we remain extremely vulnerable to assault on trains, mass transportation hubs, theaters, sports arenas and as we have all seen, places like Mall of America," Mooreland said.

"This country's security depends upon our intelligence gathering ability, our capacity for innovation and our commitment to work together to share information effectively and to act swiftly. During World War II headlines in newspapers all across the country served as a daily reminder of that global struggle. There are no daily headlines today because we are not fighting a particular country nor do we know where the enemy is. Moreover, for years, we have given our enemy a wonderful ally, apathy.

"That indifference, if you will, or lack of national focus is what the enemy counts on. Today, three weeks after the latest attacks, America is again vigilant and angry. Americans again want revenge. But our enemy has slipped back into his cave or under a rock where he patiently waits for apathy to sap our national will. But by waiting, he has given us an opportunity to thwart his efforts and destroy his dreams.

"To do so we must act swiftly and decisively with new laws, new technology, better training, and more people," Mooreland said.

"I'm going to give you a brief overview of the national picture, highlighting what successes we've had, and offering an opinion – our opinion - of what we might expect in the future. My colleagues are here to answer any of your questions about their agencies' activities as well as respond to technical questions.

"Mr. Chairman, since September 11, 2001, we have had some minor skirmishes, and foiled more than plots, including five attempts to destroy our embassies in France, Italy, Bosnia, Yemen and Singapore," Mooreland said. "We've closed down so-called Islamic charitable foundations, legally searched thousands of homes and offices, seized about $400 million in terrorist finances. We've frozen an additional $600 million in assets and we've taken into custody more than 10,000 terrorist suspects. Tragically, we've also suffered two more major attacks.

"At Westchester Airport, terrorists slipped onto airport property and fired six stinger missiles at selected targets causing maximum damage," Mooreland continued. "At Mall of America, two men disguised as sound stage technicians who were well known to mall security were able to detonate a very powerful bomb in a strategic location. We now believe that because there were additional explosions, two on the third floor and one in each of the parking garages, that others were involved.

"For a time, we focused our efforts on airport security. As the immigration controversy bubbled to the surface, we shifted some of our emphasis. It is not likely there will be another plane hijacking, certainly, not four in one day. The attack at Westchester Airport three weeks ago showed conclusively that security can be compromised by a group or groups who know how and where to look for weaknesses even in places where security is supposed to be airtight. Will there be another attack? Most likely. We just don't know where and we don't know when."

"Mr. Chairman, if I may?"

"The chair recognizes the co-chair Mr. Bartholomew."

"Thank you Mr. Chairman. Mr. Secretary, when two or three men get inside the perimeter of an airport and systematically launch six missiles, it leaves me wondering what security was in place at the time. Can you comment on that?"

"Congressman, security at Westchester Airport was not airtight. No airport has airtight security protection against a missile attack."

"Are you saying that any airport in the country can be attacked in such a manner?" Bartholomew asked.

"Sir, these missiles have a range of about three miles. To prevent such an attack a defense would have to be established that would reach beyond the airport perimeter in most cases," Mooreland said. "To put that in perspective, any building that is within a line of sight of three miles is vulnerable to such an attack."

"I see. So you're saying that even the capitol building where we sit today could be attacked."

"That is true, sir under certain circumstances. May I continue?"

117

"Please do, Mr. Secretary." Sen. Featherstone said.

"Thank you, Mr. Chairman. My top deputies and I have always remained concerned about airport security. So, at my request, Terry Daly and the FBI Counter-Terrorism Division planned and undertook an operation to deliberately breach the security of a number of airports. They were successful at the baggage areas, refueling and catering operations, passenger security and aircraft maintenance at airports in New York, Dallas, Houston, Philadelphia, Miami, Los Angeles, Detroit, Chicago, Dulles here in Washington and others.

"What they succeeded in doing is disquieting, to say the least. As we have learned an attack on the control tower of an airport has devastating results. Coordinated attacks on several airports would deal air transportation in this country a blow from which it might never recover."

"Mr. Secretary, we all know security at Westchester Airport was breached," Sen. Featherstone said. "Hell, that's why the attack was successful. What I want to know and what the American people want to know is how in the hell could such a thing happen especially since we focused on airport security? And over the last three or four years we have been given dozens and dozens of warnings of possible attacks. Why weren't we warned this time?"

"Mr. Chairman, we received no warnings for either attack. The terrorist cells responsible for these attacks were unknown to us. These latest attacks represent a change in their methods of operation. We believe this was caused by the articles published by the New York Times on the SWIFT program. The cells changed locations and methods of financing and became more circumspect in their communications. Terrorists need money, lots of it, to finance their daily living, their communications networks and to buy expensive weapons such as those used at the airport. As I said, these latest attacks represent a change in their methods. For example, one of the attacks was conducted by suicide bombers; the other by terrorists who are still alive and at large. We are doing everything we can to find them," Mooreland said.

"Mr. Secretary, tens of thousands of people are dead and tens of thousands more injured and all you can do is tell us that you are trying to find the fiends who did this. I recall the head of one of your agencies telling us not long ago that his agency's sole responsibility was prevention and that responsibility was taken seriously by all the other agencies. What went wrong, Mr. Secretary? Who didn't do their jobs?" Sen. Poindexter asked.

"Senator. I hope you are not implying that the agencies in my department are negligent," Mooreland said.

"Well it sure looks that way to me."

"Senator, the agents in the FBI are routinely working 70 and 80 hours a week. They give up Saturdays and Sundays, holidays, and cut their vacations short trying to protect this country. And why is that, senator? They do that because they care. The fact of the matter is that we are being asked to do far more than we have the manpower for."

"Mr. Secretary, are you asking for more agents?" Sen. Fumer asked.

"Yes sir. That and a lot more."

"Is this a shopping trip, Mr. Secretary?" Sen. Fumer continued. "Do you expect to use the recent attacks as ammunition in the hopes Congress will give you everything you ask for? I seem to recall a couple of years ago that the FBI somehow managed to, shall we say, misplace a number of weapons and laptop computers. Why should we give you more hardware when you keep losing what you have?"

"Mr. Chairman, I resent this senator's remark. It is accusatory and uncalled for. We have asked the Congress for additional appropriations for more manpower and better technology and we've been turned down turned down five times in the last six years. I'd like to ask the senator how many secretaries he has. How many, senator?"

"The number of people on my staff is irrelevant to this hearing, Mr. Secretary," Sen. Fumer said. "We're talking about the attacks of three weeks ago and the FBI's failure to stop them. Those are the facts. And we want to know where the breakdown was."

"Blaming an understaffed agency that is handcuffed by outdated equipment and encumbered by outrageous laws or the lack of effective laws is not only unfair, it is wrong, senator. The Congress has refused to deal with the immigration problem and by doing that has openly permitted millions to break the law."

119

"Mr. Secretary, we are trying to find out what went wrong. And we want to know why the terrorists weren't stopped and why the alert level wasn't raised," Sen. Fumer said.

"We have reason to believe that the cells responsible for these attacks have been here for years, perhaps even before the attacks 10 years ago," Mooreland said. "There was no way for us to know of their existence."

"What makes you so sure of that?" Sen. Poindexter asked.

"Two of the men who blew up the mall worked for a sound systems company for five years. They were Saudi citizens whose Visas had expired. In other words, they were here illegally."

"They had been here for five years, they were illegal aliens and your agency couldn't locate them?" Sen. Claxton asked.

"That's one of the problems we are asking you to fix. You see, Senator, being an illegal alien is not a crime and apparently Congress doesn't believe that entering this country illegally is a crime either. So the employers of the two bombers were not required nor were they interested in turning them in. They were good employees so why rock the boat?" Mooreland responded.

"Mr. Secretary, what happened at the Mall? How could that have been prevented?" Sen. Featherstone asked.

"Mr. Chairman, up until just three weeks ago in most Malls across the country there was no prevention security. No shopping bags were searched and there were no metal detectors. If there had been that Mall might be standing today. But we don't have the authority to order anyone to install security devices. Today, procedures are changing.

"Many malls are now searching bags and have installed metal detectors. But that won't stop a terrorist from detonating a bomb at a mall entrance before he gets to the metal detector," Mooreland said. "And since we don't conduct personal searches, a terrorist could strap on 40-50 pounds of high explosive and blow himself up along with dozens of others.

"The terrorists could be employees of the malls. No one knows if or how many terrorists work in malls or shopping centers or for their vendors. Based on what happened at Mall of America, we have to assume that some have been there for years. And frankly I doubt

120

employees at most malls go through a security checkpoint. That's a serious weakness that we at the federal level cannot control. And for those managing the malls it is a huge expense."

"Mr. Secretary, let me ask how you would improve security at our malls so that another attack like the one we've just experienced won't ever happen again?"

"Senator, there is no way we can guarantee that we will not suffer another attack. But we can make a coordinated effort on a number of levels to make such an attack very difficult. Doing such a thing will take additional resources, courage and political resolve."

"What exactly do you mean by political resolve, Mr. Secretary?" Rep. Harlan Bard asked.

"I'll be direct, Congressman. We need new laws. Our current immigration laws are , ah, well, they are in need of tightening." Mooreland said. "That means some members of Congress are going to have to make a choice, defend America or allow America's enemies free access."

"Mr. Secretary, how will changing the immigration laws – tightening them to use your words – help prevent terrorist attacks in the future?" Rep. Lillian Snyder asked.

"Madam Congresswoman, we have terrorists in sleeper cells in this country today because our immigration laws are so weak they enable illegal aliens to stay here, even those who are guilty of crimes. Some are even repetitive criminals.

"Mr. Chairman, I had intended to address the subject of immigration a little later, but now seems as good a time as any. Earlier I said that our national security begins at our borders. Current immigration laws are designed to permit the downtrodden and persecuted to seek a better life and to allow foreign students to get a superior education so that they may return to their own country and apply what they have learned," Mooreland said.

"That is no longer reality. We all know that hundreds of thousands of foreigners either enter this country illegally every year or simply do not leave when their visas expire. It isn't just individuals who cross the border in the dead of night who concern us. Most of them come here for employment to better the lives of their families. What is of great concern are the people who disappear when their visas expire. Here are some cold facts for you to digest:

121

"To the best of our knowledge of the more than 36 million illegal aliens in this country more than three million including at least 250,000 from the Middle East have overstayed the expiration date on their visas and continue to live here illegally. It is our best guess that at least 10 percent are involved in plots against this country," Mooreland said.

"Remember 15 of the 19 September 11, 2001 hijackers came from Saudi Arabia and were here illegally or with expired visas. And the two men who worked for that sound stage company who helped blow up the mall in Bloomington, Minnesota were also Saudis with expired visas. We have apprehended about 10,000," Mooreland said. "If my math is correct that means about 15,000 are unaccounted for. And as a result of the exposure of the SWIFT program they may have gone deep underground making them even harder to find.

"Yet we continue to issue thousands of new visas a year to people living in Iraq, Iran, Syria, Libya, Egypt, the Philippines, the Sudan, Afghanistan, Pakistan and Somalia, countries in which al Qaeda thrives. I am sure all of you are aware that we have a Diversity Visa lottery system that permits 55,000 applicants and their families to get green cards each year. Where do these people come from?

"Nearly 1,700 came from Egypt and more than 3,000 came from Iran, Sudan, Libya and Syria, the very countries who sponsor terrorism, permit terrorists to train on their soil and who offer refuge to terrorists on the run. We have a serious problem here that could have cataclysmic consequences. We are providing an open door and an open invitation to thousands of potential terrorists to come to our shores every year. Hell, the only thing we aren't providing is valet service for them.

"Let's look at the Diversity Visa lottery rules? What does it take? First, they have to have a clean criminal record. Also required is a high school diploma or a couple of years of work experience, and a clean bill of health. The application process is inordinately simple. No forms to fill out, just submit a letter with biographical information and a photo. None of this alleged documentation is checked by anyone. In other words, all of the documentation can be forged.

"The welcome mat we have installed on the southern border includes water towers and rescue beacons equipped with alarms so illegal aliens can summon help. That welcome mat extends to the state and local level where there are laws that actually encourage illegal aliens. The 700 miles fence Congress approved a few years ago covers one third of the southern border. That's like building a prison wall with one side missing.

"Some states give aliens subsidized education, driver's licenses and free medical care. Talk about incentives! These are accorded to people who shouldn't be here at all. Many of the suspects we have apprehended for other crimes – and there are thousands of those even at the federal level - tell us how easy it is to get into this country.

"When an illegal alien is apprehended, he or she is handed over to the Citizen Immigration Service for further action. More often that not, no action is taken. More than a quarter of a million people who were ordered deported as long as a year ago still live here in the U.S. Since they are not detained, they promise to show up for a hearing and that's the last we see of them"

"Mr. Secretary," Sen. Feinberg interrupted, "we have no evidence that any of these people are plotting against us. These people may be hiding so they can stay here in the United States rather than return to an oppressive atmosphere in their own country. It may be that simple. Have you considered that?"

"Senator Feinberg, one of the snipers that terrorized this area for three weeks about seven years ago was an illegal alien who was turned loose by the then INS in clear violation of a federal law. A moment ago I said we had taken into custody some 10,000 people we suspect are engaged in terrorist activities. More than 2,000 of them are Middle Easterners who came here on student visas that have long since expired. Legitimate students don't enter this country on student visas to attend a university, and never show up for class.

"There are still thousands of these so-called students who registered and then disappeared. When we discussed this with officials at institutions with the greatest number of foreign students, their response was almost universal.

"They merely said 'we don't take attendance.' When we questioned them about where these students were living, their response was 'most like to live off campus.'

"The universities either don't care or don't feel the need for better control of their students. Advance payment of tuition eliminates the one area where a university takes a solid interest in its students. Money talks even in academia. One more point, it takes nearly six months for the CIS to even respond to the universities that do report foreign students who skip classes.

"I want to call your attention to another serious problem with CIS," Mooreland said. "As you may know there is a Board of Immigration Appeals. It can reverse a CIS ruling. And it usually does. This Board is not elected and unfortunately is largely unaccountable to anyone, even Congress. Even the media are almost unaware of it. This group has tremendous power that has unfortunately been abused.

"For example, in one case that is particularly disturbing, a Haitian woman was convicted in the beating death of a baby, served two years of her sentence and was freed. The then INS, now the CIS, wanted her deported as a convicted criminal alien and won a deportation order. But the woman claimed deportation would be a hardship on her family," Mooreland recalled.

"The Board of Immigration Appeals concluded that her crime, and I quote, did not constitute a crime of violence, unquote. The baby died of injuries to the head, abdomen and chest. And now a convicted criminal alien is free to live in this country."

"The CIS is not represented here and cannot rebut your charges. I would ask that you please confine your remarks to the areas of your responsibility," Senator Featherstone said.

"Sir, the CIS reports to me. But I do not have the authority to change the rules under which it operates. And I have no authority to challenge the Board of Appeals. What I am saying here is public knowledge. And it makes no sense to me to have federal agents running around the country trying to round up people the CIS or rhe board of Appeals keeps turning loose."

"Is the President asking us to tighten the regulations on visas or compel the universities to keep closer tabs on their foreign students?" Sen. Featherstone asked.

"They are not mutually exclusive, Mr. Chairman. The President wants changes in immigration laws and procedures. Let me move to another serious concern. This is related to the illegal alien situation. It's our port security. Hundreds of foreign tankers and cargo ships arrive each day at our ports and harbors," Mooreland continued. The agencies I talked about – Customs, the Coast Guard and the

Border Patrol must screen arrivals at 351 ports of entry including airports, seaports and border entrances.

"Some of the states represented by this distinguished panel have major seaports. The threat of an explosive device – even a nuclear device – being smuggled in a container ship into New York City, Philadelphia, Houston, Port Arthur, San Francisco or Los Angeles is very real. We do have agreements with a number of countries. Under the Container Security Initiative container ships are pre-screened before they leave for our ports," the secretary continued.

"There are inherent risks. For example, we don't know how thorough the foreign screenings are. We don't know who the screeners are, how well they have been trained or - and this is key - whether they can be bribed. Even the ships themselves are a threat. A small tanker carrying 80,000 barrels of crude can do enormous damage.

"There are nearly two thousand miles of unguarded wilderness that separate the United States and Canada. A terrorist could slip across the border at any one of dozens of places and blend into our society. Bear in mind that Canada has the most liberal immigration policy in the entire free world. Almost anyone is allowed into Canada.

"Another problem is related to hiring and training," Mooreland continued. "Aside from pilots and crew, few airline and airport employees undergo a thorough background check. Before the first September 11 attacks most of the people who handled passenger screening and who x-rayed our carry-ons worked for private companies. Now they are federal employees. Their previous employers didn't bother to check their backgrounds or figured it was too costly.

"In general, airport security clearance people, the ones who check all of us for weapons, sharp instruments and who x-ray our carry-ons, are poorly trained, poorly motivated and poorly supervised. And because they are now federal employees, they can't be fired, not even the one who let a gun get by him," Mooreland said. "But before we blame them entirely for failures or breaches, we should understand that they are victims too.

"They have been accused of racial profiling because they paid special attention to Middle Eastern males between the ages of 20 and 45, people who exactly match the profile of the hijackers who brought down the twin towers and I might add, all of the Taliban fighters now being detained. To avoid charges of profiling, they now pay special attention to the most unlikely people like an 85-year-old woman who is bound to a wheel chair. And they have even asked a woman to drink her own breast milk to be sure it wasn't poison," Mooreland continued.

"We have allocated most of our FBI resources toward making it safe to fly and investigating leads. Unfortunately that means less attention is focused on intelligence gathering. It's our opinion that any new attacks will not come from the air, but from the ground as it did in Westchester County. Our country, to use a military term, is a target rich environment.

"Theaters, sports arenas, ball parks, train stations, bridges, tunnels and of course, malls, are all inviting targets," Mooreland said.

"Near as I can tell, Mr. Secretary, we've got police all over the place at those locations," Rep. Richard Loveless said. "What are we supposed to do, stop and frisk everyone?"

"I'm sure everyone here has seen police at balls parks and sports arenas," Moore responded. "And they are pretty effective at preventing coolers, packages and the like from being brought into those facilities. But that won't stop a guy with 50 pounds of HMX or another high explosive hidden under a ski parka or overcoat on a cold December day at a football stadium.

"And then there are the thousands of facilities all across the country where no such security is provided, places like Grand Central Terminal and Penn Station in New York, Union Station in Washington or dozens of other rail, bus stations and airports such as Dulles and National here in D.C.? No one searches bags or suitcases except before loading on airlines," Mooreland went on.

Senator Claxton gasped. Her eyes found Sen. Feinberg's.

"That would be extremely inconvenient," Sen. Poindexter interrupted. "You simply cannot search the bags of everyone entering an airport, rail or bus station. There are police on patrol."

"The police can only be really effective if they suspect something. I'd rather be inconvenienced than killed. Attacking those facilities would not only kill hundreds, perhaps thousands of people, but their acts would trigger a chain reaction closing all train, subway and bus stations, and probably airports as well. Destroy and disrupt. Destroy and disrupt.

"I'm sure you recall the terrorist Sheik Abdel Rachman," Mooreland continued.

"The FBI nailed him for the first World Trade Center attack in 1993. But the charge didn't stick. Not enough evidence. But we did convict him of conspiracy to destroy a number of places and he's now serving a life term. Anyone here remember what his targets were?"

Mooreland looked around the table. No one responded. "Mr. Owens."

"Mr. Chairman."

"The chair recognizes FBI Director Roy Owens."

"Thank you Mr. Chairman. Sheik Rachman planned to destroy the George Washington Bridge, the Lincoln and Holland tunnels, the UN building and the largest federal building in New York. At the time, we didn't think it was possible to do that. Now we know it is," Owens said. "Grand Central Terminal, is arguably not as great a symbol as the World Trade Center, but it's a symbol nonetheless and a landmark. It's used by more than 425,000 commuters each day. And we have no way to control who comes into the terminals or what they carry. People with baggage and packages come and go all the time.

"A suicide bomber or bombers with a couple of suitcases of explosives could destroy the terminal crippling rail transportation for everyone living north of the city," Owens continued. "If another bomber did the same thing a few blocks away at Penn Station, the effect would isolate New York City for weeks."

"Don't you think you are being overly dramatic, Mr. Owens?" Senator Fumer asked.

"The attacks on the towers 10 years ago and the airport attack three weeks ago have had an incalculable effect on the airline industry. We believe it is logical to assume an attack on those rail facilities might generate a similar reaction?

"Let's for the moment assume you are right, Mr. Owens. We can't search every person in Grand Central, or x-ray every bag. The public wouldn't stand for it," Sen. Poindexter said.

"We realize that, Senator," Mooreland replied. "That's why we believe it's necessary to deploy all the security technology that's available right now. And we should assume that not only are those places targets but tunnels and bridges, too. Anyplace where an ordinary looking person could cause extraordinary damage. Anyplace where security is not tight because it means inconveniencing a lot of people."

The hearing droned on for another hour before Mooreland turned to explosives.

"The first World Trade Center attack in 1993 was carried out with fertilizer bombs, deadly, but low grade. If they had used the same amount of C-4 or worse, HMX, in that truck, the building certainly would have collapsed. The loss of life would have been three or four times the number lost when the towers collapsed eight years later.

"The terrorists in Israel and elsewhere are using weapons grade explosives like C-4 which they buy from Iran, Syria, North Korea, Russia and other places. 500 pounds of C-4 detonated in Grand Central Terminal would destroy the building."

"Are you an explosives expert, Mr. Secretary?" Rep. Pete Gomez asked.

"No sir, but Terry Daly is and so are Fritz Thompson and Eliot Schweikert. Anyone want to weigh in here?"

"If I may," Thompson said.

"Certainly. Would you identify yourself, please," the committee chairman said.

"Mr. Chairman, I am Assistant FBI Director Fritz Thompson, head of the Los Angeles Office. Before joining the FBI I was a demolitions expert in the Army and then head of the bomb squad on the LAPD. Every explosive is rated by how fast it expands.

"TNT, for example, expands at the rate of between 21,800 and 22,400 feet per second," Thompson stated. "Amatol, the main ingredient for military bombs, has an expansion rate of between 14,800 and 21,100 feet per second. C-4, the short name for Composite 4, has 1.34 times the explosive force of TNT. It expands at the rate of 26,400 feet per second. Sixty-six pounds, or 30 kilograms can bring down a 10-story hotel if properly placed. One pound can bring down a two foot thick tree."

"Mr. Thompson, the manufacture of C-4 is carefully regulated and possession is tightly controlled." Sen. Poindexter said. "How would terrorists get possession of enough C-4 to blow up a train station?"

"Senator, laws regulating the manufacture or possession of dangerous materials or an illegal substance never deterred anyone intent on buying, selling or using them. Our drug policy is all the evidence you need on that score. So are the six missiles used at Westchester Airport."

"Enlighten us, please. How can explosives in large quantities be smuggled into this country?" Rep. Stuart Carlson asked.

"Congressman, C-4 is a plastic explosive. It can be shaped to resemble harmless things like pottery, or lumber, candles, any number of innocent looking objects. So unless bomb-sniffing dogs are employed at all entry points 24/7, smuggling C-4 into this country isn't very difficult. And C-4 is so stable, it can be hit with a hammer. It takes a detonator to make it work."

"Mr. Thompson. This is fascinating in a macabre way," Sen. Featherstone declared. "Please continue."

"As powerful an explosive as C-4 is – and a small quantity was strong enough to seriously damage the USS Cole – there is an even more powerful plastic explosive called HMX. It is made from one of the main ingredients of C-4. And its expansion rate is 29,900 feet per second. That translates to more than five and one half miles in a single second. At that speed, anything propelled by it, even a match or a paper cup is lethal. Its power, in a word, is awesome. That's what was used at the Mall of America."

"Mr. Thompson, where do terrorists get this stuff," Sen. Claxton asked.

"From a variety of countries that supply arms and munitions to terrorists or anyone else who has the money," Mrs. Claxton. "Ironically, C-4 was introduced to terrorists courtesy of a renegade ex-CIA agent named Edwin Wilson. In the 1970s he was convicted of shipping 21 tons of the stuff to Libya for use in their terrorist schools."

"Twenty-one TONS?" Sen. Featherstone exclaimed. "Did you say tons?"

"That's correct."

"Where in the world did he get that amount of explosives," Rep. Bitterman asked.

"I honestly don't know. But he certainly was in a position to know if such an amount existed. But that was C-4. The terrorists have graduated. As I said earlier, they are now using HMX, the most powerful conventional explosive on earth. A few innocent looking suitcases containing 500 pounds of that stuff would easily destroy Grand Central Terminal or Penn Station," Thompson declared.

"You people keep mentioning train stations. Should we be worried about them especially?" Sen. Claxton asked.

"Absolutely. And for a variety of reasons. First, like the towers and the Pentagon, they too are symbols of our great nation. Second, destroying one or two would affect transportation all across the country. Third, such an attack would kill and injure thousands if carried out at the right time of day, like rush hour."

"Mr. Secretary, I don't question your statement that the twin towers and the Pentagon were symbols of our nation's greatness. And the rail terminals might even qualify. But I fail to see how Westchester County Airport is a symbol of our nation. Could you comment on why terrorists would attack a small regional airport instead of one of the more tempting targets you mentioned?"

"Certainly, Mr. Chairman. By itself, the airport wouldn't qualify. But supposing it was just one of a number of airports that were scheduled to be attacked on the same day?"

"My God, Mr. Secretary, are you trying to tell us that was part of a larger plot?"

"That's the theory the FBI is working on, Mr. Chairman. And although we have no hard evidence as yet to support that conclusion, it makes absolute sense. Imagine the effect on this country if LaGuardia, Newark and JFK along with Westchester were all attacked on the same day."

"Thank you Mr. Secretary," Sen. Featherstone said. "I want to make sure you have a chance to give us the president's recommendations. Does anyone else in your group want to add anything?"

Phil Maranda, raised his hand and was recognized by Senator Featherstone.

"Thank you Mr. Chairman. I am Assistant FBI Director Philip Maranda. I head the Miami FBI office. I promise I'll be very brief. Mr. Secretary, I would like to add to your testimony with respect to immigration. I apologize to you and the Director for not briefing you on this, but this is a theory that may have some validity and it's one we are not ignoring in Miami," Maranda began.

"Mr. Maranda, excuse me, before you begin I want to make one final point, to emphasize the seriousness of the situation," Mooreland said.

"We haven't even talked about a nuclear threat. We've all read that our intelligence sources estimate that some Middle Eastern regimes, notably Iran, now have nuclear capability and are perfectly willing to sell one or more to the highest bidder. With our open borders, foreign agents and terrorists could bring in suitcase-sized nuclear weapons.

"If terrorists explode one of those it won't be just a couple of towers that collapse. It'll be half a city. And that city could be Washington. I'll leave it to your imagination as to how catastrophic that would be and what level of response we'd see from our government."

"I don't want to minimize what you say, Mr. Secretary, but I simply don't believe these countries have that capability," Sen. Fumer declared. "If they had wouldn't they have used it by now?"

"With few exceptions these nations have plenty of money. I think that it would be very naïve to think that nations like North Korea and China have not made their weapons and weapons technology available. For the right price, of course," Mooreland said.

"There's an old saying in the military: never underestimate your enemy. As far as smuggling such a device into this country, it's quite easy, actually. The weapons can be brought here in innocent looking pieces and assembled."

"How would they get the plutonium or other radioactive material here without its being discovered?" Sen. Fumer asked.

"Any number of ways, Senator. Perhaps the easiest is through a sealed lead lined container in a diplomatic pouch. Airport security does not check for radioactivity. We have no Geiger counters checking luggage or containers. It could arrive by ship surrounded by shielding and hidden deep in a container. Our customs people have the resources to check only one in 100 containers.

"Mr. Mooreland. How concerned are you about a nuclear threat?"

"Sen. Fumer, I am very concerned. Historically this country has never responded against any nation without overwhelming evidence. Any terrorist who uses a nuclear device isn't going to be around to answer questions or leave much evidence. That may leave us with a city that has been destroyed and no enemy country to deal with. That means it could happen again and again. That's all I have, Mr. Chairman. Thank you for your attention. I'm sorry for the interruption, Mr. Maranda."

"Mr. Maranda, you have the floor," Sen. Featherstone said.

"Thank you Mr. Chairman," Maranda said. "I think there's something else we need to consider. Since I am Latino, I thought this should come from me. So far we have been taking very close looks at men with darker skin with Middle Eastern passports as they more closely fit the terrorist profile. What we are overlooking are other people with dark complexions such as those traveling from Latin countries."

"What the hell do you mean," Rep. Gomez asked. "Are you trying to tell me there are terrorists coming here from peaceful places like Peru, Brazil, Costa Rica or the Dominican Republic? That's ridiculous."

"It's not only possible, Congressman, but highly probable. Sir, I mean no offense. Let me lay out a scenario for you. A terrorist training school that teaches its students Spanish. sends these people to a Latin country on some bogus business deal," Maranda went on. "From there they can easily enter the U.S. And I believe that's exactly what they are doing."

"A school for terrorists where they teach them Spanish? That is far fetched," Rep. Gomez said.

"Why not," Maranda replied. "The key here is that although they have darker complexions like mine, they are not regarded with suspicion because of their passports. And speaking English with a Spanish accent or switching between the two languages would throw off most customs inspectors."

"Mr. Maranda," Rep. Gomez interrupted. "I'm sorry. I find this difficult to believe."

"Congressman, I am asking you to examine all possibilities. Don't rule anything out. You've heard the expression *money laundering*? Think of this as people laundering. Terrorists think out of the box. We should too.

"Nearly all of the terrorists in this country are from the Middle East and all of them speak English very well. Training some of them to speak Spanish would not be difficult or time consuming. And we know these people have the resources to forge any documents they want or need."

"**Jesus Christ**, that's it," Terry Daly uttered.

"Something wrong, Mr. Daly?" Sen. Featherstone asked.

"Ah, oh, nothing Senator. I'm very sorry for the interruption." On his yellow note pad he wrote two words: *Tony Rodrigo* and showed the pad to Roosevelt Ewing. "Would you excuse me for a moment."

Daly left the room and called Special Agent Robert Turner from his cell phone.

"Turner."

"Bobby, did you get anything on Antonio Rodrigo?"

"Nothing yet. No wants or warrants and his motor vehicle record is clean too," Turner said. "I've got his home address and the address of his employer Pantone Associates in Manhattan. I'm waiting for replies from Interpol and Scotland Yard."

"Good. I'll be in the office tomorrow. I've got a hunch about this guy. I'll talk to you first thing in the morning." Daly hung up and called his wife.

"Hello," Ellen Daly said.

"Hi, honey. We're nearly finished with Congress. Did you find out anything else about this guy Rodrigo?"

"Not much. Angela apparently doesn't know much. She did find out that he comes from Madrid, Spain. He told her his parents are both dead, he's a U.S. citizen now and he went to Temple University. Oh, and he's 38 years old and never been married. Can't figure why a guy that good looking hasn't been grabbed. By the way, Angela is wondering why you are so interested. I think you are scaring her, Terry."

"Thanks, honey. You know me. I like to place a name with a face. That's all. See you tomorrow."

Daly hung up and called back Special Agent Robert Turner.

"Turner,"

"Bobby, Terry. Rodrigo says he is a naturalized U.S. citizen and a Temple University graduate. Check with State and make an official inquiry with the university."

"I'll get right on it."

-Chapter Twelve-

Daly returned to the meeting thinking about Rodrigo.

"Ah, there you are Mr. Daly," said Sen. Featherstone. "I think we have all the information we need at this point. We're just about to hear Secretary Mooreland's recommendations. Mr. Secretary, if you please."

"Thank you, Mr. Chairman. The president believes that substantive changes are needed in our immigration policy and the way we deal with foreign visitors who are here illegally. He is suggesting these changes as part of a comprehensive package he will send to Congress that includes requests for additional funds for more personnel, better training for existing personnel, and the deployment of new technology.

"The terrorists who flew into the towers and the Pentagon and at least two who helped destroy the Mall of America had been in this country for years. All of them were well financed. It's also obvious that they are receiving illegal weapons and explosives in large quantities. That is a huge concern to us. It's also obvious that they are using the internet to communicate.

"We've armed airline pilots and equipped senior flight attendants with stun guns. All planes are now equipped with hidden video cameras that on command from either the plane or the ground can send images to the ground when an incident occurs on an aircraft," Mooreland said. "But a terrorist bent on hijacking a plane can exploit weaknesses in the system as federal agents did over the last few months. That's why we need low frequency radar and personal x-ray for passenger screening.

"Our overburdened and understaffed FBI and Border Patrols must be reinforced and given the latest technology. The Border Patrol needs unmanned aircraft, similar to the drones we use in Afghanistan armed with video and infrared for day and night work to extend their reach. The thousands of miles of unguarded border leave us vulnerable to the smuggling of alien agents, terrorists, and their weapons. That double fence needs to be finished along the entire length of the border.

"Immigrants who entered this country and those who have overstayed their visa expiration dates represent a very serious threat to national security. We have to tighten the rules governing visitation to this country, and put in place a coordinated mechanism for ensuring people depart when their visas expire. And we need a no-nonsense approach to rules breakers. We believe that aliens convicted of any crime should be deported after they serve their sentence.

"Included in this proposal will be a request asking that the issuance of visas will be transferred from the State Department to the Department of homeland Security," Mooreland said.

"And just why would you want to do that?" Sen. Budreaux asked.

"I'd rather not get into that, senator."

"Well, "I'd like to hear the reason why such a shift in function is needed, if you don't mind, Mr. Secretary," Sen. Claxton said. "I'm sure this entire panel would like to hear that."

"Very well. Mr. Chairman, the Justice Department has asked that State deny the issuance of visas to anyone who might be a terrorist. State has refused."

"That seems reasonable to me, Mr. Secretary. Denying anyone the right to come to this country based on suspicion without proof is reprehensible," Rep. Budreaux said.

"With respect, Congressman. No foreigner has the RIGHT to visit this country. It is a privilege. And to your second point, the law states that the burden of proof is on the visitor, not on the State Department."

"State has been doing this for decades. I see no reason to change that responsibility," Sen. Featherstone said.

"I'll be direct, sir. State is not abiding by the law. It's that simple."

"Are you saying the State Department is violating the law, Mr. Secretary?" Sen. Claxton said.

"Senator, I am saying that State is not abiding by the law," Mooreland replied. He waited politely for a rejoinder. When none came he continued.

"The president is asking for strict accountability by employers and institutions that deal with immigrants and foreign visitors. This would include requiring all colleges and universities to keep track of their foreign students on a monthly basis and to report to the FBI any failure on the part of any student to report," Mooreland continued.

"Businesses would be required to register all foreign employees whether they are here temporarily or permanently. Any foreign national not complying with initial registration and with monthly reporting, would be taken into custody and subject to deportation. Any business employing illegal aliens would be fined and their owners subject to imprisonment," Mooreland said.

"As an aid to law enforcement people the president is proposing a digitized National Identity Card for all citizens over 12 and all visitors over the age of six. This card would be produced when requested by a law enforcement officer.

"The National ID Card would contain a photo taken by a special retinal camera to prevent forgery and would provide such information as name, date of birth, nationality, address and in the case of foreign nationals, the date their visa expires. Law enforcement people would also be empowered to do random checks to make sure everyone keeps their address up to date.

"Those who are stopped would be asked to produce some other government issued photo ID such as a driver's license unless, of course, they are obviously too young. Police cars would be equipped with a card swiping device enabling the officer to get vital information instantly," Mooreland said.

"Finally, the President wants a new border law that would prevent anyone from a nation that sponsors terrorism from gaining admittance to this country. That would include students."

"That's outrageous, Mr. Secretary," said Sen. Feingold. "We cannot and we should not prevent legitimate students from coming here to get an education."

"Senator, students who come here from such places as Iran, Syria, Libya, North Korea, Somalia and Cuba are not seeking an education. Their regimes know an educated student is dangerous. These so-called students come here to teach us a lesson, a lesson in terror," Mooreland said.

"President Barnes knows there is substantial political risk on both sides of the aisle with respect to personal x-ray, new immigration laws and the retinal photo National ID Card. But he is willing to take the heat and to back all of you who stand behind this legislation. Ladies and gentlemen, this is not about party politics, it is about nothing more basic than national security. So, if I may, I'll try to address your concerns."

"Well as I see it, Mr. Secretary, we are going to become a police state," said Senator Fumer. "The only things that are missing are storm troopers dressed in brown uniforms. I've seen that personal x-ray and it reveals, ah, well just about everything."

"I agree," Senator Feingold chimed in. "I'm not going to submit to that and I'm damn sure my constituents won't either. Mr. Secretary have you thought about the potential for abuse of such laws and the repercussions?"

"Mr. Chairman, may I address these concerns, please."

"Please do."

"Thank you. Let me first ask you all a question. Would you submit to a personal x-ray if you know it will reveal any weapon?"

"That's not the issue, here, Mr. Secretary. The issue here is personal privacy. These machines are so thorough they can detect the underwire of my bras," Sen. Feingold said. "It will also indicate if someone is wearing a medical prosthesis. That's damn personal. Besides, existing machinery detects weapons"

"Yes, senator, it is personal. But I'd rather have that level of detection than risk an aircraft full of people hitting another building. To address your second point existing detection machinery isn't always adequate," Mooreland replied.

"Perhaps, Mr. Secretary, but we have no guarantee that it will stop everything. And as far as the National ID Card is concerned, we might as well start wearing yellow Stars of David on our sleeves. A National ID card is a total invasion of our privacy. It's ludicrous," Sen. Feingold said.

"Senator, do you have a driver's license with your photo on it?"

"Well, yes, but driving isn't a right. It's a privilege."

"Until a few years ago, senator, photos were not required on a driver's license. Now all states require photos. A photo provides verification and also helps prevent fraud. There is little difference between a National ID Card and a driver's license, except that an ID covers everyone including non-drivers," Mooreland explained. "The only real difference is that it would reveal the card holder's nationality."

"Mr. Secretary, how do we prevent people from the Middle East or from India or even Latin America from being profiled?" Rep. Gomez asked.

"Law enforcement people should always have the ability to investigate. That's their job. Profiling has to be discussed in context. Remember, the twin towers and the Pentagon were attacked by Middle Eastern men between the age of 22 and 40, not by persons of any other ethnic background. And not by females. Those who carry the card are legitimate. Those who don't are..."

"Are what, criminals?" Rep. Gomez said raising his voice.

"I didn't say that, senator. Let me put this in context. If you are stopped by an officer for a traffic offense, and you cannot produce your driver's license, what happens?"

"You get another summons," Rep. Gomez answered.

"That's not quite true. Roy correct me if I am wrong, a suspicious officer has the right to take you into custody. Roy?"

"That's correct, Mr. Secretary," the FBI director said. "And in a considerable number of highway traffic offenses, the driver is arrested. That ensures that the defendant will be identified so the proper paperwork can be completed and justice served. If the police didn't have that authority, the defendant could just drive away."

"All of you know that there are probably millions of undocumented workers who come from many Latin American countries. Are they going to be arrested when they show up to get their card?" Rep. Gomez continued.

"That's up to the Congress, senator. There is no legislation requiring that as of now. As I've stated repeatedly being an illegal alien is not a crime, although many believe all illegal aliens should be deported. Whether they will be deported is not for the FBI to say, it's for CIS. And new legislation to prevent that can be written into this initiative protecting the people you are talking about," Owens said.

"Do you believe all aliens should be deported?" Rep. Gomez asked.

"Are you talking about people who are here illegally, Congressman?"

"Yes, people who are undocumented workers."

"I am amused by the term sir. Do you call an armed bank robber a thief? To your question, yes, Congressman. Frankly I do. If we don't deport them you encourage the practice and you make fools of those who have adhered to the rules. If illegal aliens know they can get amnesty and a fast track to citizenship with free education and medical benefits along the way, that is a solid incentive for people trying to enter our country illegally."

"Mr. Owens, I'm curious about something," said Sen. Poindexter. "Nowhere in this session have I heard any reference to the FBI internet snooping device ah, Carnivore, I think it's called. How come?"

"The President believes employing Carnivore Two may not be necessary. At any rate he hasn't made up his mind."

"Seems to me Carnivore is just another excuse to invade people's privacy," said Sen. Poindexter. "It also seems to me that the FBI wants a laundry list of tools to look up every skirt and into every computer and lock up everyone who isn't lilly white. I'm surprised you didn't ask for a super infrared machine so you can see how many people there are in a house and what they are doing.

"I think the Secretary and the FBI Director are overestimating the situation. If they need more agents and some training for the airport people, I think Congress should go along with that. But I'm not in favor of legislation approving the use of technology that invades our personal lives. This is still America."

"Mr. Chairman, I'd like to respond to that."

"Certainly, Mr. Secretary."

"Mr. Chairman about three weeks ago more than 40,000 people were killed. That's more than one half of the number killed in the entire Vietnam War. And the Mall death toll may rise significantly because a third of the more than 30,000 who were injured are still in critical condition. Two American cities have suffered catastrophic losses. Thousands of families are grieving and nearly every major medical facility in the Midwest is overtaxed because of this tragedy. So, Senator, I don't think we are overestimating anything."

"I think it is outrageous to target people who only want to come here to learn from us so they can take what they learn back to their countries to improve their standard of living," Sen. Feingold added. "Students are not terrorists. At least not most of them."

"Students from Iran, Libya, Syria, North Korea, Sudan, and Yemen are not sent here by their totalitarian governments to learn anything," Mooreland said. "Their purpose in sending students is to infiltrate and destroy our nation."

After two more hours of grilling, Sen. Featherstone interrupted. "We've run out of time. Thank you, Mr. Secretary. Thank you distinguished senators and congressmen and women. Does anyone else have anything to add? I'll entertain one more question from each member of the committee, if necessary?" Hearing none, the committee chairman said, "Very well. Ladies and gentlemen, if you have nothing further, we'll adjourn this session. Thank you all for coming."

Outside, Owens, Daly and his assistants gathered around Secretary Mooreland.

"Mr. Secretary, it looks like all we're going to get from them is authorization to hire more agents and improve training for the airport people," Daly said.

"Don't give up, Terry, the president hasn't weighed in on this. He told me he's going to address the nation about security and I'm sure he'll bring up many of the things we discussed today."

"That won't matter," said Carter Brown. "This joint bunch of stuffed shirts will bottle this up in the two committees where it will die."

Mooreland and the FBI agents knew Brown was right.

"So, if that happens, we...?" Daly asked.

"We do what we've been doing," Mooreland interrupted.

"Mr. Secretary, we can't ask our field agents to continue to work 70-80 hour weeks," Owens said. "We're already losing agents to high paying corporate security jobs and if this continues we will lose a lot more. Just how much are they expected to sacrifice when they get no cooperation from a bunch of suits whose only concern is re-election?"

"Just what do you suggest? Do you have any alternatives?"

"Yes," Daly said.

"Anything you would care to discuss?"

"Not now."

-Chapter Thirteen-

"Lucy, get me William Burdette, please."

"Right away, Mr. President." Lucy Vernon, president Barnes's secretary said. Moments later CIA Director, William Burdette was on the phone.

"Yes, Mr. President."

"Bill, I know this very short notice. But are you free for dinner tonight?"

"I don't have anything pressing, Mr. President," Burdette said.

"Good, we'll have dinner in my private dining room. I've got something I want to discuss with you. Say about seven?"

"Seven's fine, Mr. President."

The president hung up without saying goodbye. *Can I do this? How can I justify this?*

He was interrupted by the voice of his secretary. "Mr. President, the vice president is here to see you."

"Thanks Lucy. Send him in please."

"Mr. President," Richard Dillon greeted his boss as he entered the Oval office.

"Dick, thanks for coming over so quickly. Sit down, please. Would you like coffee?"

"Please."

"Lucy, please get us some coffee and ask Fred to stop in." Harold Barnes shut the door and sat across from the vice president. After some small talk about families, the President began. "Dick, I want to talk about our so-called immigration policy. We simply have to make changes, tough changes before we have another catastrophe on our hands. I want your thoughts about what should be in the bill to Congress."

President Barnes was interrupted by a soft knock.

"Your coffee, Mr. President," Vernon said. Right behind her was Fred Randolph, the president's chief of staff. As was his style, he did not offer to help until the President stood to help his secretary.

"I'll take that Lucy," Randolph said taking the tray. The president sat down and began repeating what he had told the vice president.

"As both of you know, Phil Mooreland testified behind closed doors before the Joint Committee on Homeland Security. He told them what we all know, that our immigration laws are hindering law enforcement, while enabling the continued influx of illegal into this country. He briefed them on what this administration believes is necessary to win this fight against terrorism. And you know what that bastard Featherstone told him? Featherstone told him, he would not even listen to many of the proposals for changing the immigration laws. He said that even after he heard how many illegals are from the Middle East," the president said.

"When I spoke with him just a few days after your speech, Mr. President he as much told me he wasn't going to make it tougher for the quote downtrodden unquote to get into this country. Shit, he even quoted some of the stuff from the Statue of Liberty, "give me your tired you poor," etc. I didn't mention it to you because I thought he was just pontificating as he often does," the chief of staff said.

"I know he has the power to hold up legislation, but I have the sworn obligation to protect this country and I can't do that if Congress won't give me the laws," the president said.

"I believe in compromise and give and take as much as anyone. Hell, I've done that all my political life, But the time for compromise is past. Hell, there is no goddamn reason why an illegal alien should be allowed to stay in this country. I want 'em out of here. And I want a national ID Card, and all of the other tools the FBI asked for. All of them."

"You may get some, more people, perhaps some of the equipment, but that's all in my view," Randolph said. "Certainly not Carnivore Two, the personal x-ray and the National ID card..

"Somehow we have to isolate some of these senators and change their minds, perhaps with the threat of going to their states to talk to their constituents to tell they are unsafe without the safeguards we are proposing.

"The liberals know that today's illegal aliens are tomorrow's grateful voters so they are not about to lower the number of passengers on that gravy train," Randolph said. "Featherstone, Claxton, Fumer, Feingold and Representative Gomez among others won't buy into it. Period," Randolph said.

"Do either of you think a national TV address would help persuade them?"

"Sir, you did that on September 11," Randolph said. "That hasn't weakened their resolve."

"I agree with Fred, Mr. President," the vice president said.

"What do you think about the idea of visiting their home states?"

"That would take weeks. And the media might have a field day with that tactic," Randolph said.

"Well, goddamn it, we have to do something. These attacks scared a lot of people. It really hit home. Look at what it's done to shopping. And what's left of the airline industry is in a shambles. Hell, our whole economy is in the toilet. Americans expect us to do something. And fast."

"I think we need to focus on what we know we can do," Randolph said.

"Mooreland's anti-terrorism report lists so many places that are defenseless it makes this country look like a shooting gallery. It's appalling. Malls, theaters, ballparks, stadiums, train and bus stations, bridges and tunnels are all prime targets. Well I'm going to do something. If we're going to have an attack on my watch it won't be because we didn't try seriously to prevent it," the president said. "I don't want to be awakened some morning or be called out of a meeting to be told that one of our cities has disappeared. Desperate times call for desperate measures."

"Mr. President, as I assess the votes I think we'll be able to get more manpower for the FBI and the border patrols and money for some of the new technology, like the ah, drones and maybe even the low frequency radar. They might even go for finishing the fence. But that's about it," Randolph said.

"That's not good enough. We have to do a lot more. And it may require changes in the way we think and act. I'm sick to death of political correctness. Illegal immigrants pose a serious threat to our national security not to mention to our economy. At first I was against the national ID card, the personal x-ray, and the new carnivore, but after looking at the casualty reports from the mall attack alone, they make sense to me."

"Sir, some say a National ID Card would lead to profiling," Randolph said. "Featherstone, Feingold and Fumer are dead set against the personal x-ray and Carnivore. Fumer thinks Carnivore is a device for the Gestapo. I think those are dead on arrival."

"Featherstone, Feingold and Fumer, eh. The three F's. Featherbrains. If we are to win this war, I'm convinced we need everything: people and tools," the president said. "Dick, I haven't heard anything from you."

"Mr. President, I agree with you. We need changes. But I also think Fred is right. We might get most of what we want through the House, but not the Senate. And if there is another attack they'll blame us. But we may have an opportunity here. Perhaps we should approach this from another direction. I think the American people are scared and angry," the vice president said. "I think we need to be bold, to go outside the box and be, ah creative."

"You've got my attention, Dick."

"The one critical element we lack in this war seems to be accurate and timely information. We must find a way to allow our federal law enforcement officials to get better information and to use it to dismantle the remaining terrorist cells," Dillon said. He paused to see if Randolph would interrupt. "So what I'm proposing is we extend the interrogation sessions, keep terrorist suspects on ice for a month or two in isolation to give us time to act on their information."

"Christ, Mr. Vice President, with all due respect, that is outrageous and blatantly illegal. It's also unconstitutional. The

146

Supreme Court was adamant about that. I'm rather surprised you would even think of such a thing."

"Perhaps, Fred, but you have to admit the vice president's idea is intriguing," the president said. *Intriguing as hell. It would seem I have an ally. I wonder how far he's willing to go?*

"Mr. President, please. Think of what you're saying," Randolph said.

"Fred, we've never fought a war like this. Our enemies don't wear uniforms so we can't tell them apart from ordinary people. That makes them spies in my view or at least enemy combatants out of uniform. Either way, they don't deserve Constitutional protection."

"Sir if you do this and word leaks out you'll be impeached."

"In the court of American public opinion I'll bet 8 out of 10 Americans would stand up and cheer. But I'm getting ahead of myself. It seems to me we won't need to do that if we get what we're asking for through Congress. I admit it doesn't look promising, but we have to try. Fred, see what you can do. Let me know who you think might jump," the president said. "In the meantime I'd like to hear more of what the vice president has in mind. Go on Dick."

"Mr. President, Fred's right. Thanks to the Supreme Court, terrorism suspects must be afforded the right to counsel, the right to confront an accuser and the right to a fair trial," the vice president said.

"Exactly," Randolph said. "Anything less would be unconstitutional."

"I see two ways to address our immediate concern and perhaps even deal terrorism a serious blow. First, we allow federal agencies greater leeway in their arrest procedure."

"What do you mean by leeway? We can't change the laws without Congress, Mr. Vice President," Randolph said.

"I'm aware of that." Dillon took a sip of coffee and cleared his throat. "I'm talking about taking terrorism suspects to a safe, secure place for interrogation."

"You mean kidnap them and hold them prisoner without a lawyer," Randolph said. "Ever hear of Habeas Corpus?"

The president rose, poured himself a cup of coffee and looked out the window. "Fred, Dick and I took an oath to preserve and defend the Constitution. Included in that oath was our vow to defend this nation against all enemies foreign and domestic."

"So you're recommending we break the law?" Randolph said.

"Not break the law, Fred, but carry out one part of the oath with a little more vigor than the other part," the vice president said." It seems that when we preserve and protect the Constitution we leave the nation vulnerable. Since the Constitution isn't under attack, maybe we should shift the emphasis to protecting and defending this nation against all enemies foreign and domestic. By doing that we protect the Constitution."

"I want to hear more," the president said.

"I would rather not be privy to this Mr. President."

"Very well, Fred." Randolph rose, looked at both men, lowered his head and left the room.

"You have the floor, Dick."

The vice president laid out his ideas. When he was finished he was perspiring profusely, emotionally caught up in the boldness of his thoughts. "You and I have been friends for 12 years, Harry. I never had political ambitions, let alone wanting to be vice president. And I sure as hell never thought I'd be suggesting that the President of the United States should break the law."

"I know, Dick. Kind of exciting isn't it? Thank you for discussing this with me," Barnes said. "For both our sakes, please keep this to yourself."

Lucy Vernon waited at the door while vice president Dillon passed. She entered and shut the door.

"Don't forget, Mr. President, you are having dinner with Mrs. Barnes and guests in the residence," she said.

"Oh yes, thank you, Lucy. Oh damn, wait a minute, I'm having dinner with Bill Burdette in my private dining room. I'm glad you reminded me. He likes filet mignon, salad, baked potato and a California red. Oh, Lucy, I don't want to be disturbed by anyone or anything unless it requires the immediate attention of the President of the United States. I'll call Alecia. Thanks Lucy."

"You're welcome, Mr. President," Vernon said. She closed the door. *I wonder how any woman can put up with being married to a president?* Vernon dialed the Secret Service Command Desk. "This is Lucy Vernon. I am leaving for the day in about a half hour. The President is having dinner in his private dining room and he does NOT want to be disturbed by anyone unless it is a national emergency requiring the attention of POTUS."

"Yes, ma'am. One minute, please." The agent verified the line Vernon was using as that of the president's secretary. "Two uniformed agents will be dispatched right away, Mrs. Vernon."

She looked up to see Fred Randolph and Bill Sellers, Chief White House Counsel on their way to the door to the oval office.

"The president left instructions that he does not wish to be disturbed… by anyone, Mr. Randolph."

"Would you hand me your intercom phone, please," Randolph said testily.

"He's on the phone right now. Please wait a moment."

"Look here, Lucy. I have to see him right away. That means NOW," Randolph said raising his voice. "This is about national security."

"You'll have to wait until he is off the phone, Mr. Randolph," Vernon said keeping her voice under control. *What does the president see in this bastard?* "Please gentlemen make yourselves comfortable."

Inside the Oval Office, President Barnes called his wife.

"White House Residence."

"Sam, it's me. Is Alecia there?"

"Yes, Mr. President. She is standing right here." Samantha Alford, Alecia Barnes', personal assistant and life long friend, handed the phone to the First Lady. She quietly retreated and shut the door behind her.

"Hi honey. Sam and I were just going over the final details of the dinner tonight. Oh, please don't tell me you are calling to tell me you can't make it."

"I'm sorry, dear. I had a last minute meeting that because of the hour I had to change into a dinner meeting. It won't take too long and I should be able to be there for dessert."

"You promised, Harry. Greg and Nancy will be very disappointed. We haven't seen them in two years, you know."

"I know. And I'm dying to see them again. I'll make it fast and be there for dessert."

"Please do try dear. Goodbye."

"Bye, honey." President Barnes hung up. Seconds later the intercom buzzed.

"Yes."

"Mr. President, Mr. Randolph and Mr. Sellers are here, sir. They want a few moments to talk about national security." As she talked, Vernon nodded to the two Secret Service officers who had stationed themselves at the entrance to her office. That did not escape the notice of Randolph.

So Randolph ran right to the counsel to get him to persuade me not to do this. "Lucy," President Barnes said loudly on the intercom so the two staffers could hear his voice. "Please tell Mr. Randolph and Mr. Sellers that I am having dinner with my family tonight and that I do not wish to be disturbed. Tell them I'll see them in the morning."

Vernon almost corrected the president on his dinner engagement. "Yes Mr. President, I'll tell them." She placed the phone in the cradle and said, "I assume you heard him. He'll see you in the morning. He's having dinner with his family and friends tonight."

Randolph started to say something and thought better. He glanced at the secret servicemen *Yeah, then why are there two uniformed guards here. Something is going on? Why am I being left out of the loop?*

Randolph and Sellers turned on their heels, nodded in the direction of the two guards and walked down the hall. Out of earshot, Sellers asked, "if he's having dinner with the family in the residence, why the uniforms? They're only summoned when he's there and Lucy is gone for the day."

"Good question, Bill. Damn good question. Something's going on."

Vernon filed two letters and made some notes on her calendar which she locked away in her desk. Then she knocked on the door to the Oval Office, opening it when instructed.

"Mr. President, if you don't need me, I'll be heading home. Two Secret Service men are in my office."

"Thank you, Lucy. Please come in and shut the door." Vernon entered the office, shut the door and leaned her back against it. "You know Lucy, Fred Randolph is a good man. But at times he's a demanding pain in the ass. And he likes to intimidate people. I hope he wasn't a problem."

"I work for you, Mr. President, not Fred Randolph. I don't care if he is chief of staff."

She started to give the president her opinion of Randolph, but changed her mind. "Will there be anything else, sir?"

"Security is aware that Burdette is coming?"

"Yes sir. He'll be escorted."

"Good. Tomorrow, make sure that his presence here is NOT on the log. Understand?"

"I understand, Mr. President. I'll deliver that instruction personally."

"Thanks, Lucy. I don't know what I'd do without you. Have a nice evening and I'll see you in the morning."

Vernon started to open the door but pushed it shut. She turned and looked at the man she would give her life for.

"You know Harry, there isn't anything I wouldn't do for you. Please remember that." She opened the door. "Good night, Mr. President," she said pulling the door behind her. She smiled at the secret service agents and picked up her purse. "Good night, gentlemen," she said as she walked by. "Remember, his instructions. He's not to be disturbed unless it's a national emergency."

Harry Barnes removed his glasses and rubbed his eyes. *That's the first time she called me Harry since I was elected governor.* He smiled and looked out over the lawn. *Harry, you are about to take the biggest chance of your life.* He closed his eyes and thought about how he got to the White House campaigning on winning the war on terrorism and maintaining morality in the White House. The campaign flashed through his mind. His thoughts were interrupted by the phone.

"Yes."

"Mr. President. Don Briggs, Secret Service POTUS Detail, sir. Mr. William Burdette is here for your seven o'clock appointment. He's a little early. Should I have him wait?"

"No, Don, bring him up, please." Barnes hung up. He took off his jacket and hung it on the chair behind him and turned to look over the lawn. It was one of his favorite views.

Briggs escorted William Burdette, CIA director to the private entrance to the Oval Office. He knocked softly and then used his key to open the secure door. "Mr. President, Mr. Burdette, sir," he announced. Burdette thanked Briggs, entered the office as Briggs shut the door behind him.

151

"Mr. President, it's good to see you," Burdette said with a broad smile.

Barnes quickly rose and warmly greeted his old friend. "Bill, the spook business must agree with you. You look wonderful. And cut out the Mr. President stuff. We're alone and we've been close friends for more than 30 years."

"Nearly 35, Harry. How's Alecia? How are the kids?"

"Alecia's great. Harry, junior is doing fine. Chris hates having the Secret Service around her but she's getting used to it."

"Where is she?" Burdette asked.

"She's an intern at Duke Medical Center. Doing very well. How's Donna?"

"She's a doctor? Jesus. I remember her as a toddler and you pushing her baby carriage. Donna's taking Martha's death very hard. She's visiting our son-in-law and the grandchildren up in Minnesota. Those murdering bastards have taken two members of her family. Donna's brother was killed in the Pentagon on 9/11/01. I'm worried about her."

The president nodded and expressed his condolences. "Bill, when I heard the news about Martha I was devastated. Alecia and I watched her grow up. She was like a daughter to us. We are heart broken. She was so sweet. It was horrible, just horrible. God I hate those bastards."

"Thanks, Harry. And please thank Alecia for her help and her prayers."

The two talked about family and were interrupted by Don Briggs who knocked softly on the private door. He unlocked it and announced, "Dinner will be ready in about a half hour, sir. Would you and Mr. Burdette like some wine?"

"Yes, Don, that would be wonderful," Barnes answered as he put his arm around Burdette. The two walked across the hall to the luxurious private dining room.

Briggs poured a glass of white wine for the president and looked at Burdette, "it's red you prefer, isn't it?"

"Yes, Don. Thank you. You have a good memory." Burdette accepted the glass from Briggs.

"You like your filet medium, don't you sir?"

"Yes. Now I am impressed. It's been a couple of years, hasn't it?" Burdette asked Briggs.

"I think so sir. But I don't deserve any special credit. I like my steak the same way."

Turning to the president, he said, "Mr. President, is half an hour sufficient time?"

That will be perfect, Don. Thanks."

Briggs excused himself.

"Good man, Harry."

"He's first rate, Bill. Bright and loyal to the core. Reminds me of a young lieutenant in Army Intelligence in Nam. You know how much I value loyalty."

"Harry, why do I get the feeling you are about to ask me to do something."

"You always had a suspicious nature about you. I like that. And you are right. I am going to ask you to do something, but not for me, for the country." President Barnes said. He and Burdette sat close to each other in the dining room and the president began. He stopped talking when Briggs arrived with dinner. Sensing he had interrupted something important, Briggs served the food quickly and departed. The president resumed.

"Bill, I want you to hear me out. We've been through hell and we think we might be hit again. The public is scared and I don't think the senate is going to help. So, I think our conventional methods have to be, ah, changed. We were successful at Midway because we broke the Japanese code. And when we captured Enigma, we were successful in defeating the German U-Boats. I want to break the terrorists anyway I can. And conventional methods aren't working."

"Harry, what are you implying?"

"I'm not implying anything. I'm talking about extracting information from any suspect who is here illegally. Since I probably can't get the liberal left wingers in the Congress to pass legislation changing the alien rules, we have to resort to other means," President Barnes said. "I would rather violate the so-called rights of a thousand illegal aliens than have a small number of them blow up American cities. Hell, in my opinion illegal aliens shouldn't have any rights anyway."

"So what are you suggesting?"

153

"Our immigration laws are so loose the terrorists use them against us. We're forced to play with one hand tied behind our back and if there are any rules in this war, they sure as hell don't apply to bin Laden, Hezbollah, Islamic Jihad, the PLO, Hamas or any others. . So, I'm suggesting we even the playing field by changing the rules, or rather by ignoring them," Barnes said.

"What rules are you referring to?"

"The ones that gives these bastards the same rights and privileges as Americans. Since we desperately need information, I'm suggesting we obtain it in unorthodox ways, if necessary. No public procedure. No lawyers present during questioning and no media sniffing around," Barnes said.

"Just so I'm hearing this correctly, Harry, you're talking about suspending Habeas Corpus, the right to be represented by counsel and self incrimination. Jesus, you're talking about asking people to disobey the law, to circumvent the Constitution. With all due respect it goes against everything you and I stand for."

"Bill, we just suffered a colossal defeat, with more casualties in one day than in any battle in the Civil War. They have so many targets from which to choose. We simply have to change the rules of engagement. You're the only man I trust, the only man who can get this done. Hell, your agency is the...."

"Harry, my agency is prevented by law from operating in this country. That's number one. But what you are asking is, is, hell I don't know how to describe it."

"Bill," the president said as he poured another glass for himself and refilled Burdette's glass. "Fred Randolph reminded me of that this afternoon when the vice president brought this up. The FBI has virtually assured us of the inevitability of additional attacks perhaps even more devastating than the mall. They're convinced that business in Westchester County was part of a larger plot that went bad. The next attack may even be nuclear. That's why we have to do this. No one will know what is taking place. Your men are too good for that.

"I believe in the Constitution. But our Congress, our laws, our ultra liberal courts and even our own free society are working against us, thwarting our efforts," the president continued. "Lincoln violated the Constitution during the Civil War when he suspended Habeas Corpus. And our government violated the rights of thousands of Japanese Americans when it interned them during World War II. Someone once said 'desperate times call for desperate measures.'

"Desperate enough to violate the Constitution and break who knows how many federal laws?" Burdette asked.

"If it means saving perhaps tens of thousands of lives, how can we be wrong?"

"You said there were two things we need to do. What's the second?" Burdette asked.

"I want you to get inside the Saudi mission in New York City."

"Are you serious?"

"Yes. Bug their phones, intercept their packages, open them and reseal them. Intercept their radio traffic and put your cryptographers on it. Follow their people. When one of them takes a shit, I want you to know about it."

"May I ask why?"

"FBI agents found incriminating evidence on one of the Stinger missile crates they found at the airport on the day of the attack."

"What kind of evidence, Harry?"

"Just a shipping tag with the address of the Saudi UN Mission in English and Arabic."

Burdette's eyes widened. He took a healthy swallow.

"The cops who found the crates have been told the information is classified top secret and that revealing the information would be a serious crime. Even though congress hasn't authorized it, I'm going to tell the FBI to employ Carnivore II. What I need is additional evidence to prove beyond any doubt that the Saudis are behind this."

"We've suspected them for quite some time, Harry. I heard that we had something, but this... Shipping tags on the missile crates have all the earmarks of a smoking gun."

"Possibly. But they could claim that the tag was a plant by someone trying to discredit them," the president said. "And there are a lot of countries who would take the word of the Saudis over ours. Certainly the Times and the Washington Post would. Anyway we are withholding that from the public until we can back it up with other evidence."

"How do we justify this if my guys are caught?"

"We don't. We deny who they are and who they work for. That's unfortunate, but that's how it has to be. Your guys know that. Once we have the proof we need, I will call in the ambassador."

"Harry, that won't do any good. He'll deny it. And you can't go public with the information without giving away where and how you got it. And you sure as hell don't want to do that," Burdette said.

"The covert information we get from the mission will be used only to break up a few of these terrorist cells and grab the plotters. There are many ways to justify an arrest if necessary. In the meantime your people can interrogate them anyway you want. We'll get corroboration from the others in the cell and when combined with physical evidence we'll have enough to talk to the Saudi government. They'll talk turkey or we'll pluck their fucking feathers. What I am after is solid evidence"

"Harry, there has to be another way," Burdette interrupted.

"Don't you think I haven't tried to think of something, anything else? The worst attack on American soil took place on my watch. And they are going to attack us again. We both know that. And we are not doing everything we can to stop them. What I am asking you to do is nothing compared to what I will have to do if we are attacked with a nuclear weapon"

"I don't want to think about that. The attack on the mall was the most sickening thing I have ever seen. And it killed my daughter."

"You and I have been best friends since our Marine Corps days. You are as patriotic as me. More so. It's impossible to get the media and the public to focus on the fact that we are at war because they can't see the enemy and they don't know where the enemy is. But right now Americans are angry and they are hurting. I want to take advantage of those emotions. I can't afford to miss this opportunity," the president said.

"Bill, I have wrestled with this for a week. Earlier today, the vice president brought it up. Naturally, Randolph said it was illegal, but the vice president was undeterred. I think he's right. Since our enemy doesn't wear uniforms or have a nation's official backing… suffice to say we can win this if we know their plans and who is behind them. The number of dead and injured from the last attacks are all the motivation I need. As of now, the gloves are off. These murderers want to be martyrs. Fine, I'll be more than happy to oblige them. But first I want to put the fear of God into the folks who support them.

"They operate under deep cover so if they disappear no one will know except their handlers. They might tip their hand, but that isn't likely. But if we break up just a few of these cells, we not only prevent them from carrying out their mission, but we might be able to break one or two of their evil brotherhood and get some useful information.

"All of the terrorist bombings in Israel over the last 20 years combined don't come close to what's been done to us," Barnes continued. "Imagine what else they have in mind? The unacceptable fact is that they are using our laws and our free way of life against us. Well, no more, damn it.

"Bill, you more than anyone in my administration has a personal stake in this. You lost a daughter and a brother-in-law. Here's your chance to settle the score and help your country."

Burdette rose and walked to the buffet. He looked up at the painting of a young woman and thought of Martha and what her death was doing to Donna. "When my brother-in-law was killed my wife was devastated," Burdette said. "She and her brother were very close. Our daughter's death hit us very hard, and almost killed Donna. I think only her grandchildren really matter now. I wanted to keep this fight on an impersonal level so that I would be able to think clearly and rationally.

"But, now that we have proof the Saudis are involved, I..., well I wanted to see how far you'd go with this, how committed you are. Now I'm satisfied. I think we can get what you need. Now I have a question, Harry. Is the FBI in on this? Do Owens and Daly know?"

"I think we can count on Daly. He hates these terrorists more than I do. He thinks our laws are laughable. And he has a personal stake too. His parents were killed in the airport attack. I'll make sure he's on board."

"OK, Harry. We'll get to work on this right away."

"Thanks, Bill. I know Martha would be very proud of you right now. I damn sure know I am. Oh, one more thing. And I don't like having to say this, but I don't want to know anything more about your methods or your plans. I just want results."

Burdette stood, nodded, smile and shook the president's hand. "What plans, Mr. President?"

-Chapter Fourteen-

After leaving the White House, William Burdette made calls to Middle East "analysts" Hank Hobbs and Vince Breen. Despite the short notice, both agreed to meet the Director at his office. Next he called security and told the supervisor to send the two men to the conference room on the director's floor. He told his driver to take his time driving him to his office to give the others time to arrive. At the gate, his ID was run through the scanner by the guard. "Jerry, wait for me, please. I will probably be about an hour, maybe a little longer," Burdette said to his driver.

"No problem sir," Jerry Arnold answered. "It's a nice night."

Burdette entered the building and presented his ID.

"Good evening, Mr. Director," the supervisor said.

"Good evening, Pete. How's that new baby?"

"Doing fine sir," Pete Finnegan answered.

"Great. I'm going to be here for about an hour. Have Mr. Hobbs and Mr. Breen arrived?

"Yes sir. They're waiting in your conference room as you instructed."

"Anyone else on the floor?" Burdette asked.

"Everyone else has left for the day," Finnegan said.

"Yes. Thanks Pete. If anyone should show up, I'm not here. I don't want to be disturbed.

Finnegan relayed the message to the other guards in the event someone arrived while he was away from the central desk. He began checking the security system video screens.

Burdette entered his office placed his brief case on the desk and opened the steel doors to the conference room. Hobbs and Breen looked up and then stood.

"Hank, Vince, come on in," he motioned. "You guys want a coke, soda, something hot?"

Both selected cokes that Burdette pulled from his refrigerator. He put some ice in three glasses and handed the cokes and glasses to the agents taking one for himself. He took a long swallow and said, "Sit down, please." Burdette waited until both men we comfortable on the leather chairs facing his desk. He rested his butt against the desk and folded his arms.

"I've got an assignment for you. Totally off the books. You'll be part of a nationwide anti-terrorism operation. Your part is risky and by that I don't mean life threatening, I mean legally, because you'll be working in this country. So if you are compromised, the firm and the government will deny any knowledge of your activities. And more than likely, you'll be prosecuted, unless of course, what you uncover is overwhelming. Now before I give you details are you willing to take the assignment?"

"No problem, sir," both answered.

"Good. Here's the background. We've long suspected the Saudis are in bed with al Qaeda and other terrorist groups. Until a few days ago we had nothing solid. But now we have physical evidence to support our suspicions," Burdette said. He detailed what had been uncovered and how far along the investigation had proceeded. "The evidence we have is important, but we need more so there is no doubt in the court of world opinion. All right, here's what I want you to do.

"Vince, since you're the elint expert, this is your assignment," Burdette said lowering his voice. "Break into the Saudi UN mission communications system, their regular and secure phones, email, cell phones, and their radio links. Find out where their vehicles are serviced and bug them. Find out where the people below diplomatic status live and bug their apartments. If anyone calls a girlfriend, I want to know where they are going and if they got laid. If anyone contacts a doctor I want to know what the ailment is. Every transmission, whether in Arabic or English, should be recorded. At the end of each shift all recordings should be handed to your hand picked translators and analysts," Burdette paused and took another swallow. Both agents did the same. "Tomorrow morning I'm ordering the repositioning of GPX-2 and GPR-3. Any questions? Vince?"

"No questions, sir."

"Tell me who you need and I'll have them transferred. Get updated photos of all of the mission people who have immunity and match them with their passports just in case we have any who have grown beards or have shaven them since their passport photos were taken. Then we'll match their conversations with their photos and build a dossier on these people. We're going to ask the NYPD to tow any Saudi vehicle violating a parking rule. When a vehicle is towed, the NYPD will notify you through a special number. Get one of your men over there and bug the car. Plant a direction finder under the car too. We might get some interesting information that way. Incidentally, towing their vehicles does not violate international law. Oh, one more thing. The FBI is going to be using Carnivore Two to intercept email from the suspects. Use Moonbeam and learn what they learn. If they have a suspect, we want to question him before they do. And with respect to interrogation, make sure the information is absolutely accurate. Clear?"

Breen grinned and nodded.

"Hank, this is your baby. Your team will be given customs clearance. Station them at Kennedy and Dulles. Customs will be instructed to detour all packages from Middle Eastern nations to a special holding room for security purposes. That's where your men will examine every diplomatic package, box and carton, everything but personal baggage. Videotape the contents and make an audio description of what you see. Make sure the diplomatic markings appear in the tape. Then reseal each package so no one knows it has been compromised. That last part is vital," Burdette emphasized. "The diplomats will be told their packages will be the last removed from the aircraft so they can be safeguarded. That will give your men about one hour for the search and the cover. Are your guys up to this?"

"Yes sir," they answered.

"What about resealing the containers?"

"Piece of cake, sir," Hobbs said. "We know what they use. And we can duplicate that easily."

"Sir, what about vehicular traffic making deliveries to the mission?" Breen asked. "Do you want them tailed when they leave? I think we should know what companies or organizations they deal with and where they are located."

"Agreed. And that brings up another point. I don't want any of your guys to know what the other group is doing or about the repositioning of the birds. Understand. If word of this gets out, we'll play merry hell with the media and Congress, not to mention the Saudis."

Burdette took another swallow. "Oh, one more thing. Vince, how many of your people speak Arabic fluently."

"Six or seven."

"One should be present on each shift. If he or she hears anything remotely hinting at an attack or something hostile, I want to know about it immediately. Understand. They're to call you wherever you are and you are to call me with all the information."

"Sir, there's a problem with that."

"How so?"

"Sir if we get information that we act upon we may compromise the entire operation by inadvertently telling them we knew something."

"Sort of like the choice Churchill had to make when he found out the Nazis were going to bomb Coventry. If Churchill had warned Coventry he would have avoided thousands of casualties. But he would have alerted the Nazis that England had broken Enigma. I'm aware of that. If the information can thwart an attack or enable us to do major damage to their cause we'll have to risk our being discovered. And even if we are discovered by the Saudis I doubt they'll bring this to public attention and risk exposure."

"Is that all, sir," Breen asked.

"I know I'm asking a lot. But I think you know how important this is. In my opinion and the opinion of others, the attack on the Westchester County Airport was part of a larger plot that went awry," Burdette said. "They waited eight years before attacking the towers a second time. I hope this time they wait long enough for us to nail them. All we need is a couple of legitimate suspects that we can interrogate privately. Our role is to gather information and evidence others can act on. Nothing more."

Hobbs and Breen shook hands with the CIA director who accompanied them to the door to his office. He pulled his communicator from his belt. "Pete?"

"Yes sir, Mr. Burdette."

"Mr. Hobbs and Mr. Breen are leaving my office right now."

"Thank you sir," Finnegan answered. "I've got them on the monitor."

"Hank, Vince, good luck and God speed." Burdette closed the door and returned to his desk. He gathered the Washington Post and his brief case and turned out the light before securing his office door. *I hope to God Harry is right.*

-Chapter Fifteen-

When Angela Hart arrived for work Monday morning she checked her voice mail, turned on her computer and went to the small cafeteria for coffee and a bagel. On her way, she passed the darkened cubicle of Antonio Rodrigo. She looked at her watch. It was 7:35. *He's almost never late. I wonder if he is ok.*

"Good morning, Angela," said Tim Robbins, Hart's boss. "How was your weekend?"

"Hi, Tim. The weekend was great. I... ah, how was yours?" Hart asked deciding not to tell Robbins she had a date with Tony.

"It was good. My wife and I went to a party Saturday and then we had friends over yesterday. I grilled steaks. Great weather.

"For sure. I went for a long walk. Felt good."

"Listen, after you finish your coffee, would you and Tony come to my office. I want you both to bring me up to speed on your projects. Is the layout for Gray's publication finished?"

"I have four and a half pages to do, Tim. There are several stories still to come and some artwork. Tony told me he was going to come in yesterday to finish up the McLaughlin Liquor Company magazine. *Whoops, I don't think I should have said that.*

"He did? That's great. OK, bring me what you have so far." Robbins said over his shoulder as he headed to his office.

Hart buttered her bagel, then scraped off most of the butter wiping it from the knife before throwing the paper towel away. *I better be careful. Tim might not appreciate my dating Tony.*

The computer screen in Rodrigo's cubicle was still dark. *Wonder where he is? Is he embarrassed to see me after the weekend?*

She stared at her computer screen and the half completed page 11 of *Horizons*, Gray's publication. She was thinking about Saturday night. *I never knew a man could be so gentle, so thorough. His hands were wonderful. I have never been so turned on by a man after only one date. I hope he doesn't think I'm a slut.*

"Angela, did you talk to Tony?" Robbins was standing with one hand on the cubicle wall, the other in his pocket. He sounded annoyed.

"I haven't seen him. I don't think he's in yet. I think he was planning to drive in today and may have run into traffic," Hart said.

"Alright, I'll look at yours first. Print out what you have and bring it to my office right away. Maybe Tony will get here before we're done." He waited a moment until Angela began printing the first page of the magazine.

Hart scooped up the client's dummy and the pages that had just come out of the printer and headed for Robbins' office. She knocked on the open door and entered taking a seat at the conference table. Robbins made a couple of notations on a pad, picked up his coffee and sat down next to Hart.

"Do you need another cup before we begin?"

Seeing an opportunity to delay the meeting in the hope Rodrigo would arrive, Hart said, "Yeah. Mine's cold. How about you?"

Robbins took a long swallow and handed his cup to Hart. "A little cream, no sugar, please."

"Sure. Be right back." She disappeared down the hall praying Rodrigo was at his desk. Her heart sank when she passed his cubicle. She poured the coffee and hurriedly returned to Robbins office.

Tim Robbins was 51 years old. He had worked as an art director for a large ad agency for nearly 25 years. When his first wife, Sally, persuaded him to cut back on his hours so they could spend more time together, he went to his boss, hoping he would understand. Instead, his boss thought he was being disloyal and let him go. Two months later, on September 10, 2001, he was named an assistant art director for Pantone Associates. The next day, Sally, his childhood sweetheart and wife of 22 years, was killed in tower one while attending a breakfast at Windows on the World.

Robbins was devastated by Sally's death. Sally was the only woman he had ever dated. John Pantone, the owner of Pantone Associates was horrified at Robbins' loss and gave him two weeks off with pay even though he had been an employee for only one day. Pantone's gesture earned Robbins' unswerving loyalty that paid off handsomely as Pantone quickly became one of the most recognized publication design and pre-press houses in New York. In less than three years Pantone's business had tripled and Robbins had risen to Senior Art Director. Pantone and Robbins became good friends.

Tim and his second wife Pam had been married less than a year. Pam was a highly successful owner of a real estate brokerage in Bay Head, NJ where the couple lived in a beautiful house on Barnegat Bay.

Pam had sold Spencer and Lois Ryan their vacation home in Mantoloking. Through a friend in the business, Pam found a lovely one-bedroom apartment in Manhattan where Tim stayed four nights a week. Since her busiest time was on weekends, during the week she often stayed in Manhattan for two or three nights where they enjoyed the theater, fine dining and each other.

Hart was in awe of Tim Robbins. In her opinion, he was not only a superb art director, he was also a gentleman and a friend, a rare combination in business. She worked hard for him and he recognized her effort.

When Hart returned to Robbins office, he was studying the layouts. Rather than disturb him, she waited in the doorway until he looked up. "Ah, there you are," he said. "Angela, this is very good so far. I like the way you have subtly carried this logo and theme from the front page through the book. When will you get the rest of the copy?"

"Not sure, actually. Gray's management is reviewing the material now. That might take several days or longer. Maybe I'll get them in time to finish the layouts over the weekend. Most of the photos have been scanned and separated."

Hart didn't mind when Robbins gently put his hand on hers. "You're a hard worker, Angela. Hard work has its place, but so does play time. I learned the hard way that life is too short. You have to make time for yourself."

"I don't mind. Besides I like Gray. They are fun to work with. Any changes they make are well thought out and meaningful, not just for the sake of change. So I don't mind working weekends. Besides, it's quiet and I get a lot done," Hart said.

"Keep track of your hours and I'll give you comp time when you need it. OK?"

"That's great Tim, thanks. But you don't have to do that."

"And you don't have to come in this weekend. Hey, look who's here."

"Sorry I'm late, Tim," Tony Rodrigo said. "I tried to call you from the car but got pulled over for using a cell phone while driving. The officer didn't believe it was an emergency. But he let me off with a warning. Hi Angela."

"Good morning Tony," Angela said, deciding not to engage him in any conversation for the moment.

"Tony, get yourself some coffee and what ever else you need and then bring the McLaughlin magazine here. I want to see where we are."

"Sure, Tim. Either one of you want anything from the cafeteria?"

"Not for me. Two cups are all I can handle," said Robbins.

"No thanks," said Hart. "Tim, anything else for me?" She watched Rodrigo disappear down the hall.

"That's all I have."

Rodrigo dropped his coffee off in Robbins' office and retrieved the layouts from his cubicle. When he sat down, he slid them over to Robbins.

"Angela said you were coming in yesterday to finish these."

"Yeah, I like this client. They have a good art director and a pretty competent editorial staff," Rodrigo said.

"Working with professionals makes life a lot easier," said Robbins as he began looking over the layouts. "By the way, they have good things to say about you. You are very conscientious and deadline oriented."

"That's important in the publication business, especially when they have to mail it to their employees after its printed," Rodrigo said..

Robbins caught the word *Labour*. "Did they proof this?"

"They proofed the galleys, but not the pages. Why, something wrong?"

"No big deal, but the word *Labour* is misspelled. There's no *u*." Robbins took his red pen and scratched a vertical line up through the *u* ending it with a delete mark.

"I asked them about it. That's the way they want it, Tim. The story is about the English labor market and the English, ah British, use the letter *u*."

"Well, the customer is always right," Robbins said writing stet over the correction. "Good catch, anyway. The layouts look sharp. They going out today?"

"I'm going to make one last pass and then take them to their offices on Park this morning."

"Will you be at the press OK?"

"They haven't said anything about that, but I think the art director Ann Dunn wants to go so she'll probably ask me to go with her, show her the ropes. Do you know her?"

"Sure. She's very good. And good looking as I remember. She's one of the people over there who think so highly of you. Mentioned your great work several times."

Robbins handed the layouts back to Rodrigo. "Incidentally, we're taking on two new clients, Time Warner, and Altria," Robbins said.

"Altria. Wow! Doesn't get much bigger than that. What are we going to do for them?"

"What we do best. Designs, layout and pre-press."

Robbins pressed his speakerphone button and the intercom extension for Hart's office.

"Angela Hart."

"Angela. Tony's here with me. Can you come over for a few minutes?"

"Sure. Right away."

Hart dropped what she was doing and hurried to Robbins office. She got half way and retreated to pick up a clipboard for notes if needed.

"Hi, what's up," she said slightly out of breath.

"Good news. We've taken on two new clients. Big clients. Time Warner and Altria. John and I both agree that you two should be the art directors," Robbins said. "Angela, we're giving you Time

Warner. They're starting a new employee publication, six times a year initially. They are going to need original design work for their front page and they'll need page design, layout and pre-press work. Your contact is Vera Perry, a senior editor over there. She told me she'll call you when she's ready."

Tony, Altria wants a whole printed package for their under age no smoking campaign. Includes flyers, brochures, posters, design and pre-press. Your contact is, ah, a woman named Brianna Russell. She's a public affairs director. She'll be calling any day to arrange for the planning meeting. You two will back each other up so keep each other fully informed. Questions?"

"Tim, what if we're out of town doing press a Ok on the day they want to meet?" Hart asked.

"I told both clients you were finishing up some projects and would be available on a part time basis next week. We can adjust, if necessary and I can fill in on either one if either or both of you are away at the printer," Robbins offered. "Where is *Single Maltings* being printed, Tony?"

"On my recommendation, McLaughlin just signed a new contract with Quad Graphics in Saratoga Springs. This will be the first time for their publication, but. I've used Quad for several other clients."

"That's where we're printing Gray's *Horizons*," said Hart. "Hey maybe we'll both be there at the same time."

"Nice college town," said Robbins. "You two behave yourselves. Where do you stay?"

"There's a fairly nice Sheraton about 3-4 miles from the printer. That's where I stay," said Hart.

"I've never stayed there. I usually stay at Brackett House, a fabulous place the printer allows his clients use it at no cost," Rodrigo said.

"Anytime a vendor offers to pay for anything other than a meal you should check with the client. Some clients shy away from that kind of relationship with a vendor. OK, if there's nothing else. I have a meeting with John in about 15 minutes."

Rodrigo and Hart walked back to Rodrigo's cubicle.

"Everything OK, Tony?"

"Sure, why?"

"Well you seemed a little distant, that's all. I had a great time Saturday and I hope you did too."

Rodrigo stopped at his cubicle entrance and put his hand on Hart's shoulder. "I had a wonderful time. But I didn't want to give Tim even the slightest hint that you and I, ah, were together over the weekend. OK?"

"Thanks, Tony. I appreciate your protecting my privacy. Want to go for a walk at lunch?"

"If I get *Single Maltings* done. Then we can drop the layouts off at McLaughlin's and get a sandwich. How's that?"

"Cool. Call me when you're ready." Hart didn't wait for a reply as she headed for her cubicle. Bridget MacDonald, the assistant art directors' secretary was waiting.

"Good morning Angela. A woman named Ellen Daly called. She wants you to call her back right away. She says you have the number," MacDonald said.

"Thanks. Oh, and good morning to you, Bridget," Hart put her clipboard down on her layout table and dialed the Daly's phone number.

"Hello."

"Good morning, Ellen. It's Angela. I'm returning your call."

"Hi Angela. Thanks for getting right back to me. Listen, Terry asked me again last night if you had any more information on this man Tony Rodrigo. Terry is sure he knows him from somewhere and was embarrassed because he couldn't remember."

Why would an FBI agent have a reason to know a graphics artist? Seems strange.

"I've worked with him for five years, Ellen, but Saturday was the first time I've been out with him. I don't know much more about him other than what I've already told you. Tony's a nice guy and I like him a lot." Angela looked up. Rodrigo was at the entrance to the cubicle.

"Hi. What's that all about?"

Hart put her hand over the phone. "Hi Tony. Got to go, Ellen. Bye."

"Hi. Who's asking about me?"

"Actually it's her husband who is interested. You remember, the guy I introduced you to at the zoo."

An alarm went off in Rodrigo's brain. *Asking about me once may be ok, but this is beyond coincidence.*

"Oh, sure, him, the FBI agent." Changing the subject, he said, "If you are going with me to McLaughlin's, you better tell Tim."

"Good idea. I'll call him in a couple of minutes."

Hart and Rodrigo didn't talk much on their way to McLaughlin's.

Rodrigo's mind was far removed from the job and from the attractive woman with him. She slipped her hand into his as they walked.

"Earth to Tony. Earth to Tony. Where are you?" she mocked.

"Angela, I have never been arrested. In fact, the closest I've come to even getting a traffic ticket was this morning when I got stopped for talking on my cell phone. So, why is this FBI agent so interested in me?"

"He thinks he knows you or your face from somewhere, that's all. Is that worrying you?"

"Well, sure. Wouldn't it worry you? No one I know has the FBI snooping into their lives. I'd like to know why. I sure as hell haven't done anything wrong." Rodrigo replied trying to get Hart to see him as a victim.

"Look, if this is bothering you, I'll tell Ellen and ask her to stop asking questions."

"NO," he said sharply, causing Hart to stop and stare at him. "I mean, what I mean is, there's no point in getting her angry. Just tell her that what you've told her so far is all you know." *I'm sure you don't know anything that will hurt me.*

"Whatever. I don't like the idea of her asking questions either. Makes me feel creepy and disloyal. I'll just tell her you are great in bed," Hart laughed.

"Angela!"

"I'm kidding, Tony. I won't say anything. I promise."

Rodrigo and Hart arrived at the entrance to the McLaughlin Building.

"You'll have to get a visitor's badge if you want to come up, or you can wait by the desk," Rodrigo said.

"I'd like to come up if that's ok. I've never been here before."

Rodrigo entered the revolving door first followed by Hart and the two strode to the reception desk. "Tony Rodrigo to see Ann

Dunn," Rodrigo said to the guard. "This is Angela Hart. She works with me."

"One moment, sir," the guard replied. Quickly she looked up the extension for Ann Dunn. "Ms. Dunn, this is reception. There is a Mr. Rodrigo and a Ms. Hart here to see you." The guard listened as Ann Dunn relayed instructions. "OK, thank you Ms. Dunn." The guard pointed to the register. "Please sign in. Ms. Dunn will be right down.

If you like, you can wait here or have a seat over there."

"Thanks. We'll wait right here," Rodrigo said.

Moments later a tall and very attractive, black-haired woman in her 40s appeared. "Tony, my assistant said you were on the way. Good thing you called. I was on my way out for the rest of the day. Hi, I'm Ann Dunn. I'm the art director at McLaughlin."

"Hi I'm Angela Hart, a colleague of Tony's," she said. "It's an honor meeting you."

"Nice to meet you too, Angela. Why don't you both come with me." Dunn led the way. "How do you like this unseasonable weather, Angela?"

"I don't mind warm weather," Angela said. It's the humidity I mind. It frizzes my hair."

"Mine too. That's why I keep it in a ponytail. Have you been with Pantone long?"

"About five years," said Hart. "I do the same kind of work as Tony."

Dunn motioned for them to enter the elevator. When the door closed, she took off her suit jacket. She noticed Rodrigo's gaze shift to her bosom. "Too warm for jackets," she explained. "I prefer business casual like you guys, but our CEO is a nut about suits even for women. Doesn't say it in writing, but he doesn't need to."

The floor bell rang. When the doors opened Dunn exited first deliberately giving Rodrigo a clear view of her backside. Hart didn't catch on but she inadvertently spoiled the view by exiting in front of Rodrigo. They followed Dunn to her office.

"Grab a seat," Dunn said pointing to the chairs at the conference table. "It's just about lunchtime. I can order something from the management dining room. Just tell me what you want. Sandwich, salad, anything."

Before Hart could reject the offer, Rodrigo said, "That's very kind, Ann. We are in kind of a hurry. This way we can eat while we work." Hart stared at Rodrigo, annoyed that she hadn't been asked.

Dunn summoned her assistant. "Monica, you know Tony Rodrigo. This is Angela Hart, one of his colleagues. Angela, this is my assistant Monica Soto. Monica, we're going to eat here while we go over the layouts Tony did for *Single Maltings*." After they exchanged greetings, Hart ordered a salad; Rodrigo ordered a hamburger with fries. Dunn ordered the pasta special and told Soto to order for herself too. The three began with some small talk.

"Tony's recommended we use Quad Graphics up in Saratoga Springs, Angela. Are you familiar with them?"

"Sure. Great printer. They go out of their way to please their clients. Do you do press OKs?"

Dunn looked quickly at Rodrigo. "Not often. I know I don't have to with Tony there, but I enjoy a day out of the office and I should get to know them. Saratoga Springs is an easy drive from my apartment in Hartsdale. Tony says he stays at the printer's guest house. Is that where you stay?"

"No. I stay at the Sheraton City Center. It's only a couple of blocks away from the guest house. They have a decent restaurant and there's a lovely old place called The Olde Bryan Inn right at the end of their parking lot if I don't feel like driving," Hart explained.

"That's good to know. Ah, here's Monica."

Dunn's assistant laid the food, napkins and utensils on the table and asked what soft drinks the group preferred. She excused herself to fetch the drinks.

"Why don't we get started," Dunn said opening the envelope containing the layouts. She arranged pages one and eight and two and seven on the table and began studying them interrupting her concentration only long enough to take a forkful of baked ziti. "Hmm, this is good. How's yours?"

"The salad's fine," Hart said.

"The burger's just the way I like it and the fries are good too. Not as good as McDonald's, but very good," Rodrigo said.

Some 45 minutes later, Dunn completed her review. "These look terrific, Tony. I'm going to ask Chris Corman, our editorial Director, to have one last look. What's the tentative press date?"

"Monday, the 17th. I'll messenger the film up to Quad on Friday, the 14th so they can make the blueprints. I'll check the blues on Sunday. Then it's a matter of their scheduling actual press time. When do you want to come up?"

"Well, since this is the first time we've worked with Quad, I think I'll go up on Sunday too. That way I can see the whole process from beginning to end."

"Fine. I'll let them know. Where would you like to stay?"

"That house sounds nice, Tony. But I'm leery of that. I'll stay at the hotel. Monica," Dunn raised her voice to be heard outside her office.

"Here, Ann," Soto said as she poked her head into Dunn's office.

"Would you make a reservation for me for Sunday night, the 16th at the Sheraton in Saratoga Springs?"

"Sure."

"Ann, I always make a reservation for two nights just in case we get a very late press time or in the event they have a problem," Rodrigo said.

"Really," Dunn seemed surprised. "Does that happen often?"

"Once in awhile. I don't want to drive three hours after a late press OK. And you can always cancel the second night," said Rodrigo.

"Good thinking. Monica, make the reservation for Sunday and Monday nights.

Tony, do you want Monica to book your room too?"

"Sure, why not. Angela says the hotel is nice. We'll give it a shot."

"Monica would you also book a room for Tony for the same nights? Oh, wait a minute. Would you two excuse me for a second?" Dunn said. She picked up her purse and followed Soto to her desk. "Monica, when you get the hotel on the phone, let me speak to them, please."

"Sure Ann. I've got an errand to run. Mind if I leave for a few minutes?" she asked as she dialed the number.

"No, you go ahead," Dunn pulled her credit card from the wallet in her purse. When the hotel switchboard answered, Soto handed the phone to Dunn.

"Hi. My name is Ann Dunn from McLaughlin Beverages in New York City. I want to book two rooms for Sunday and Monday,

October 16 and 17." Dunn looked around and cupped her hand over the phone. "I want connecting rooms. Got that, *connecting* rooms." she whispered and then in a normal voice gave the hotel clerk her credit card number.

"Ok, Tony, all taken care of," Dunn said as she returned to her office. "We have rooms for Sunday AND Monday nights. I hope there is a good seafood restaurant there."

"There are a bunch," Rodrigo replied. "They even have one called The Wishing Well that serves lobster. OK, so Chris Corman will call this afternoon or tomorrow. Right? Once I have his final editorial changes, I'll check in with you no later than Friday."

"Sounds like a plan. I'm looking forward to a day or two out of here," Dunn said as the three rose. "Angela, it was very nice to meet you. I hope we see each other again soon."

"Thanks Ann. I hope so too. And thanks for the lunch. Please thank Monica for us."

"Will do. I'll walk you to the elevator. You know maybe the three of us might meet in Saratoga Springs together. Might be fun." As the elevator door opened, Dunn shook hands with Rodrigo and Hart. "Have a great week."

Outside, Hart stopped Rodrigo. "OK, you promised to tell me about yourself. Where you come from, your family. You know."

"When did I promise that?"

"Tony, if you want to keep your life a deep dark secret that's fine. But I'd like to know why. We have worked together for years and on the first date we fall into bed. It was great. And I'm glad we did. But I think I have a right to know a little more about the guy I slept with. Don't you?"

"Me llamo Antonio Rodrigo naci en Madrid. Mis padres son muertos. Vine a este pais y fui a la escuela fina del arte de Temple University. Soy solo. No tengo una religion y voto solamente en elecciones presidenciales. Oh, en caso de que usted se este preguntando, tengo treinta cinco anos, cuidadano naturalizado y nunca me he casado."

"Terrific. My Spanish is rusty. Would you mind translating for me?"

Rodrigo laughed out loud. "My name is Tony Rodrigo. I was born in Madrid. My parents are dead," Rodrigo said. "I came to this country and went to Temple University's fine arts school. I'm single.

175

I don't have a religion and I only vote in presidential elections. Oh, in case you are wondering, I am 35, a naturalized citizen and I have never been married. OK?"

"Yeah, You don't have to cop an attitude with me, you know."

"I'm sorry. I don't feel well. I have a headache and my stomach is upset. Must have been that burger. I'm going to head home. Would you please tell Tim?"

"Sure. You know, you don't look well," Hart said feeling his forehead. "You better get some rest."

Rodrigo smiled and then headed across the street to the parking lot a few blocks away.

He didn't even say goodbye. Hart headed back to the office.

Less than 90 minutes later Rodrigo opened the door to his apartment and hastily turned on his computer and joined the chatroom. Atta, or one of his assistants, was on line. He typed the message: *Competition still inquiring. Please call. Acknowledge.*

Rodrigo grabbed a Pepsi from the fridge and returned to the computer. There was a message from NYGAL. *Will call at 3:40.*

Rodrigo looked at his watch. It was 3:34.

Without bothering to turn off his computer, Rodrigo raced outside and down to the phone several hundred yards from his building. He was still out of breath when the phone rang.

"Yes," he answered.

"Juamah."

"Dhahran."

"What's the problem?"

Rodrigo explained that he overheard part of the conversation in which his name had come up. "I asked her and she told me that the FBI agent's wife was still asking questions. I have a bad feeling about this."

"Stay calm. They have nothing on you so it's unlikely they will want to question you. Just be very careful what you say to this woman. Don't give her anything that can be traced."

"OK." Rodrigo hung up. Something bothered him. Shit. I told her I went to Temple University. They can trace that.

-Chapter Sixteen-

Special Agent Robert Turner was waiting in Terry Daly's office when Daly came in.

"Good morning, Terry," Turner said cheerily.

"Good morning, Bobby. I somehow get the feeling that you are about to tell me something I really don't want to know. Is this about Rodrigo?

"Yup."

"What do you have?"

Turner opened the file. "First, CIS has nothing on him. Never heard of him. I checked with State. They never issued a visa. And they checked back 29 years."

"Jesus. I was right."

"There's more," Turner said.

"Wait a second. Pat, ask Carter and RE to come in, will you," Daly said to his secretary. "Hold on a second until they get here."

Turner delayed his report. He and Daly talked about Washington and Daly started to give him and overview of the meeting. He was interrupted by the arrival of Brown and Ewing.

"Bobby has some interesting news about this guy Rodrigo, the one I've been wondering about. Go ahead Bobby."

Turner greeted the two deputies, repeated the information he had given Daly and then added, "Not only has the government never heard of him, but Temple University never heard of him either."

"Are you sure?"

"No question. They checked the list of graduates of the Tyler School of Fine Arts going back to 1970. Then they checked several other schools too. Nothing. But, he does have a Social Security number"

"Probably bogus?" Daly said. "But why would a guy lie to a girl he's dating about something so simple as his country of origin, his citizenship and where he went to college?"

"I don't know, but it doesn't pass the sniff test," said Brown. "What we need is his photo and prints. Should we have a talk with him?"

"Not yet," said Daly. "Bobby, find out where he lives and you and RE get over to his apartment. Put a bug on his phone and see if you can get something from his computer. Be quick and be neat. Don't leave anything behind. Use the phone company decoy."

"Boss, you know we can't do that without a court order," Brown said.

"I know. But we're not going to use this as evidence, only as a lead. Let's see where this takes us," Daly said.

Turner and Ewing put on phone company uniforms and went to the underground garage to the FBI truck with Verizon markings. Turner drove up the Deegan Expressway as Ewing prepared a phony work order in the event it was needed. They parked the truck in front of the 949 Palmer Avenue address in Bronxville and walked to the entrance. The door was locked.

"Don't alert the super," Ewing said. "He might say something to Rodrigo. Pick an apartment number on a different floor and dial the number." Turner pushed the button for 2C.

"Yes, who is it?" said a female voice.

"Verizon, ma'am. You know, the phone company. The super isn't available and we need to check the main cable to the building," said Ewing. "We don't need access to any apartment." The occupant of 2C pressed the button unlocking the door. There were two hallways one on each side of the lobby. "Take the left. I'll take the right. See what the numbers are."

"This side," Turner called out after a moment. He held the elevator door for his partner.

"I hope this guy doesn't have electronic security."

At the door to 3H, Ewing stood behind Turner to shield his skillful use of locksmith tools. Inside, Ewing shut the door and whispered, "I just hope no one saw us."

"I hope this guy doesn't come home now. We better get to work," Turner said.

Turner went into the bedroom, found the phone and placed the bug inside the speaker. Ewing booted the computer and checked the desktop and "c" drive.

"This is curious," he said. "The guy has AOL AND holy shit, a T-1 line. Do you know how much that costs?" He found no trace of any records. He carefully searched the desk for disks and found none.

"This guy apparently doesn't use this thing very much or he erases all his messages," Ewing said. "There's no record of any word processing or use of any software application. I can't get into his email without the password or without using Carnivore. And we're not authorized to use Carnivore."

"I'd use Carnivore in a heart beat. If he is up to something I want to know before something goes down," Turner said.

Ewing wrote down the phone number. "While we're here, let's turn the place. Check the other bedroom."

Turner slowly opened the bureau drawers to ensure no pins were set to alert Rodrigo should one fall out of place. The bureau contained underwear, t-shirts, socks and shorts. Expensive suits, sports jackets, a half dozen pairs of slacks, several dozen shirts and some tasteful colorful ties filled the closet. On the floor of the closet were three pairs of dress shoes, docksiders, sandals and a pair of running shoes. Turner failed to see a concealed door to a small compartment. The top three drawers of the second bureau contained long and short sleeved polo shirts that offered more evidence that Rodrigo was a careful and stylish dresser. Frustrated, Turner joined his partner in the kitchen.

"I'd say this guy eats out most of the time. There's nothing but soda and beer in the fridge, and a few snacks," Ewing said. "You get anything?"

"Nothing. He's a smart dresser, expensive clothes and that's all we know. I sure hope he likes to chat on the phone. Are you finished?" Turner asked.

"In a minute," Ewing said. He opened the dishwasher and pulled out the top drawer. Several glasses lay waiting to be washed. "See if you can find a plastic bag, Bobby."

Turner opened several drawers and found a box of food storage bags. He pulled one and held it open. Spreading his hand on the inside of the glass Ewing picked it up and dropped it into the bag that Turner sealed.

"Make sure we're clean and let's get out of here," Turner said. "I think we better use the stairs. No sense running into a curious neighbor trying to use the elevator."

Turner carefully placed the bag containing the glass into the Verizon tool kit. The two agents made a visual sweep of the apartment before leaving.

At the door, Ewing looked through the visitor identification peephole. The corridor was empty. Outside, they jumped into the truck. Turner listened for the ring on the bug receiver as Ewing dialed Rodrigo's number. "Got it," he said and disconnected. Ewing picked up his secure cell phone and dialed Daly's private number.

"Daly."

"All set boss. No problems and no one saw us. I don't think we are going to get much on this guy. He appears to be very careful."

"How do you know that?" Daly asked.

"Nothing in the bedrooms, no photos, no personal stuff, no bills or records. And no food in the kitchen, just snacks. There's nothing on the computer, either. No record of any work. Either he erases everything from the hard drive and its backup, or he doesn't use the computer except for email. But I did find something curious."

"What's that?" Daly asked.

"He uses AOL. That's not unusual. But what is unusual is he uses a very expensive and private T-1 line."

"T-1 line. How many people you know have their own T-1 line in their residence?" Daly asked.

"No one I know could afford it. By the way, I picked up a dirty glass from the dishwasher. I'll have it dusted for prints and checked for DNA."

"What kind of email has he been writing?"

"Can't access that without Carnivore," said Ewing. "Do I have your permission?"

"What do you think?"

"OK, whatever you say," Ewing said. He knew by the answer that Daly didn't give him permission. Nor did he say no either. He thought briefly about telling Daly using Carnivore was a bad idea, but changed his mind.

"RE, I'll notify the "e" boys to start monitoring the bug," said Daly. "Let call this operation Conquistador in honor of the country he never lived in."

After returning to his office Ewing closed the door and called special ops.

"Jim Meyer," said the cheery voice on the other end.

"Jim. This is RE. Ah, Roosevelt Ewing, A-T Detail."

Meyer checked internal phone ID. "RE it's been a long time. I keep missing you at weapons requal. How've you been?"

"Just fine, Jim. My boss keeps sending me on details when I have a requal date. I'll get there soon. Want me to call you?" Ewing asked his FBI Academy roommate.

"Yeah. Give me about a week's notice so I can jiggle my schedule and get away from this nightmare."

"Will do. Listen, Jim, we're tracking a suspect and we need to use Carnivore Two. Terry Daly is aware of this if you have to verify."

"I trust you, RE. Ever use Carnivore Two before?"

"I'm familiar with the original. What's the difference?"

"Much better than Carnivore. Tracks and records email messages and instant messages from the sender and receiver. Stacks them by date and time and cross checks them by the name of sender and receiver.

"Then, using the screen name of each person in a chatroom, it will find each person's real name and address and credit card used to pay for the ISP. All I need is the person's name and ISP. Who is the perp and when do you want to activate?" Meyer asked.

"His name is Tony Rodrigo. That's probably short for Anthony or Antonio. He uses AOL." Ewing said. "He also has his own T-1 line."

"T-1 line! Wow! I'll have to get the details from the phone company for that. In the meantime give me the perp's address and phone number.

Ewing gave Meyer all the information he requested and asked for reports by email.

"OK, RE," Meyer said. "We'll activate what we call a Carni Coupling in a couple of minutes."

"Thanks, Jim. Oh, by the way. We may want to do a Carni Coupling on anyone he gets an email from. Is that possible?"

"That's automatic, RE. Carnivore Two records Instant Messages from the sender and the receiver and tells us their real names. I don't think the internet service providers know we can do that."

"Thanks. Hope to see you at the range real soon."

Ewing opened the door to his office and walked through the cubicle grouping to Daly's office. "All taken care of on my end, boss."

Daly looked up, his face first indicating curiosity, then satisfaction. "Great. The "e" boys will monitor the bug when sound activates it. Bobby," he said to the agent standing behind Ewing, "anything else on Rodrigo. Anything back from latent prints?"

"Nothing yet, boss. I don't think we'll get anything either from our boys or Interpol or the Yard. And probably nothing from Mossad either."

"If we have to we can pick this guy up on immigration charges."

"Big fucking deal," Ewing weighed in. "That's like ticketing him for riding his bike on the frigging side walk."

"True. But that will prevent him from running. Check his bank records and credit cards. He has to have a credit card if he has AOL." Daly ordered. "And then see if he has a cell phone."

Ewing called Preston Sandford at AOL and obtained the credit card company Rodrigo used to pay his internet bill. A call to them resulted in an email containing Rodrigo's activity report for the last six months and the name of the bank Rodrigo used. The bank faxed a copy of the last six month's activity. Ewing printed out the email and put the fax and emails side by side on his desk. Some numbers jumped out at him.

"Jesus Christ," he uttered. He took the sheets to Daly's office. Thrusting the papers onto the desk he said, "Take a look at this."

Daly followed where Ewing was pointing. "Well I'll be damned. Will you look at that?"

"Look at what?" Turner asked.

"This bank statement for our friend Rodrigo. The latest one shows he has a balance of more than $90,000."

"90 K is a lot of money for someone who is a graphic artist. RE, did he have any other accounts, savings, money market, anything like that?" Turner asked.

"No other accounts. But look at the activity. He has six straight monthly deposits of 50K. That's 300K. And each month there's a withdrawal of exactly $30,000 in cash plus others. There's a distinct pattern here.

Looking closer, Daly said, "let's find out where these deposits came from. Maybe we can nail this guy on an income tax rap. There is something illegal going on here you can bet on that. The question is what?"

Daly, Turner and Ewing were soon joined by Carter Brown. Ewing brought Brown up to date. "I have to admit, boss, you have a nose for the bad guys," Brown said..

"I can smell shit miles away," Daly said. "And this guy is beginning to stink. Every single one of these deposits was in cash. Who the hell sends 50 thousand dollars in cash through the mail? And what does he do with the cash he withdraws? RE, you're the expert here. Start with the bank and get his entire banking history. Let's see where that leads. Bobby, put a tail on him and put his apartment under surveillance.

Daly returned to his office and the stack of reports.

Ewing began to compile a financial dossier on Rodrigo. According to bank records, he had been depositing huge amounts of money each month and withdrawing somewhat smaller amounts. All transactions were in cash and were always the same. He had no checking account indicating he paid all of his bills with cash or a money order. His credit card expenses were automatically deducted from his bank account as were his monthly utility bills and apartment maintenance.

Ewing verified Rodrigo's Social Security number on the bank statement with Social Security in Washington. But he drew a blank with the IRS who reported that Rodrigo dutifully declared his income from his job and made additional quarterly payments.

The 1040 indicated that Rodrigo was a Graphics Consultant and his non-corporate income was from a personal services contract with *Saudi Arabia!*

He called Daly.

"Terry, our friend Rodrigo lists huge amounts of income from, get this, Saudi Arabia. He has a personal services contract as a graphics consultant."

"I suspected we'd find something like that. And that isn't illegal. Keep digging."

-Chapter Seventeen-

"Pantone Associates. This is Tony Rodrigo."

"Tony, hi, it's Ann Dunn. How are you?"

"Hi Ann," Rodrigo responded looking at his door to see if Angela was nearby. "How are you? Is anything wrong?"

"No, nothing's wrong. Chris Corman signed off on the copy. There are a few changes. Listen, you live in Westchester, right?" Dunn said, biting her lip.

"Yeah, why?"

"Well, if you like, we can arrange to meet at Grand Central, and I'll give you the layouts. Save you a trip over here. If you have time, we can have a drink at a bar in the terminal. If that's too noisy for you, we can meet in Westchester somewhere. I get off in Hartsdale, where do you get off?"

"Bronxville," Rodrigo replied. "I think Hartsdale is three or four stops after that."

"Hey, if you want a quieter place, we can both get off in Hartsdale and have a drink and I'll drive you home."

Rodrigo thought about Dunn's taking her jacket off in the elevator. A plan began to hatch.

"Tony, are you still there?"

"Yeah, sorry, Ann, someone just handed me a note. Listen, I've been out walking. Just got back from a client," Rodrigo lied. "I would like to go home take a shower and change. Would you mind if I met you at your place, or some place near you?"

"Not at all. In fact, that's a good idea. I'll go home, shower and change into something more comfortable than this suit. Let me give you my address," Dunn said delighted that Rodrigo was so willing.

Rodrigo copied the address, tore the paper from the pad and put it in his pocket. "What time, Ann?"

"I can be ready by seven. Why don't we make it for dinner? My treat," Dunn said.

"Seven is fine. I'm leaving now anyway. Going to catch the 4:50. We can discuss who pays over a drink."

"Deal. I know a neat seafood restaurant over in Eastchester. It's terrific! Or, if you're not afraid to try my cooking, we can eat here. But you have to bring the wine. Your choice."

Rodrigo's thoughts turned erotic. "Tell me what you plan to serve and I'll bring the wine. Jeans Ok?"

"Be yourself and wear what makes you comfortable. We'll have salmon, a salad and roasted red potatoes. How's that sound?" Dunn asked hoping it met with his approval.

"Sounds wonderful. I'll get a bottle of chardonnay."

"You know, I think I'll get out of here early and catch the 4:50 too. What car will you be in?" Dunn asked.

"I usually sit in the last car, the one closest to the track entrance."

"Save me a seat if you can. I'm almost ready to leave. "

"OK, see you in a bit. Bye"

"Who was that?" Angela Hart asked.

"Oh hi, Angela," a startled Rodrigo replied. "I didn't see you there. That was Ann Dunn. She called to tell me she has the layouts ready for me. We're going to meet on the train so she can give them to me and save me a trip to her office."

"Why can't she just messenger them over here?"

"Actually, I never thought of that. Maybe she wanted to save her company some money. Who knows?" Rodrigo responded weakly.

"Yeah, probably. Well, I have a couple of things to finish and then I'm out of here too. See you tomorrow."

"OK. Maybe we can have lunch."

"Fine," Hart said as Rodrigo turned off his desk lamp.

Rodrigo sat on the aisle in the last double seat in the last car and began to read *The New York Times* when Dunn appeared. "This seat taken?" she asked coyly.

"Actually, it is. I was saving it for a very attractive art director with long dark hair."

"By coincidence," Dunn answered, "I happen to be an art director. And I have long dark hair."

"Then you must be the one," Rodrigo smiled pointing to the adjacent seat. "Please sit down, madam art director."

Dunn placed her brief case in the overhead rack as Rodrigo folded his newspaper and stuffed it between his hip and the window. The two began talking. Rodrigo asked Dunn about her company and how long she had been employed.

"I've been working there 18 years," Dunn said. "Started as an art assistant right out of college. Now I have a staff of eight including the web page designers. I love the company. They have been very good to me. What about you, Tony?"

"Nothing special, really. Been at Pantone a few years. Really like the job and my boss, Tim Robbins. He says he knows you. Speaks very highly of you."

"I've known Tim for eight or nine years. He's a great guy. Lost his first wife in the world trade center attacks. That was tough. But he's ok now," Dunn went on.

"Mind if I ask a personal question?" Rodrigo asked changing the subject before it became an issue.

"You can ask. And if it isn't too personal, I'll answer. How's that?"

"Fair enough," Rodrigo replied. "What I want to know is how come a beautiful, talented and well dressed woman doesn't have a husband."

"Never really had the time. I've concentrated on my career. And now that I'm fairly successful... well maybe it's too late," Dunn answered. "You know this is new for me. I've never dated a business associate before. I hope you don't mind my calling you."

"Mind? Are you kidding? To be truthful I've wanted to ask you, but because you are a client, I didn't think I should. I'm not sure Tim would approve."

"Tim doesn't have to know. And as long as we're telling the truth, I'll be honest too. I find you very attractive and I just decided to take a chance."

"I'm glad you did."

"Tickets, please," said the conductor. Rodrigo and Dunn showed their monthly commuter passes.

"Do you have a girlfriend, Tony?" Dunn asked changing the tone.

"No. I date every now and then, but no one special. And I'm not married, if that is worrying you."

"I guessed you weren't married. Are you and Angela good friends?"

"We're friends. We work together on some projects and we have lunch together sometimes. Stuff like that," Rodrigo lied.

"She's a good looking woman and she has a great body."

"I suppose."

"Oh come on, Tony. Oh never mind. I'd like to be 25 again."

"Ann, don't take this the wrong way, but I think you look great. And you have a great figure." Rodrigo looked across the aisle at the passengers who were keenly interested in their conversation as were the passengers sitting in the seat in front. "Ah, we better change the subject. Too many nosey people," he whispered.

Dunn laughed. "I'm making you nervous. You're blushing," She put her hand on Rodrigo's thigh for a moment. "I'm sorry. I didn't mean to embarrass you."

Rodrigo seized the moment and closed his hand over hers. "I'm not embarrassed," he whispered. "And you do have a great body. You are, ah very, very attractive."

"Thank you, sir," Dunn replied. "Now it's my turn to blush. Maybe we should wait until later to get better acquainted." Dunn moved her hand from under Rodrigo's and asked him for a section of the paper. The two began reading.

"The next station stop is Bronxville. Bronxville, next," said the conductor.

Dunn rose to allow Rodrigo to get up. "You can have the paper, Ann. I'll see you at seven."

"Thanks, Tony," Dunn replied taking the paper. "Wait a minute. I forgot to give you the layouts." She pulled her briefcase from the overhead rack, opened it and handed Rodrigo the envelope. "Chris told me the changes are straightforward and clear. I have a photo copy. If you have any questions, call me."

Rodrigo clutched the layouts and headed for the door. Dunn watched and was a little surprised at her thoughts.

Rodrigo entered his apartment and stopped dead. He sniffed. He walked around and inhaled deeply. *What is that smell. Is it perfume?* In the kitchen a drawer was slightly open. When he looked at the clock his thoughts turned to the coming evening with Dunn, and her tight slacks and he hastily went to his bedroom, hung up his slacks and tossed the rest of his clothes into the hamper. After his shower, he changed into jeans and a polo shirt and then put a toothbrush, shaving kit, cologne, a change of underwear and a clean shirt in a paper bag. The phone rang and Rodrigo let the answering machine screen the call.

"Hi Tony, it's Angela. Just wondered if you felt like hanging out. But you may not be home yet. I'm still at the office. Give me a call at home."

Not tonight. Rodrigo pulled the door shut and walked to the elevator.

Dunn found her car in the commuter lot and raced to the supermarket picking up salad material, 16 ounces of fresh salmon, an onion and a bag of red potatoes.

When she got home, she went to her bedroom, put on a CD and hastily disrobed, throwing her clothes on the bed. Before she stepped into the shower she tucked her ponytail inside her shower cap, adjusting it in front of the mirror.

She studied her figure. She was in good shape for her 5 foot 8 inch frame. Small love handles had developed on her sides, but her breasts showed no signs of her nearing her 41st birthday. She cupped them and turned and patted her right buttock. *No cellulite yet.*

The shower felt good. She closed her eyes and let her mind drift with thoughts of Rodrigo. Her hands wandered over her body. *Tall and suave. I wonder if...*

Rodrigo had trouble finding a place to park near the liquor store making him anxious, and 10 minutes late. He parked in the driveway of Dunn's center hall colonial. *She must make a nice salary to afford this.* He left the car unlocked and grabbed the bag with the wine leaving the paper bag with the clothes and toiletries on the front seat. He rang the bell waiting politely for about a minute before ringing it again.

Dunn opened the door. She was draped in a large blue towel.

"Tony, I'm sorry. Please forgive me. I ran a little late. I'm not finished dressing. Make yourself comfortable. The paper's on the table in the family room and the TV controller is around somewhere." Dunn raced upstairs showing Rodrigo a substantial portion of her long legs and just enough of her bottom.

"You don't have to get dressed just for me," Rodrigo joked.

Dunn stopped at the top of the stairs, looked at Rodrigo below and grinned. "I'll bet. You'd like that. You men are all alike. Oh, you can put the wine in the fridge and if you like make yourself a drink. The liquor is in the cabinet next to the microwave."

"What do you have?" Rodrigo asked.

"Anything you like. Make me a Jack Daniels on the rocks, please. I'll be down in a second."

Rodrigo put the wine in the fridge and pulled the familiar Jack Daniels bottle from the shelf. He searched several cabinets before finding the glasses that he half filled with ice. He took a long pull from his drink before pouring hers. The warmth spread slowly in his stomach and he began to relax. He carried both drinks into the family room and deliberately chose the sofa sitting in the middle. He was reading the front page of *The Times* when Dunn walked in wearing jeans and a t-shirt.

"Sorry Tony," she said taking the drink from him. "Thanks. This will hit the spot."

They clicked glasses and said "cheers." Rodrigo was admiring Dunn's form as she took a healthy swallow. He averted her eyes when she caught him looking at her chest. She was not wearing a bra.

Dunn brushed by him deliberately letting her breast touch his arm as she went to the kitchen. "I'm going to prepare the potatoes," she said. "Do you want to make the salad?"

She stopped in her tracks and turned to see Rodrigo staring at her behind. Dunn smiled and walked over to him. "That's twice I caught you leering at me. Do you like what you see?"

Rodrigo put his drink down and placed his hands on her shoulders and nodded. "Very much."

"I'm glad. Because I like you too." She tilted her head and they kissed. One hand clasped her drink; the other found the back of his head. Rodrigo inhaled sharply and encircled her waist drawing her charms to him. Their tongues touched tentatively at first gently exploring. Dunn moaned and pushed Rodrigo away gently. "I'm starved," she said patting his face before turning toward the kitchen.

Rodrigo gave her bottom a gentle pat, "Tease," he whispered.

"Actually you'll find I'm not a tease, Tony, but if we start, we'll miss dinner. And I am hungry." She let his hand linger and felt him squeeze her cheek. "I've got a fat butt," she said responding to his playfulness.

Emboldened by her comments, Rodrigo slipped his hand inside the waist band of Dunn's jeans. She turned to him and kissed him removing his hand gently. "Eat now, play later," she said.

Rodrigo took full advantage of the close quarters in the kitchen as he and Dunn prepared dinner. Each time he walked behind her he slipped his hand over her bottom.

Dunn smiled and thought about touching him intimately.

"Ann can I ask you another personal question?"

"Sure, same rules apply. If it's not too personal, I'll answer."

Rodrigo paused, then asked, "Do you go to work braless?"

"Hmmmmm. Sometimes. When I know I won't be taking off my suit jacket I sometimes wear a silk blouse. The silk feels good on my skin. Satisfied?"

"I guess so. I think you were wearing a bra in your office the other day."

"I was. Why all this interest in bras?"

"Well I couldn't help but notice that you aren't wearing one now and I wondered if, ah why?" Rodrigo said.

"I find bras restricting. You guys should have to wear them." She laughed. "I hope you aren't complaining."

"Not at all, believe me."

"So do you like me, better this way," Dunn asked looking down at the nipples poking against the t-shirt. She edged closer to him and he took the hint putting the paring knife down.

Rodrigo slipped his hands under her shirt and moved them gently to her breasts, letting his thumbs roll over the hardened nipples. Dunn sighed. "You have warm hands, Tony. You're making me hot."

He dropped his hands and slipped them inside the back of her jeans. She was wearing no panties. His hands cupped the cheeks of her bare bottom. "God you feel good. I want to see you naked."

Dunn pulled her head back and looked directly into his eyes. "I can tell you're excited. I want you too. But I want to eat first. Please. I am starved. I only had a cup of yogurt all day."

Rodrigo removed his hands. Patting a cheek he said, "dessert."

By 9 the two had finished dinner and Dunn rose to clear away the dishes. "That was lovely, Tony. You grilled the salmon perfectly."

"I really liked those potatoes. The sautéed onions made them really special," Rodrigo said as he began washing the pan in which the potatoes had been roasted.

Dunn rinsed the plates and placed them in the dishwasher. "Would you like some more wine," she asked pouring a half glass for herself. "We have plenty."

"I'll take a little, please."

They finished the kitchen cleanup and carried their glasses into the family room. Dunn surprised Rodrigo by turning off the light. "Let's go upstairs for dessert."

They put their glasses on the dresser and fell into each other's arms. After a short kiss, Rodrigo removed Dunn's shirt. She fumbled for his buckle and soon had his pants down by the ankles. He stepped free and she yanked his underpants. He stepped out of his boxers and raised her head to kiss her. While they embraced he unbuttoned the top of her jeans and pulled the zipper down. The jeans fell to the floor. Before she could step free, Rodrigo scooped her up and gently placed her on the bed.

"Let's pull down the spread first," she said jumping off. With the spread on the floor and the fitted bottom sheet exposed, the two melted together in a hot kiss as their hands ranged over each other.

Dunn moaned slightly as she was rolled onto her back and Rodrigo began kissing and licking his way down to her breasts gently sucking both nipples. He rolled his tongue over each breast before returning to the nipples. He continued lower and began moving his tongue over the lips of Dunn's sex. "Oh God," she moaned. "Right there."

Within minutes, Dunn was writhing in orgasm. "YES, YES, YES," she hissed through clenched teeth.

Rodrigo stopped, allowing Dunn to come down from her climax. He rolled onto his side and held her closely, his right leg over her.

"That was wonderful. Absolute heaven," Dunn whispered. "You are a man of many talents." They lay holding each other as Dunn's breathing returned to normal. She kissed Rodrigo and said "Your turn." She rolled Rodrigo onto his back and slowly lowered her face to the chest, the stomach and finally to his half rigid organ. "I'll have him standing tall in a moment," she said as she engulfed him. She was right. Having achieved her goal she moved to a sitting position astride Rodrigo's hips and impaled herself on him.

Rodrigo groaned as Dunn began the slow rhythm. He held her hips and guided the pace.

Within minutes she knew he was close and so was she. The pace increased with the urgency. At last Rodrigo exploded followed seconds later by Dunn. She dropped her head to the pillow next to him.

"That was spectacular," Rodrigo said. They were completely spent.

Dunn lay still for a time before rolling off Rodrigo. "What time do you want to get up tomorrow?" she asked Rodrigo.

"I have to go home to change. Better set the alarm for 6."

"Six? I usually get up at 6:45. You are costing me an extra 45 minutes of sleep," she whined in a joking manner before setting the alarm.

"It's only a little after 10 so you'll get a good seven hours," Rodrigo teased. "Did I tire you out?"

"We can go again, if you like," Dunn said hoping Rodrigo would decline the offer.

"I'll take a rain check," he said.

"Sounds delicious." She pulled the sheet over them snuggling next to him. Rodrigo held her close and the two kissed passionately.

"I'm beat," she whispered. "Let's get some sleep." She turned out the light.

Angela Hart put the phone down after getting Rodrigo's answering machine for the fourth time. She opened the cabinet over the fridge and removed the phone book turning to the D's. She found the address of A. Dunn, the only Dunn in Hartsdale. The Westchester map revealed the address off Central Park Avenue, a short drive from her apartment.

Tentatively, Hart turned on to Maplewood Road and stopped to study the numbers.

Number 39 is odd so it has to be on the left. She drove two hundred yards as the numbers came down to 45. Three houses away she spotted Rodrigo's car. She accelerated and drove by. *The lights are off. They're in bed. That fucking bastard.*

-Chapter Eighteen-

Before the alarm went off, Rodrigo had showered and shaved and returned naked to the bed where Ann Dunn lay after silencing the radio.

"Good morning," Rodrigo said as he eased himself along side Dunn's naked body.

"Hmmmm. Good morning, Tony. Did you sleep well?" She turned to him.

"Do you know the only thing better than sleeping the sleep of the just?" Rodrigo asked.

"No, what?"

"Sleeping the sleep of the just after," Rodrigo chuckled as he rolled Dunn on top of him.

"Hey, no fair. You showered," Dunn hummed as she rolled off. "And you shaved too. What time did you get up?"

"I've been up for about a half hour," Rodrigo said. "I'm an early riser and I don't need a lot of sleep."

"Too bad," Dunn said. "You could have showered with me and maybe we could have found time for play."

"Didn't you complain last night about getting up so early? And now you want to play?"

"I'm wide awake and seeing your naked body turns me on. Last night was unbelievable. It's been over a year for me, Tony."

"That's hard to believe. You're an incredibly sexy woman. Most men would love to change places with me." Rodrigo said.

"The only men I see are those I work with. I am not a bar person," Dunn replied running a hand along Rodrigo's cheek.

"What about the internet? Ever considered using that to attract a guy?"

"I considered it," Dunn said. "A girlfriend of mine tried it and found a great guy. They've been going together for several months. I'm not that trusting. There are a lot of creeps out there."

Rodrigo put his arm around Dunn and caressed her bare bottom. "I love to touch your fanny," he said patting one cheek.

"Well I love to have you touch my fanny," Dunn purred. "Tony I was thinking. We're going to spend two nights in Saratoga Springs. I'd love some company."

"Company? As in this kind of company?" Rodrigo asked as he caressed her breasts.

"Yes, that kind, but I'd also like to spend some time together seeing the town, dining in some nice places, taking walks. Stuff like that. There will be some down time and I'd like to get to know you better."

Rodrigo felt a stirring in his groin. "I know one thing we could do," he chuckled. He kissed Dunn passionately and quickly turned and rolled out of bed. "But I have to go. Got to get home and change."

"So does that mean yes?"

"Why not."

"Wonderful. Want to drive together?" Dunn continued as she slipped out of bed. "We can take my car."

"Yeah. You drive and I'll find places to put my hands."

"And just where would that be?" she teased, cupping her breasts.

"You'll find out. Seriously, I've got to go or I'll be late." He meant to kiss her quickly, but Dunn put her hands on his butt and held him tight. Her tongue found his. He almost succumbed to her charms before gently pushing her away. "I really do have to go." Rodrigo put on his clothes and combed his hair.

Dunn pulled her robe from the closet and put it on as she and Rodrigo walked downstairs. "Don't forget. If you have any trouble with Chris's edits, or you don't understand something, call me."

"I will."

She kissed him at the door as his hands roamed inside the robe. "Tony, make love to me right here. You can be a little late."

"I'd love to, Ann, but I have to finish *Single Maltings* and get the film made." He gave her fanny a smack before opening the door.

"Bye Tony," she said holding the robe closed..

"Bye Ann. Thanks for a wonderful evening."

Rodrigo arrived at the office at 8:30. He made some coffee and settled down with the layouts carefully making the changes page by page. When he had finished, he reviewed each change checking the kerning to make sure the text broke correctly. Satisfied, he took another sip of his coffee and called the imaging department.

"Imaging, this is Jason."

"Jason, Tony Rodrigo. I've got the final changes on *Single Maltings*. I'll print a hard copy and then send you the files in a couple of minutes. You made all the color seps so all we have to do is make the film and proofs. Can you do that today?"

"If everything checks out, we should have the film by late this afternoon, Tony. When do you go to press?"

"I'm planning to take the stuff with me on Sunday. We go to press on Monday."

"Send the file as soon as you can and we'll get started. Call me about 2 and I'll give you a progress report."

"OK, sorry for the short notice. I just got the final corrections last night. I had to input them this morning," Rodrigo explained.

"It'll be tight. We have Angela's *Horizons* pub on the schedule too and she is trying to get a press date for Monday or Tuesday. But I think we can handle it," Jason Pulver said.

Damn, Angela and Ann in Saratoga Springs at the same time. Shit "Did Angela send her files yet?"

"She said she would send them by 10 this morning."

"That's cool. Since I have a definite press date, please do the film for *Single Maltings* first. OK?"

"That's the plan, Tony. We'll get started as soon as we get the file."

"You'll have the file in 10 minutes." Rodrigo hung up and began printing a copy of each page of *Single Maltings*. When the last page had come from his printer, Rodrigo sent each page file to the Imaging Department. Then he called Pulver.

"Imaging. This is Jason."

"Jason. I sent the files. I'll have the hard copy dropped off as soon as I can get a company messenger here."

"Wait a second," Pulver said. "OK, the files are coming through. We'll get started right away."

"Thanks."

Rodrigo picked up his coffee cup and went to the pantry. He poured another cup and grabbed a donut from the box that Tim Robbins brought in every day for his staff.

"Good morning, Tony," Angela Hart said coolly.

"Hi Angela. How are you?" Rodrigo asked, taking a bite from the donut.

Do you care, you bastard. Here I am sleeping with you, protecting you from Ellen Daly and you jump in the sack with another woman. "I'm fine, thank you," she said sweetly turning on her heels to return to her office.

What the hell did I say? He quickly caught up with her. "Angela, what's wrong?"

"You don't know?" Hart asked.

"All I did was say good morning and ask how you were and you cop this attitude."

"I called you five times last night."

Shit, here it comes.

"I left four messages. Where the hell were you?"

"I was busy. I had dinner out and got home after 9:30. I went to bed without checking my messages," Rodrigo lied. "And I didn't check them this morning. What did you want?"

"It's not important. Now excuse me I have to try to get a press date." Hart tried to brush past Rodrigo who blocked her path.

"If it's not important, then why are you so upset?" he asked.

"I'm not upset. I just don't like being lied to."

"What are you talking about?"

"I think you know perfectly well. You weren't home last night and you weren't at a restaurant either. So you figure it out. Now, please let me get by," Hart seethed.

Rodrigo let her pass without saying a word.

She returned to her cubicle and alerted the Imaging Department she was sending her files. Jason Pulver informed her Rodrigo's film and proofs would be produced first and that he probably would not get to her work until late afternoon. "If I have to stay tonight I will, Angela. It will be ready for final proof tomorrow."

"Thanks, Jason. I really appreciate it."

198

Hart looked over the rim of her cubicle and saw Rodrigo. Seeking to avoid another confrontation she hurried to the pantry and poured another cup of coffee. When she returned, the phone was ringing.

"Pantone Associates, this is Angela," she said.

"Angela, good morning, it's Vera Perry from Time Warner. Have you got a minute?"

"Yes. Good morning, Vera. I was expecting your call this week."

"I wanted to call earlier, but I've been putting out little fires here. Anyway, did Tim speak to you about our project?"

"He did. No real details, though," Hart replied.

"We're planning a new employee publication. Eight to 12 page tabloid. Initially it will be every other month, then possibly monthly. What we need is an original front page design using the Time Warner logo, and some carry through design for continuity. Then we'll need layouts and pre-press," Perry explained.

"Do you know what kind of paper you plan to use? Will there be color art or just black and white. Line drawings or process?"

"I don't know about the paper, but it should be a good quality offset. And it will be process color, up to 2 photos and or art per page on average."

"Do you have a printer in mind?" Hart asked.

"We have used a printer in Pennsylvania. Brown Printing. Do you know them?"

"Yes," Hart replied. "We've used them. If you like I can give you the names of 2-3 other printers and once you've determined the specs, the frequency and the number of copies, we can do an RFP. Oh, sorry, that's a request for proposal."

"Wonderful. Do you guys handle RFPs?"

"We can, but most clients prefer to prepare the RFPs themselves because they sign the printing contracts. But we can offer technical help and answer the printers' questions," Hart explained.

"All right, fill me in on the details when we meet."

"I'm finishing up a job now, Vera. Trying to get a press date for next week. Can we meet Wednesday or Thursday, the 26th or 27th? My schedule is wide open both days."

199

"Hang on a minute." Perry turned her calendar to the week of the 24th. "Wednesday the 26th is good for me. How about I come to your place and we can chat? Then you can give me a tour and show me what you guys do. Is 10 OK?"

"Ten's fine. And I'll give you a guided tour," Hart replied.

"Look forward to it. See you then, Angela. Goodbye."

"Goodbye Vera."

Hart found the number for Quad Graphics in her computer file. She called and asked for the representative who handled Pantone's accounts.

"Quad Graphics, this is Lee."

"Lee, good morning. It's Angela Hart at Pantone."

"Hi, Angela. What's up?"

"We're finishing *Horizons* and we need a press date next week. I can have the film shipped or I can bring it with me on Sunday," Hart said. *Please have some press time.*

"Angela, let me call scheduling. I'll get right back to you."

"Fine, Bye."

Hart accessed the *Horizon* files and sent them to Imaging. She began printing a copy of each page. The phone rang. It was Lee Baxter at Quad Graphics.

"We can fit you in late Monday or Tuesday, Angela. Did you know Tony is printing *Single Maltings* next week?"

"Yeah. He told me. When you say late Monday, how late do you mean?" Hart asked.

"Probably late enough to be early Tuesday, I'm afraid. You know how this business works. But we'll try to fit you in earlier if there's an opening. When are you planning to come up?"

"I was planning to come on Sunday," Hart said. "I'll have the film and proofs with me. Then Monday sometime I can look at the blues. Is that OK."

"Sure. I'll make sure our Plate Department knows the film is coming. What time will you get here Sunday?"

"I should be there before noon. That way I can get a nice lunch and take a long walk"

"Sounds like a plan. I'll see you on Monday."

"Great Lee. Bye."

Hart found another number and dialed the Sheraton City Center in Saratoga Springs. She asked for reservations.

"Reservations. How may I help you?"

"Hi, I need to book a room for Sunday and Monday nights, October 16 and 17. My name is Angela Hart from Pantone Associates in New York City."

"One moment please." While waiting for the clerk, Hart pulled the printed copies of *Horizons* from her printer and put them in the manila envelope labeled Imaging Dept. She put it in her out box, then put it back on her desk. *I better walk this down there myself.* "Ms. Hart," the hotel clerk said, "you have a room for both nights, departing on the 18th. May I have your credit card number, please?"

She removed her corporate credit card from her wallet and read the number to the clerk who repeated it and then gave Hart her confirmation number. Slipping the number into the pocket of her calendar diary, she turned off her computer and went to the elevator. Rodrigo was waiting and chatting with Tim Robbins.

"Good morning, Angela," Robbins said.

"Hi Tim. I'm on the way to imaging to give them the hard copy of *Horizons*," she explained. "We're going to press early Tuesday I think."

"Oh, that's wonderful. Tony tells me he is going to be there at the same time with *Single Maltings.* Maybe you two can drive up there together."

"That would be terrific, Tim," Rodrigo said. "But Ann Dunn, McLaughlin's art director, already asked me to drive with her since it's her first trip."

"Well, maybe Angela can go along with you. It's up to her, of course. Anyway you two can work that out," Robbins said.

The elevator door opened and Hart and Rodrigo stepped in. Neither said a word until the door had closed and they were safely out of Robbins' hearing.

"If you want to drive up with us, I'll ask Dunn since she volunteered to drive," Rodrigo offered.

"No thanks," Hart said. "I'm sure you don't want me along."

"What's that supposed to mean?"

"Tony, I'm not stupid. And I don't like being lied to. I know where you were last night. It's your business if you want to sleep with her, but you won't be sleeping with me again. Ever!"

"Who said I was sleeping with her?" Rodrigo asked.

"No one had to say anything. I just know. OK?"

"What do you know? I told you where I was last night."

"Tony, I don't like being lied to. I saw your car at Ann's house last night."

Shit. Now she's following me. "I'm not lying. I didn't say I wasn't at Dunn's house. I went there to pick up the corrections she received from the editorial department. I brought them in here first thing, made the corrections and sent the files to imaging."

"Yeah, well when I drove by I didn't see any lights on," Hart said defensively wishing she hadn't admitted she was there.

"We were at the kitchen table and she was going over the changes. The kitchen is in the back of the house. I hope you are satisfied."

Wanting to believe Rodrigo, Hart caved in. "OK, I believe you. I'm sorry I distrusted you but I called you last night to see if you want to come over. I was lonely."

The elevator door opened and the two exited at the entrance to imaging. The receptionist was not at the desk. "It's OK, but I really don't appreciate being followed or being checked on."

"I'm sorry, Tony. It won't happen again. I promise," Hart said.

Rodrigo said nothing as the receptionist appeared. "Hi Tony, hi Angela," she said.

"Hi Bridget, is Jason around?" Hart asked.

"He's making film for Tony," Bridget Rourke said. "Go on back if you want."

Hart took the easy way out. "Just give him this, Bridget. It's the hard copy for *Horizons*. He has the file and he promised he'd make film for me as soon as he finishes Tony's work. I've got to run. I've got another appointment."

"OK, Bye."

Rodrigo waived at Hart as she got on the elevator. After she waived back, Rodrigo turned to enter the Imaging Department bumping into Rourke. "Oh, sorry, Bridget. Didn't see you."

"No problem. You should bump into me more often," said Rourke who was five feet four inches tall and weighed over 200 pounds.

202

Don't hold your breath. "I have to see Jason right away, Bridget." Rodrigo slipped past and walked down the hall to the manager's office. He could feel Rourke's eyes boring into him.

Rodrigo watched Jason Pulver make the magenta, cyan, yellow and black film for pages one and 12. When the four film sheets had been developed, Pulver placed them in correct order one on top of another over a sheet of the same paper on which *Single Maltings* would be printed. The proof came out perfectly. Pulver handed it to Rodrigo who studied it making sure the registration was correct.

"Looks great, Jason."

"Thanks, Tony. Sure wish I was going to Saratoga Springs with you. It's a nice town. Quad is a great printer." Pulver said.

"You know, that's not a bad idea. The art director of McLaughlin is going. This is her first experience with Quad. If you went along, it might send the right message to the client that we really are concerned about the quality of our work," Rodrigo said. "Do you want me to ask Tim?"

"I can't this time, Tony. Too much work to do. But maybe we can swing it for the new clients."

"OK let me know and I'll ask Tim. Listen, I'll touch base with you around 1:30. Looks like you might be finished by then."

"Might be, but you never know. The tolerance in lining up the film sheets for the proofer is very close. One mistake and we start over. But give me a call about 2 just to be safe."

"Two it is," Rodrigo said. He put the proof down on the light table and left the Imaging Department. Hart was standing in the elevator lobby when the doors opened.

"Tony, can we talk?"

"Sure. Let's go to your office."

She led the way and sat down in her chair. Rodrigo sat on one of the two guest chairs. "Would you mind if I went with you?" Hart asked.

Trying to be diplomatic, Rodrigo replied, "Tim's idea was a good one. But he didn't know that Ann Dunn was going along and that *Single Maltings* would be printed before *Horizons*. Your job might run two or ten hours later and I don't think Dunn wants to wait around. I'd love your company, but well, I'm caught with the client. I'm sorry, Angela."

Hart thought a moment and said, "You're right. It's ok, I'll manage. Maybe we can have dinner together Sunday night."

"Sure. That would be nice." *I better find a way to avoid this. I don't want Ann to know I've slept with Angela.*

"When are you leaving for Saratoga Springs?"

"Sometime Sunday, but the exact time is up to Ann. She's driving. And I have a few household chores: laundry, dusting. Shit like that."

"Yeah, me too. I'll call your room when I get to the hotel and we can hook up for dinner."

-Chapter Nineteen-

Tony Rodrigo was excited at the prospect of spending two nights with Ann Dunn at Saratoga Springs. Dunn had asked Rodrigo to spend Saturday night with him at her home before driving north, but Rodrigo begged off using the planned two days away from home as an excuse to catch up on chores. Dunn didn't mind. It only increased her desire. She told Rodrigo to be ready by 9:30 Sunday morning so the two could have a leisurely lunch before checking in at the Sheraton.

Using a chatroom, Rodrigo (MILLERMAN) sent an email message for Atta (NYGAL) at 9:00 a.m., "Will be in SS for two days, back on Tuesday." Atta understood what SS meant. He tolerated the necessary inconveniences.

When ATTA was unavailable an assistant always monitored the chat room looking for familiar screen names. "Will miss you. Have a good time. I have nothing planned."

Dunn was on time and gave Rodrigo a hug and a kiss when he emerged from his apartment. Rodrigo gaped at Dunn's three-month old Infiniti Q-45, but was even more impressed with her tight gray slacks and a white blouse. The top three buttons left were open revealing no bra. He dropped his bag in the trunk and slipped into the luxury car beside Dunn who leaned over to open the glove box to give Rodrigo a clear view of her breast.

Few subjects were unexplored as they drove north on the New York State Thruway and the Northway, stopping once for coffee. It was a few minutes past 12 when they arrived in Saratoga Springs.

"Which way to the printer, Tony?"

"Straight down Broadway to the fork, then make a right."

When they pulled into the parking lot, Rodrigo told Dunn to park as close to the door as possible.

"I'll only be a couple of minutes. It doesn't make a lot of sense for you to come in since management isn't here on Sunday. I'll just drop this stuff off, find out when the blues will be ready and be right out."

"OK," Dunn said.

Rodrigo grabbed the envelope and disappeared inside. Dunn turned on a CD.

She was lost with the music when Rodrigo returned ten minutes later.

"The blues will be ready by 10:30 tomorrow," Rodrigo said. "I'll call our account rep at 9:30 so we can arrange for you to meet the plant manager and get you on a tour of the plant while I check the blues. Then maybe we can hook up with some people for lunch."

"That's great, Tony. Thanks. And speaking of lunch, I'm famished. Where are we going to eat?"

"Let's go back to the hotel. The Olde Bryan Inn is at the end of the hotel parking lot about 150 yards away. They have nice sandwiches, great salads and good soup," Rodrigo said.

"Great idea," said Dunn. "I'd like to take a walk after lunch. See the town."

"OK." Rodrigo directed Dunn back to the Sheraton. She pulled her car into a slot vacated by a car with a Vermont license plate. She held Rodrigo's hand as they walked to the restaurant.

"That was very nice. Good choice," Dunn said as they emerged from the restaurant. They retrieved their luggage from the car and entered the hotel where Dunn told the clerk she had made reservations for two under her name. Rodrigo appeared nervous looking around the lobby. Dunn noticed, but said nothing.

Each signed the credit card slips and received their digital keys. Rodrigo led the way to the elevator. "Why are you so nervous?" Dunn asked.

"I'm not nervous. I was just looking for Angela. She said she would be here this afternoon."

"Oh. Why don't we leave a message in her room and ask her to join us for dinner?"

Rodrigo knew he couldn't say no. Dunn would ask why and Angela would be very angry. "She may not have checked in yet so I'll call the desk and leave a message. They'll give it to her when she checks in."

On the 4th floor, Dunn led the way to rooms 456 and 458. Without saying a word about having arranged for connecting rooms, Dunn opened her door and said, "I'll be ready in about 15 minutes, then we can go for a walk and work off lunch. Want to tell Angela we'll meet her in the lobby at seven?"

"OK. I'll knock on your door in 15 minutes."

Rodrigo entered his room, dropped the luggage on one of the queen beds and called the desk. To his relief, Hart had not yet checked in. In his message he included a suggestion for casual dress.

When he hung up, there was a knock on the inner door. Rodrigo hesitated, then unlocked the connecting door. There stood Dunn. "Do you believe we have connecting rooms?" she said. "Should we use your room tonight, or mine?"

"We better use mine."

"Why?" Dunn asked.

"I might get a call from either Angela or the printer."

"Good thinking. Give me a minute to change shoes."

"Good idea. I'll put on something more comfortable too," Rodrigo said.

When they returned from their walk, the message light on Rodrigo's phone was blinking. He listened to the message and returned Hart's call, "Hi. I was out for a walk. I think Ann's taking a nap," he said, winking at Dunn. "We're going to meet at seven in the lobby. I'm going to take a shower before laying down for awhile."

"I was hoping you would come to my room for a little while, but we can meet after dinner."

Rodrigo frowned, but said, "Sounds like a plan. See you at seven." He looked at Dunn who was unbuttoning her shirt. Rodrigo hung up. Dunn took off her blouse and threw it at Rodrigo. Rodrigo picked up the phone, raised a finger to indicate he would be ready in a moment, and dialed directory assistance. Then he called The Wishing Well restaurant and asked if lobster was on the menu. "Great. I'd like to make a reservation for three at 7:30. The name is Rodrigo." He smiled as Dunn removed her slacks and panties."

"Should we play now or later?" Dunn asked as Rodrigo placed the phone in the cradle.

Rodrigo turned Dunn around and kissed her neck while his warm hands held her soft breasts. "Now and later."

"I was hoping you would say that. Let's shower first."

Hart was waiting in the lobby dressed in a patterned skirt and tan blouse. When Rodrigo arrived she asked if he had seen Dunn.

"I told her to meet here at seven. It's only 6:55." Rodrigo replied. "I guess she hasn't come down yet."

The elevator chimed and the door opened. Dunn appeared wearing dark blue slacks and a red and white striped blouse. Her hair was swept back in a long ponytail. Rodrigo remembered it cascading across his chest and stomach as she kissed his body. "Hi Angela, how are you?" Dunn asked. "How was the trip?"

"I'm fine, Ann. Good to see you again. The drive was great. Took about 2 ¾ hours with a stop."

"That's about how long it took us. I feel energized after that nap. And I'm also hungry. Tony, where are we eating?"

"I made a reservation at a restaurant about five miles from here. They have lobster if you're in the mood for that." Rodrigo responded.

"Thanks for including me," Hart said. "Do you want me to drive?"

"You just got in," Dunn said. "I'll drive. Give you a break."

On the way to the restaurant, Dunn asked Hart about her printing job. "I dropped the film off before I got to the hotel," she replied. "They'll call me tonight and let me know when I can review the blueprints. What about *Single Maltings*?"

"The blues will be ready at 10:30 tomorrow morning," Rodrigo said. "I'm going to try to get Ann on a tour and introduce her to the plant manager."

"That's great. Ann, you'll like Dick. And the plant is impressive, nearly a million square feet," said Hart.

"I love the smell of printing plants," Dunn said.

"There it is," Rodrigo said.

The owner greeted the three and took them to their table in the small dining room. Rodrigo and Dunn ordered Jack Daniels on the rocks and Hart ordered a vodka tonic.

"I'm going to have the lobster," Rodrigo said. "I've been thinking about that all day."

The two women studied the menus for a few moments. When the waitress returned with the cocktails, Dunn ordered lobster and Hart ordered a filet mignon.

"I'll have the biggest lobster you have," Rodrigo said.

Dunn took a long swallow of her drink and let the warmth settle in her stomach.

"Have either of you ever thought about flying here?" she asked. "The flight is only about 40 minutes."

"Sure," Hart said. "Our customer rep Lee Baxter told me when we first started using Quad that he would arrange for a pickup at either the train station in Albany or the airport if we decided to fly. I enjoy the drive but it's nice to know the option to fly was there."

"Where do they fly out of?" Dunn asked.

"LaGuardia and Westchester. Well just LaGuardia now." Hart said.

"Have you heard anything about when Westchester will be back in service?" Dunn asked.

"Not for months," said Hart. "I hope they catch those bastards and give them the death penalty."

"Me too," said Dunn. "My company lost two managers in that attack. We also lost three people in the World Trade Center attacks."

Rodrigo finished his drink and signaled for the waitress to bring another.

"What do you think, Tony?" asked Hart trying to get him back into the conversation.

"About what?" Rodrigo asked.

"About the attacks? Haven't you been listening to us?"

"Oh. Oh, that. What can I say, except I'm glad I wasn't there at the time. I've flown into and out of Westchester about a half dozen times."

"What do you think should happen to the guys who did that?" Dunn asked.

"Do they know who did it?" Rodrigo asked.

"Not yet, but what do you think should happen to the terrorists? Should they get the death penalty?"

"Didn't they blow themselves up? Rodrigo asked playing dumb.

"No silly," Dunn said. "These guys used some kind of missiles. The guys in the shopping mall blew themselves up."

"Oh yeah, now I remember," Rodrigo said.

The waitress appeared with Rodrigo's drink. He took a swallow and swirled the contents with his finger before licking it.

"Well, what do you think?" Dunn asked again.

"I think you should have ordered Jack, Angela. It's good isn't it Ann?"

"I give up, Tony, you're impossible," Dunn said.

I thought she would never stop.

"You ladies ready for another round. We have time," Rodrigo said.

The women emptied their glasses. Dunn nodded and Hart said, "me too."

Later in the hotel parking lot, Hart asked to speak to Rodrigo in private. Dunn said good night to both and went inside.

"I want to see you tonight. Do you want me to come to your room or ...?"

"I'd love to Angela, but I am very tired. Maybe tomorrow?"

"Just be honest with me. Are you going to see Ann tonight?"

"Not unless she's waiting for me in my room. Now that would be interesting."

"Be serious. Look I know I don't have the right to tell you what to do, but I was hoping we could take advantage of our being away together and..."

"I would like to do that too, but I'm not sure we should take the chance with Ann around. She and Tim are good friends and if she gets a hint of us together, she might tell Tim."

"How would she know?"

"Supposing she has a question and calls my room and I'm not there?"

"OK, then I'll come to your room."

"But supposing she decides to come to my room. If you are there. Well..."

"Tony does she know your room number?"

"Probably. Remember, she made the reservations. And she was at the counter when we checked in. Hell, I don't know, but I'm not willing to take the risk. When we're home we can meet at your place any time. It's a lot safer," Rodrigo said.

"Funny, I never thought you were afraid to take a chance. You know what we do on our own time is our business."

"You're right, it is, but remember we are not on our own time, we are on company time and Pantone is paying our expenses," Rodrigo said.

Hart sighed. "OK, you're right. But I do want to see you again. I want you to make love to me. That night was special."

"It was wonderful." Rodrigo took her hand and they walked into the hotel. Rodrigo was grateful that Hart pushed the button for the third floor and not the fourth. When the door opened, she kissed Rodrigo passionately. "There's a lot more where that came from. I'm in room 326 if you're interested."

Rodrigo returned the kiss and cupped her buttocks in his hands. "I'd really like to but we can't take the chance."

He released the door and returned her blown kiss. When the elevator door opened on the fourth floor, Rodrigo sprinted to his room wanting to be inside in case Hart came looking for him. Once inside he quickly shut the door.

"I was wondering about you," Dunn purred. She lay naked her hair splayed across the pillow.

She rose to help him undress. "You smell of her perfume, Tony."

"I know. She gave me a good night hug at the elevator and then she kissed me."

"WOW. She kissed you. Wonder what's on her mind?" Dunn asked.

"Probably the same thing that's on ours," Rodrigo said as he stepped out of his underwear. Dunn knelt in front of him and caressed his excitement.

They made love again the next morning after showering. Then Rodrigo said, "we better get dressed and get over to the printer."

"What's the hurry?" Dunn asked.

"No hurry. But I would like to get you on a tour while I check the blues."

The phone rang. Rodrigo told Dunn to be quiet. "It's either the printer or Angela."

Dunn giggled.

Rodrigo put his finger to his lips and Dunn stopped. "Yes," he said.

"Good morning. Thought you'd like to know I'm naked. Wish your warm body was lying next to me right now. I can think of several things I'd like to do."

"Good morning, Angela. What's up."

"Wanna come to my room and play?"

"Ann is probably trying to call me right now. We have to get to the printer."

"Too bad. My breasts are waiting for your touch and I would love to feel you inside me," Hart said boldly. "Just think what you are missing."

"What time are you going to the printer?" Rodrigo asked changing the subject.

Suspecting something was amiss, she confronted Rodrigo, "Is she there with you?"

"SHE is going to call me when she is ready. And then we are going to the printer."

"I'm sorry Tony. I just…"

"I have to hang up, Angela. Dunn is a client and she might be calling right now," Rodrigo said winking at Dunn. "We were supposed to be at the printer by 10:30 and it's ten after. I have to go. I'll see you later." Rodrigo hung up without waiting for a good bye.

Hart was angry with herself. She walked into the bathroom and turned on the shower. *You idiot. You made a fool of yourself. He is all business because of Dunn.*

Rodrigo had finished reading 10 of the 12 pages of the blues when Hart walked into the client room.

"Hi. Where's Ann?"

"She's on a tour of the plant. I asked Lee to show her around. Ann was really interested in how they make the plates without film. When will your blues be ready?"

"Melissa told me the blues would be right up. What are you guys going to do after you're finished here?"

"Ann wanted to see some battlefield near here. Something about the revolution."

"Saratoga. The Battle of Saratoga was fought here over 200 years ago in the American Revolution. If I remember my history, it was very important," Hart said.

Rodrigo was confused. "Revolution?"

"Yeah. We fought the British and that's how we gained our independence. Don't you know anything about American history?"

"A little. Remember I'm from Spain. They don't teach American history over there," Rodrigo said. "Why did this country fight the British?"

"We wanted to be free of the king of England," Hart replied. "We didn't want a foreign power telling us what to do."

Be careful. "Listen I have to finish this and get it back to Melissa."

After reading the pages, Rodrigo signed off, replaced them in the envelope and took them to Melissa, the assistant account representative filling in for Lee Baxter. "All done, Melissa. Do you have a press schedule yet?"

Melissa Cordell pulled up the schedule on her computer. "Nothing yet. I'll check with scheduling when I take the film down to the plate room."

"OK. If, I'm not here, leave a message for me at the hotel or call my cell."

"Will do. Are you going back to the lounge?" Cordell asked.

"Yeah."

"Would you give these blues to Angela for me. I'll take your stuff down to the plate room right now." Cordell handed the envelope to Rodrigo.

Rodrigo returned to the client lounge where Hart was reading a magazine. "Here are your blues, Angela. Ann's not back yet?"

"Not yet." Hart put the blueprints on the proof table and began reading. Rodrigo began playing a game on the computer.

"Hi guys," Dunn said as she returned from the tour.

"Good morning, Angela," Baxter said as he shook hands with Hart.

"Morning Lee. Melissa got the blues for me. They look great so far. Should I bring them to your desk when I'm finished?"

"Yeah, or give them to Melissa if I'm not there. I have a meeting in about 10 minutes. If she is away from her desk, give them to the receptionist and she'll page Melissa."

"Will do. Hey Ann, Tony tells me you're going to see the Saratoga battlefield. Mind if I tag along?" Hart asked.

"Not at all. How soon will you be finished here?" Dunn asked.

"Ten minutes max."

"OK, we'll wait."

She read a magazine and Rodrigo played hearts on the computer while Hart completed the review of the blueprints. She clipped the "Ok to print" order to the blues, signed it and put everything into the large blue envelope and delivered the package to the receptionist.

Rodrigo and Dunn were chatting about dinner plans when Hart reappeared.

"OK, I'm ready. Sorry to keep you waiting."

"No problem," said Dunn. "Have you ever been to the battlefield site?"

"Yes, but it's been years. My parents took me there when I was a young teenager," Hart replied. .

"How should we get there? Can we leave a car here and all go together?" Dunn asked.

"I think it's easier to go back to the hotel and drop off a car. The battlefield is about 15 miles south of town," Hart said.

Rodrigo climbed into Dunn's car and she followed Hart back to the hotel.

"Doesn't look like we're going to have a romantic dinner for two tonight," Rodrigo said.

"We just can't cut Angela out, Tony. After all, she is a colleague. And I'm sure Tim Robbins would not approve of your abandoning her."

"You're right. That wouldn't be fair. But I think I'm going to have a difficult time with her after dinner."

"Oh, And why would that be?"

I knew I shouldn't have said that.

"Well, how in the world can I get time alone with you without telling her? She's going to feel left out of the picture. You know what I mean?"

"Of course. And I admire you for thinking of her. That's very sweet. But tell me something. What do you think of her? Are you attracted to her?" Dunn asked.

"Why?"

"I just want to know. I like you very much. I think you are bright, articulate, well traveled, interesting, very good looking, very sexy and a hell of a lover. There, I've revealed my inner most thoughts. Now what about you?" Dunn asked.

"Is this conversation confidential?" Rodrigo asked.

"After what I just told you. Absolutely. I hope you'll keep what I've told you to yourself."

"I will," said Rodrigo.

"Ok. So now, turnabout is fair. What's your opinion of me?"

"I think you are a great art director. Tim Robbins does too."

"That's not what I mean. What do you think of me as a woman?" Dunn pursued the issue.

"OK. I like you. A lot. I've always liked you. And after the other day when you took me by surprise by calling me and asking me to join you for a drink, and then everything that happened afterward, well I, ah I thought you were very special."

"Thought I was or think I am?" Dunn asked.

"Ann, I was not a virgin. But being with you was something I had only dreamed about."

"Really?"

"Yeah, really. For me it was like being with a celebrity. I was in seventh heaven," Rodrigo said.

"Did I disappoint you?"

"No. Not at all. You were soft and sexy and warm and uninhibited. And I knew you wanted me. That was very flattering."

"I did want you. It took me more than a year to understand my feelings and that gave me the courage to finally call you. I've never done that. And I have never slept with a man on the first date," Dunn said. "Was I good for you? I mean I know you were satisfied, but beyond sexually satisfied, was I good for you?"

"Yes. The sex was great. But I also just enjoy being with you. You are a beautiful woman, and you are interesting. You dress well, you are very smart and have accomplished a lot. I don't know how to describe my feelings. Maybe it's because I feel privileged to be able to work with you on one level and then make love to you on another. That's pretty awesome," Rodrigo said. "I know I like you, and the other night was very special. So was last night."

"As long as we are going to be completely honest, I should tell you that you gave me the most intense orgasm I've ever had."

"If I hadn't worked all day, I think we could have done better."

"I think so too," Dunn said. "I am looking forward to it. I don't want to scare you, but I think I'm falling in love with you."

"I am very attracted to you. And I love the way you look at me. I love the way you feel, the way you smell and the way you taste. I never knew a woman could be so uninhibited, so daring. This is new to me, and it is terribly exciting," Rodrigo said. It was the truth. He had never had feelings like this.

"I've never been inhibited. Probably part of my art training and a healthy attitude about sex taught to me by my parents. And over the years I've learned that I am a hedonist. I love sex. And with the man I love it is exhilarating."

"A hedonist, eh. Is anything taboo?

"No. Nothing. By the way, do you like candlelight baths?" Dunn asked.

"Not by myself."

Dunn laughed out loud. She had pulled next to Hart who was looking at Dunn and Rodrigo. "No, I meant with a companion."

"Are you inviting me to take a bath with you?" Rodrigo asked.

"Wouldn't you like that?" Dunn said as Hart sped off. Dunn followed.

"I am your servant," Rodrigo said, putting his hand on Dunn's thigh. She did not remove it, but instead parted her legs. Then she thought better of it. "We better not. You'll get me hot. And the hotel is just ahead."

She followed Hart into the parking lot. Rodrigo slid into the back seat, Hart sat next to Dunn. They chatted about their interest in graphic arts and Dunn's rise to her position as art director. For perhaps the first time in his life, he admired a woman for her professional achievements as well as her ample charms and smoldering sexuality.

After the battlefield tour Dunn asked Rodrigo what he thought. "I didn't realize Americans preserved their battlefields, except for maybe Gettysburg," Rodrigo said.

"Saratoga was a great American victory, Tony. It changed the course of the war," Hart said.

"That foreign officer, ah Kosciuszko, I think his name was. Did they name that Kosciuszko bridge after him?"

"I think so. I don't know what he did to deserve the honor, but I doubt there was another fellow named Kosciuszko," Dunn said. The three laughed.

"Hey guys," Hart said changing the subject. "What are we going to do for dinner tonight? Anyone have anything in mind?"

"What about the Waterfront? It's on the Lake. Very nice," Rodrigo suggested. His cell phone rang.

"Hello."

"Tony? It's Lee Baxter. We caught a break. We're plating now and we'll be ready for you at about 5. How's that?"

Rodrigo looked at his watch. "Terrific, Lee. Any idea when you can get to *Horizons*?"

"The plates are being made as we speak. I left a message at the hotel. We're running both on the same press. After we're through with yours, we have a free standing insert to print. Then we'll run *Horizons*, probably about 2-3 tomorrow morning," Baxter said.

"OK, I'm in the car with the ladies and I'll relay the message. Thanks Lee, we'll see you at five." Rodrigo disconnected. "Ann they'll be ready for us to check color at about 5. Should be finished no later than six if there are no web breaks. Angela, your plates are being made and you should be on press sometime around two or three tomorrow morning."

"Shit," Hart said. *Now there's no chance to be with Tony tonight.* "I really didn't feature having to get up at that hour."

"Look at the bright side, you can go back to bed, sleep late and just drive home," Rodrigo said.

I'd rather sleep late with you. "I suppose," Hart sighed.

"Ann and I will do the press OK and meet you in the hotel lobby between 6:30 and 6:45. We'll call you from the printer to give you an update."

"Thanks."

After arriving at Quad Graphics, Rodrigo led Ann inside to the huge press at the far end of the room. He greeted the lead pressman who handed him the first sheets. Rodrigo began looking at the color comparing it to the proofs. He was pleased that the color was nearly perfect after making adjustments to the yellow and magenta.

"One or two adjustments to the cyan and we should be finished," Rodrigo said as he told the pressman to lower the intensity of the cyan.

"It looks pretty good, Tony," Dunn said. "You have a good eye. I was never very good at this."

Rodrigo smiled at Dunn and almost put his arm on her shoulder. Instead he took a last look at another sheet before signing "ok to print" with his initials. The pressman placed the final sheet in front of him alongside the one on which the color change was indicated. Rodrigo checked both and then checked the new sheet against the color proof. "Dead nuts on," he said to the pressman. "Whoops, sorry Ann."

"I've heard the term before. It's OK."

Rodrigo signed the sheet, shook hands with the pressman. "Can we take about a dozen press copies with us? They don't have to be trimmed," Rodrigo said.

While the pressman was gathering the copies Rodrigo asked Dunn "How long will you need to shower and change for dinner?"

Dunn looked at her watch and said, "I can be ready by 7:00, or eight if you have something else in mind."

Rodrigo chuckled. I'll tell Angela to meet us in the lobby at 6:30. We can have dessert later," he said as he dialed the number of the hotel. Hart's phone was busy so Rodrigo left a brief message.

After returning to the hotel from dinner Hart excused herself. "I better get a couple hours of sleep before they call," she said. "Good night, Ann. Good night Tony. If I don't see you tomorrow, have a pleasant trip."

"I'm going to the bar and have a nightcap," Rodrigo said hoping Hart noticed he was not going upstairs with Dunn

"I'm going to bed too," said Dunn. Walking around the battlefield tired me out." She entered the elevator with Hart as Rodrigo walked across the lobby to the bar. He waited about five minutes before returning to the elevator. When he entered his room he could smell Shalimar. Dunn was sitting on his bed. "I wasn't lying. I told Angela I was going to bed and I am. I just didn't say which bed."

As Rodrigo approached he could tell even in the dark she was naked. "I want to take a fast shower."

"Good. I'll join you."

-Chapter Twenty-

Dunn pulled her car into an open space on Palmer Avenue in front of Rodrigo's apartment. "Are you going to invite me up? I'd love to see your place."

Rodrigo thought about making love to Dunn. She pleased him in every way possible. But he was exhausted after five sessions in two days. He held her face between his hands. "I'd love to, but you've worn me out. I need some time to recuperate."

Dunn thought about teasing him, but changed her mind. "You were wonderful Tony. No woman in the world could be more satisfied than I am. Will you call me?"

"Yes. I promise. I've never felt like this before. You are intoxicating."

"So are you. Everything you do to me is special. It's probably for the best that I not come up because to tell you the truth I am very tired too," Dunn said.

The pair kissed and held each other for five minutes as Rodrigo's hands explored Dunn's breasts to the amusement of several passersby. Two of the witnesses were Special Agents Scott Weathers and Bernard Tillman. They had arrived at Rodrigo's apartment about an hour before Dunn drove up and were parked behind Dunn. Weathers and Tillman were amused by the steamy scene, but neither knew that the man they were watching was their quarry.

They were relying on a sketchy description given them by Terry Daly. But Rodrigo had his back to them and was wearing sunglasses and a baseball cap. When Rodrigo finally got out of the car, Dunn inadvertently gave the two agents the help they needed.

"Goodbye Tony," she yelled. "Thanks for all your help on the press OK. Say hello to Tim Robbins for me."

"So long, Ann. I'll tell Tim you said hello and I'll call you."

"I think that's him," Weathers said. He jotted down the make and model of Dunn's car and the license number while Tillman took photos of Dunn. "Let's make sure. Wait a few minutes and then call his apartment. He might tell us his name. While you do that let's see where this woman lives."

Tillman put the camera on the seat and pulled out his cell phone. He looked at his watch and let three minutes elapse before dialing. Weathers had turned onto Central Park Avenue cautiously following Dunn.

"Hello," Rodrigo said.

"Good afternoon. This is Walter Jones from Smith and Rothstein Investment Company. Is Mr. Anthony Rodrigo there?"

Taken momentarily off guard, Rodrigo identified himself. "This is Antonio Rodrigo."

"Mr. Rodrigo. How are you today, sir?"

"I'm sorry I don't take unsolicited investment calls," Rodrigo said before hanging up.

"Now I know why telemarketers hate their jobs," Tillman said as he put his phone in his breast pocket. "That was our man."

"Good, as soon as we find out where the woman lives we'll come back and sit on this guy," Weathers replied.

"Why not ask the uniforms to get the information on the woman?" Tillman asked.

"Daly's orders, we want as few people in on this as possible," Weathers replied. He followed Dunn to Maplewood Road. She turned into her driveway and drove the car into the garage. Weathers continued past her house and Tillman wrote down the house number 39.

"Now all we have to do is find out what town this is. Let's ask this guy walking the dog," Tillman said.

Weathers slowed and Tillman opened the window. "Excuse me sir. I think we are lost. What town is this?"

"Hartsdale. What are you looking for?" the man asked.

Tillman looked down at his notes to give the man the impression he was reading directions. "We're trying to find Beech Street in Yonkers," he said.

"I don't know about Beech Street, but if you get back on Central Park Avenue and head south. You'll go right into Yonkers."

After thanking the man, Weathers retraced the route while Tillman called the office. "Jeremy, it's Bernie Tillman. Run an address for me. Who lives at 39 Maplewood Drive in Hartsdale?"

It took Special Agent Jeremy Burns 25 seconds. "The occupant's name is A. Dunn. Need anything else?"

"Yeah. Run a check on her. She if she has anything besides traffic offenses. I doubt you'll find anything, but you never know." Tillman wrote down the name next to the address. "A. Dunn. Rodrigo called her Ann. Ann Dunn. They must be business associates," he said to Weathers.

When Rodrigo entered his apartment, he put his bag down and booted his computer. After logging into AOL, he checked for messages on his own domain spotting a message from NYGAL. He typed Glad to be back from SS. Atta's assistant, writing as NYGAL sent a smiley face. Rodrigo knew his message had been understood. Rodrigo waited five minutes to see if there were instructions then logged off.

He called the office and left a message for Tim Robbins that he had returned from the press ok. Then he pulled a ginger ale from the fridge and sat on the sofa with The Times.

In the elint section FBI Special Agents Jim Meyer and Roberta Wisniewski were monitoring Rodrigo's email and phone conversations. Meyer saw the message and was puzzled that there was no answer. Then he saw the smiley face. He instructed Carnivore to monitor the traffic.

The phone interrupted Rodrigo's perusal of *The Times*.

"Hello."

"Tony, it's Tim Robbins. How are you? Any problems? Was Ann pleased"

"Hi Tim. *Boy was she pleased.* Everything went extremely well. Ann was very pleased. She really liked the printer. Complimented us on our choice. I arranged a tour for her and she met the plant manager and a couple of other people there. She was impressed." Rodrigo said.

"That's terrific. Nicely done, Tony. Listen there is no need for you to come in today, but tomorrow please call Brianna Russell at Altria. She called this morning. She wants to meet with you next week to discuss the under age no smoking campaign if your schedules mesh."

"That's good news. I am really looking forward to working on that. Do you know anything I should know about her, or about the company?" Rodrigo asked.

"John and I met with her several weeks ago. All I know is she is the public affairs director for Altria and she is very bright. When she and I first talked, she said they are looking for all sorts of printed materials that carry a theme. Nothing specific about quantities or deadlines," Robbins said. "You can find out a lot about the company on their website."

"Do you want me to call her now?"

"She isn't expecting you to call today, but that would be helpful. Maybe you two can at least arrange a meeting and discuss some preliminary things. I'll give you her number."

Rodrigo jotted the number down on the margin of The Times editorial page. He repeated it to Robbins. "Anything else for me?"

"Did you see Angela there?"

"Sure. She was scheduled to go on press some time early this morning. I was tired so I went back to the hotel. But when she looked at the blues she said everything was ok," Rodrigo said. "I'm sure the press run went off without a hitch or she would have called."

Special Agent Wisniewski was taking notes of the conversation as it was being recorded.

"OK, Tony. See if you can hook up with Brianna. I'll see you tomorrow."

When Rodrigo hung up, he opened his briefcase, copied Russell's number down on a small pad and picked up the phone.

"Brianna Russell's office. This is Sam," said a husky female voice.

"Hi. This is Tony Rodrigo from Pantone Associates. I am returning Ms. Russell's call. Is she there?"

"Mr. Rodrigo. One moment please. Brianna, it's a Tony Rodrigo from Pantone. He said you called him," Samantha MacFarlane said.

"Oh good. Thanks, Sam," Russell said returning to her desk. She removed the earring from her left ear. "Brianna Russell."

"Ms. Russell, it's Tony Rodrigo from Pantone Associates. I'm returning your call."

"Hi, Tony. First please call me Bree. I wasn't expecting your call today. Tim said you were at a press ok upstate."

"I was. Just got back. How can I help you?"

"How's your schedule next week? I want to talk about the new under age no smoking campaign we want to unveil. Lots of thing to design like brochures, a booklet, some posters, inserts and P.O.P's, ah, sorry point of purchase, materials."

"I can rearrange my schedule to suit you, Bree. You tell me when you want to meet and I'll be there."

"That's very sweet of you Tony. How about, a week from today? That's Tuesday the 25th at 10? I'm at 41st and Park."

"Terrific. That's only a few blocks from here."

"OK, when you get inside, go to the security desk and tell them you're there to see me. They'll buzz me and I'll send Sam down to get you. Sam's my assistant," Russell said.

Rodrigo wrote the instructions on the pad. "Fine, next Tuesday at 10 at 41st and Park. See you then, Bree."

Special Agent Wisniewski wrote down the time and place of the meeting.

Rodrigo sat at his computer and checked the chat room to see if any members of his cell had sent anything. He scanned the names currently on line and quickly spotted NYGAL. "My friend just returned from 48th trip to favorite haunt. Weather lovely," said NYGAL's innocent looking message.

Rodrigo withdrew from the chat room and went to the hall closet. He used a putty knife to open the small tightly sealed secret door. Inside were documents possible intended targets, technical information on explosives and their placement, the names, addresses and phone numbers of the cell members and some notes. On one of the notes was a calculation about the number of trips needed to bring in the required amount of HMX. The number 48 matched the number in the email. Atta was telling him they now had more than five tons of HMX, enough to complete their assignments. He hoped Atta would contact him soon.

FLOWERPOT asked NYGAL where this marvelous place was that would attract someone 48 times. Ever ready, NYGAL responded, "Bermuda." FLOWERPOT answered, "Been there three times. It was good, but not good enough to visit 45 more times. Where did you stay that was so special?"

NYGAL typed "Always the same place" and signed off.

Special Agent Meyer wondered out loud, "That's a good question. What place in Bermuda is so special that you want to visit it 48 times?"

"What?" asked Terry Daly who had just entered the Elint section.

"Hi. I'm monitoring Rodrigo's email. He's in a chatroom using an alternate screen name MILLERMAN. Someone named NYGAL wrote that a friend just returned from a 48th trip to Bermuda. No one visits any place 48 times, do they?"

"Ever been to Bermuda?" Daly asked.

"Sure. Went there on my honeymoon. And I've been back. But 48 times! That island is so small you can see everything in a week." Meyer said.

"I agree. Find out who NYGAL really is. These guys are clever. I'm sure they use code and this may be worth following. Got anything yet, Roberta?"

"Nothing specific. We're just getting acquainted." Wisniewski answered. "Anything I should look for?"

"Not sure. Just be on the lookout for anything unusual. Most phone conversations are fairly routine. Be wary of conversations that are surreptitious or don't seem relevant. We may find something when we find out who NYGAL is. I'll be in my office if you need me," Daly said.

Atta knew that the longer he waited after the aborted attempt on September 11, the greater the opportunity for discovery even though the cell was asleep. Since most cells operated independently, he did not know the cell members who attacked the Westchester Airport, but he was certain they survived. That meant an intense investigation focused on two or three Arabs. He thought about asking Riyadh, but quickly dismissed that.

Instead he asked one of his assistants if MILLERMAN was still logged on.

"No," the assistant said.

Atta told his assistant to get some coffee and he composed an email to ARODGO.

"How was your weekend? Tell me when to call?"

Rodrigo had returned to his computer and was going to send Ann Dunn a funny email when Atta's message came through. He checked his watch and typed *"5:15."*

When Meyer alerted Wisniewski that Rodrigo was expecting a call at 5:15 Wisniewski changed tapes. At 5:05 Special Agents Tillman and Weathers were watching when Rodrigo left the building at 949 Palmer Road and walked to the pay phone near the hospital. The phone rang at 5:15. He and Atta exchanged passwords.

"How soon can you be ready?" Atta asked.

"I don't know. Have the four packages arrived?" Rodrigo asked referring to the four Saudi students who would be driving the vans.

"Only two," Atta responded. "The other two were not shipped. We have inventory on hand that we can use."

Rodrigo knew that meant using staffers from the Mission. "How do you want me to handle?"

"Use the original business plan we discussed," Atta said.

"What businesses do you want the product shipped to?"

"Use your judgment" Atta said. "Let me know as soon as you can when you'll be ready to pick up the product." The line went dead.

"Come on, call. Call, dammit," Wisniewski said as the clock showed 5:20. "No call yet," she said to Meyers.

Tillman and Weathers observed the call from the public booth. When Rodrigo left the phone, Tillman obtained the number and called Daly with the information.

"There's a pay phone on Palmer about 150 yards from Rodrigo's apartment building," Daly said to Roosevelt Ewing. "Rodrigo apparently uses that instead of his own phone."

He gave Ewing the number and ordered him to tap it.

"Right. Out for now."

Daly went to the elint room and told Wisniewski that Rodrigo was using a pay phone and that it was going to be tapped.

"Without a court order?" Wisniewski asked.

Daly smiled.

At the CIA Headquarters in Langley, Breen and his staff were monitoring phone and email communications from the Saudi UN Mission in New York. Moonbeam told him that ARODGO and MILLERMAN were both screen names used by Tony Rodrigo and that he lived in the Bronxville section of Yonkers. Moonbeam also identified NYGAL as Talal Farham, a functionary in the Saudi Mission.

Now this looks interesting. Our guy chatting with a Saudi in the Saudi UN mission. Carl Pickett made some notes.

CIA Agents Bump Masterson and Chuck Corrigan monitored the phone conversation between Farhan and Rodrigo. Masterson called Breen.

"Vince, it's Bump. We have a Saudi employee in their UN mission talking to Rodrigo about shipping some product. Since when is a UN Mission in business and shipping products. And these guys are using passwords."

"Are you recording?"

"Yeah."

Get a voice rec on Farhan and monitor all his calls. We may be on to something."

-Twenty-one-

Jameel Subaey read the letter from Tony Wattes, the building manager. "Mr. Winter and Mr. Wall, Concord Contractors will be painting a number of apartments in the coming weeks. Your apartment is scheduled for painting beginning Monday. Please make sure all your valuables are secured. To minimize the inconvenience to you we also will be replacing the sink and the dishwasher at the same time. Please make sure the dishwasher is empty and nothing is left in the sink. Thank you for your cooperation."

"Faisel, they're going to paint this apartment next week," Subaey said. "We have to get rid of the weapons before Monday." Hamed took the letter and read it.

"There's no reason to panic. We'll put these two in the car with the others until the painting is finished."

"If we are in a collision or the car is stolen, they might be able to trace those weapons right back to us and from there they could link us to the airport attack because of the missing magazine," Subaey said.

"All magazines are the same. But just to be safe we'll take everything to the weapons should be taken to Abdelaziz," Hamed agreed. He called Abdelaziz Saleh his handler in the Saudi Mission in New York.

"We've been notified our apartment is going to be painted starting on Monday," Hamed said. "We can't risk keeping the tools here."

Unknown to Hamed and Saleh, Carl Pickett, an Arabic speaking CIA agent monitored the conversation and quickly traced the call to a cell phone owned by the fictitious W & W Sales in White Plains. He alerted Vince Breen.

"We've got a guy in the Saudi Mission named Saleh, Abdelaziz Saleh who is talking to a man with a White Plains based cell phone," Pickett said. "They're talking about having to remove tools from an apartment that is scheduled to be painted. That doesn't make a lot of sense. Why would someone have to remove tools because an apartment is being painted? I think we may have something here. I think tools is a code word."

Breen pulled up a chair and waited for the next translation.

Saleh quickly agreed that the weapons should be removed from the apartment. "Take the tools apart and put them in a gym bag. That won't attract any attention. Then bring the bag here. I'll make sure someone is available to pick it up when you arrive. Call me when you are a few blocks away," Saleh ordered.

"I want to do this as soon as possible," Hamed said. When can I bring them to you?"

"Bring them tomorrow morning at 10."

"Will do. Tomorrow at 10," Hamed said.

"I've never heard of tools that needed to be protected by diplomatic immunity," Breen said after reading the translation. "This doesn't pass the sniff test."

Breen alerted the surveillance teams. "Overlook, this is Bobcat. A rental vehicle will be bringing a gym bag to the mission tomorrow morning at 10. The gym bag probably contains weapons. These guys are supposed to call the mission when they are a few blocks away. We'll alert you when they do that."

Nine-year-old Evan Gifford was looking out the window of his second floor apartment when he saw Hamed and Subaey go to their SUV in a parking space nearly below his window. Gifford waved hello, a gesture Subaey missed. He and his partner had run into the curious youngster several times before. Hamed finally introduced themselves as secret agents working undercover. He told Gifford to say nothing to anyone and they would make him a junior agent. Gifford was thrilled.

Subaey was so intent on returning the weapons to the mission he failed to notice the youngster peering at him. When Subaey opened the trunk Gifford's eyes went wide in disbelief. It was the first time he saw a real AK-47. Hamed held the Nike gym bag open for Subaey who quickly dismantled the weapons into three pieces and put them and the magazines inside the bag that contained two other rifles, four handguns and a quantity of ammunition. Subaey zipped the bag.

"What do we tell Abdelaziz when he asks about the missing magazine?" Subaey asked.

"I'll tell him we were only given five. He won't know," Hamed replied.

It had been several weeks since the attack and there had been no mention in any of the press reports of a magazine being found at the scene. "Besides it can't be traced back to us," Hamed said as he looked up and spotted Gifford watching them. The youngster waived and Hamed waved back. "That kid on the second floor is watching us. He may have seen the guns," Hamed said.

"What do we do?"

"I'll handle it." Hamed motioned for Gifford to come down to the car. The youngster disappeared from the window and soon joined them in the parking lot.

"Hi Agent Gifford," Hamed said. "Remember us? This is agent Winter and I'm Agent Wall," Hamed said, using the last names of their alias. "Do you remember the day we first made you a junior secret agent?"

"Sure."

"And you remember we told you not to say anything, that it would be our secret?" Hamed asked.

"I haven't said anything to anyone," Gifford said.

"Are you sure?" Hamed pressed. "Maybe you said something to your parents."

"Not even them," Gifford said. "I can't talk. I'm a junior secret agent."

"Exactly right, Agent Gifford. I know you were watching the parking lot looking for bad guys. How long have you been watching?"

"For a few minutes," Gifford replied.

"Good agents remember what they see," Hamed said. "So tell me what you saw."

"I saw one of your secret agent guns," Gifford said. "Agent Winter took them apart and put them in that bag."

Hamed was ready with an explanation. "That's right. We put them in a bag so people won't get frightened. Some people don't like guns."

"I know. My mother says all guns should be outlawed. But Secret Agents are supposed to carry guns. Isn't that right?" Gifford asked.

"That's right. And good agents don't talk about it. So we are relying on you to keep our secret. OK?" Hamed asked. "Can we count on you, Secret Agent Gifford?"

"You can count on me Agent Wall. I won't say a word to anyone. I promise"

"That's very good, Secret Agent Gifford. And you should be rewarded." Hamed reached into his pocket and pulled out a roll of money. He peeled off a five and handed it to the youngster. "This is for helping us keep our secret, Secret Agent Gifford. Agent Winter why don't you wait in the car," Hamed said.

Subaey closed the trunk. "See you later, Secret Agent Gifford." Subaey saluted Gifford. Gifford's heart swelled as he returned the salute. Subaey got into the car smiling.

Hamed asked Gifford about his folks, what they did, whether he had any brothers and sisters and where he went to school. Each time Gifford mentioned a member of the family, Hamed reminded him, "Remember, Secret Agent Gifford, not a word to anyone."

Gifford asked him about the FBI but the questions were so leading, Hamed had no trouble filling in answers.

"Do you guys work in New York City?"

"Yes, Agent Winter and I work in a big building in the city. But sometimes we work out here too looking for clues the bad guys leave behind." After a few minutes, Hamed looked at his watch and said, "I have to go now, Secret Agent Gifford."

"OK Agent Wall. Thanks for talking with me and telling me all about the FBI."

"Remember we're not FBI agents. We're secret agents. We work in the same building as the FBI. That's why it is so important for you to keep our secret. OK?"

"WOW! You really are secret agents."

"You are a very good junior secret agent." Hamed put out his hand which Gifford shook. Hamed put his hand to his lips, "Remember, sshhhh."

Gifford watched as Hamed's car left the parking lot. He looked up and saw his mother opening the window. She told him to come inside.

"What were you doing with those men?" Mrs. Gifford asked.

"We were just talking," Evan said.

"I know dear. What were you talking about?"

"Just stuff."

"What kind of stuff, Evan?" Mrs. Gifford said.

"I can't tell you."

"Why can't you tell me? I'm your mother."

"I'm sworn to secrecy. They made me a junior secret agent."

"That's very nice. You'll make a very good secret agent. But good secret agents answer their mothers' questions."

"I'm not supposed to tell anyone, not even you or dad," Evan said.

"Well the secret agent must have made a mistake, because it is ok to tell your father and me any secret you want to. And you know we won't tell anyone."

"You promise, mom?"

"I promise. So what were you talking about?"

"We were talking about how neat it is to be a secret agent. They get to carry guns and they go after the bad guys."

"I know they chase the bad guys, but were they carrying guns?" Mrs. Gifford was becoming slightly alarmed.

"They put them in a big bag in the back of the car."

Sensing this might be a tale Evan was making up, Mrs. Gifford asked, "Evan police officers wear their guns on their hips. Why would secret agents put their guns in a bag?"

"Agent Wall told me they did that to hide the guns so people wouldn't be scared. The guns were special."

"Special? How so?"

"Mom, you wouldn't understand. You're not an agent."

"No I'm not. But now that my son Evan is an agent he needs to be extra truthful with his mother. Tell me about the guns, please. Were they the same as the guns police officers carry?"

"Police officers don't carry machine guns. Only special agents carry machine guns," Evan Gifford said.

"Machine guns? How do you know that?"

"They're the same kind of guns I saw in a Clint Eastwood movie when he was a marine sergeant. They go…" Gifford made a noise to imitate the firing of an AK-47.

"I know you are a secret agent. But are you sure. Did you see one?"

"Did I? I saw two of them. Agent Winter took them apart. He had extra bullets too."

A growing uneasiness crept into Mrs. Gifford. She wondered if her son was telling the truth. *Why would he make that up?* She decided to take him at his word and change the subject.

"OK Mr. Secret agent, I have work to do, why don't you get started on your homework."

Mrs. Gifford made sure her son was engrossed in his homework before she went to the bathroom and called her husband on her cell. She tried to keep her voice under control as she relayed the incident.

Patrick Gifford listened. He was a recent night school law graduate and was clerking for one of the judges in White Plains. "OK, honey, I'll get right back to you. I'm going to talk to judge Driscoll."

"About what," Forest Driscoll said as he appeared at Gifford's door.

Gifford relayed the story.

Judge Driscoll leaned against the door jam. "I wonder if this has anything to do with what happened at White Plains? The police reports said one of the items they found was a fully loaded AK-47 magazine. You know what, I'll call the police and you call your wife and tell her to stay in the apartment."

Driscoll phoned police headquarters and identified himself. In a calm voice he explained the situation. "I'm not sure whether this is some kid's wild imagination, or whether he's on to something," he said.

"We'll send a car over there. What's the apartment number?"

"Hang on, Captain. Pat, what's the apartment number?"

"What's their apartment number, Judy? The judge wants to know."

"I don't know. I'll have to ask Evan. Hang on, I'm going to put the phone down.

"Evan," she said as she went to the dining room where he was reading. "Do you remember the names of the two agents?"

"Sure Mom, Winter and Wall."

"Do they live in our building?"

"Yeah. I'm not sure what apartment. But I can find out. Their names should be on the directory at the entrance."

"You really are a good secret agent. Go find out for me, will you."

Evan Gifford ran out the door and down the fire stairs. Breathless, he was back in less than five minutes. "They live in 516, mom. But why do you want to know?"

"I wanted to know just in case I ever needed a secret agent, that's all. Thank you Mr. Junior Secret Agent. You are going to make a very good Secret agent."

Evan beamed while his mother disappeared into the bathroom and shut the door. "Their names are Winter and Wall and they live in 516. I don't know their first names," she told her husband who relayed the information to the judge.

"We'll send two cars, judge," the police captain said. "Can you get us a search warrant?"

"Absolutely." He instructed the captain to have one of the patrol cars stop at the courthouse. He relayed the information to Gifford who was still on the phone with his wife.

"Stay in the apartment and make sure Evan doesn't go out," Gifford said to his wife.

They hung up and Judy Gifford returned to the kitchen where she was working on her shopping list. From the kitchen she could see the parking lot. A police cruiser pulled in and parked in an empty slot. Sergeant Mike Reynolds radioed the captain and was told to wait until he received a message that the other car was in the front of the building. When the second car with two men arrived, all four officers went into the building.

In the rear, Reynolds and officer Curt Mendicini walked up the fire stairs. Officers Matt Pinto and Ricardo Jiminez entered the main entrance and rode the elevator. When the elevator door opened they waited for their backup to finish climbing the six flights from the basement. All four walked uneasily to 516.

Reynolds knocked on the door. Mendicini and Jiminez stood to one side of the door, officer Pinto waited on the other side, their hands on the butts of their automatics. Reynolds knocked again. He waited a few seconds and knocked a third time.

"Rick, get the building manager and tell him we have a warrant to enter this apartment. Don't tell him what we're looking for. I'll wait here. Matt, you and Curt go downstairs and move the cars a couple of blocks from here. We don't want to scare these guys away. Then get your asses back here so we can search this place," Reynolds said.

When officers Pinto and Mendicini returned, the manager was engaged in a conversation with Reynolds.

"This is an exclusive building, sergeant. We have doctors and lawyers, diplomats, even a judge living here. So I would like to know what these two guys have done," Tony Wattes said.

"We want to ask them some questions, Mr. Wattes. That's all."

"Well, if that is true, why do you need a search warrant?"

"We have the warrant in case they refused to cooperate. Strictly routine, Mr. Wattes. Now if you'll let us in, sir, we can get started," Reynolds said.

Wattes opened the door and entered the apartment first calling out the names of Wall and Winter. "They're not here, sergeant. Why don't you come back when they return?"

"Thank you for your help Mr. Wattes. Give me your cell number. We'll call you if we need you." Reynolds copied the cell number. "Get started in the living room," he said to the officers. "Be careful. Don't make a mess."

A slow methodical search of the living room, dining room, hall bath and kitchen turned up nothing. "OK, let's split up. Rick you and Matt take that bedroom. Curt and I will look in here," Reynolds said referring to the master bedroom.

"Looks like this hasn't been used, sarge," Jiminez said.

"Toss it anyway. Ya never know. Then, have a look in the other bedroom."

Mendicini booted the computer in the master bedroom. AOL's sign-on plate showed two screen names: *Winterstorm* and

Wallpainter. "Hey sarge, we have two screen names here. What are the last names of the guys who live here?

"Winter and Wall, why?"

"The screen names are *winterstorm* and *wallpainter* and Mr.*wallpainter* has an automatic sign on."

"No shit," Reynolds said. "Sign on and let's see what we have."

"Hmmm. That's interesting. No messages waiting and none in the sent folder," Mendicini said. "Let's see if he has any notations on his calendar." Mendicini went back eight months and then flipped through the next eight months of the calendar. Nothing. And the only email addresses that appeared at the top were harmless yahoo shopping on line and several entries for a dating service.

"Anything saved?" Reynolds asked.

The C Drive revealed no saved text or files. The computer was clean. "Nothing sarge."

"What about disks? Did you find any?"

"I'll check the desk."

"OK then let's finish turning this room. I'll get the closet. When you finish with the desk, look in the bureau."

The closet contained suits, shirts, jackets, slacks, shoes and ties. One of the shoes was out of alignment with the others so Reynolds looked behind and under each. He found what he was looking for behind a shoebox. "Curt, look at this." Reynolds uncovered a small door fitted tightly to the surrounding wood. "You got a knife?"

Using Mendicini's Swiss Army knife that he wedged into the crack, he pulled the door open. Without being asked, Mendicini handed the sergeant his flashlight. Reynolds shined it into the small opening. It was empty.

"Now why does anyone have a secret hiding place like this and not keep anything in it?" he asked.

"Doesn't add up to me," Mendicini said.

"Me neither. Let's see what the others found." Reynolds resealed the compartment and the two joined the other officers in the second bedroom.

"Anything?"

"Not much," Pinto said. "Just bills. No papers. No mail. Nothing else, not even a check book. It's weird. I've never seen anything like it."

"I have," Reynolds said. "This is what people operating undercover do. I think we're on to something. I'd sure love to know where they took those guns. OK. Let's play a hunch they'll be back shortly. While we're waiting, let's take another look. Slowly and carefully."

Each car that arrived at the mission was carefully scrutinized by overlook. The plate numbers were surreptitiously run through the FBI motor vehicle records using Moonbeam. When Hamed drove his SUV into the mission, Moonbeam revealed the vehicle had been leased from an agency in White Plains.

"Bingo," Overlook called Breen. "We've got something solid, Vince. The SUV just entered the Saudi Mission."

"Good work," Breen alerted the operatives waiting in a car and a van on Lexington Avenue. "This is Bobcat. Overlook, I want you to follow the SUV when it leaves the mission. Stay close. Pickpocket go to the White Plains address and wait for the SUV."

The van eased into traffic and headed to the suburban address.

Carl Pickett's partner, Grady Hatten called the auto dealer, identified himself as an FBI agent and asked who rented the vehicle. The leasing manager told him it was a man named Cliff Wall and gave him the address. "The SUV was leased by a Cliff Wall. Here's his White Plains address," Hatten said to Breen.

Breen relayed the information to the surveillance and snatch teams.

Inside the Saudi Mission, Abdelaziz Saleh put the rifles, handguns and ammunition in the security office. He was troubled by Hamed's apparent overreaction to the painters. Both Hamed and Subaey appeared to be agitated and stressed and that might lead to a mistake that would compromise the Saudi mission.

"I'm sending you back to Riyadh," he said. "I want you to return to your apartment pick up your clothes, whatever you need that fits into one large bag. Then make absolutely sure you leave nothing that can be used to track you. Be back here by 3 p.m. I'll get you on a flight to Riyadh tonight or tomorrow night. Understood?"

Both men nodded. They kissed and left the building.

"Overlook to Bobcat. The SUV is leaving the mission. New York license Whiskey Charlie Juliet three, niner, six, niner."

"Roger overlook. Follow him. Stay close. Pickpocket, did you copy that."

"Roger. New York license whiskey, Charlie, Juliet, three, niner, six, niner. We're at the White Plains address."

When the SUV drove into the parking lot it was followed by a gray Ford sedan. A dark blue van waited nearby, its engine running. When the SUV pulled into a parking spot, the van moved to a spot behind the SUV blocking it. Two men dressed in blue jump suits got out and waited. When Hamed and Subaey got out of the SUV, they were hustled into the van where they were bound, gagged and blindfolded by George Vladik and Dan Moretti. They were forced to sit on the floor as the van left the parking lot and made its way toward a New Jersey suburb.

-Chapter Twenty-two-

Subaey and Hamed sat blindfolded on the floor of the van, their hands and feet securely bound and their mouths taped. Vladik and Moretti kept an eye on them while Gerald Simpson directed the driver Cory Walker. All were former CIA agents recruited for special ops by Vincent Breen.

"Bobcat, this is pickpocket," Simpson said. "We have the merchandise. No problems. Proceeding to factory."

"Bobcat confirms. Proceeding to factory with merchandise." Breen was pleased with the snatch operation. He called CIA Director William Burdette on his private secure line.

"Burdette."

"Breen. We've picked up two people who dropped off a large Nike gym bag at the Saudi Mission. We've been monitoring their communications and we have strong reason to believe the bag contained weapons or maybe explosives. They used the term tools in their phone conversation and they were jittery about maintaining possession of those tools. It doesn't seem logical anyone would drop off tools surreptitiously at a UN mission unless they wanted to ensure the so-called tools were beyond the reach of the law. We'll know soon enough."

"Good work. You're probably right. Get to work on them as soon as possible," Burdette said.

"They're being taken to a small warehouse in Carlstadt. No neighbors. If they know anything, we'll get it from them. It won't take long. What do we do with them after we get what we need?"

"Keep them on ice until we can check out their story," Burdette said.

"OK, boss. I'll get back to you."

When the van approached the garage of the warehouse, Simpson tapped the code and the door opened. Inside, four men sat playing cards. Like Walker, Simpson, Vladik and Moretti, Frank Guidice, Petra Uvanov, Gunther Williams and Stanislaus Sobaleski were former agents and double agents who were paid handsomely to freelance for the CIA. Guidice, Uvanov, Williams and Sobaleski were experts at extracting information. Their methods ranged from clever questioning to innovative barbarity. Even though Uvanov and Sobaleski spoke fluent Arabic, they planned to conduct the interrogation in English to fool their "guests" into thinking they could use Arabic to secretly communicate among themselves.

After taking the wallets and watches from the prisoners and stripping them to their undershorts, Walker and Simpson guided Hamed to a steel chair; Vladik and Moretti put Subaey in a similar chair in the second room. When the prisoners had been secured, their blindfolds and gags were removed. Uvanov watched over Hamed while Guidice went to the room where Williams and Sobaleski prepared to work on Subaey. Guidice deliberately wasted an hour with Williams and Sobaleski discussing sports. Then Guidice returned to the room where Hamed waited.

"What the fuck is going on?" Hamed asked. "Who the hell are you guys. Why are you treating us like this?"

"Mr. Wall, your friend is being very cooperative. Now it is your turn. We are going to ask you some questions," Guidice said calmly. "And we want truthful answers. If you cooperate and give us what we want. You'll be released unharmed."

"What kind of questions?" Hamed said.

"What's your real name?"

"Cliff Wall."

"That's the first lie. Lie to me again, and you will regret it." Guidice said.

"Now, who is Abdelaziz Saleh?"

"I never heard of the man. What is this all about?"

240

"Mr. Wall, Mr. Winter says you know Abdelaziz Saleh. I'm going to give you just one more chance," Guidice said. He moved directly in front of Hamed. At 6 feet 3 inches 220 pounds, Guidice was an imposing figure. He removed his jacket and shirt revealing a muscular upper body and powerful arms. Guidice interlaced his fingers and stretched his hands then rested them on Hamed's knees. "Who is Abdelaziz Saleh?

"I don't...." Hamed never got the third word out of his mouth as Guidice's right hand crashed into Hamed's stomach knocking the breath out of him. The left hand smashed Hamed's jaw splitting his lip, breaking one of his teeth and knocking him to the floor in his chair. "I don't know what you want," Hamed wheezed when he had recovered his breath. Blood dripped from his chin as Uvanov righted the chair.

"It's simple. You have information and I want it. And believe me when I tell you, I am persistent. Save yourself a lot of trouble and a great deal of pain. Now we'll ask again. Who is Saleh?"

Though he was genuinely frightened by the size and power of his assailant, Hamed was more frightened of the consequences to his family if he told Guidice what he wanted to know. He tried a different tack. "I only know him from a phone conversation. I don't know anything about him."

"Where does he work?"

"I don't know?" Another blow to his bare stomach sent Hamed's chair to the floor. Uvanov, even larger than Guidice, easily returned the chair to its position. Guidice bared his teeth. "I know you know where he works because Mr. Winter said you talked to him today on the phone."

Genuine panic swept over Hamed. *He talked. Coward. Allah will make him wish he was dead a thousand times.* "All I did was call a number I didn't know where I was calling."

Guidice sighed "Mr. Wall, you have continued to lie to me and I am getting impatient. You may enjoy pain. That's good because we have much more painful methods for getting the information we want. And we also have drugs. I know you know where Saleh works because Mr. Winter said you visited the Saudi mission today and dropped off some weapons. Isn't that true. And before you deny it stop and think what will happen if you do. What will it be, Mr. Wall?"

"I dropped off some tools, that's all. I don't know anything about weapons. And I don't know a man named Saleh."

Guidice was tempted to break Hamed's jaw. Instead he said to Uvanov, "Hook him up."

Wearing gloves, Uvanov ripped the undershorts from Hamed's body. An alligator clip was attached to one of Hamed's testicles, another to his penis. Hamed cried out in pain.

Holding the terminal, Guidice said, "this will be very painful. And I can turn up the juice so high it will fry your nut." He made sure the current was on low power before closing the switch.

Hamed's body stiffened but he kept silent. Guidice killed the power and increased the voltage. Again the current surged through Hamed's genitals.

His scream bounced off the soundproof walls.

"What's it going to be, Mr. Wall, a crispy dick or some information?" Guidice said.

"I can tell you nothing," Hamed said through clenched teeth.

"That's too bad." Guidice again increased the power and closed the circuit. Hamed's body convulsed. His screams assaulted Guidice's ears. Then silence as Hamed lapsed into unconsciousness.

"He's out," Uvanov said.

"That should just about do it. When he comes to, let's put the two of them together."

Guidice went to the room next door where Williams and Sobaleski were questioning Subaey.

"I'm going to bring his friend in now."

"Good idea," Williams replied.

Guidice returned to the other room where Hamed had regained consciousness. Guidice and Uvanov carried Hamed's chair and placed it alongside Subaey. "Perhaps you two will be more comfortable together," Guidice said. "Mr. Wall, as you know, we have learned quite a bit from Mr. Winter here. And as you can see he is untouched. Now we want you to verify the information. Is Abdelaziz Saleh your contact at the Saudi mission?"

Hamed looked at Subaey and switched to Arabic. "What the fuck did you tell him? Keep your mouth shut."

"I didn't tell him anything," Subaey said in Arabic

"Then how did they know Saleh is our contact?"

242

"I don't know. I haven't said anything," Subaey said. Guidice looked at Uvanov who smiled. The plan was working. Guidice walked behind the prisoners and stood next to Sobaleski.

"Mr. Wall, don't you find it interesting that Mr. Winter told us all about the weapons you took to the mission," Guidice said "He even mentioned that in your haste to leave the airport you attacked, you carelessly dropped a full 30-round magazine. That was very careless, Mr. Wall. And he told us all of that without any, shall we say, persuasion."

Hamed exploded. "You bastard. I will kill you," he said in Arabic.

"I didn't tell them anything," Subaey said. "Nothing."

"Then how do they know so much?" Hamed asked. "The only way they could know about the weapons and the airport is if you told them. If we get out of here alive I will kill you and I'll have your family killed, you traitor."

Subaey's mind raced trying to find something, anything to persuade Hamed he was telling the truth that the information was already known. "If you think I am lying, then how come he keeps calling you Mr. Wall and me Mr. Winter? They don't know our names."

In Arabic, the names Winter and Wall are pronounced Winter and Wall. Sobaleski quickly wrote what Subaey had said and passed the information to Guidice. "Mr. Wall, Mr. Winter has been very cooperative so we're going to give him something to eat and drink. But you have been lying to us. That of course means more pain and suffering until we get what we need. You can avoid that."

Hamed thought that Subaey's explanation made sense. He was about to forgive his partner. Guidice decided to take a chance.

Mr. Wall, Mr. Winter said you each fired three stinger missiles and that he took out the control tower. That was nice shooting, Mr. Wall. That's a much smaller target than the terminal that you hit."

Hamed seethed. If there were any doubts about his partner spilling his guts they were dispelled. Forgetting they had left behind the six crates the missiles were stored in, Hamed said, "That is all the proof I need, Jameel. You will die a slow death."

"Since Mr. Winter appears to be much more cooperative, let's move Mr. Wall back to his quarters." Guidice said. He and Uvanov picked up the chair and carried Hamed into the adjoining room. Uvanov shut the door.

"Mr. Wall, it's clear that you don't want to cooperate with us. All we wanted was your Saudi contact. Now you sit here by yourself for a few minutes while I have a nice chat with Mr. Winter."

Guidice and Uvanov returned to the room where Subaey was sitting silently. Mr. Winter, I don't think your partner is very pleased with you. In fact, I'll bet he intends to kill you. I don't want to let that happen. I'm going to make you an offer. You tell us what we want to know and the U.S. government will give you a new identity and a safe place to live away from people like Mr. Wall who want to harm you. What do you say?"

"He'll kill my family," Subaey said.

"Not if you tell us where they live. We'll have them flown here to join you," Guidice said.

Subaey fell silent thinking about his options. "How do I know you are telling me the truth," he said finally.

"You'll have to trust me just as I am trusting you that you are telling me the truth," Guidice said. "You think about that, Mr. Winter. We are offering you and your family a nice safe home and money. No one will ever know where you live."

Subaey knew now that he had no choice. Hamed would not believe anything he said.

And al Qaeda vengeance was merciless.

"What do you want to know?"

"You are being very sensible," Guidice said. "And we will guarantee that your friend in the next room will not kill your family. He will be held here until your family joins you and then he will be put on trial and executed or sent to prison for the rest of his life. My assistant will set up the video camera and CD recorder. OK, let's start with your real names and where you came from."

"My name is Jameel Subaey. My friend's name is Faisal Hamed. We are Saudis. I'm from al Dammam; Hamed is from al Khobar."

"Are you members of al Qaeda?

"Yes."

"On September 11 was your assignment to destroy Westchester County Airport?"

"Yes."

"How did you do that?" Guidice asked.

"With missiles. We had six stinger missiles. Faisel fired three and I also fired three."

"Where did you get these missiles?"

"From the Saudi mission."

"How did they get them into the mission?" Guidice asked.

"I'm not sure, but I think they were brought here by diplomatic courier."

"Were there any other plans to attack other airports or buildings on the day you attacked the Westchester airport?" Guidice asked.

"Yes. Other members of our cell were supposed to attack JFK, LaGuardia and Newark."

"Do you know the other people in the cell and where they are located?"

"No. We are not told that information."

"Who is your main contact and where is he?"

"Our contact is Abdelaziz Saleh. He is Deputy Charge D'affairs at the Saudi UN mission."

"You recently visited that mission with a large gym bag. What was in the bag?" Guidice asked.

"Four automatic rifles, four pistols, ammunition and some magazines."

"Automatic rifles? You mean AK-47's? Kalashnikov's?"

"Yes."

"Did you have them with you when you attacked the airport?" Guidice asked.

"Yes."

"Why?"

"To kill anyone who interfered."

"Is Faisal Hamed your boss? Does he take orders from Saleh?"

"Yes."

"How long have you been in this country? How did you get here?"

"We have been here six years. Hamed came in through Mexico. I came in through Canada."

"Are either of you here legally?" Guidice asked.

"No."

For nearly two hours Subaey answered questions. Guidice appeared cordial offering the terrorist operative water and some fruit.

"That's it for now, Subaey. We're going to check out your information. Williams, you and Sobaleski take Subaey to his quarters and keep an eye on him. Petra, let's have a talk with our friend Faisal Hamed," Guidice said.

Uvanov and Guidice opened the door between the two interrogation rooms and were greeted by an empty chair.

"Shit. The fucker's bolted," Guidice said. "Go after him. He's naked and injured so he'll be moving slowly to avoid being seen. If you don't find him within an hour, drive to the Mission and watch the entrance. He must not be allowed access to the mission or anyone in it."

Guidice called Breen.

"Bobcat."

"Pickpocket." One of our guests has left our company."

"Shit. How the fuck did that happen?" Breen asked. "Wasn't anyone watching him?"

"He cut the ropes on the rough edge of the chair," Uvanov called to Guidice after examining the ropes. Guidice repeated the information to Breen.

"I've got four guys out looking for him. He's naked. They'll find him," Guidice said.

"They better. When you get him under control ask him who Talal Farhan is. Farhan works at the Saudi Mission. He may know or work with Saleh," Breen said.

When Breen hung up he called Carl Picket and explained the dilemna.

"Hamed may try to contact Abdelaziz Saleh at the UN Mission. If he does, he may give us his whereabouts. At that point scramble the transmission so Saleh can't give him instructions. Then let pickpocket know where Hamed is."

Less than five minutes from the warehouse, the four former agents came upon a small gathering. Dan Moretti got out and walked to the edge of the group. "That's right officer," a witness said. "I was walking my dog and this naked guy comes out of nowhere and goes to a car that stopped at this light. He opened the door and before the driver could react this guy slugged him and pushed him to the other seat. Then they drove off."

"What kind of car was it," the officer asked.

"It was a Chrysler PT Cruiser. It looked like an old station wagon, you know the one with the wood sides," the pedestrian said.

"What about the driver? What was he wearing?"

"A light gray shirt and a light gray matching tie. Couldn't see anything else."

Moretti went back to the car. "We're looking for a Chrysler PT Cruiser that looks like an old fashioned station wagon. Our friend Hamed slugged the driver and took the car and the driver with him. He'll probably take this guy clothes and then kill him. The driver was wearing a light gray shirt and a matching light gray tie.

"You know that color matching design crap. He may ditch the tie or he may want to look like a businessman. Either way, he's wearing a gray shirt. Cory let's get to the Saudi mission. He probably won't try to enter before tonight but we can't afford to take the chance. We have to make sure Hamed never gets there "

Speeding slightly, Walker drove through the Lincoln Tunnel into the city parking in a vacant diplomatic spot on Lexington Avenue a block from the Saudi mission. Moretti put a U.S. Gov't Official Business sign on the dashboard and the four men got out. Each man took up a position where they could see each other's backs and easily stop someone from entering the mission. Each carried a hypodermic filled with a sedative.

It was well after dark when the Saudi mission received a call from someone requesting Abdelaziz Saleh.

"He's in a meeting," the operator said.

"This is Mr. Cliff Wall. I must speak to him. It is urgent, an emergency." Hamed said in Arabic.

"The operator buzzed the conference room and told Saleh about the call. Saleh excused himself, walked down the hall and entered his office.

"Yes."

"Khobar."

"Ras Tanura. Where are you? You were supposed to be here hours ago" Saleh said.

"The FBI is on to us. They still have Subaey. I got away. Subaey talked. They know everything, even your name."

"I see," Saleh said. "Where are you?"

"In a restaurant on 45th. I don't have any ID."

"Get here as fast as you can. "Someone...."

Picket electronically interrupted the conversation preventing Saleh from telling Hamed there would be someone waiting outside to get him clearance into the mission. Pickett called Moretti.

"Dan, this guy won't have any ID on him so the cops won't let him within 25 feet of the entrance," Pickett said. "He'll probably try to find another phone. That's when you can grab him."

Using the intercom, Moretti alerted the team. "He's on his way. When he gets to the police barricade, they'll probably turn him away. Any dark skinned guy turned away who's wearing a gray shirt has to be our man. Follow him and when it appears safe, hit him with the needle."

When Hamed approached the police barricade, he told the cops he was a Saudi. But with no ID and no letter from the Mission, he was told to leave. Vladik and Simpson followed Hamed to a phone booth. After Hamed dialed the number Vladik forced the door open, jammed the syringe into Hamed's arm and pushed the plunger. Hamed's eyes went wide and he started to sag. Vladik propped him up, and replaced the phone as Simpson arrived. "My friend is drunk," Vladik said loudly so the three passersby could hear. "Sir, will you give me a hand?" he said to Simpson

"Sure."

Assured that nothing appeared to be wrong, the passersby continued on their way. Simpson spoke into his intercom mike. "Dan, we're in a phone booth near Marconi's Spirit shop on 43rd. Bring the car."

Abdelaziz Saleh came out of the Saudi mission and approached the commander of the police security detail. "Has a man asked you for admission, Captain," Saleh asked.

"Yes sir, just a few moments ago. He didn't have any ID so I sent him on his way."

Despite a growing alarm, Saleh managed, "Thank you captain" before returning to the Mission.

Walker and Moretti arrived across the street from the phone booth. Vladik and Simpson each put a shoulder under Hamed and carried him to the waiting cat. Moretti opened the door. "He didn't get a chance to call," Vladik said. "He'll be out for several hours."

With Hamed safe between Vladik and Simpson, Walker drove away. Moretti called Breen. "Bobcat, this is pickpocket. We have the merchandise you ordered. Proceeding to the factory."

"This is Bobcat. Keep a close eye on merchandise. We don't want anyone stealing it."

"Understood. Out."

Everyone was visibly relieved when Cory Walker pulled into the warehouse and shut the door. Hamed was pulled from the vehicle and carried to the chair from which he had escaped. This time his arms were secured to the arms of the chair by Velcro straps. He was stripped of his stolen clothing.

When Hamed regained consciousness he realized what had happened.

"Ah, I see you are now awake, Faisel," Guidice said. "You caused us quite a bit of trouble."

Hamed cursed his captors in Arabic.

Guidice resisted the urge to smash the terrorist. "Your partner told us everything. In fact he told us so much that we no longer have any use for you. So unless you feel like cooperating…"

"What do you intend to do?" Hamed asked.

"That depends upon you. If you talk and corroborate what Subaey told us, we'll be very considerate. If not, well, no one will know where you are and no one will admit to missing you. You'll just disappear. No martyrdom for you. We'll bury you with some pigs."

"I will tell you nothing."

"You don't have to. We know all about what you did at the airport. And we know who your contact is at the Saudi mission. We know a great deal in fact. And what we are considering is letting your Saudi friends know that you talked and that Subaey died before he would give up any information," Guidice said.

"They would not believe you."

"Perhaps not. But you can believe they will no longer trust you . I don't think they will be pleased. Do you? By the way, do you have family in Arabia? I pity them," Guidice said.

"They will kill my family."

"Like I said, Hamed, that's a pity. But it doesn't have to be that way. You can save them. It's up to you."

Hamed knew al Qaeda would find his family. Death for him would be swift, but his wife and daughters would be raped and tortured.

"What do you want me to do?" Hamed asked.

Guidice turned on a video light and the camera. "When I tell you, talk into the camera.

I want you to tell us who you are, who you work for, how you got here, what your assignment was, how you carried it out, and what you are planning next. Tell me how you get your weapons and explosives. Don't leave anything out." Guidice started the DVD recorder.

When Hamed was finished, he was given some fruit and more water.

"One more question. Who is Talal Farhan? He works at the Mission."

"I don't know him."

"Are you sure? Has Saleh mentioned his name?"

"I don't know him. And I don't know if Saleh knows him. He has never mentioned Farhan's name to me."

Guidice decided Hamed was telling the truth. He took the disk from the machine, left the room and called Breen.

"Breen."

"Vince, it's Frank. We got it all. From both of them. I have it on disc. Hamed says he doesn't know Farhan."

"Stream it to me as soon as you can. Make a copy of the Disk and send me the original."

Breen called CIA Director Burdette. "Our two friends are Jameel Subaey and Faisel Hamed. They told us everything, names, dates, methods, everything except where they plan to attack next. They haven't been told that. And they are both al Qaeda. Both have met bin Laden."

"The one who got away. Did he talk to anyone?"

"He talked to his contact in the Saudi mission, a man named Abdelaziz Saleh. He's the Deputy Charge D'affaires there."

"Are you sure of that?"

"Yes," said Breen. "Both Subaey and Hamed confirmed that."

"He has diplomatic immunity. I wonder if your two have immunity."

"Doubtful. Both are here illegally. What do you want me to do with them?" Breen asked.

"Keep them secure. See if you can punch holes in their stories. And stream that disk to me and have a messenger bring me the original as soon as possible."

"Understood. One more thing. My guys monitored a conversation between a man at the Saudi mission named Talal Farhan and a guy named Tony Rodrigo. They were talking about delivery of a product, strange conversation for a mission employee. These guys also use email chat rooms to talk."

"Very interesting. Do you think Farhan and Saleh work together?" Burdette asked.

"Possibly, but Faisel Hamed says he never heard of Farhan and never heard Saleh speak of him."

"Do you believe this Hamed?" Burdette asked.

"I don't think he had any reason to lie. He gave us an awful lot."

"Alright. Stay with it," Burdette said..

"Roger that."

After Breen hung up, Burdette called the White House and was put through to the President.

"I hope you have good news for me, Bill," President Barnes said.

"I think I have the proof you need about the Saudis, Mr. President. My team leader is sending a video stream in a few moments and I'll have the disk tomorrow. We also picked up some electronic intelligence involving another man in the Saudi mission," Burdette said.

"Sounds fascinating. Any holes, any wiggle room for them?"

"Not for the two my men are holding. They confessed. They're both al Qaeda operatives. One of them got away briefly and talked to his Saudi contact. So the contact knows we know something. How much we're not sure. But they know they have been exposed. Incidentally, these two guys admitted they blew up the airport and both independently named the Deputy Charge D'affairs as the guy who gave the orders. They also said they know there are other cells being run from the mission but they didn't know who was running them or who the members were," Burdette said.

"I know a few people who should see this, Bill. Thank you for your help. I want you at a meeting early tomorrow. Bring the disk with you."

"Yes sir."

"Is there anything left to clean up?" the president asked.

"Yes sir. Our friends. They are being kept on ice for now."

"OK, the attorney general will want to chat with them, I'm sure of that." the president said. "Thank you, Bill. You did a great job. I look forward to seeing you tomorrow."

"I'll be there by 7, Mr. President."

Barnes buzzed his secretary Lucy Vernon.

"Lucy, I want you to arrange a meeting for 7:30 tomorrow morning. Please ask Nancy Hanks, General Watson, Randolph, Secretaries Collins and Mooreland, Rivera, Roy Owens and attorney general Mike Armistead.

"Very well, sir."

-Chapter Twenty-three-

"You all know each other, so let's get started," President Barnes said. "This morning I received videodisks in which two men, both Saudis, both here illegally, confessed to the rocket attack of the Westchester County Airport. Both admit that attacks on other airports were planned on the same day, but were called off for some reason that is unclear. Furthermore, they named the Deputy Charge D'Affairs at the Saudi UN Mission as being their contact. In my view their confession and other evidence gathered by the FBI leaves little doubt about Saudi involvement in terrorism. Play the disk please."

The President and his security team watched Jameel Subaey's confession. When the disk concluded the president said, "The other disk is similar. It's a confession by this man's accomplice, a man by the name of Faisel Hamed. Since he essentially says the same things and admits to the same crime, in the interest of time I suggest we skip that and devote the rest of the meeting to deciding exactly what we should do. Alan."

"Mr. President," Secretary of State Alan Collins began, "I must admit I am stunned by this. And it raises many, many questions. Where are these men being held? If the FBI doesn't have them, who does? How was this confession obtained? Is there a link to the attack on the Mall?"

"I have been assured that the recording is authentic," the president said. "I did not ask how the confession was obtained and I don't care to know. The two men are admitted terrorists who attacked one of our airports and killed more than 400 people. That makes them our enemy. For now they are being held in seclusion."

"Mr. President, these two men must be handed over to Justice," said Attorney General Mike Armistead.

"I agree, Mr. President," Homeland Security Secretary Phil Mooreland said. "The case must be turned over to the FBI immediately. Even though this man Subaey denies any knowledge of other cells, he could be lying. It is possible he could lead us to the people planning the other airport attacks and maybe even tell us who attacked the mall in Minnesota."

"Before we make something formal out of this – and make no mistake we will do that – I want to develop a comprehensive strategy, a plan for dealing with the Saudis, with Congress, with the UN and finally with the American people," the President said.

"Sir, we can work on a strategy while the FBI is investigating the case and questioning the terrorists. These could be accomplished at the same time," Mooreland said. "The correct procedure is to have the FBI take them into custody without delay. Am I right, Terry?"

"Mr. Secretary, thank you for the tremendous vote of confidence in the FBI," Daly said. "I'm Terry Daly, head of the counter terrorism department of the FBI. Director Roy Owens is under the weather and asked me to sit in for him. I was at the airport about an hour after the rocket attack. And even though I agree with what you suggest, Mr. Secretary, I think we can concede that whoever has custody of these two men has done a masterful job of extracting information, probably better than the FBI, or at least as good. We should also consider that when they are turned over to us the case becomes public and in fact becomes a criminal case precluding us in the FBI from discussing it in relation to other cases involving terrorists or that might otherwise be related."

"He's right, Mr. President. FBI investigators in this case cannot discuss facts with other investigators working on other terrorism cases. "That is stupid and outrageous," Mooreland said. "Is that why you are suggesting the suspects not be turned over to the FBI?" Mooreland asked.

"Sir, under current law, turning them over to the FBI will actually hinder the FBI investigation," Daly said. "Right now we are free to use the facts we have in that case to help us in other cases. If they are charged we will no longer be free to do that. And when it becomes known that they are being charged with the rocket attack on the airport, the media circus will begin. All of the nets will want to interview you, Attorney General Armistead, and Director Owens and about who these guys are, where they came from, how we found them, what we learned, what charges will be filed, what kind of trial they will have and where will it be held. And the victims' families will weigh in as well."

"Mr. Daly, are you advocating that they shouldn't be turned over to the FBI?" Fred Randolph, the president's chief of staff said. "Because if you are, you are advocating breaking the law."

"I am not advocating we break the law at all, Mr. Randolph. I am merely advocating that we take our time enforcing it. The president said he wants to develop a strategy for dealing with the Saudis, the Congress, the UN and the American people. I believe that will be difficult, if not impossible, to do with the distractions caused by the media."

"Mr. President, you and I have discussed this before," Nancy Hanks, National Security Advisor said. "I strongly believe that since we are in a war against terrorism, we are justified in treating those we apprehend as members of a foreign military and holding them for a military tribunal, not criminal trial,

"That's pretty thin, Nancy," Armistead said. "They weren't apprehended on a battlefield fighting our military."

"Perhaps not. But since they did use military weapons, and since al Qaeda stated they are at war with us and they said they belong to al Qaeda, it isn't such a stretch to hold them as representatives of a foreign military organization. That will enable the FBI to continue its investigation unheeded and give us time to develop the strategy the president wants."

Mr. President, if it isn't too much trouble, I think we all would like to know who is holding these men. Is it the FBI?" Randolph asked.

"Where they are, who has them and how we deal with them is secondary right now though I will be blunt in telling you I want the death penalty for both of them. No deals and no weaseling," the president said. "But right now we have to focus on the larger picture dealing with the Kingdom of Saudi Arabia and with the UN," the president said. "Alan?"

"Mr. President, the Deputy Charge D'Affairs is immune to prosecution. We can declare him persona non grata and order Saudi Arabia to send him home or ask the Saudis to strip him of his immunity," Collins said.

"That's all?" the president asked. He looked around the room. Everyone nodded.

"Well I have a different view. Under orders, this man planned and directed the attack that caused the deaths of hundreds and the destruction of an American airport. And he probably, no make that certainly, knows the whereabouts of the people who were supposed to attack the other airports. Immunity or not, he's not going to get away with it, not as long as I am president."

"Sir, " Collins said. "If the Saudis agree to strip him of his immunity it will be a show of support and a condemnation of terrorism. If they won't release him they can rightfully be accused of hiding a terrorist thereby supporting terrorism. And we can ask the Security Council to condemn Saudi Arabia and order them to turn over Saleh to us."

"There's not much chance the UN will play ball with us after we unilaterally sent some of their delegates home," Randolph said.

"Mr. President, perhaps the UN will side with us when they see that we have unimpeachable physical evidence that ties the Saudi Deputy Charge D'affairs to the airport attack," Daly said.

"What kind of evidence?" the president asked.

"We obtained from customs the records of all diplomatic pouch deliveries over the last two years and the names of the individuals who picked them up," Daly said. "According to customs records, Abdelaziz Saleh signed for six crates marked "beach umbrellas" last April."

"Beach umbrellas? What do they have to do with this, Mr. Daly?" General Beverly Watson, senior military advisor asked.

"These weren't beach umbrellas, general. Those crates contained stinger missiles."

"Oh come on, Daly, how the hell do you know that? I seriously doubt customs searched the crates?" General Watson asked.

"General, six empty crates labeled "beach umbrellas" were found at the airport along with the empty missile launchers. They were the original crates in which stinger missiles were shipped. And one of the crates had the address of the Saudi UN Mission written in English and Arabic and the customs number on it. That number matches the number in the customs records."

"It would appear we have a smoking gun," Armistead said.

"On the other hand, it could be argued that Saleh had no knowledge of the contents of the crates and that he merely signed for them," Hanks said.

"That might be true, Nancy. But there is no getting around the fact that the Deputy Charge d'affairs accepted a package containing missiles and that means someone in the mission facility was expecting them," Barnes said. "Personally, I don't believe that someone as important as the Deputy Charge'd'affairs signs for packages or goes to the airport to pick up packages unless there is a very good reason. No, he knew what they contained alright."

"In any case, it is damaging information as you suggest," Armistead offered. "The Saudis may claim they do not know Hamed and Subaey, but they cannot deny a mission official picked up six crates that contained missiles."

"That's good work, Daly. Thank you," the president said. "Now the larger question is what do we do next? Do we call in the ambassador?"

"If you do take that next step, Mr. President, I don't think it would be wise to tell him we have two Saudi nationals in custody," Shanks said. "There is no point in providing that information unless we have to. It will be interesting to see how they respond to the customs records and the fact that those crates delivered to the mission were the same crates found at the airport."

"Mr. President, I know the ambassador very well. He's clever, bright and he plays hardball. He'll deny everything and accuse us of falsifying records to embarrass his country," Randolph said.

"Sir," Collins said. "If he decides to play hardball, as Fred puts it, I am prepared to tell him we will present the evidence to the Security Council and request a resolution demanding that the Saudis give up Saleh so he can stand trial."

"And what will the Security Council do? They cannot force the Saudis to give up Saleh," Randolph said. "If they do anything at all it will be a minor rebuke or maybe a condemnation of Saudi Arabia."

"Fred's right, Mr. President. A condemnation has the same force as a slap in the face," Hanks said. "But on the other hand that would be a terrible blow to Saudi pride. We must also consider the possibility that China or one of the other permanent members will veto the resolution in return for Saudi oil."

"Suddenly, what seemed so simple a few minutes ago, now seems terribly complex. Just exactly what can we do if someone does veto the resolution?" the president asked. "This guy was behind one of the most heinous acts ever committed in this nation, the cold blooded murder of hundreds of innocent people including women and children. With the evidence we have he'll be condemned by the entire world

"Mr. President, what should we do if Saleh decides to flee the country?" Daly asked.

"Can we legally prevent him from leaving?" Barnes asked.

"No," Collins said. "Not unless the Saudis agree to revoke his immunity."

"So he can just leave?" Barnes asked.

"Yes sir," Collins replied.

"Alan, I don't care what international law on diplomacy says. We're going to detain that bastard and put him on trial."

"If we do that we'll be breaking international law. That trial will be illegal in the eyes of the world. That makes us no better than Saleh," Hanks said.

"I hope you are not comparing what I would do with what the terrorists have done. If this bastard is allowed to flee the country, Americans would be outraged. Alan, call the ambassador in and make our case. Tell him we want Saleh," Barnes said.

"Our next step will be based on what the Saudis do. Fred, will you, Phil and Terry join me in the Oval Office for a few minutes, please."

"Mr. Secretary, the ambassador of Saudi Arabia is here to see you sir," Vicki Stevenson, Collins' secretary said.

"Ah, show him in, please, Vicki."

"Mr. Secretary, it is an honor to see you again sir. You are looking well." Ambassador Abdul Sulieman said.

"Thank you Mr. Ambassador," Collins said as the two shook hands. "I want to thank you for coming on such short notice. Please sit down, Would you like coffee, tea?"

"Coffee, please," the ambassador said.

Collins asked Stevenson to bring in coffee. The two men shared small talk while she poured the Arabica from a silver pot that she placed on a silver tray on the ornate table.

"Would you like cream and sugar, your excellency," Stevenson asked.

"One lump and very little cream, please."

When Stevenson finished she withdrew closing the double doors to Collins' office. The two sipped. The ambassador broke the silence. "To what do I owe the pleasure of this meeting, Mr. Secretary?"

"Mr. Ambassador, I am deeply troubled. I have learned that one of the officials in your mission is implicated in the attack on the airport several weeks ago."

"Surely you are mistaken, Mr. Secretary. I have known my staff for years. They are all honorable people. Who is the individual about whom you speak?"

"His name is Abdelaziz Saleh, the Deputy Charge d'affairs, Mr. Ambassador."

"I see. What evidence do you have to support such an allegation?"

"Last April, Mr. Saleh signed a customs document taking possession of a shipment of six crates under diplomatic immunity," Collins said. "Those crates turned up at the airport. They contained the missiles that were used in the attack."

"Forgive me, Mr. Secretary, but how can you be sure the crates were the same?"

"One of the crates found at the airport was stamped with the address of the Saudi mission and had the customs seal and document number on it. The crates were labeled "beach umbrellas," Collins said. "They are the same beach umbrellas Mr. Saleh signed for. There is no doubt about that."

"Mr. Secretary, if what you say is true, what is it you would like me to do?"

"My government wants your government to waive Mr. Saleh's immunity and turn him over to us."

"My government will not do that, Mr. Secretary. Surely you can understand that if we were to do what you ask we would be demonstrating to the world that the United States has inordinate power over the Saudi government. That would diminish our stature."

"On the contrary, Mr. Ambassador if you turn Mr. Saleh over to us your country will be making a statement that it denounces terrorism and terrorist acts and that mission employees will not be allowed to hide behind diplomatic immunity. Your country will be praised," Collins said.

"My government has a long standing policy, Mr. Secretary. We will not permit our diplomatic personnel to be arrested or harassed by any government. If there is any wrong doing, we will investigate and take appropriate action."

"Appropriate action. Every terrorist suspect your country has arrested has been released. No trials. Nothing. That's hardly appropriate action," Collins said.

"The individuals were investigated and no evidence of any criminal action was found."

"Mr. Ambassador, the president has instructed me to tell you that if your government fails to cooperate in this matter, we will take this to the United Nations Security Council."

"If you do that Mr. Secretary, there may be serious consequences on the world petroleum market. In addition you will be embarrassed because whatever resolution you seek will be vetoed. Was there anything else?"

"No, Mr. Ambassador. Thank you for coming in."

"Good day, Mr. Secretary."

When ambassador Sulieman returned to the mission he asked his secretary to summon Abdelaziz Saleh. While awaiting Saleh's arrival, Sulieman called Prince Abdulla in Riyadh.

"The American government has proof that Saleh was involved in the attack on the airport. I'm afraid the evidence is very strong, your highness. The Secretary of State has demanded we turn Saleh over to them for trial. If we fail to do that, they will present their charges to the UN Security Council and it will become public. They will then ask for a resolution requiring us to surrender Saleh."

"We will deny the allegations and claim the Americans are trying to discredit us. As luck would have it, we sit on the Security Council this year. We also have several friends who will veto such a resolution in return for oil," Prince Abdulla said. "That, of course, is what I would prefer. You have to get Saleh out of America as soon as possible."

"Very well, your highness," Sulieman said. "I'll get Saleh out of the country tonight on my plane."

The ambassador called Talal Farhan. "The Americans are planning to make a case before the UN Security Council. I want you to create a major diversion that will occupy the press and the authorities for some time. Activate your cell immediately," Sulieman said. "We may have a security breach Talal, so be very careful how you communicate with them. Use a public phone."

"What are the targets, your excellency?" Farhan said.

"Pick the ones where you can do the most damage and inflict the most casualties," the ambassador said.

"Yes your excellency. It will be done."

"You wanted to see me, sir?" Saleh asked as he knocked on Sulieman's door.

"Ah, Abdelaziz, yes. Come in please. Would you like coffee?"

"Thank you sir"

Sipping his coffee, Sulieman studied Saleh making the young Deputy Charge D'affairs squirm. "Abdelaziz," the ambassador began, "The American Secretary of State told me that they have overwhelming evidence linking you to the airport attack. I'm surprised at the carelessness of you and your people. Leaving a missile launcher crate with our address on it is inexcusable. I'm relieving you and sending you back to Riyadh today."

"Sir, I think you should know the Americans have captured two of my men Faisel Hamed and Jameel Subaey."

"What! How did that happen? Were they careless? Did they talk in a bar someplace?" Sulieman asked.

"They were being very careful. When they were notified that their apartment was going to be painted they brought their weapons to the mission to avoid discovery. They rarely went out together in public. Sir, this is very strange. It could not have been the FBI or local police because there's been nothing said publicly about their being arrested."

"Who do you suppose is responsible?" Sulieman asked.

"I don't know sir. It could be the CIA. Hamed escaped briefly and called me. He does not know who is captors were. I told him to meet me at the entrance to the Mission, but he never showed," Saleh said.

"I think they recaptured him. Hamed said Subaey talked and told them a great deal including the fact that I was the person who ordered the attacks."

"You fool. Why didn't you tell me this sooner?"

"You weren't available earlier. And then you were out meeting with the Secretary of State," Saleh said.

"Secretary Collins did not mention Subaey and Hamed. Most puzzling. We can't take any chances. We've got to get you out of here now. Get your things. I will have you driven to the airport within the hour. You'll take my plane. I'll cancel my visit to Los Angeles," the ambassador said.

After Saleh left the office, Sulieman called the private hangar at JFK Airport and ordered his plane prepared.

"Mohammed, I want you personally to see to it that the plane never reaches Riyadh. Understand?"

"Yes ecellency," Mohammed Hassan replied. Hassan, a blood relative from the same tribe, who was handpicked by Sulieman, handled travel arrangements for the Saudi Mission in New York and the Embassy in Washington. Hassan ordered the plane prepared. While it was being fueled, he disabled the fuel indicators on all four tanks so the gauges would give false readings to the pilots.

They should run out of fuel over the Atlantic.

Vince Breen and Bump Masterson were keenly interested in the phone conversation between the prince in Riyadh and the ambassador.

"This goes right to the highest levels of their government," Breen said.

"I think they're panicking," Masterson said. "Let's hope they do something stupid."

"Yeah, that means we've got them and they know it. Now they're trying to cover their tracks. The boss needs to know this."

"Excuse me for interrupting, Mr. President. There's an urgent call for Mr. Burdette."

"Thank you Lucy," Burdette said. "May I, Mr. President?"

"Certainly, Bill."

Burdette picked up the phone on the president's desk. "Burdette."

"Breen. The Saudis are trying to get Saleh out of the country. They're flying him out in less than an hour on the Ambassador's private plane."

"Shit. Any chance you can disable that plane?"

"Not enough time, sir."

"OK, thanks." Burdette hung up. The president was staring at him. "Mr. President. That was one, ah, can we talk in private, sir?"

"Will you gentlemen please excuse us? Just wait in Lucy's office. I'll be with you in a few moments," the president said.

When Burdette finished briefing the president, Barnes said, "Can we stop them?"

"Not likely, sir, unless you want the FAA to quarantine the plane," Burdette said.

Using the intercom, the President said, "Lucy, ask Randolph to call Sally Borders at FAA and tell her on my orders to have JFK quarantine any Saudi private plane trying to leave JFK," Barnes said.

Randolph opened the door and walked into the Oval Office. "Mr. President, how is it that the director of the CIA knows Saleh is trying to leave the country?" Randolph asked.

"You're wasting time, Fred. After you have talked to the FAA you and the others rejoin me here and I'll inform you of what is going on."

An anxious Saleh packed lightly and was on his way in the Ambassador's car in 10 minutes. When he arrived at the hangar he was greeted by Hassan.

"Mr. Saleh, the plane is fueled and waiting," Hassan said.

"Thank you Mohammed," Saleh said as he boarded the Grumman G-5 and sat in one of the luxurious seats facing forward. The pilot closed the door and informed Saleh where the lavatory, refrigerator and liquor cabinets were located. Saleh stood and made himself a stiff drink as the pilot returned to the cockpit. He and the co-pilot went through their checklists as Saleh fidgeted in his seat gulping down his drink. At last the first engine whined to life. Saleh poured himself another drink and took the bottle with him to his seat. The co-pilot radioed the tower asking permission to taxi.

"Kilo Sierra Alpha One Zero Zero, Kennedy Ground. Taxi runway 4 left."

The G-5 entered the que with commercial airliners. When it reached the number one position, the co-pilot radioed the tower, "Kilo Sierra Alpha One Zero Zero, ready for take off 4 left."

"Kilo Sierra Alpha One Zero Zero, cleared for takeoff 4 left. Contact Departure Control on 120.4."

"Roger. Kilo Sierra Alpha One Zero Zero cleared for takeoff 4 left."

The pilot pushed the throttles to the stop and watched as the rpm's rose rapidly. He released the brake. "Kilo Sierra Alpha One Zero Zero rolling." The sleek G-5 screamed down the runway and roared into the air.

"Kilo Sierra Alpha One Zero Zero, Departure Control. You are clear to 3,000, 015 degrees.

"Kilo Sierra Alpha One Zero Zero, 3,000, 015 degrees."

"Kilo Sierra Alpha One Zero zero this is Departure Control. You are clear to one zero thousand. Maintain heading of 015. Contact Boston Center on 174.three. Good day."

The FAA station chief entered the tower. "If a Saudi private or government plane asks for permission to taxi tell him his plane has been temporarily quarantined and he's to return to the hanger," said Larry Munoz.

"Too late, sir. A Saudi government G-5 just left two minutes ago," the air traffic controller said.

"Shit." Munoz returned to his office and called Washington. The message was relayed to FAA Administrator Sally Borders who flashed it to the White House.

"Mr. President. We just missed him. The Saudi plane is airborne. I'm sorry." Borders said.

"Thank you, Sally," the president said and hung up. Turning to the group who sat in silence, he said, "What are the rules of engagement for a civilian aircraft? Just kidding. The bastard has gotten away."

"What is going on Mr. President?"

Barnes sat on one of the sofas. "What I am about to say doesn't leave this room. A while back I asked Bill Burdette to conduct a no holds barred investigation to find the perpetrators who attacked the airport. I didn't ask how he did it and I don't want to know. And you are not authorized to ask. But suffice to say, he has succeeded in nailing the two responsible and in having them give up their boss. We now have proof that the Saudis are directly involved.

"Why did I do that? Because gentlemen our laws were and are working for the enemy. We now know that attacks were planned on three other New York metro area airports as we suspected. I wondered what such an event might do to this country and after considerable thought I decided to ask for Bill's help."

"Mr. President, you broke the laws of this country by ordering the CIA to operate within our borders," Randolph said. "And I'll bet the methods they used were anything but kosher."

"Mr. Randolph," Burdette said, "there are times when we spend too much time playing within the rules. At the end of the day all that matters is that we have nailed the guys responsible for the attack on the airport, exposed their leader, and probably prevented additional attacks. We have also determined there is no doubt that the Saudis are involved."

"This is a country where we live under the rule of law, Mr. Burdette. And you have broken the law. Mr. Daly, Mr. Armistead, what are your views?" Randolph asked.

"Mr. Randolph don't lecture me about the rule of law. Your sanctimonious bullshit about playing within the rules is how we got hurt the first time ten years ago and how we got hurt again," Burdette said. "My wife lost a brother ten years ago. A few weeks ago we lost a daughter and Terry Daly lost his parents who were killed by these heartless bastards. Terrorists don't play by the rules. The only way to fight terrorism is to throw away the book they so skillfully use against us. Sorry for the interruption."

"Fred, all I really heard here is that Bill Burdette has two Saudis in custody awaiting disposition," Daly said. "And they have confessed."

"Burdette, how the hell did you do to get the confessions from these two men?" Randolph asked.

"We asked politely and they agreed to confess." Everyone laughed.

"This is not funny. Mr. President if Featherstone, Fumer or Claxton find out about this they'll leak it to the liberal press and you'll likely be impeached."

"I view my most important job as protecting the American people and I will do just about anything to accomplish that job," the president said. "I seriously doubt anyone will want my head after they learn that the men we are holding are responsible for the airport attack. I don't need to remind you that my political enemies are very vulnerable because of their unwillingness to cooperate or act on legislation I have proposed. So I'll take my chances. What remains to be decided is a criminal trial or military tribunal. Mike?"

"I think a tribunal is appropriate because it accomplishes our goals. It will enable the FBI to widen their investigation and will keep the media at bay.

"Agreed. Bill as soon as you can, turn them over to the military. Gen. Watson will give you instructions. In the future all foreign terrorist suspects will face a military tribunal," the president said.

"Mr. President, I think this is unwise. We open ourselves to severe criticism and a possible Constitutional challenge," Randolph said.

"You are very naïve, Mr. Randolph," Burdette said. "Perhaps if you had suffered the loss of a family member or seen first hand the carnage that these bastards created you might be more of a patriot than a whining bleeding heart liberal. Mr. President, I'll make the arrangements with Beverly."

"Very well, Bill." The two shook hands.

-Chapter Twenty-four-

When Rodrigo returned to his office from his meeting with Briana Russell at Altria, he found an urgent message from Talal Farhan (Atta): Urgent. Use outside phone.

"I have to run an errand," he said to one of the secretaries assisting the designers. Exercising extreme caution he deleted the message, turned off the computer and left the building by the rear entrance. He headed to Grand Central Station where he knew his conversation would be covered by the public address system. On his way he "window shopped" at several storefronts to see if he was being followed.

At the station he selected an end booth to minimize the chance of anyone overhearing. He and Farhan exchanged passwords.

"Can you talk?" Farhan asked.

"Yes. I'm at Grand Central in a booth with a door."

How ironic, using one of the targets. "The American government may be closing in. We have to act immediately. Tell Tariq to make arrangements with Yousef to pick up the product and transport it to Dossari's, New Jersey place as fast as possible," Farhan said.

"Where do the deliveries go?" Rodrigo asked.

"The top four places on your list. I do not want you involved in the deliveries. All of them should be made during the morning rush hour to ensure we have the maximum number of customers. It should take four vanloads to transfer all of the product to Dossari's office," Farhan said.

"I'll get started right away," Rodrigo said.

"Keep me informed," Farhan said. "But be careful when you call."

"Will do." Rodrigo hung up and called the office notifying the secretary that he wasn't feeling well and was going home.

CIA Operative Bump Masterson was monitoring Talal Farhan's conversations. When he heard the passwords, Dhahran and Juamah, he called Vince Breen on the intercom. Breen hurried to the monitoring room.

"They're talking about products again, boss. And this time they used Muslim names Tariq Dossari and Yousef. The materials are supposed to be taken to Dossari's place somewhere in New Jersey and then delivered to quote the top four places on your list unquote."

"Where are the materials to be shipped from?"

"They didn't say," Masterson said.

"I'll bet a year's pay it's from the Saudi mission."

"Here's something rely strange. This guy Farhan says all the deliveries should be made during the morning rush hour to ensure the maximum number of customers."

Masterson replayed the conversation for Breen.

Breen picked up his radio. "Overlook, this is Bobcat. Are you still in position?"

"Roger Bobcat, what have you got?"

"Some vans will probably be entering the mission some time today to make pick ups. I want you to follow one of them. It will probably go to a place in New Jersey. When it gets there, let me know ASAP and alert Pickpocket. I'll tell them to expect your call. Got that?" Breen asked.

"Any van in particular?"

"Follow the first one so you'll be in position to watch the arrival of the others. Stay cool."

"Roger Bobcat. Overlook out."

"Pickpocket, this is Bobcat."

"Go head, Bobcat, this is pickpocket."

"Overlook is going to follow a van leaving the Saudi mission sometime today. It's destination is a place in New Jersey, hopefully near your location. He'll call you the minute the van stops. I want you to back him up, but keep a low profile. Got that?" Breen asked.

"Roger. Will await Overlook's message. Pickpocket out."

Breen walked to his office and called Burdette on Burdette's private line.

"Yes," Burdette answered.

"Breen. I think something is going down. We monitored a phone conversation between a Saudi mission employee named Farhan and a man named Antonio Rodrigo. They talked about taking product to a place in New Jersey and then Farhan said he wanted the product delivered during the morning rush hour to the top four places on their list. Farhan mentioned two Muslim names Tariq Dossari and a guy named Yousef. I've got my surveillance team ready to follow one of their vans when it leaves the mission," Breen said.

"Good work, Vince. I agree with your assessment. Stay with this," Burdette said.

Rodrigo called Frank's Used Furniture and Furniture Repair. Tariq Dossari using the alias Frank Petrocelli answered and the two exchanged passwords.

"We've got our assignment," Rodrigo said. "Have Yousef pick up the materials and bring them to your shop today. It might take as many as four loads, perhaps five. Ahmed will meet you at your office and drive one of your vans to help with the pickups. Yousef will join you on your last trip." Rodrigo decided not to share the information about the students.

Bump Masterson passed the information along

Rodrigo hung up and walked to gate 107 where he boarded the train to Bronxville. In his apartment, he opened the tiny compartment in his closet and withdrew the papers identifying the targets. Grand Central Terminal was listed as number one. Rodrigo thought about Ann Dunn who used the terminal every morning and decided to substitute number five, Penn Station, for number one.

Al Hafra was waiting when Petrocelli backed the van to the loading dock. Inside the building near the rear door were ten boxes labeled copy paper, bond paper, and office supplies. Each of the 10 boxes contained 250 pounds of HMX. When they were loaded, three filing cabinets were wheeled into the van to foil a cursory search at the tolls.

Petrocelli shut the rear doors and drove away. Moments later, Ahmed Humaidi backed his van to the loading dock. Later

269

Petrocelli and Humaidi returned to pick up another load. Humaidi loaded first and waved as he departed. A half hour later Petrocelli and Hafra finished wheeling the last of the boxes into the van. Petrocelli had no way of knowing that 360 pounds of HMX were missing.

He pulled the van into the parking lot of the small business bearing the name of his alias and parked to the right of the other vans. Humaidi was waiting inside the office. A car drove into the parking lot and parked in the last slot. Rodrigo jumped out and walked to the rear door.

The four men chatted. Petrocelli volunteered to bring back food from the diner and took their order. At the last minute Rodrigo offered to help carry the food and beverages. The two walked to the Cedar Lane Grille some 200 yards away. They paid no attention to the car and van parked across the street.

Over dinner Rodrigo identified the four targets, substituting Penn Station for Grand Central Terminal. "Two students will be arriving shortly. Since they are the least experienced, I will accompany them to Penn Station. Tariq will attack the bridge, Ahmed's target will be the Holland Tunnel and Yousef will destroy the Lincoln Tunnel."

"What about Grand Central?" Humaidi asked.

"It's not on the list. We would have to dilute the amount of the explosives to add a fifth target. These four will isolate New York from the west and the south. And the effect will force them to shut Grand Central for weeks. Ahmed, you've been studying the targets, tell us where the weak points are."

"The most logical spot is the midpoint of the tunnels and the bridge. The tunnels will be at their deepest point where water pressure will be the highest. The force of the explosions will take the path of least resistance that in this case is toward the openings on the East and West side of the tunnels.

The tunnels slope downward and curve and they will be choked with vehicles. The blast should generate enough pressure to breach the roof of the tunnels and open them to the Hudson River.

"Each of the four large cables on the bridge has a capacity of 350,000 tons. At the midpoint of the bridge the cables are closest to the roadbed. Tariq should stay in the right hand lane to be close to the cables. The explosions will badly weaken or destroy the two cables on the New York bound side. Large holes will be opened in the upper and lower deck that will further weaken the integrity of the suspension system. The bridge should collapse."

"And the rail station?" Rodrigo asked.

"One of the bombs should be detonated in the center of the waiting room," Humaidi said. "The other at the lower level near the PATH entrance."

"I've got two very large sports bags on wheels," Dossari said.

"I bought two college sweatshirts with Rutgers and Princeton on them," Rodrigo said. "The students will look like college students wheeling the suitcases."

"Should the vans be stopped when we detonate the bombs?" Hafra asked.

"Only at the bridge," Humaidi said. "Tariq, make sure the van is as close to the cables as possible. You won't be able to stop long before security is all over you. In the tunnels, rush hour will slow you. It isn't critical to be right at the center, just close. Look for the sign on the wall New York/New Jersey. That's the midpoint."

"When are the students coming?" Hafra asked.

"They should have been here. I'll call."

Rodrigo went to Petrocelli's private office, shut the door and dialed the mission. When Farhan came on the line, the two again exchanged passwords.

"All is ready in New Jersey," Rodrigo said. "We will move tomorrow morning. Where are the other two?"

"The students will be driven to the first location on your list at 8," Farhan said.

"That is not a good idea. I prefer the fifth instead," Rodrigo said, referring to Penn Station. "There will be more customers. How will they get the product?"

Farhan thought for a moment. "Agreed. The students will go to number five. We have the product here. They will bring it with them and be there by 8." Satisfied, Rodrigo hung up and explained the changes.

Breen alerted Burdette. "They're going to move tomorrow morning."

"Are you sure."

"That's what Rodrigo said," Breen said.

"Alright. Thanks."

"One more thing. There's been a slight change in their plans. They changed one of the locations from number one to number five. I don't know what that means. But Rodrigo suggested it."

"We'll nail them all, Vince. Thanks," Burdette said.

-Chapter Twenty-five-

"Terry Daly's office, this is Pat Clinton"

"Is he there? This is William Burdette."

"One moment, sir," Clinton said.

"Terry, it's Mr. Burdette."

"Thanks, Pat." Daly closed his office door. "This is Daly."

"Terry, Bill Burdette. How are you?"

"Fine. Bill. And you?"

"Just fine, thanks. I want to thank you for supporting me in the meeting. Randolph is an arrogant jackass."

"I agree. And I also believe these bastards should be tried before a military tribunal, not a criminal court. How can I help you Bill?"

"I didn't want to mention this in the meeting because of Randolph's probable reaction. I hope I can trust you. Anyway, my boys have been monitoring some conversations. We have reason to believe terrorists are going to strike four targets in the New York metro area tomorrow morning at rush hour," Burdette said.

"Where, for Christ's sake?" Daly jumped out of his chair.

"We don't know exactly," Burdette said.

"The New York metro area is a big place."

"We've made it a little easier for you. My boys followed a van, that picked up what these guys called product or materials from the Saudi UN mission on Lex. They drove to a small office building in Teaneck, New Jersey and parked in the lot in the rear. There are at least four men inside the building," Burdette said.

273

"We can't do anything based on that, Bill."

"I know. For what it's worth, one of the guys in the phone conversation we monitored is a guy named Talal Farhan. He works in the Saudi Mission. The firm can't do anything legally and I hesitate to get the local uniforms involved. If these guys are planning to blow something, they have to be totally surprised or they might set off the explosives prematurely. That's why I called you."

"That's still not enough to go on. Do you know who this guy Farhan was talking to?"

"Yes, a fellow named Rodrigo."

"Rodrigo. Tony Rodrigo?

"That's the man. Do you know him?"

"That's the guy we've been building a case on. He's an illegal alien. Give me the address," Daly said. "We can pick him up on suspicion."

"It's 705 Cedar Lane in Teaneck, a small two story place called Franks Office Furniture Repair, something like that," Burdette said. "My team tells me the vans parked in the rear have not been unloaded. So whatever was picked up at the mission is still in the vans."

"Thanks, Bill. Thanks very much."

"Good hunting."

"Thanks," Daly said. He opened his office door and yelled.

"Carter, get a tac team together. Assault weapons, vests, helmets, everything. We move in 30 minutes."

Brown called the field desk supervisor. "This is Carter Brown. Anyone still in the office?"

"Are you kidding me?" Jack Wardell, the supervisor said. "This isn't a nine to five job."

"I know. I want all available agents in battle dress in the garage in 25 minutes. Full gear. This is a live terrorist situation. How many people do you have?" Brown asked.

The supervisor did a quick count. "We have 15, 16 including me."

"OK, get moving. Wait a minute. Make sure four of your people are in plain clothes."

"Jack can give us 16 including himself. They'll meet us in the garage in 25," Brown said to Daly. Both men began changing.

"RE," Daly said, "ask Pat to pull up the Bergen County, New Jersey map and find out where Cedar Lane is in Teaneck. You get the police chief in Teaneck on the horn ASAP. Then call Roy, tell him what's happening and tell him I'll check in when we have surrounded the target building."

Clinton was printing the Bergen County map when the Teaneck Police answered the call.

"Lieutenant Fugate."

"This is the New York FBI office, please hold for Assistant Director Terry Daly. Terry I have a lieutenant Fugate Teaneck PD on the line." Clinton next called Owens and briefed him on the developments.

Daly told Fugate who he was and asked if he was in charge.

"I can't give that information over the phone. I have no way to verify who you are," Fugate said.

"Is your chief there?"

"He's off duty."

Off duty? "Lieutenant, is he at home?"

"I'm not at liberty to say."

"If he is at home, I want his phone number right now."

"Sir, I cannot give you the number. It's private," Fugate said.

"Fine, lieutenant. Call the chief and ask him to call me." Daly spelled his name, repeated his FBI position and gave Fugate his number. "We'll be leaving here for Teaneck in 10 minutes."

"Sir, I...."

"Lieutenant, I don't have time to explain. My advice is to call the chief right now. Is that clear."

The lieutenant called the chief and gave him the number. Chief Morton Fasow was annoyed at the interruption, but he called and was put through to Terry Daly.

"Daly."

"This is Chief Fasow, Teaneck PD. I don't like the way you talked to my desk officer, I don't give a shit if you are FBI."

Daly ignored the comment. "Chief, listen carefully. I am Terry Daly, Assistant Director and I head the anti terrorism department at the bureau. In less than 10 minutes an FBI Tac Team will be leaving Manhattan for Teaneck. We're going to need your help. When I get to the Fairleigh Dickinson parking lot at Route 4 and River Road I want all the patrol cars you have in service and all the men you can muster to meet me. I will brief you when you get there."

"What the fuck is this all about, Daly?"

"I'll brief you when we meet, Chief. All of your officers must be in uniform. No plain clothes. I don't want my guys worrying about people they don't know in civilian clothes. Understand?"

"This better be on the level."

"I assure you it is, chief."

"Alright how many men do you need?

"Enough men and cars to block traffic in both directions within 500 yards of 705 Cedar Lane and all side roads in between. If you don't have enough cars to do that, ask the County Police for help, or the fire department. And chief, this is not a cakewalk. This could be, well, catastrophic if we don't do this right, so do not attempt to do anything until we get there. Understood?"

"Understood."

"Good," Daly said. "Give me your cell number. I'll call you when we cross the bridge. One more thing, chief. I'll need a street map. Ours isn't detailed."

Fasow gave the number to Daly and then called Fugate. "Frank, Mort. Get everyone in off patrol. I want all available uniformed personnel to meet me in the parking lot ASAP No plain clothes. And we'll need all available cars too. "

"But...."

"Now Frank. This is an emergency."

Seven minutes later 22 uniformed officers stood in formation in the Teaneck Police Department parking lot.

Fasow who rarely wore his uniform, stood in blue with a white shirt, three stars gleaming on each collar.

"Gather around." His cell phone jingled. "Fasow."

"Chief, Terry Daly. We've crossed the bridge. We're on route 4. How long will it take us to get there?"

"No more than 10 minutes."

"Good, see you then," Daly said.

"Alright, listen up. We're going to meet an FBI Tac Team in the college parking lot on River Road. We'll be briefed there. Captain, send a car there right now to meet them. Everyone else will follow. No cars left here. This is not a drill, gentlemen. Let's move."

Eleven police cars were in the parking lot when two vans and four carloads of FBI Agents arrived with Captain Rogers. Terry Daly got out of the lead vehicle accompanied by Carter Brown. They exchanged greetings with Chief Fasow and two captains. "Here's the town map, Sir," Fasow said. "Now would you mind telling me what this is all about?"

Daly spread the map over the hood of one of the patrol cars. "Chief we have at least four terrorist suspects inside 705 Cedar Lane. In the rear are vans that we believe may contain large quantities of high explosive. That's why we want the area clear," Daly said. "Show me where 705 Cedar Lane is located?"

Fasow looked at the map and pointed. "About here, between River Road and Catalpa"

"What's behind 705?" Daly asked.

"There's an unpaved road back there. Does it have a name, Paul" Fasow asked Captain Paul Rogers.

"No, sir. It's used as an access road for the apartment garages. It runs from Cedar Lane, actually from a municipal parking lot, to Catalpa," Rogers said.

"Chief, when you block off Catalpa, place a patrol car just north of that dirt road so no one can enter. My team will cover the front and rear of 705. We'll prevent these people from reaching the vans. I want you and one of your officers with me to relay any messages to your men. Station one of your captains on Cedar Lane about 500 yards east of the building and use your cars to block all the side roads in between. Windsor road looks like a good spot. Put the other senior officer on the west side of River Road about the same distance. Is Pommander the only side road on the west side?"

"That's right sir, but if you want 500 yards clearance, we'll have to block the other side of the Hackensack River Bridge and that is Hackensack's jurisdiction," Fasow said.

"Call them and tell them to do it on my say so. If they won't, you do it and I'll send one of my special agents with your patrol car. Order one car to block off River Road at least two blocks north of Cedar and another at least two blocks south.

"I want all residents and businesses evacuated from inside this quarantine line," Daly said, pointing to the East and West perimeters. "Set up the road blocks, then evacuate everyone as quickly and as quietly as possible. We have some special agents in civies who will handle the evacuations from the buildings within sight of 705. That way, anyone watching won't see any uniforms.

"Carter make sure both captains have an agent with them for liaison. Chief, tell your captains to let you know when their men have completed their assignments and all the roads are blocked. We'll move when the area is cordoned off and the civilians evacuated. Better brief your men and get them moving. No sirens and tell your men to avoid driving past 705 to get to the east side. Use another road. One more thing. No shooting without a direct order from me. Clear?"

"Yes sir." The chief and his two captains returned to their men gathered around several of the cars. Fasow counted the side roads and requested the fire department to provide four trucks and the county police to block River Road.

Captain Rogers took his group to Windsor Road where he set up his command post. He then directed cars to block off the side roads beginning with Catalpa working West. Fire Department trucks blocked Windsor, and Belle.

Captain Lauretta Boggio led her five men and one agent in two cars. One car blocked Pommander. Boggio and two officers entered the Cedar Lane Diner and directed everyone to walk to the bridge. After the diner was cleared, Boggio's team accompanied by the FBI agent then blocked the Cedar Lane Bridge.

One van load of agents entered the parking lot connecting the dirt road behind Cedar Lane. A special agent began knocking on apartment doors Another alerted the residents of the apartment complex at 709 and directed them to the municipal parking lot where a police officer accompanied them to Captain Boggio's position. When Daly was notified that the north side of Cedar Lane was clear he directed Carter Brown and six heavily armed agents to take up position to block access to the vans while covering the rear of 705. Two spotlights were set up to illuminate the rear and side doors.

On the south side of Cedar Lane the evacuation was somewhat more complicated. Two agents, a man and a woman, posing as solicitors, went to each residence identified themselves and directed the occupants to leave by the rear, and make their way to River Road or to Windsor and wait behind the police lines.

Inside 705 Rodrigo and his team amused themselves. Ahmed Humaidi watched television. Tariq al Dossari, who had removed the paper cups and plates from the diner, sat observing the backgammon game between Yousef al Hafra and Tony Rodrigo. Occasionally he would glance out the front window.

When Fasow notified Daly that the evacuations had been completed and the roads blocked, Daly called his boss, FBI Director Roy Owens and filled him in on the details.

"We're ready to move, Roy. All civilians evacuated."

"Take them down," Owens said. "Get back to me when you have them. Good luck."

Daly radioed Fasow. An armored FBI van and two cars rounded the corner of River and parked across the street from 705. Agents quickly set up a spotlight at the front and rear of the van. From inside the van, Daly gave the signal for the spotlights to be turned on. He picked up the microphone.

"Attention occupants of Frank's Used Furniture and Furniture Repair at 705 Cedar Lane. This is the FBI. You are surrounded. You have two minutes to come out with your hands on top of your heads."

Rodrigo hit the floor turning over the backgammon board spilling the dice and round pieces. Al Hafra dropped beside him. "What do we do?" he asked. "The weapons are in one of the vans."

"Try to get to the vans. Maybe we can get at least one."

Humaidi and al Dossari also dropped to the floor after turning out the lights and the TV. Humaidi crawled toward the rear door. When he opened it, he saw three laser beams. The back room was bathed in light. Humadi slammed the door and rolled to the side. "We can't get to the vans," he yelled.

Al Dossari crawled to the side door, but it too was illuminated.

"You have one minute. Come out with your hands on top of your heads." Daly said.

"All the doors are covered," al Hafra said,

Al Dossari crawled to the window on the west side and slowly raised it.

"I think the closest van has three guns," He said. He stood on a chair and eased himself out using the chimney to conceal himself from the street.

"Thirty seconds," Daly announced. "This is your last warning."

279

Al Dossari dropped to the ground, and placing the van between himself and the agents in the rear, he slowly crawled to the vehicle 20 feet away. Raising himself to his knees he pulled the door handle. It was locked. The keys were inside the office. He dropped to the ground. "Shit."

"Times up. Give them the gas," Daly said.

Three agents aimed carefully at the front windows and fired teargas grenades. All three grenades crashed through the windows and began fizzing. Within seconds al Hafra and Humaidi began coughing. Rodrigo held his breath and used his shirt to shield his eyes. He crawled to the bathroom to wet his shirt.

"Let's go," Daly radio. Covered by Chief Fasow and an officer and agents with automatic weapons, five agents in gas masks, led by Daly rushed the front door. In the rear, two agents with clear fields of fire covered Brown as he and three other agents rushed past the vans and crashed through the back door.

At the sound of the gas grenades smashing into the windows, al Dossari rolled under the van. When the three agents rushed by him, he crawled to the other side, got to his feet and ran toward the dirt road.

"Freeze. This is the FBI. Lie down and put your hands on your head," The loudspeaker blared

In the glare of the spotlight, al Dossari couldn't see who was talking or how many there might be. He knew at least one gun was trained on him, the laser beam dotted the middle of his chest. Meekly, he lay down.

While one agent covered him, another cuffed him and lifted him to his feet. He was thoroughly searched and pushed to the rear. "We have one in custody," Special Agent Cary Woodruff said. "The vans are secured."

Al Hafra and Humaidi yelled their capitulation and were forced to the floor. Daly placed his back against the east wall. When he peered around the corner he saw the bathroom door being closed. "Here," he said to Brown and Bobby Turner. Brown trained his gun on the door as Daly jumped past and took up a position on the far side. "You, inside. Drop your weapons and come out. NOW."

With nowhere to run, Rodrigo opened the door and was quickly grabbed by Turner and Daly and thrown to the floor. As Rodrigo was cuffed and searched, agents scrambled to the basement and the second floor. The three suspects were led out the front where converging officers and agents took over. Brown stood by the door to the basement; Daly by the stair to the second floor. "Clear" came the call from the basement followed by a similar declaration from the second floor.

The lights were turned on and the agents began searching the building. Daly spoke into his communicator. "This is Control. We are clear. All suspects are in custody. Maintain your positions until we determine the status and contents of the vans." Daly walked across the street. "Rodrigo," he said to the tallest. "Remember me. I sure as hell remember you."

Rodrigo's eyes looked venomous.

"Where are the keys to the vans?" Daly asked. He asked again. Then he strode to Humaidi and with his face up against the face of the smallest suspect, he snarled, "Where are the fucking keys to the vans?"

"Don't tell him anything," Rodrigo ordered.

Daly pushed Rodrigo against the side of the FBI van, "Shut your fucking mouth, you murdering bastard. Get this guy out of here," he said to an agent.

"Now you murdering lowlife coward, where are the keys to the vans?" he hissed to Humaidi.

Humaidi looked into Daly's cold eyes.

Daly took out his 9mm pistol and held it against Humaidi's crotch. "You better tell me where the keys are or I'll blow your balls off."

"In the… the d-d-desk," Humaidi stammered. "Top drawer on the right."

"What's in the vans," Daly asked jamming the gun into the terrorist's crotch.

"I don't know."

Daly pulled the gun back and then slammed it into the terrorist's crotch. Humaidi yelped and sank to his knees. He was quickly lifted by an FBI Agent and a police officer wide-eyed with fascination over the brutal interrogation. "Last chance, fucker. Are there explosives in the vans?"

"Y-y-yes," the terrorist moaned.

"Are they wired to explode?"

"N-n-no."

"Plastic stuff?"

"Yes," Humaidi said.

"Control to Turner. Bobby, the keys to the vans are in the top right hand drawer of the desk," Daly said. "The vans contain plastic explosives. Open the vans carefully. If you see any small light of any kind or color, don't touch anything and get the hell out of there. Understand?"

"Roger, control. I've got the keys."

Daly approached the patrol car in which Rodrigo was being held a short distance away. The other suspects were secure. Daly opened the door and told the agent to take a break. "Rodrigo. I knew I was right when I saw you at the zoo. I never forget a face. You're one of the murderers who escaped us in Afghanistan. Well, I've got a big surprise for you. We know who you are working for and it's going to be a pleasure bringing them down."

Rodrigo surprised even Daly when he screamed invectives and vowed he would see them in hell before he talked. "You will never stop us. We cannot lose with so many willing to die for Allah and Jihad," Rodrigo said.

"Coming from you, that's laughable. Willing to die. Sure. You gave up without a fight," Daly said.

"Control, Turner. First van is loaded with plastic stuff, lots of it. I also found three automatic weapons and a carton of magazines. Grenades too."

Brown brought the fourth suspect to the street. Each was now in a separate car under the watchful eye of an FBI Agent.

"Control, Turner. All four vans contain what looks like C-4. I've never seen this much of the stuff in my life. Must be thousands of pounds. There's enough here to take out a whole city block."

"Did you check for detonators?"

"Checking now."

Daly looked into the first two cars. He found Humaidi in the third and opened the door

"Same rules apply," he said without pulling his weapon. "Where are the detonators."

"In the glove compartments."

"Are they rigged?" Daly asked.

"No."

"If they are and one of my team is hurt... Control to Turner. The detonators are in the glove compartments. I've been told they are not rigged. But be careful."

Daly slammed the car door and strode over to Chief Fasow. "We have this under control, chief. I want to thank you and your department for all your splendid help."

"Glad we could be of assistance, sir," as he shook Daly's hand. "Sorry about admonishing you. I didn't realize how serious this was."

"It's Terry, chief. I probably would have done the same thing."

"Control, this is Turner. All detonators are secured."

"Roger that, Bobby. Out. Carter, assign two men to each van and have them drive to the NYPD bomb disposal dump. I want these vans closely guarded," Daly said. As Carter issued the orders, Daly asked the chief for a police escort to the New York side of the bridge. Then he called NYPD HQ and requested an escort for the four vans and guards.

"Chief," Daly said. "I left a forensic team in there gathering evidence. As soon as the vans are out of here, you can let the residents go back to their homes and release the road blocks."

"Will do, Terry. Please call me Mort."

"Thanks Mort." The two shook hands. "Oh, one more thing. If the media come snooping, and we know they will since they monitor police radios, refer them to my office. OK?

"No problem."

On the way back to the office Daly called FBI Director Roy Owens on his secure phone and filled him in.

"There's another Saudi from the UN mission involved in this, Roy," Daly said. "He's an official of some sort, a man named Talal Farhan. I don't know yet if he has diplomatic immunity.

"How in the hell did you learn about this New Jersey place?"

"From the unlikeliest and most welcome of sources. But I'd like your assurance you'll take no action, Roy," Daly said.

"You have it."

"It was Bill Burdette. The firm's been monitoring phone conversations and that's how he learned this was going down. Since the CIA can't make any arrests he called me. I told him that his suspicions weren't enough to go on until he told me the other man on the phone was Tony Rodrigo, a guy we've been building a dossier on. We know he's illegal and has forged identification so we decided to move," Daly said. "Anyway, when one of the suspects tried to enter one of the vans, that gave us the right to search. Now we have weapons and explosives charges we can throw at them. Funny thing, the vans were locked and the guy left the keys in the office."

"That's ironic. Terry, that was good work. Congratulate your team for me. Oh, one more thing, while you were having all that fun out in New Jersey, we received a report that the Saudi jet carrying our friend Abdelaziz Saleh is missing over the Atlantic."

"That should please the president. But I sure would have liked the chance to question him," Daly said. "I'll give you a complete report on this in the next several days."

Daly called Burdette. "We got them, Bill. We hit the jackpot. Enough plastic to level a city block or two, automatic rifles, grenades and ammunition. I'm grateful."

"I'm glad you nailed them. Our working together does help, doesn't it?"

"Funny thing. This guy Rodrigo. I met him at the zoo a few weeks ago. He was with a friend of my wife's. I recognized him, but couldn't place the face."

"Recognized him? From where?" Burdette asked.

"I was in Afghanistan. We nabbed Rodrigo and some of his buddies. Fully armed. Hot barrels. Anyway, they escaped when an F-16 dropped some ordinance and distracted us."

"Well, if it's any consolation, they probably would have been let go anyway by some bleeding heart liberal judge. Take care, Terry."

-Chapter Twenty-six-

At seven the next morning, Khalid al Hazmi and Nawaf al Midhar, the two "students" from Saudi Arabia met with Talal Farhan in his office at the UN Mission. Unaware that Rodrigo had been taken into custody, Farhan talked about the mission, its goals, their belief in what they were doing to achieve martyrdom and the absolute necessity for total success. Al Hazmi and al Midhar were dressed in jeans and college sweatshirts under waterproof jackets that they left unzipped to ensure the college names were visible. Each had a jumbo sports equipment bag and a suitcase and a luggage carrier. Inside the equipment bags were 150 pounds of HMX. The medium sized suitcase contained 30 pounds of HMX into which hundreds of screws had been embedded.

"Your sacrifice today will be remembered forever," Farhan said. "You and your fellow martyrs will rock satan to its very foundations, instill fear into the hearts of all Americans and show the world that Islam will triumph. You are going to destroy Grand Central Terminal one of the most famous rail stations in the entire world and a national landmark in the United States.

"Khalid, I will drop you off first at the Lexington Avenue entrance. You are to walk across the concourse and go downstairs to the food court area. There you will get something to drink at one of the shops. Read your chemistry textbook and keep the luggage cart near you.

285

"Nawaf, you get off at the 42nd street entrance. Go straight down the ramp and stop at the information booth in the center of the concourse."

Farhan showed al Midhar a primitive drawing of the concourse in which the information booth was prominently displayed. "Take one of the long schedules from the rack and walk about 30 feet from the booth so you won't be blocking anyone and drawing attention to yourself. Open the schedule and study it. Don't look around. Look at your watch. After a few minutes look at the arrival/departure board on the wall. If anyone asks if they can help, politely refuse and thank them. Any questions?"

"What should we do if a police officer stops us?" al Midhar asked.

"Tell the officer you are a college student and you are waiting for a friend who has invited you to his home." Farhan explained. "Khalid, it isn't likely you will be questioned, but if you are, tell them you are on your way to a friend's home in New Canaan, Connecticut. Anything else?"

"No," both men answered.

"The timer is set for 8:10. If anyone tries to interfere, do not wait for the timer. Understood."

Both men nodded.

"Allah Akbar," Farhan said and shook their hands.

It was raining harder when the three men climbed into a Mercedes with diplomatic plates. The CIA tail called Breen and was instructed to follow the car. At Grand Central, Farhan's driver parked in a "no standing" zone and opened the trunk. Farhan helped al Hazmi load the sports bag and the suitcase onto the luggage carrier. The two men hugged. Al Hazmi entered the terminal. Farhan's chauffeur drove around the corner stopping at the 42nd street entrance. After loading the cart, al Midhar hugged Farhan and turned toward the terminal. Farhan jumped into the Mercedes.

"Let's go. Get in the left lane as soon as you can and make a left on Fifth. We have less than 10 minutes."

That morning, Terry Daly was late. During the night, a car had downed a utility pole near his home and the power in most of his neighborhood in Larchmont was knocked out. Carter Brown called Daly's home.

"Hello," Ellen Daly said.

"Good morning, Ellen, it's Carter. Has Terry left for work?"

"Good morning, Carter. Yes he was late. He left about 10-15 minutes ago. We had a power outage and the alarm didn't go off on time," she said.

"Thanks," Carter hung up and informed the staff assembled in the conference room. They began pouring through reports. Brown called the duty desk and asked that they pick up the four prisoners being held at the Rikers Island jail.

When Daly's train arrived at Grand Central, he bounded onto the platform moving swiftly between commuters to the food court where he stopped at one of the restaurants to get some bagels for the staff as an apology for keeping them waiting.

"Terry, is that you?"

Daly turned. It was Angela Hart. She was accompanied by a beautiful woman with long black hair, somewhat older.

"Hi Angela. How are you?"

"I'm fine, thank you. Terry, this is Ann Dunn. My company is working with hers on some projects and she and I take the same train. Ann, this is a good friend Terry Daly."

"Good morning Ann. It's very nice to meet you," Daly said cutting Hart off before she could mention that he was an FBI agent.

Dunn flashed a quick smile and took Daly's proffered hand. "I've got to run. I have a nine o'clock meeting," Dunn said. "Nice to meet you Terry."

"I'm going to get some coffee. Would you like to join me, Terry?"

"I can't, Angela. I really have to get to the office. I'm late for a meeting. *We have Rodrigo.* Good to see you again. Nice to meet you Ann," Daly said, but Dunn, walking briskly, was on the stairs to the main concourse

Daly headed for the subway.

Hart sat down and ordered coffee and a bagel with cream cheese. She didn't notice a "student" in the green windbreaker who just seated himself on a stool. He was reading a textbook.

The 7:08 out of Chappaqua was seven minutes late because of weather problems. Larry Kirkman, Robert Costa, Lois Ryan and Gray Bostwick were among the first to exit the second car. Harry Kaufman helped Briana Russell remove her heavy briefcase from the overhead rack before the two stepped onto the platform.

Behind them were Walter and Vera Perry. Vera had left her umbrella on the floor beneath her seat and her husband waited while she waded through the throng to retrieve it. They were some 30 yards behind the others when they left the train. Dr. Keith Slack who was scheduled to work in his New Jersey office, was not on the train.

Daly was standing in a jammed subway car of the #4 train bound for Federal Plaza. The doors closed and suddenly the lights went out, not an uncommon occurrence on the subway. The train shook violently then slowed to a stop.

The concussion came seconds later, diminished by concrete and distance, but loud enough to cause visible concern among the passengers. Even though he could see no fire or smell smoke, Daly knew immediately it was an explosion. Dunn was walking briskly on 42nd street striding past the Grand Hyatt when the bomb detonated. The window she had just passed shattered as its contents blew on to the busy street. Dunn was knocked off her feet.

Khalid al Hazmi disappeared, vaporized in a huge flash and a deafening roar. The shock wave blasted through the food court annihilating everyone. Benches and kiosks splintered, their pieces destroying counters and food service equipment and shredding human flesh everywhere. The ceiling above al Hazmi buckled upward, opening a large hole in the floor above. Then it collapsed bringing injured commuters from above through the gaping hole.

The Perrys and other passengers entering the lower lobby from arriving trains were obliterated. Passengers further down the tunnel were blown to pieces. The mammoth blast crushed the eardrums of those left barely alive 400 feet down the platform. One train, moving slowly to its destination, was smashed to a halt by the unseen shockwave knocking all the standing passengers off their feet.

Seated passengers facing forward were slammed into seats, wall separators or fellow passengers facing rearward. They suffered agonizing whiplash, a momentary pain that was extinguished forever by the shock wave.

The motorman and many in the first car were shredded by glass in the front of the car. Dust and debris reduced visibility to a few inches. The tunnel reeked of blood.

On the main concourse above, al Midhar and more than two thousand commuters including Kaufman and Russell were knocked to the floor or down the stairs. Shouts and screams filled the air. Some, badly shaken, but otherwise uninjured, struggled to their feet. But there was no time to run.

Al Midhar was in mid prayer when he joined his companion in death. There was nothing to mute the force of the blast before it reached the ceiling 100 feet above. Much of the ceiling lifted and hung, the weakened steel groaning. Then it crashed to the floor bringing with it hundreds of tiny lights that portrayed the heavens at night. What was left of the information booth and hundreds of commuters was buried under tons of debris.

A giant hole was all that remained of the six story glass windows on the west side as hundreds of pounds of shattered glass and bits of steel frame scarred the buildings on the other side of Vanderbilt Avenue, riddled scores of pedestrians and destroyed more than 20 vehicles. Shards from the huge windows on the East side severely injured pedestrians blocks away.

The 20-foot high arrival/departure board splintered, its tiny pieces adding to the carnage and the darkness caused by the dust and ash. Fourteen ticket clerks were pulverized by the armored glass windows that ironically were there to protect them. One interior wall stopped moving only when it slammed into another interior wall. Between the walls were a bakeshop and more than a hundred commuters.

Kirkman, Costa, Ryan and Bostwick were knocked to the ground by the first thunderclap. All four were on their knees struggling to comprehend what had happened. They were 15 yards from the terminal exit when the second bomb detonated. All four died instantly, their bodies tossed like dolls into the heavy doors leading to 42nd Street

Outside on the sidewalk pedestrians walking by the terminal doors were dismembered by glass and steel. Some pieces smashed through the window of the museum in the Altria building and the discount store under Park Avenue. Stunned motorists drove wildly onto the sidewalk or into oncoming traffic.

At the Vanderbilt Avenue entrance to the terminal, a cab was overturned in the semi circular driveway. Its hot engine ignited gasoline flowing onto the pavement underneath other waiting cabs. Drivers, stunned by the explosion, were unable to extricate themselves from their cars in time to avoid the exploding gas tanks. Within minutes, the passenger drop-off area was engulfed.

The Grand Hyatt Hotel next door to the terminal trembled. Chandeliers in the lobby ceiling swayed violently and crashed to the floor. Huge cracks appeared in the east wall above the second floor. Chunks of plaster and wood plummeted to the busy registration desk below striking guests and employees alike. The reverberations shattered the glass wall overlooking the lobby entrance. Unsuspecting guests leaning against the railing plummeted 25 feet on to arriving guests. Shelves in the bar overlooking 42nd street collapsed. The aroma of a potpourri of spirits filled the lobby mixed with the odor of gore. All elevators stopped and the lights went out. The injured and uninjured alike began screaming.

Dunn sat on the sidewalk dazed from the first blast. On both sides of the street pedestrians were running screaming hysterically. As she struggled to her feet, the second blast knocked her flat. She lay on the sidewalk with her hands over her head as debris landed on the sidewalk. A woman who was struck by glass fell over Dunn her body falling on Dunn's head. She lay unconscious underneath the badly injured office worker.

Down in the subway, Daly waited patiently for the train to begin moving. Other passengers, normally unconcerned by the temporary darkness, were chatting nervously about the noise and the rocking caused by the tremors racing through the ground. An off duty motorman came into the car and tried to explain there would be a short delay. As he passed, Daly stopped him, identified himself, and asked him if they could talk in private.

"Follow me," the motorman said.

Daly followed him to the rear of the car where they entered the motorman's compartment. Daly shut the door. "Do you have radio contact with anyone," Daly asked.

"Sure," the motorman said.

"Good. I want you to contact your dispatcher, your engineer, someone and find out what's going on."

"Ain't nothing wrong, sir," the motorman said. "We'll be moving in a few moments."

"I can't tell you how important this is," Daly said. "That noise was probably a bomb. The safety of everyone on this train may depend on your acting right now."

"You serious, ain't ya?" the motorman said.

"Very."

"Look, this is a subway. We get lots of noise and lots of shaking down here. That don't mean we got trouble." When Daly didn't reply, the motorman picked up his radio and called the motorman running the train.

"Mike, what we got? This is Dom. I'm in the third car."

"I'm talking to dispatch right now."

"I got an FBI man here. He thinks sumpin's wrong."

An interminably long two minutes ticked by. "Dom," the motorman said, "Somebody blew up Grand Central. Power's out. We got to get everyone out and up on the street. Now!"

"No shit."

"No shit. Move. No telling if there's another bomb," the motorman said.

"You was right," Dom said to Daly. "We got to get everyone out of here."

Daly was already on the move. When he reached the street by an emergency stairway, sounds of dozens of sirens filled the air. When he looked north on Park Avenue he was stunned. The terminal, a New York City landmark, was a wreck, its roof gone and huge pieces of the south side missing. Thick black smoke rose from the hole. The street below was chaotic. Panicked pedestrians tried to dodge emergency vehicles, weaving their way through debris and damaged trucks, buses and cabs.

After finding his cell phone useless, Daly entered a drug store flashed his ID and used the store phone to call the office.

When Pat Clinton answered Daly had to fight to keep himself under control. "Pat, put Carter or RE on, please."

"This is Carter, Terry. Where are you?"

"I'm in a drug store on Park Avenue near 39th."

"Why didn't you use your cell?"

"Grand Central has been bombed, Carter. It's almost unrecognizable. Cell service is out."

"Holy mother of God! Are you OK?"

"Yeah. I'm OK."

"What do you want us to do?" Brown asked.

"Get a full team up here. The works. Tell them to bring extra clothing and ask Pat to make reservations at a hotel four or five blocks south or north of the terminal. There won't be any mass transit for some time."

"What about Rodrigo and the others? Brown asked. "We've got them in the holding cells."

"Keep them there. I want to find out what Rodrigo knows about this. I'll be there as soon as I can but that may be an hour or so," Daly said. He picked up his brief case, went outside and looked for a cab. Traffic on Park was stopped. Drivers stood outside their cars and stared.

City, State and Federal authorities acted swiftly. All subway service going into Grand Central was stopped backing up train traffic on all three lines. MTA officials worked calmly to prevent panic and collisions. Penn Station and every bridge and tunnel leading into Manhattan were closed. Ferries headed for the city we turned back.

On the orders of the governor, three battalions of the 42nd Division of the New York National Guard were activated and the troops ordered to help police at the bridges, tunnels and airports. The three remaining area airports – Newark, LaGuardia and JFK – were closed and air traffic was diverted to Philadelphia, Baltimore, Hartford, Boston and Washington. Manhattan was isolated.

Daly walked along 35th Street to Fifth Avenue and then to Broadway. Fire, police and EMS vehicles choked north-south avenues and east-west streets as the drivers maneuvered their way to Grand Central, their sirens and horns adding to the agony of a stricken mid-town. Wrecked vehicles, debris from the terminal roof and walls and the bodies of the dead and dying, littered 42nd, 43rd and 44th streets, Vanderbilt and Lexington Avenues.

Realizing no cab could get through, Daly called the office again from another store. "Carter, better send a car. Meet me on 30th and Park. That should be far enough south."

"Will do."

Ninety minutes later, Daly, disheveled and in shirtsleeves was seated in an interrogation room. He pressed a button and ordered, "Send him in."

Dressed in prison orange, Tony Rodrigo, his hands in cuffs held by his side with a chain, was ushered in by two agents. He was offered something to drink and told to sit down. The waist chain was unlocked.

Daly looked up. "Did you know the bastards who blew up Grand Central?"

The look on Rodrigo's face indicated complete surprise.

"Let me be very clear. Just so you know who you are talking to and how serious I am, my parents were killed when your fellow al Qaeda brothers attacked the airport in White Plains. So I don't think you want to risk pissing me off. We've been to your apartment in Bronxville and we found a list of targets written on Saudi Mission stationery. On that list was Grand Central. That ties you to the crime Rodrigo and that means you get the needle along with your other friends and the two guys who blew up the airport. So tell me, who blew up Grand Central. Don't tell me you don't know."

Rodrigo didn't answer. He was sure the FBI Agent was confusing Grand Central with Penn Station

Daly stood up and loosened his tie. "Do you know who I saw in the terminal this morning about 10 minutes before the bomb went off?"

Rodrigo was silent.

"You work with her. It was Angela Hart. She was going to the food court to get some coffee. It's possible that your friends just killed her."

Angela doesn't use Penn Station.

"She was with a woman named Ann, ah Dunn. Do you know her?" Daly asked.

Rodrigo gasped. "Did you say Ann Dunn?"

"Yes. Do you know her?"

Rodrigo hesitated. He must have said Grand Central. Ann uses Grand Central. That bastard Farhan bombed Grand Central. He double crossed me…

"I asked you, do you know her?"

"Yes. We worked together. My company has a contract with hers."

Daly pressed, "She may not be dead. She had a meeting and didn't stop for coffee. How well do you know her?"

Shaken and near tears, Rodrigo put his hands to his face. His body shook. When he regained his composure, he said, "that bastard double crossed me."

"Who? Who double crossed you?"

"Before I tell you anything I want to know if she is OK. She works at McLaughlin Corporation," Rodrigo said.

Pressing the intercom Daly said, "Pat, call McLaughlin Corp and see if a woman named Ann Dunn is there. I'd like to talk to her. Don't tell anyone it's the FBI calling. Rodrigo, while she's trying to reach Ann suppose you tell me about the double cross and who double crossed you."

"Just so you understand me, Daly, I am not afraid to die. I only want two things. I want to know if Ann is OK and I want to make sure you get that double crosser Atta."

"Atta?"

"That's his code name."

"What's his real name?"

Clinton knocked and opened the door. "Terry, according to McLaughlin Corporation, Ann Dunn was scheduled to be at work today. She did not show up".

Rodrigo's eyes watered. Daly jumped in.

"Pat, she may not have been able to get to the office. There's a lot of confusion. Try again later. In the meantime I need information."

Rodrigo was thinking about the special moments with Dunn. The sadness and anger boiled up. It was true, he really liked Ann, admired her, and, yes, loved her. "What do you want to know?"

"Start with the name of the guy who double crossed you," Daly demanded.

"It was Atta. That's a code name. His real name is Talal Farhan. The target was Penn Station. We agreed and then he changed it," Rodrigo said.

"And he works in the Saudi mission."

"Yes."

"Does he have diplomatic immunity?"

"I don't know."

"Carter, take over. I'll be back in a couple of minutes. Rodrigo, if you want to know about Dunn you better cooperate," Daly said. He went to his office and called Roy Owens.

"Roy, Terry. Carter and I are interrogating the chief of the cell we took down yesterday in New Jersey. His name is Tony Rodrigo. He claims he worked with a guy in the Saudi Embassy named Talal Farhan. His code name is Atta. He said Farhan was the guy who ordered Grand Central bombed. The original target was Penn Station."

"We're getting the preliminary reports on Grand Central right now," Owens said. "I'm about to go into a meeting with Mooreland and the President. I'll get back to you after the meeting. Keep working on this guy."

Daly returned to the interrogation room. "Anything new Carter?

Daly was astonished at the enormity of the plan of which only 20 percent had been completed. The other three agents in the room were riveted.

"Who else in the mission knows about these plans?" Daly asked.

"Abdul Sulieman, the ambassador," Rodrigo said.

"The Ambassador? You're certain of that?"

"Yes. Atta, I mean Talal used the name Abdul several times during our conversations. Sulieman is the only man named Abdul in the mission."

"How fitting." Daly responded. "Do you know where Sulieman gets his orders?"

"No."

"Where did the explosives come from?" Daly asked.

"They were brought in from Saudi Arabia by Yousef al Hafra in diplomatic packages. Al Hafra is one of the men with me last night. He works at the mission and has an apartment there."

"Are you telling me your man smuggled thousands of pounds of plastic explosive into this country in diplomatic bags?" Daly asked.

"Yes, but he didn't know what was in the bags. Farhan kept him in the dark in case someone started questioning him. He brought in more than 10,000 pounds."

"Did you know Abdelaziz Saleh? Do you know anything about the cell he ran?"

"No. I never met him. The cells are separate and do not communicate with each other for security reasons." Rodrigo said.

"So you knew nothing about the attack on the airport or the Mall?"

"No."

"Where does the money come from that you deposit in your account?"

Rodrigo was surprised by the question. "You know about that?"

"Yes. We know about that."

"It comes from Washington, I think. But it is mailed to me from the mission," Rodrigo said. "That's all I can tell you."

"Carter, get another guy in here. I want you to join me in my office.

Daly called Pantone Associates and asked for Tim Robbins, Hart's boss.

"Tim Robbins. How can I help you?"

"Mr. Robbins, this is Terry Daly. Is Angela Hart there? I am a friend of hers."

"No, she's not. We haven't seen her and we are very worried she may have been involved in the attack on the terminal," Robbins said.

Daly elected not to tell Robbins that he saw Hart moments before the explosion. "I hope that's not the case, Mr. Robbins. Thank you."

Daly looked up at Carter. "Well, this is a first. We now have indisputable evidence that the Saudis were behind the attacks on our country. But the question is, how do we deal with it?"

"I think that's the president's call."

-Chapter Twenty-seven-

A grim President Barnes looked at the faces of those seated around the crisis room table. Present were Secretary of State Alan Collins, National Security Advisor Nancy Hanks, Chief of Staff Fred Randolph, Attorney General Michael Armistead, Secretary of Defense Lawrence Needham, CIA Director William Burdette, Senior Military Advisor Gen. Beverly Watson, Homeland Security Secretary Philip Mooreland and FBI Director Roy Owens.

"What have you got, Phil?" the president began.

"I'd better let Roy fill you in, Mr. President. He just got off the phone with the New York office."

"Mr. President, last night, as you know, Terry Daly's team took down a terrorist cell. Apparently, they didn't get them all as we've just learned they hit us again. The leader of the cell said the plan was to blow up the Lincoln and Holland Tunnels, the GW Bridge and Penn Station. Apparently, at the last minute they changed their plans and blew up Grand Central instead of Penn Station. The cell leader whose name is Tony Rodrigo said he was unaware of the switch, that he was double crossed by a man who works in the Saudi Mission."

Owens paused and looked around the room. The President had leaned forward in his chair and was about to say something. Owens continued, "Rodrigo said this guy's name was, ah," Owens looked at his notes, "Talal Farhan. But that's not the most interesting part. Rodrigo also said another guy in the mission knew about the plan.

Anyone ever hear of the name Abdul Sulieman?" Owens asked for effect.

The president gasped.

"The Saudi ambassador to the UN? You've got to be kidding," Secretary of State Collins said.

"Rodrigo said he was certain because he was the only man named Abdul in the building," Owens responded. "And that's not all. Rodrigo said a Saudi mission employee named Yousef al Hafra brought the explosives into this country using packages covered by diplomatic immunity. This guy al Hafra was in Rodrigo's group when they were apprehended yesterday. Under questioning, he corroborated Rodrigo's story."

"Why wasn't I told about this right away?" Collins asked.

"I just got the information minutes before coming into this meeting, Mr. Secretary," Owens responded.

"Mr. President," Collins said, "we better be right on this one. Accusing an employee is one thing, but the ambassador?"

"Let's look at what we have," President Barnes said. "We've got physical evidence pointing to the mission. We've got videotapes of two suspects who named the Deputy Charge D'affairs and we've got two more confessions including one from a mission employee who named another mission employee as their contact and implicated the ambassador."

"Too bad we couldn't talk to their Deputy Charge D'affairs," Hanks said.

"I'll bet that was no accident," the president said. "How do we get Farhan, Alan," Barnes said.

"I'll check the mission's personnel roster. Excuse me for a minute," Collins said.

Collins called his office and asked for the undersecretary for the Middle East. "Chris, does the Saudi UN Mission have an individual named Talal Farhan?

Chris Chamberlain checked the computer data. "Yes sir."

"Is he D.I.?"

"No sir. They requested that, but we told them they had filled their quota," Chamberlain said.

"Have they made a move to declare him immune in the wake of the death of their Deputy Charge D'affairs?" Collins asked.

"Not yet sir. Don't know if they will do that."

"Thanks, Chris." Collins hung up. "He's not immune."

"How do we get this bastard?" the president asked.

"I'll have to make a formal declaration of our accusations with the demand he be turned over to us," Collins said.

"And if Sulieman refuses, then what?"

"Legally, he can't. Under UN rules any employee of any foreign mission or embassy can be formally charged with a crime. As long as he or she does not have immunity, the foreign mission or embassy must surrender the individual," Collins said.

"Make it happen, Alan. I want that cowardly mother behind bars. When he talks, we can nail the ambassador. Alan, tell the ambassador we are making a formal request for Farhan," the president said.

Collins nodded and again turned his chair to the phone on the credenza and relayed the instruction to Chamberlain.

"Secretary of State Collins wishes to speak with the ambassador," Chamberlain said to Ambassador Sulieman's deputy.

"This is Ambassador Sulieman," came the reply after a short wait.

"Please hold for the Secretary of State." Chamberlain hung up.

"Mr. Ambassador, Alan Collins. How are you today sir?"

"We are in mourning, Mr. Secretary. You may have heard that my deputy charge d'affaires is missing. He was aboard my plane when it went down somewhere over the Atlantic," Sulieman said. "He was a decent man. But in the wake of your accusations, I had to relieve him and send him home."

"I'm very sorry for your loss, Mr. Ambassador." *Relieved him my ass. You sent him home to make sure he wouldn't talk and I'll bet you made sure the plane went down.*

"I'm glad you called, Mr. Secretary. I want to replace Mr. Saleh. The man I have in mind is Talal Farhan. Can you arrange diplomatic immunity for him?"

Doesn't waste any time, does he? "I'm afraid not, Mr. Ambassador. Mr. Farhan is the reason why I called. He is wanted for questioning. I am requesting you to surrender him to us."

The ambassador was shaken. "Mr. Farhan is a friend of the royal family. Surely you must be mistaken"

"There's no mistake, Mr. Ambassador. I am sending two State Department Security people over to the mission to pick him up."

"I cannot allow that, Mr. Secretary. First it was Abdelaziz Saleh. Now, Talal Farhan. This harassment of my people has to stop. It is offensive."

"Mr. Ambassador, I am afraid I am going to have to insist. We have four men in custody who were plotting to blow up several New York City landmarks. Mr. Farhan has been implicated as being their leader and the individual who directed the attack against Grand Central," Secretary Collins said.

"Since he does not have diplomatic immunity, you must turn him over to us." Collins decided not to let the ambassador know he was also a suspect.

"I will question him myself. And if what you say is true, I will turn him over to you."

"Just like that. If he denies it, then what will you do?"

"Nothing. His word is good enough for me," the ambassador said.

"As I said, Mr. Ambassador, I am going to insist. We want Farhan. Since he does not have diplomatic status, UN rules and international law are clear on this. You must surrender him."

"I believe we have concluded this conversation, Mr. Secretary," the ambassador said.

"Before you hang up Mr. Ambassador, I want you to know that Mr. Farhan will not be permitted to leave the mission unless he is in our custody."

Sulieman declined to reply. He hung up and called Talal Farhan to his office.

"You wanted to see me, Mr. Ambassador."

"Yes. The reason why the other targets have not been destroyed is because your men have been arrested. And two of them have talked. They named you as the leader. The Secretary of State has demanded we surrender you to the U.S. government. I can delay that, but in the end I will have to comply since you do not have diplomatic immunity."

"What if I am not here, Mr. Ambassador?"

"The secretary said you will not be permitted to leave the mission."

"You can contact our embassy in Washington and ask them to send the Royal ambassador's car. It can take me to Washington and from there I can get back to Riyadh. Surely the Americans would not dare to stop a car belonging to the royal family," Farhan said.

I am certainly not going to request the royal ambassador's car and I can't take the chance that they won't seize you in that car embarrassing the royal family. I have other plans for you. "That is an excellent suggestion. Pack some of your things. We'll get you to Washington and then in a few weeks we'll fly you home."

"Thank you excellency."

After Farhan left Sulieman's office, the ambassador summoned the chief of security. Mahmood Rashid to his office. "Mahmood we have a security leak and I want you to take care of it personally."

"Of course, your excellency. What is it you want me to do?"

"This is top secret, Mahmood. I want you to silence Talal Farhan."

"Silence him your excellency? May I ask why?" a surprised Rashid asked.

"He may talk to the Americans and if he does we will be compromised."

"When do you want me to do this?"

"The Americans will not allow him to leave the mission. Do it here and get rid of the evidence," Sulieman said. "Make sure no one sees you."

"I understand."

Rashid excused himself.

Farhan was packing when Rashid asked him to accompany him to the security office in the basement to pick up documentation changing his name to Adnan Maladi.

When Farhan entered the security office he thought it odd that a shower curtain had been laid out on the floor. As he turned to ask about it, a single shot was fired into his head. An hour later Rashid returned to the ambassador's office.

"Excellency, the problem has been taken care of. He will disappear with the rest of tomorrow's garbage."

The ambassador smiled.

Sulieman stood at his office window overlooking the entrance to the mission. State Department and FBI agents had moved into position to prevent vehicles and personnel from entering or leaving the mission without a search or and ID check. Sulieman asked his administrative assistant to call the Secretary of State. He was patched through.

"I left a message for Mr. Farhan to report to me Mr. Secretary. When he did not respond, we searched the building thoroughly. He is not on the grounds," the ambassador reported. "His clothes are here so it is likely he has gone out, perhaps to shop."

"Thank you for calling, Mr. Ambassador. Until he is found and surrendered I have authorized the search of every vehicle leaving the mission. If he tries to leave the country, he will be arrested. *I hope you are not planning to do away with this bastard too.*

"The search of any vehicles bearing diplomatic plates is strictly against international law."

"You are right, of course. But we will demand the driver and all passengers carry appropriate ID. Good day, Mr. Ambassador," Collins said. He reported the developments to the meeting assemblage.

"There is nothing more we can do, Mr. President." Collins said.

"I have a mental image of Grand Central, Alan. If you think I'm going to let protocol stop me from getting this bastard you are mistaken. You have my direct orders. Stop and search all vehicles entering and leaving the mission. I'll take responsibility," the president said. And I think the next step is to put some heat on Sulieman through the UN Secretary General."

"All he will do is quote the laws and tell you the mission is foreign territory and tell you to dismiss the guards immediately," Collins said. "The only thing you're going to do is stir up the UN and the media."

"You may be right. But he'll do something behind the scenes. He cannot ignore the issue." Barnes pushed the intercom and asked his secretary to place the call."

"Mr. President, I was going to call you this afternoon to express my condolences. I am deeply sorry for the losses your country has suffered," the secretary general said.

The hell you are you sniveling bastard. You're delighted.

"Thank you, Mr. Secretary General, for your kind words. I am calling on a related matter. It seems sir that we have irrefutable evidence that members of the Saudi Arabian mission to the UN were involved in two of the recent terror attacks on our country. I am calling to tell you this because I also want to inform you that the Saudi ambassador is shielding one of his employees who directed the attack on Grand Central. We have sealed the mission and until we have him in custody we will search every vehicle."

"Mr. President, international law applies here. You cannot seal any mission and hold its occupants prisoner. And you cannot search any vehicle bearing diplomatic plates."

"I understand your position completely, Mr. Secretary General. I hope you understand mine. Thousands of Americans were killed in those attacks. We know that one of the mission employees was responsible for directing the attacks and another imported the explosives under diplomatic immunity. That too is against international law. That is all the reason I need."

"I sympathize with your situation, Mr. President. But international law is quite clear on the matter. You cannot seal the mission."

"Mr. Secretary General, international law also applied when the Iranians stormed our embassy in Teheran and took our personnel hostage. The UN said nothing. When our embassies were attacked in Africa the UN said nothing. When the Cole was bombed the UN was silent. How is it that International Law applies now and not then?"

"I repeat, any action taken against a sovereign nation's UN mission will be viewed very gravely," the secretary general said. "Bring your evidence before the UN. The Security Council will handle it."

"Thank you, Mr. Secretary general. I wish you a pleasant day." *Have I got a surprise for you.*

President Barnes, Randolph, Mooreland, Collins and the chief speech writer Lisa Cunningham began working on the president's address to the nation.

"Good evening. As you know by now, our country has suffered another devastating attack. The bombing of Grand Central Terminal in New York City was a heinous act carried out by cowardly murderers who have no regard for human life.

"While we do not have final figures, our best estimates are that more than 5,000 people were killed or injured and hundreds more are missing. A national landmark was destroyed, a city devastated once again.

"When the Mall of America and Westchester County Airport were attacked some weeks ago, I sat here in this chair and outlined how the United States would respond. We ended diplomatic relations with the Palestine Liberation Organization, Iran, the Sudan, Syria and Libya.

"I ordered their embassies and missions closed and their personnel sent home. The United Nations vilified our country and me for my actions. But the United Nations has yet to condemn those terrorist acts in Minnesota and New York.

"The murdering terrorists who destroyed The Mall of America and Westchester County airport were illegal immigrants, leaving no doubt that there is a link between terrorist attacks and illegal immigration. I determined to address that problem to make this country safer. Accordingly, I sent to the Congress a comprehensive bill that would tighten our laws, and give our law enforcement people the new tools they need to track down the people who threaten us. I asked for bipartisan support.

"One of the proposals would have eliminated what is known as a Visa lottery. This law permits 55,000 people per year with unverified documentation to circumvent our immigration laws by simply having their name chosen in a lottery. Using this mechanism, hundreds have come to our shores from the countries we suspect of being friendly to terrorism including the nations with whom we no longer have relations.

"I also asked congress to make it a federal crime to enter this country illegally or to stay in this country once a visa has expired. As we have seen for years, illegal immigrants get free medical care, send their kids to our schools and get social security benefits. And they are given the fast track to become citizens. In fact, in a number of states, illegal immigrants already vote. To put it simply, we are rewarding people for avoiding the lawful immigration process.

"Our best estimate is that there are more than 30 million illegal aliens in this country. To make matters worse, ninety percent of foreigners who were ordered deported are still here. In some cases they remain here as the result of direct intervention by members of congress despite the fact that exhaustive investigations support the CIS judgment that the individuals should be deported.

"I am not and never have been an opponent of immigration. This country was built by immigrants. We draw our strength from our diversity, something our enemies cannot understand. We invite people from other countries to come and build a home. The legend on the Statue of Liberty that begins with "Give me your tired, your poor" is as true today as it was when the statue was erected in the 19th century.

"But I am an opponent of reckless immigration laws that permit our enemies free access to our shores to murder us in cold blood. And I am an opponent of reckless immigration laws that do not provide a penalty for being here illegally and that permit people who are here illegally to stay and apply for residency.

"The vast majority of immigrants are law abiding, hard working and peace loving people. Tougher immigration laws will not prevent these people from coming to America. But the new laws will make it much more difficult for a terrorist to slip in unnoticed.

"The bill I sent to Congress contains a provision for establishing a national ID card that would be carried by all Americans 12 and over and by all foreign visitors. The card is no different in most respects than a driver's license.

"It would include the individual's name and address, a photo and a digitized code to prevent tampering. If the individual was a foreign national his or her fingerprints would also be included. Congress in its infinite wisdom declared such a card was unnecessary.

"So where do these proposals stand? Unfortunately, Congress apparently sees no danger from illegal aliens despite the fact that nearly all the terrorists who have attacked our nation, were in this country illegally. The toll is frightening and it is mounting. To date nearly 50,000 people are dead as a result of these attacks and tens of thousands have been injured. Let me put this in perspective. The populations of 99 percent of our cities including the capitals of Wyoming, Vermont, South Dakota, Maine and Montana are smaller than the number of casualties our nation has suffered as a result of terrorism.

"Tonight I am again asking that Congress move quickly on this legislation. And I am asking you to call your representative and your senators and urge them to pass this legislation.

"When I talked with you after the 9/11 anniversary attacks I promised that we will eliminate terrorism which I called the scourge of the 21st century. I issued a strong warning to the countries who harbor, support and finance terrorists and to those who would murder innocent men, women and children to advance their cause. Perhaps some did not hear that warning. Perhaps some chose to ignore it. The warning bears repeating. Expect no mercy. You will get what you deserve, death and destruction.

And now, please join me in a moment of silent prayer for the victims of the bombing and their families and for those who are assisting them. Thank you, and may God Bless America."

-Chapter Twenty-eight-

Senate Majority Leader Robert Fennel and Senator John Featherstone, chairman of the Senate Homeland Security Committee sat in Fennel's office discussing the president's speech. National polls showed nearly 80 percent of the American public wanted changes in the country's immigrations polices and laws and nearly 75 percent were willing to accept a National ID card.

"I will not by God be coerced into changes that are not needed," Fennel said to Featherstone. "If we give something, we're going to get something in return."

"The public will be demanding our heads if we fail to act on Barnes' proposals," Featherstone said. "He practically has them believing we are responsible for the attacks."

"I've been in the senate for nearly 23 years," Fennel said. "No president is going to bully me into doing something that I think is bad for the country."

"Not to mention bad for the party."

"Sir, excuse me. Fred Randolph is on the phone," Fennel's secretary Winnie Ross, said.

"Thanks Winnie. This is Senator Fennel."

"Bob, it's Fred Randolph. The president has asked me to invite you and other Congressional leaders to a meeting at the White House. I left a message with Senator Featherstone's office. They told me he is with you. The president would like to invite him as well. The meeting is at 8:00 tomorrow morning."

"Thank you Fred. Tell the president I will be there. Hang on a second." Fennel put Randolph on hold and told Featherstone about the meeting invitation.

"Could be interesting, if not entertaining," Featherstone said.

"Fred, Senator Featherstone will be there too."

"Excellent. Thank you, Senator Fennel."

By eight, the Congressional leaders were seated in the White House Conference room. In addition to Senators Fennel and Featherstone, invitees included ranking minority member Senator Walter Poindexter, Speaker of the House Craig Welbourne, ranking minority member Sharon Goodfellow, Secretary of Homeland Security Philip Mooreland, Secretary of state Alan Collins, Secretary of Defense Lawrence Needham, Attorney General Michael Armistead, National Security Advisor Nancy Hanks, the Chairman of the Joint Chiefs Admiral Troy Warren, and Vice President Richard Dillon. The president's chief of staff was noticeably missing.

"Good morning, ladies and gentleman. Thank you for coming on such short notice. The information I am about to share with you is extremely sensitive and potentially explosive as you will see. After I am finished I'd like your thoughts on how we should act on this information.

"We now have solid information that connects the Saudis to terrorism in this country."

President Barnes looked around the room. All eyes were riveted on him.

"We know who was responsible for the attack on Westchester County Airport. The two terrorists who fired the missiles are in custody and have confessed. We have their confessions on video. They named Abdelaziz Saleh, the Deputy Charge D'affairs of the Saudi UN mission as their handler, and that man personally signed for six crates that came through customs with diplomatic immunity. Those crates contained Stinger missiles and were later found at the airport with customs markings on one along with the address of the Saudi Mission. Unfortunately, Saleh died in a plane crash.

"The FBI has also taken into custody four men who plotted to blow up the George Washington Bridge, the Holland and Lincoln Tunnels, and Penn Station. They were found at their safe house in New Jersey with vans loaded with high explosives, enough to level every building within 500 yards. One of the men in custody is an employee in the Saudi mission. Two others are Saudi citizens. And two other men from that cell were responsible for the explosions that destroyed Grand Central Terminal.

"The UN mission employee the FBI arrested is a man named Yousef al Hafra. He and the cell leader Ahmed al Akbar, named another Saudi mission employee, a man named Talal Farhan, as their handler and they said the explosives came through our customs in diplomatically sealed containers. Al Akbar is also known as Tony Rodrigo. Now, this is where it gets tricky. Both Rodrigo and al Hafra said the Saudi Ambassador to the UN was involved in the plot."

The president was pleased at the reaction to his naming Sulieman.

"Ambassador Sulieman told Secretary Collins that Farhan was going to be elevated to Saleh's slot as Deputy Charge D'Affairs, but Collins refused to grant immunity and demanded that Sulieman surrender Farhan. Sulieman refused and accused us of harassing Saudi mission employees. In a subsequent conversation with Secretary Collins, Sulieman said that Farhan had left the Mission. The FBI has been hunting him ever since.

"Attorney General Armistead says we have solid evidence to indict all six terrorists and Farhan. The ambassador is, of course, another story. But it would help our case if we find Farhan and he talks."

"I don't have to tell you that when the announcement of the arrests is made, the media and the public will be demanding action, possibly military action against Saudi Arabia. So before that occurs, I'd like to hear what you have to say."

Everyone in the room was silent.

"Let me put it this way," the president said. "We will prosecute the terrorists in a military tribunal, not in a court. That's my decision. And I believe we have enough evidence to prove that Saudia Arabia financed them and gave them their orders."

"Aren't there diplomatic avenues we can explore before we resort to military action," Senator Featherstone asked.

"John, the Saudis refuse to hand over a mission employee in direct violation of international law. Given their stand, what diplomatic channels are left?

"Mr. President, as I said I think we have enough evidence to convict the terrorists and Farhan, but linking the ambassador is thin without the testimony of Talal Farhan," Armistead said.

"That may be true, but the evidence found at the airport and the testimony about where the explosives came from inextricably links the mission and Saudi Arabia to these crimes," the president said. "The ambassador is in charge of the mission."

"When the public is given that information, they will demand military action, especially after what you said in your speech the other night," Rep. Goodfellow said.

"I don't agree," Senator Poindexter replied. "We have six terrorists. We should put them on trial for murder and terrorism. That should be sufficient."

"We could send ambassador Sulieman packing," Speaker Wellbourne said.

"If you do that you better be prepared for an oil embargo," Admiral Warren said.

"Mr. President, it would appear we are in a chess game," Secretary Mooreland said.

"We have to be prepared for any counter move they may make. Of course, if you elect to act militarily, they won't have any options."

"If we do something that precipitates an oil embargo and then we attack, it will look as if we are only after their oil," Hanks said. "That might not sit well with a number of our allies, and it certainly won't sit well with members of OPEC."

"It appears to me that the bottom line is this: If we do anything resembling a threat, the Saudis stop the oil. If we act militarily, they stop the oil," Featherstone said.

"If that is the case, and I'm not saying you're wrong, John, then we have nothing to lose by taking military action," Vice President Dillon said. "Would the House and Senate go along with that?"

"Based on what I have heard this morning, I am confident the Senate would back the president. Would you agree, Bob?" Sen. Featherstone asked.

"Yes, I think the American people would want us to hit back," Sen. Fennel replied.

"What about the House?" Barnes asked.

"I am certain the House will support military action," Speaker Wellbourne said. "You have presented a compelling argument for that even if the Saudis surrender the ambassador and recall everyone in that nest on Lexington Avenue."

"What's your view Sharon?" the president asked.

"The threat of another war with a Middle Eastern country only inflames the militants and drives them to more terrorism," Rep. Goodfellow said.

"Surely you are not recommending appeasement?" Secretary Needham asked.

"Not at all. I think we should consider both what we hope to gain and what we might lose if we were to go to war. Saudi Arabia is home to two of the three most holy places in Islam. If we damage either of those we will inflame the entire Middle East," Rep. Goodfellow replied.

After 90 minutes of spirited discussion, President Barnes rose. "I want to thank you all for your ideas and your support. I will study all of them. I promise that if I decide to use military force I will ask Congress for that authority. Rest assured, this administration will DO something. You can take that to the bank."

As the group started to file out of the room, Secretary Needham approached the president. "Mr. President, may I have three minutes of your time?" he asked. Senator Featherstone paused, looked at the secretary then changed his mind and filed out with the others.

"What's on your mind, Larry," the president asked as the conference room doors were closed.

"Mr. President, I think you should place the issue before the United Nations General Assembly yourself. Present the evidence and explain our right to self defense," Secretary Needham said. "If the Saudis don't move first by expelling their ambassador to defuse the situation, the UN will be forced to act. If in the unlikely scenario where neither acts, you can order the ambassador arrested and turn him over to the World Court. If the Court declines to hear the matter, you still have the option of military force."

"Legally, we cannot arrest the ambassador. And they can still play the oil embargo card."

"I don't think they will do that. Their economy is in poor shape. They need the income. And such an obvious political move would make them look petulant in the face of hard evidence," Needham said.

"Thanks, Larry. I want you to tell the Joint Chiefs to begin quietly preparing for military action. And I mean quietly. And make sure they understand what Rep. Goodfellow said about the holy places."

"Yes sir."

The President, accompanied by three Secret Service agents returned to the oval office stopping at the entrance to his secretary's office. "Lucy, ask Lisa, Fred and Al Collins to come in please."

"Mr. President, I have Mr. Burdette on your private line."

"Thanks, Lucy." The president shut the door and picked up the phone. "What's on your mind, Bill?"

"Mr. President, we have absolute proof of Sulieman's involvement."

"What do you mean, absolute?"

"On my authority I asked two of my men to case his residence."

"You did what? Jesus, Bill, if they were seen or left anything behind we'll have more shit thrown at us than we can shovel in a hundred years. He's an ambassador, for Christ's sake."

"Mr. President, my men aren't careless. They left nothing behind and they left everything in its place. Before they touched anything they took digital photos of the room and the desk to make sure everything would be replaced exactly where it was found."

"What did they find?" the president asked.

"A lot of coded stuff. It looks like cell locations, members, and target lists. And some other files. They photographed every page."

"You said it was coded. Can we break the code?" the president asked.

"We won't have to. My guys found a wall safe behind a painting. They opened it and guess what they found?"

"A code book, I hope," the president said.

"Exactly. They photographed that too and then put it back. They're working on decoding what they found."

"When you have it decoded, get together with Owens and Daly. We should try to nail everyone at the same time so no one has time to disappear."

"Agreed. I'll get right on it. What are you going to do about the ambassador, Mr. President?"

"I'm hoping the UN will handle that. If not, then…" Barnes let his voice trail off."

"I understand," Burdette said.

The president's secretary knocked and entered the Oval Office. "Mr. President, Lisa, Fred and the Secretary are here."

"Thank you Lucy. I'll talk to you later, Bill. Come on in. I have decided to address the United Nations General Assembly to tell the world about the Saudi treachery. Al, please arrange a date for me and then come back and let's get started on a draft," Barnes said.

Two days later, acting on the decoded information taken from Ambassador Sulieman's residence, FBI agents in 14 cities arrested more than 150 al Qaeda terrorists and confiscated large quantities of explosives and weapons and sophisticated computer equipment. That afternoon, President Barnes addressed the UN.

"Mr. Secretary General, distinguished members of the United Nations General Assembly I am grateful to you for allowing me to address this august body. As you know, a few days ago, cowardly murderers again attacked my country destroying a facility almost within site of this building. That attack should be of enormous concern to you because 11 of your colleagues, including two ambassadors and nine other people who worked here in this building were among the nearly 6,000 victims.

Since September 11, 2001, the United States has been at war against terrorists and the people who would hide them, train them and finance them. We have met with some success, and we have suffered horribly. Since the first attacks a little over ten years ago, terrorists have taken the lives of more than 60,000 innocent men, women and children in this country and injured at least that many.

After the first attacks, then President Bush declared we were at war with terrorism and said no matter how long it took, we will not falter, we will not fail. The evil cowards who destroyed a shopping center in Minnesota on the 10th anniversary of 9/11 took their own lives. But the two individuals who attacked the small regional airport not 20 miles from here have been taken into custody and have confessed their crimes.

In their confession they named the Deputy Charge D'affairs at the Saudi UN mission as the man who directed and probably planned the attack and handled the importation of the missiles that were used to carry it out. Those missiles came to this country under the protection of diplomatic immunity. The empty launchers and the shipping crates were found at the airport with the U.S. customs documentation number attached to one along with the address of the Saudi mission on Lexington Avenue. The Deputy Charge D'affairs signature was on the customs release form for those crates.

Unfortunately, he died several days ago when his plane went down over the Atlantic.

Less than 24 hours before the George Washington Bridge, the Holland and Lincoln Tunnels and Penn Station were scheduled to be destroyed by a terrorist cell, FBI agents arrested four men at a location in New Jersey and impounded vehicles containing nearly 10,000 pounds – 5 tons – of a very powerful explosive known as HMX. Unfortunately at the last minute the terrorist leader chose Grand Central instead of Penn Station and assigned that job to other members of the cell. Grand Central was destroyed the next day.

One of the men arrested by the FBI was an employee at the Saudi mission and was responsible for bringing in nearly 50 shipments of explosives from Saudi Arabia under diplomatic immunity.

He and the leader of the cell have named another Saudi mission employee as their inside contact. Unfortunately, in what has to be considered a disturbing pattern, that man has also disappeared. But the treachery does not stop there.

"Two of the men in our custody also named another person inside the mission as being directly involved in the plots. The man they named is none other than the Saudi ambassador to the UN, Abdul Sulieman."

A great stir went up in the general assembly hall. Dozens of delegates rose. Cries of surprise and shock spread throughout the assembly. Everyone turned toward Ambassador Sulieman. He rose, his face crimson, "That is a lie. This man and his Washington thugs have harassed our employees and broken international law. Now in desperation, when we would not bow to his illegal wishes to search our vehicles and seize our employees he points his finger at me," Sulieman said.

All eyes returned to the president to see the response.

"Distinguished delegates, the evidence is overwhelming. We have confessions, missile launcher crates and the empty launchers and the vans with explosives. And this morning, agents of the

Federal Bureau of Investigation in 14 cities arrested more than 150 members of Al Qaeda and seized their weapons, explosives and their plans that included bridges, tunnels, theaters, ball parks and the New York Stock Exchange in their list of targets. I have absolute confidence that all of this will lead to the Ambassador's doorstep.

The ambassador from France rose. "Mr. President, you are making an extraordinary charge, one that must be substantiated. Why do you come before us with these allegations instead of the Security Council? And why did you choose to make these allegations publicly?"

"I chose to announce these allegations publicly before the General Assembly because one of your ambassadors now stands accused of aiding terrorists. Under international law, we do not have the authority to arrest him. But this body, after it reviews all the evidence, can urge the Saudis to strip him of immunity and order his arrest. I also hope and believe that this organization is united against terrorism and that you are prepared to confront those nations that support it.

"Once the evidence is presented to this body, the United States will give you time to decide an appropriate response. In your deliberations please remember that 11 of your colleagues died in an attack that was planned, financed, and directed by one of your member nations. A weak response or no response on your part will be interpreted by us that the United Nations does not have the will to act.

"In that case, under the articles in the UN charter pertaining to self-defense, the United States will be completely justified to take military action. The choice is yours. Thank you for allowing me the time to speak to you."

When President Barnes looked over the General Assembly, Ambassador Sulieman was not in his seat. As he left the podium, he signaled to Don Briggs of his POTUS detail who nodded. Briggs brought his right hand to his face and spoke quietly into the microphone concealed in his sleeve. "Suspect has left the room. Proceed and apprehend. Repeat apprehend."

When Ambassador Sulieman and two aides entered the UN garage, they were approached from three different directions by CIA operatives. "UN Security, Mr. Ambassador," one of the agents said. "The Secretary General wants to make sure you are safe. We are to drive you to the Saudi mission." He motioned to a van parked some 75 feet away. The van pulled out of its parking space and stopped next to the group. Sulieman and his aides entered followed by the agents and the van sped through the garage.

Sulieman relaxed as the van sped south on First Avenue. He became alarmed when the van turned right on 42nd street. "The driver missed the turn," he said as calmly as possible.

"We're not going to the Saudi Mission, Mr. Ambassador," the agent said as two other agents gently pressed automatics into the necks of the ambassador's aides and relieved them of their pistols. "This van is soundproof so not even gunshots can be heard. And the doors cannot be opened except when released by a control in the front seat."

"Obviously you know who I am. Well you also must know this a violation of international law. I will protest this to the UN and to your president."

"Killing thousands of innocent commuters, airline passengers and shoppers is also against international law. We know you were behind it. My advice to you is to keep your damn mouth shut, MISTER Ambassador. And tell your goons if they make any move to help you, they will be shot."

Sulieman said something in Arabic to his aides.

"I understand Arabic, you scumbag. Tell them what I told you or you will need crutches to get out if this van." The ambassador complied.

"Where are you taking me?"

"To a nice quiet secure studio where we will record your confession and renounce your immunity," the lead agent said.

"I will not."

"I think you will Sulieman. We have people who know how to administer pain. They're as good as your people. And if you die in the process it won't matter much because no one will find your body. No one will know what really happened, but we will spread the word that your car was found on a deserted road and you were missing. The FBI will investigate, but not very thoroughly and they will find nothing. After some time, your body will be found with a note. People will assume you felt so guilty you committed suicide."

Sulieman was sweating profusely. "You'll never get away with this. My disappearance will cause an uproar in the international community, especially in light of what the president said to the UN about me. It will certainly look like I have been kidnapped."

"You have been kidnapped. And we are prepared to go to any lengths – and I mean any – to get the information we need.

"You cannot stop us. It is the will of Allah."

"If there are any additional attacks you will learn first hand we can be as unforgiving as you people. And make no mistake who will win this war.

"You don't scare me," Sulieman said.

"Not yet, perhaps," the agent replied.

Everyone fell silent as the van sped to a safe house in East Rutherford, New Jersey. It entered a gate just off Route 17 and approached a garage. One of the CIA agents pressed the opener and the steel door rose allowing the van to enter. The door closed behind them.

"A word to the wise, Sulieman. Tell your two goons if they make any attempt to escape or any noise I'll kill them."

Again the ambassador meekly complied. When the van doors slid open, the ambassador and his aides were pulled out and taken to a small room. The ambassador was taken to a second room equipped with video equipment.

"Here is the way this is going to work, Sulieman. You are going to address the members of your Royal family and the UN. You will tell them that you are speaking freely and under no duress. You will admit your involvement and name the person or persons in Saudi Arabia who gave you the orders. You will urge your government to give up all your co-conspirators. And then you will apologize to the American people.

Finally, you will tell everyone that you have agreed to stand trial for your crimes," the agent said.

"And if I don't?"

"Before we kill you, we will let you watch CNN broadcasts of the systematic destruction of your country by our air and naval forces. Then you will see our ground troops annihilate your National Guard. That is what is in store for your country if you don't name names. And how long do you think it will take us to do that? Three days? A week? Two weeks at the most. And your family may be among the rubble when we're through.

"I don't think you need to be reminded you are a man used to the finer things in life, Sulieman. As a member of the royal family you have never been subjected to subtle things like sleep deprivation or water boarding . And I doubt if you have ever suffered real pain, excruciating pain that will make you beg for death. That's what you have to look forward to. Your choice is very simple. Do what we ask or die a slow and painful death. "

"Have you no scruples, no honor?" Sulieman asked.

"Scruples? Honor? You don't know the meaning of either word. Your life depends on what you say and how you say it. You had better look ambassadorial, even regal. Your confession must be credible. I have no scruples. I have no ethics. And I will have no mercy. I hope I am getting through to you."

Sudden bright lights startled Sulieman. At the rear of the room he could see a mini TV studio. "This way MISTER ambassador." When Suliman was seated and miked, the agent said. "I want to make sure you understand that we will study this disk carefully in super slow motion and if we believe there is any attempt to deliver signals of any kind through gestures, facial expressions or words or phrases, we will proceed with the second part of the plan. And I assure you that it will not be pleasant. Do you fully grasp what I'm saying to you?

Sulieman nodded.

"You may start by telling everyone who you are. Then you will confess, explain your involvement and tell the world who gives the orders in Riyadh . Ready?

Sulieman nodded and began.

When President Barnes was seated on Air Force One for his return trip to Washington he took a call from CIA Director William Burdette.

"Bill, were you successful? Any trouble?"

"No trouble. According to my people our friend is cooperating beautifully, confessing to everything except the crucifixion."

"Excellent. Get the disk to Secretary Collins as soon as possible and get me a copy. It's going to be interesting to see what Saudi Arabia and the UN will do after they see the disk."

"I'll have it flown out tonight sir. Should we keep him on ice?"

"Yes. Thanks for a great job."

"Thanks, Mr. President. It was a labor of love for all my guys."

As Air Force One rose into the New York sky, Barnes leaned back in his chair and lit a cigar. *The Saudis have lost their knights and their queen. I wonder if they will force us to take their king?*

About the Author

William Gamble began his career as a newspaper editor in the 1960s before joining the business world. He served with the New Jersey National Guard's 50th Armored Division from 1962 to 1968. While with Exxon Corporation he served as senior communications advisor for the Arabian American Oil Company in Dhahran, Saudi Arabia between 1979 and 1982. Business honors include the Award of Excellence and two Awards of Merit from the International Association of Business Communicators and two Special Achievement Awards from Philip Morris Companies, Inc.

Gamble retired in 2001 after nearly 40 years in corporate communications and public affairs. He lives in Pennsylvania.

Printed in the United States
70596LV00003B/1-90